THE CAPE RAIDER

Jack Pembroke Thrillers
Book One

Justin Fox

Also in the Jack Pembroke series

The Wolf Hunt

THE CAPE RAIDER

Published by Sapere Books.

20 Windermere Drive, Leeds, England, LS17 7UZ,
United Kingdom

saperebooks.com

ISBN: 978-1-80055-207-4

To Luke Stevens

ACKNOWLEDGEMENTS

Although I did serve as a naval officer for a short period, I've never been to sea in a minesweeper, or a whale catcher, or even a trawler. But I have been an enthusiastic trawler of archives, libraries, museums and the arcane nautical bilges of the internet. Much of what I've gleaned about minesweeping has been liberally and gratefully borrowed from others.

For an understanding of South African minesweeping, I'm indebted to K.G. Dimbleby's *Hostilities Only*, John Duffell-Canham's *Seaman Gunner Do Not Weep*, Joe Tennant's *The Red Diamond Navy* and Jack Young's *Salt in my Blood.* In addition, *Proud Waters* by Ewart Brookes, *Allied Minesweeping in World War 2* by Peter Elliott, *Trawlers Go to War* and *Out Sweeps!* by Paul Lund and Harry Ludlam, and *Swept Channels* by Taffrail (Taprell Dorling) gave me a better grasp of wartime minesweeping further afield. SW Roskill's definitive *The War at Sea* provided the context.

For the story of South Africa's naval war, I owe a debt of gratitude to H.R. Gordon-Cumming's *Official History of the South African Naval Forces during the Second World War (1939-1945)* and C.J. Harris's *War at Sea.* The South African Naval Heritage Trust's regular digest publications, as well as those of the Simon's Town Historical Society and Cape Odyssey also proved invaluable. To learn more about wartime South Africa, I read Lucy Bean's *Strangers in Our Midst*, the many evocative accounts by Lawrence Green, *U-Boats and Spies in Southern Africa* by Jochen O.E.O. Mahncke and *Just Nuisance AB* by Terence Sisson. The naval-historical novels of authors such as

Alexander Fullerton, Alastair MacLean, Nicholas Monsarrat and Douglas Reeman have been an abiding inspiration.

For the story of German raiders, I'm indebted to Charles Gibson's *Death of a Phantom Raider*, Richard Guilliatt and Peter Hohnen's *The Wolf*, Ulrich Mohr and A.V. Sellwood's *Atlantis*, Karl August Muggenthaler's *German Raiders of World War II*, Kurt Weyher and Hans Jurgen Ehrlich's *The Black Raider*, Gordon Williamson's *Kriegsmarine Auxiliary Cruisers* and David Woodward's *The Secret Raiders*.

I spent many happy hours in the British National Archives at Kew, the British Library, University of Cape Town library, Simon's Town Museum archive, as well as the archives of the Simon's Town Naval History Museum and those of Snoekie Shellhole, attached to the Simon's Town Museum (especially their meticulously recorded personal accounts of those who served at sea during the war).

Long-suffering friends and family helped with research and offered advice on various drafts of the manuscript. In particular, I would like to thank my three wonderful editors, Amy Durant, Jenefer Shute and Rear Admiral Chris Bennett (Rtd), as well as Revel Fox Jnr, Suzanne Fox, Gail Gilbride, Penny Haw, Peter Horszowski, Paul Morris, Luke Stevens, Stephen Symons, Gillian Warren-Brown, Alan Whelan and Tracey Younghusband. A special thanks to the team at Sapere, and to my agent and friend, Aoife Lennon-Ritchie.

The principal ships and characters of this tale are entirely fictitious.

FOREWORD

When South Africa declared war on Germany on 6 September 1939, it is said that Hitler burst out laughing. At the time, South Africa's permanent naval force consisted of only three men.

The Cape of Good Hope was a critical strategic point on the sea route around the continent and would be vital during the coming North African campaign. Once Italy entered the war in 1940, the Mediterranean became too dangerous for Allied convoys and most were rerouted around the Cape. Much preparation was needed before Nazi warships made their way to Africa's southern tip. The Royal Navy base in Simon's Town had to be expanded and reinforced, and a fledgling South African Navy created almost from scratch.

First came the German surface raiders, then the U-boats. They attacked within sight of the coast and near the entrance to the harbours of Cape Town and Durban. Over the course of the war, enemy submarines, raiders and mines sank more than 150 ships in South African waters. It's an episode in the country's history that went largely undocumented. During the war, this was justified, given the need to maintain morale and keep ship movements secret. After coming to power in 1948, the Nazi-sympathising Nationalist Party did not wish to celebrate, or even acknowledge, South Africa's war achievements. For them, the future of the country looked not dissimilar to Hitler's Germany, with racial segregation being central to their post-war plans.

If the wartime actions of raiders, U-boats and convoys were soon forgotten, the exploits of minesweepers hardly received mention at all. Yet the industrious, daily sweeping by these ships kept South African ports open. Theirs was an extremely hazardous endeavour. There was no visible foe, hardly any chance to hit back — just the lottery of endless sweeping through deadly waters.

During World War II, the Royal Navy employed almost 1,500 minesweepers. They cleared channels in every corner of the Empire. They worked every day, for no one could tell when new mines had been laid. Not for them the thrust and dash of battle on the high seas. Their job was akin to that of a cleaner, dutifully sweeping the doorsteps of every major harbour, from Liverpool to Cape Town, from Mombasa to Singapore. Winston Churchill knew well the debt the Allies owed to these ships. He wrote: *The service of minesweeping is one of peculiar danger and one calculated to try the strongest nerves because of the silence and constant uncertainty of destruction in which those who engage in it must dwell.*

This is the story of one such flotilla, operating in the stormy seas off the southern tip of Africa.

CHAPTER 1

HMS *Havoc* stole towards the shore, her engines at dead slow. It was early morning, and the coast lay shrouded in a caul of smoke from the burning refinery. The destroyer was at action stations, all guns at high elevation. As Sub-Lieutenant Jack Pembroke lifted his binoculars and scanned the shore, his stomach muscles clenched. It seemed impossible.

Like insects, the beach was crawling with thousands of men. Listless hordes without order. A whole army, pressed up against the strand, trapped, waiting for slaughter.

'But, sir, it looks like the entire BEF,' Jack said.

'Thank you, Pembroke, I can see for myself,' said Captain Murray.

'It's just that —'

'I know, Lieutenant, I know.'

Jack had asked for a transfer from minesweepers in order to see action. But he hadn't expected *this* — this beach that was the setting of a rout. Perhaps, he thought, he was witnessing one of the greatest retreats in history. The annihilation of the British Army. The worst defeat since 1066?

'Lieutenant Frye, starboard side netting, if you please,' said Captain Murray. 'Tell the hands to be ready to help the soldiers aboard at the double. We'll need to look lively. I want to be in and out of this wretched beach before the vultures arrive.'

'Aye, Captain!'

Jack watched the first lieutenant dart from the open bridge and down the ladder to the well deck.

As the destroyer slid through inky water, the sound of the guns grew more insistent, the heavy bass thudding of artillery offset by the lighter kettledrums of anti-aircraft fire behind the dunes. Jack's heart seemed to be keeping time as he watched the flashes in the murk and listened to the faraway drone of bombers. The iron ring was tightening.

HMS *Havoc* edged past a gutted transport ship, lying on her side, smoking and abandoned. All around her were tin helmets, bobbing on the surface like grotesque green jellyfish. Jack realised abruptly that they were not floating: they were still attached to the bodies of soldiers who had jumped over the side wearing full kit, greatcoats and bandoliers, hoping their Board of Trade lifebelts would keep their heads above water. Jack let out a gasp and reached for the rail to steady himself as the bile rose in his throat.

To port and starboard, he watched as dozens of vessels crept towards the beach with the incoming tide. Smaller craft of every shape and kind — yachts, barges, paddle steamers — were already in the shallows. Lines of men waded out to board them. Some of the boats were down to their gunnels, barely afloat. And still they loaded more.

'By the mark, three fathoms!' came a call from the forecastle.

'Bring her two points to starboard.' The captain's voice was devoid of emotion.

'Two points to starboard it is, sir.'

'We'll get as close as we can to that makeshift jetty dead ahead.'

Jack trained his binoculars on a row of cars that had been lashed together in the shallows, then lorries in deeper water, all connected with wooden duckboards, followed by a line of rowing boats. Soldiers were clambering over this hastily prepared walkway and onto a trawler. Most of the men had discarded their greatcoats and any heavy weapons other than rifles.

By now, the trawler was dangerously close to foundering. Her skipper gesticulated wildly from the wheelhouse; a black dog on the foredeck barked throatily. After three sharp blasts from the trawler's steam siren and a roar from her engine, she backed smartly away and slewed round. Two men fell into the water, shouting. Another held onto her rail, feet dragging in the water. His mates helped to haul him aboard.

Weak sunlight was trying to break through the gloom. A mothball sat low in the eastern haze, occasionally haloed by the spatter of ack-ack flashes. HMS *Havoc* sidled up to the jetty. Jack's throat was dry; he noticed that his hands were trembling. He needed to get a hold of himself. To save an army to fight another day, that was the call.

The beach seethed: army ants in the snow, letters typed on broadsheet. Indecipherable, unfathomable. Just too many. Some soldiers milled about in aimless groups, some queued patiently, waiting for salvation, others had dug foxholes in the dunes. A few Bofors guns poked from sandbagged emplacements, but for the most part the army was naked, exposed, at the mercy of the Luftwaffe.

Jack saw bodies everywhere, floating face down like brown flotsam or laid out in rows on the beach. Abandoned ambulances stood axle-deep in sand, their doors left open like gaping mouths. He saw burning vehicles — staff cars, Bren-gun carriers, half-tracks — most of them set alight by the soldiers. A man on a dune was playing the bagpipes. The faint sound reached him on the breeze — the wail of a dying animal.

Fear. Jack could feel it growing within. Like quicksand sucking him down. Surely it wasn't meant to be like this. Would he even be able to move when called upon to act? *What's happening to me?* he wondered. *What's wrong with me?* He shrank towards the still, hard kernel of his own survival.

'Stop engines!' The captain's order snapped Jack from his inertia. *Got to pull yourself together.*

The destroyer slowly lost way.

'I can see the bottom, sir!' came a cry from the forecastle.

'Surely we must go astern, Captain,' said Jack.

'No, let her coast.'

The string of rowing boats was alongside now. Lines arced through the air and were ham-fistedly caught by the soldiers. The tall sides of the destroyer towered over the men in the boats, more dark phantom than saviour.

As the ship's prow touched the sand, *Havoc* gave a shudder and stopped.

'Needs must,' muttered Captain Murray. He walked to the bridge wing, held a speaking trumpet to his lips and called down to the main deck: 'Number One, see to the transfer of the men. Get the injured below, pack the mess decks first. As many as you can, as fast as you can.'

'Aye, sir!'

There was a great murmuring, like cattle returning home at dusk. Jack thought fleetingly of the estate, late-afternoon light on the meadows. Soldiers swarmed up the side netting. Stretchers were passed overhead. Sailors jumped down into the boats to help.

'Come on, mate, there you go.'

'Easy does it.'

'As good as home, you are.'

'One rung at a time, look up, not down.'

Jack scanned the sky. From overhead, above the layer of black smoke that poured from the destroyed refinery and burning materiel, came the unsynchronised drone of aero engines. Something caught his attention just above the beach:

an elongated object, then another, growing in size and changing shape. He went cold.

'ME-109s, sir, three o'clock low! Two of 'em!' yelled a lookout.

The 4.7-inch guns traversed as the planes roared in at mast height. One fighter began strafing the men on the beach, its machine guns spitting fire. Soldiers scattered and fell. On came the leading Messerschmitt, parting a sea of men as gouts of sand flicked up in a chattering hailstorm. Jack heard a few rifle shots in feeble riposte.

The trailing aircraft came straight at HMS *Havoc*. Her guns barked, to no avail. Jack's hands gripped the binnacle, frozen. The engine's growl filled his ears; he couldn't take his eyes off the plane. The machine guns and nose cannon fired. To his right, he felt the quadruple Vickers machine guns responding, the staccato slapping of their fire. Tracer arced up towards the fighter, but well wide of the mark.

The plane was upon them. A thundering, stammering, hateful thing. Sparks danced along the side of the bridge. Jack dropped to the deck, hands over his ears. He saw the old house on the hill. His brother and sister on the lawn. The soft plop of a tennis ball. His father kissing his mother's cheek.

The fighter split the air above *Havoc*'s mast with a bang.

'Get up, God damn it, Pembroke!' yelled Captain Murray. 'What the hell are you doing?'

Jack stood up slowly, his legs shaking. He held the rail to stop himself from sinking to his knees again. Below was pandemonium. One of the rowing boats had been ripped to matchwood and there were five men in the water, leaking blood. All of them appeared dead. The wounded were either slumped in the boats or being lifted over the gunwale. One man was screaming, a high-pitched sound that was barely human.

'Where's the RAF?' he heard someone shout. 'Why isn't there any bloody air cover?'

The strafing had spurred the men on the beach. No one heeded the commands of the tomato-faced sergeant major with the ferret moustache as they poured towards HMS *Havoc.* There was no queuing now, no semblance of order. Jack watched appalled as the slower and weaker were shoved aside, the line of boats, some awash, weighed down with men. Rats abandoning a sinking land.

'Netting, port side, they're swimming for it,' barked Captain Murray. 'And put our boats in the water port side too. They've got wounded.'

Two men were shoulder-deep, pulling a third in a life jacket, his head bandaged so that the eyes were only slits. A floating mummy. *God help us,* Jack thought.

'Get a move on! Jerry will be back!' he called.

'Fuck you, sailor boy! You know nuffing about Jerry,' shouted someone in the netting. There was dull, ironic laughter from men in the boats.

Jack's cheeks flushed. He slid down the ladder to the main deck to see if he could help, brushing past sodden, foul-smelling soldiers. He had to step over those slumped on the deck. Some were already asleep, oblivious to the chaos around them after days of retreating under enemy fire. Their indifference and dejection only heightened his anxiety. One had lost a leg and was bleeding through his bandages onto a mattress brought up from the mess deck. Everywhere, sailors tended to the wounded. Mugs of soup, fannies of tea, first-aid kits, water.

'Back to Blighty, express train, promise.'

'Home in a jiffy.' *Or in a canvas bag*, thought Jack.

Bombs were falling further down the beach. *Crump, crump, crump*. Like a jackbooted giant marching towards them. Heinkels dropped their loads unsighted through the murk. They could hardly miss: there were just too many targets. *Havoc*'s hooter sounded three short blasts and still the soldiers poured over her rails. Down below, they were packed like cigarettes; the upper deck looked as though it was made of bodies, not iron.

Jack needed to get back to the bridge. There was the chatter of machine-gun fire as another echelon of Messerschmitts streaked along the beach.

'Got to go, got to go, got to go,' intoned Jack under his breath as he fought his way through the crowd and up the ladder. There was another blast of the ship's siren and the deck began to pulse. Water churned down the flanks, but the prow remained wedged in the sand.

'Damn,' muttered the captain. 'She hardly kissed bottom.'

'We've still got the making tide, sir,' said Jack anxiously.

'Thank you, Sub, I'm well aware.'

'There are still men coming aboard, sir!' shouted the first lieutenant from below.

'We can't hang around, Number One,' said Captain Murray through the speaking trumpet. 'We're overloaded and the bow is stuck.'

Jack looked down from the starboard bridge wing. As the destroyer increased her revs, the waiting soldiers grew more desperate.

'Full astern both!'

Slabs of frothing sandy water swirled down the sides, plucking soldiers from the netting and overturning one of the boats. Whirlpools sent a trio of men back towards the beach like spinning tops. One soldier, still wearing a haversack and greatcoat, was sucked under and did not reappear. Jack saw Captain Murray staring astern, his jaw set, burning eyes shaded by his cap. The ship trembled, as though in a tug of war with the land.

A corporal clung to the keel of an upturned cutter and screamed, 'Bastards! You cowardly bastards! God save the fucking navy!'

The ship increased her quivering. Jack gritted his teeth and closed his eyes. Like one of the cows on the estate giving birth. *Come on, old girl, push, push.* At last, the propellers found proper purchase. There was a shudder, then a jolt. The prow tore free of the sand and they rocketed backwards. A cheer from the deck drowned out the curses of the men left behind.

'Pembroke, in the chartroom, if you please.'

The two officers ducked into the little cabin and bent over the table. Three escape routes had been marked out on a chart.

'Ships using Route Z, the way we came, are taking a pasting from shore batteries around Calais,' said Captain Murray. 'Admiral Ramsay suggests the long way round, Route Y, up the Belgian coast. It's more than ninety nautical miles, but safer. We follow the French shoreline as far as Bray-Dunes, then swing northeast to Kwinte Buoy off Ostend. Turn west to the North Goodwin Lightship and then south around Goodwin Sands. Dover in three hours, if we crack on. Got it?'

'Aye, sir.'

'Good.' He turned to go. 'And, Sub…'

'Yes, sir?'

'It does get easier.'

'I, I wasn't, I — thank you, sir.'

Jack felt hollowed out, lightheaded. He'd been as good as useless. He'd let himself and the men down. Bending over the table, he tried to focus on the task at hand. Brass dividers, pencil lines, coordinates. Simple mathematics.

Having studied the charts and made his calculations, Jack returned to the bridge. The decks were crammed with men who refused to go below. He looked astern and saw that Dunkirk had shrunk to a dirty smudge on their starboard quarter. High above the harbour, he could see the trails of dogfighting aircraft.

HMS *Havoc* was now part of a procession of ships making for England. She had a better turn of speed than the others and raced past minesweepers, drifters, tugs, Dutch schuits, even a Thames paddler. All their upper works were swollen and distorted with massed soldiers. *Havoc* overtook the *Emperor of India*, bright white with a head of steam as if on a pleasure cruise, towing a handful of vessels, including a rowing boat whose outboard engine had given up the ghost. A great, hodgepodge, Heath Robinson armada. It was pathetic and beautiful and filled Jack with a dose of pride after the things he'd witnessed, and felt, that morning.

Havoc powered towards salvation, engines throbbing and ventilator fans hoarsely sucking air as she knifed her way northward. Reaching Kwinte Buoy, she turned west. As she pulled away from the coast, the men began to smile. The lookouts, scanning sea and sky with their powerful binoculars, started to relax. With each mile covered, Jack felt the tension lifting. Each minute brought them closer to England and safety. A steward appeared on the bridge with mugs of kye for the officers. The sun broke through the haze and the sea appeared almost blue. Jack noticed a skua, gliding along the wave tops and calling its harsh 'hah-hah-hah'. Light brown with unstreaked belly — probably a juvenile. He must remember to buy that new bird-identification book when next in London.

'Enemy aircraft!' cried a lookout. 'Bearing red nine-oh, angle of sight six-oh!'

The alarm bell clanged through the ship, ringing short-long, short-long to warn of air attack. Jack trained his binoculars at the sky. A cluster of circling dots; a swarm of bees.

'Stukas, sir!' shouted Jack, trying to contain the panic in his voice. 'About a dozen of them.' He tracked them with his lenses. They were high, waiting for the right moment to attack.

The 4.7-inch guns followed the aircraft but could elevate to only forty degrees, so the two Vickers mountings alone would have to protect them. Tin-hatted sailors stood behind their gun-shields, watching the enemy. Jack heard the cocking of Lee-Enfields among the soldiers on deck. All faces were anxiously turned towards the sky.

The dots were overhead now. The Stukas peeled off one by one, side-slipping into their dives and plummeting towards the ship. At first, there was no sound from the enemy planes, only a loud protestation from the decks.

'Hard aport.' The destroyer was doing more than thirty knots and heeled into a sharp turn, throwing up a tall bow wave as she leant over at an alarming angle.

'Fire at will!' The Vickers guns began to stutter from aft, sending eight arcs of tracer skyward.

Jack watched the gull wings and raptor-like undercarriage of the leading Stuka as it swooped towards the ship; he could see the ugly black crosses on its wings. Now came the wailing of its siren. The voice of terror. The scream of Satan.

A Bren gun with its bipod balancing on the rail crackled into life. Rifles sounded from the deck. The men were packed so tightly there was nowhere to find cover. No one had wanted to go below: the soldier's instinctive fear of being imprisoned in a steel coffin.

Jack covered his ears and crouched down, hunching his body into a corner of the bridge. In his panic, he felt the enemy was after him personally. He wanted to bury his head ostrich-like between the wooden gratings.

The Stuka was upon them, a great eagle with outstretched talons.

'Hard astarboard!' the captain shouted into the voice pipe.

The banshee wailing filled Jack's head, filled his body. The sound enveloped him. It was as though the screaming came from inside his own chest. A black egg dislodged itself from the plane's underbelly and plummeted towards them, the sun glinting on its fins. This was it. He was paralysed. How could it have come to this? He pictured his admiral father in Cape Town, his mother in the London flat, his sister in boarding school and his young brother on a ship in the North Atlantic: the four corners that squared his love.

The 550-pound bomb struck the water alongside. Its shock wave punched the *Havoc* with a body blow, followed by the clatter of shrapnel peppering the hull and a tower of steepling water. One soldier was cut in half by the flying shards of metal, and his blood gushed across the deck and into the scuppers. There was no time to worry about the injured. The next Stuka bore down on them. Again, the siren's scream. Again, a paralysing fear, a feral cowering.

'Hard aport!'

The Vickers spat a trail of lead into the Stuka's path and the bomber sailed straight through it. Metal pecked at metal. An engine coughed, sputtered. The aircraft pulled out of its dive and wobbled back towards the coast, trailing smoke.

Havoc swung to starboard once again, a sharply angled rudder dragging her around. Another bomb went into the sea beside her, sending a curtain of spray over the bridge.

'Bring her back on course, midships.' Captain Murray's voice was calm and steely, almost laconic. *How on earth did he do it? Havoc* was tearing straight at the next bomber, approaching head-on. The captain was forcing the pilot to steepen his approach in order to hit the destroyer. The closer to vertical his dive, the closer to suicide. 'Everything you can give me, Chief!' he shouted into the voice pipe, and immediately the pulse beneath their feet increased as the ship raced towards the enemy.

The pilot hesitated, then pulled out of his dive. Both Vickers guns took advantage of the exposed belly and fired, their tracers streaking up to embrace the plane. A wing was torn from the fuselage and the broken bird cartwheeled into the sea in a sheet of flame. Cheering erupted from the decks.

The next Stuka plunged towards them.

'Starboard thirty.'

'Starboard thirty, sir.'

Tracer groped for the plane. The pilot jinked away from the glittering spray and kept on coming. Jack watched in terror as a bomb disengaged from the fuselage and sailed towards them.

The ship heeled away, but it was too late. The pod of high explosives struck HMS *Havoc* between her funnels. Jack was thrown to the deck. Around him, chunks of metal and men were wrenched from the superstructure and hurled into the air. The destroyer shuddered and began to slow, still describing a sharp turn.

More wailing, and another raptor fell upon the stricken ship. A second bomb hit right aft beside Y turret. A deafening explosion, then *Havoc* slewed to a halt and began to settle in the water.

For a few moments, Jack registered a curious silence.

'Abandon ship!' shouted Captain Murray. 'Toss everything over the side that can float. There'll be hundreds of soldiers without lifebelts.'

Now, a pair of Stukas swept low over the water, hosing the decks with machine-gun fire. Men scrambled to find cover, others jumped over the side into dark water. The bridge pinged and trembled as rounds ricocheted off the metal. Glass shattered. One of the lookouts jerked like a marionette to the puncturing of his body. A lieutenant fell to the deck, red rosettes spreading from wounds in his neck and chest.

Jack felt a blow as though someone had brushed past him. He dropped to one knee, briefly stunned.

The planes roared over the ship and kept on going towards the horizon. In the silence that followed, Jack stood up unsteadily and looked around. The bridge was a mess of broken glass, splintered wood and blood. Captain Murray was crouched over the lieutenant, using a towel to stem the blood, but it was no use. With his cap off, revealing a head of grey, the captain suddenly looked like an old man. Too old for this.

The deck began to tilt at a steeper angle. Ammunition exploded at the stern.

'Sir, we must abandon!' Jack's voice was shrill.

'Aye, Sub. There's nothing more we can do here.' Captain Murray took off his jacket and placed it over the face of the lieutenant. 'Are you all right, Pembroke?'

'I, I, can't —' Jack's body was shaking uncontrollably.

'Pull yourself together, man! We've got to get a handle on this.'

'Sir, I can't —'

'Your head. It's bleeding rather badly.'

Jack reached up to touch his temple and felt wetness. Looking down, he saw that his uniform was covered in blood. His knees scuttled themselves and he crumpled to the deck. The last thing Jack heard was the captain saying, 'Cox'n, get up here and see to the sub!'

His world turned white, then black.

Grey canvas. Rope. The smell of oil and cork. Someone was sobbing. Water lapped beside his face. A burning pain in his leg. Jack opened his eyes properly and managed to lift his head a few inches. The life raft was packed with men, mostly wounded. They were so overloaded it was barely afloat. Icy water sloshed between them. He looked down at his leg. It was unnaturally twisted — like a paper clip bent out of shape. Then a stab of pain pushed him back into darkness.

When he came round again, he saw HMS *Havoc* some way off. The wound in her side was repeatedly filled and emptied by the swell. A giant mouth slurping in water, then spitting it out. Carley floats packed with soldiers and sailors were spread out over a wide area. One whaler had been destroyed in the attack, but the second had been lowered and was swamped with survivors. Around them in the water were hundreds more men. Bodies floated everywhere. Some bobbed face up, others face down.

With each rock of the raft, Jack felt bone grind against bone as pulses of pain travelled up his leg.

''Ere, sir, 'ave a sip of water.' It was the coxswain.

'Thank you, Healy,' Jack croaked, struggling to lift his head. 'The captain?'

'Not sure, sir. 'E wanted to stay on the bridge till the last. Can't see anything up there now.'

'My leg?'

'I think it got broke when you came off the ship. A long drop. You missed the water and hit the float funny.'

Havoc was standing almost vertical now, a leaning tower with her bows pointing at the sky. Steam billowed from a funnel as the destroyer slid back into a storm of boiling water. Then she was gone. Healy lifted his hand in a clumsy salute: 'A bloody good ship, she was.'

The sea was suddenly, terrifyingly empty.

A splash of water. Jack opened his eyes. Had it been minutes or hours? He lifted a hand to his face. Wet. Fingers on rough cloth. Someone had wrapped his head in a bandage. Probably Healy. His fingers traced a decent-sized dent in his forehead. He was shivering, his body in shock. The fear rose again.

'No, no! Got to get out of here, out of here!'

'Shut up, sir,' hissed Healy, grabbing his collar with calloused, gentle hands. 'The men.'

He wanted to scream, his body shaking and shuddering on the canvas like a landed fish. Healy grabbed his jaw and jammed a morphine tablet between his teeth. Sailors were raggedly singing 'Roll out the Barrel' as Jack slid back into unconsciousness.

CHAPTER 2

Jack opened his eyes to the bright, white room. Still the same iron bedsteads and grey curtains, the same green coverlets and row of sleeping men. It felt as though he'd been back in London for months. His leg remained swathed in plaster of Paris, suspended by a rope contraption that looked vaguely nautical. The beds were occupied by other officers. Not a private room, but smaller and more comfortable than the dormitories down the corridor.

'Good morning, Lieutenant, how are you feeling today?' said the pretty nurse as she drew back the curtain beside his bed. She looked barely out of school, with a sunny face, like the day, but her careworn eyes betrayed otherwise.

'All right, thank you, Nurse.'

'Still the headaches?'

'They come and go, like the Luftwaffe.'

'And the nightmares?'

'The same.'

'Doctor will be around shortly. How's the leg doing?'

'Suspended.'

'Yes, I can see that.' She smiled indulgently.

'Your leg will take quite a while still,' said Doctor Owen, arriving to do his rounds. He ran his eye over the chart at the foot of Jack's bed and shook his head. 'A bad break. Your head wound is mending nicely, though. There'll be a scar above your temple and ear, but not disfiguring in any way.'

'Thank you, Doctor,' Jack mumbled.

'Nurse Dobson tells me you're still battling with nightmares.'

'Yes, I suppose that's a word you could use: "battling".'

'The same ones?'

'More or less. Trapped below, water pouring in. Not very original for a sailor.'

'It isn't really about originality, Lieutenant. When we're done with you here, perhaps I could recommend that you —'

'That I what, Doctor? See a psychiatrist? Get transferred to a loony hospital?'

'It's just that you might need some assistance before you get back to active service.'

'No, Doctor, I'm not bomb happy and I don't need help.' Jack turned his head to the wall in frustration and humiliation.

The days passed in a dreary cycle of doctors' rounds, bland hospital meals and tracts of empty time. Jack avoided conversation with the other patients and stared out the window looking for birds — magpies and blue tits, goldfinches and dunnocks. As he'd been told, the leg was a slow mend. His nightmares came in waves. The 'daymares', as he called them, were perhaps more disturbing. Dead shipmates appeared in the ward. They stood at a distance and watched. Silent witnesses, but to what? Or perhaps they were accusers.

Flashbacks to his last moments on the bridge were triggered by something as ordinary as someone dropping a bedpan. He would break into a sweat and feel the anxiety rise like an incoming tide, until it was lapping at his chest, his neck, his chin. 'Nurse! Nurse!'

Now she stood before him, Nurse Dobson, all in white. An angel who he treated shabbily.

'You have visitors,' she said brightly, the concern written on her face. He *must* try to be more gracious towards her. 'Your mother and your sister.'

Jack hoped his dismay did not show. With his father constantly away, serving the navy in foreign stations, he'd been funnelled off to boarding school at an early age, as had his brother and sister. His mother left the house in Hampshire in the care of servants and spent much of her time in London. She had a large social circle and a flotilla of admirers. Jack had grown up feeling like an encumbrance to the grande dame of South Kensington. If only his sister would visit on her own.

'My darling boy, how *are* you?' His mother swept down the ward, drawing inquisitive, appreciative eyes. Although in her forties, Annabel was still ravishing. She wore a pale blue dress, white hat and white shoes. His sister was in tow, a few paces behind, dressed in a brown skirt with a loose cardigan.

'Hello Mother, hello Imogen.'

Both women kissed him on the cheek and took a seat on the upright chairs set out by Nurse Dobson.

'I hope you aren't giving the nurses any trouble,' said his mother, too loudly, looking back at the row of bedridden men with a winning smile.

'The leg and head are mending,' he said softly. 'I hope to get back to sea as soon as possible.'

'Don't rush it, Jack,' said Imogen, taking his hand. 'The war can wait. We must make sure you're fit as a fiddle first.'

Jack winked at his little sister. She wasn't a baby anymore: beauty and brains in a small, explosive package. She'd just finished school and was going up to Cambridge in the autumn. With his father away and his mother often AWOL, the three siblings had been close growing up, despite the six-year age spread.

'Listen to your sister, Jack. I know you won't listen to your dear old mama. We've brought a copy of today's *Times*, chocolates, some fudge made *especially* for you by Mabel, and a book. Graham Greene's *Journey Without Maps*. It's about Africa and, seeing as your papa is there, I thought you'd be interested.'

'Mother, he's at the Cape. *Journey Without Maps* is about Liberia.'

'Oh dear, so you've read it.' She pouted.

'What news of Harry?' he asked, after a few seconds.

'Oh, he's dashing about the ocean winning fame and glory like your father.'

'Seriously, Mother, any news?'

'No, convoy duty.' She bit her lip. 'He was in Belfast last week. No word since.'

'I'll write to him.'

'Yes, do. He was so happy when his big brother joined the navy. And now that you're both in destroyers too. Well, you know what I mean.' Her cheeks flushed as she glanced at her wrist. 'Goodness, look at the time!'

The visit ended abruptly. His mother had an appointment; a driver was waiting.

As the summer drifted by, Jack could monitor the war's progress through his window. It had left the beaches of France, stretched a long, black arm across the Channel and was filling the skies above southern England with hornets. From his ward, Jack watched the dogfights and the bomber runs. RAF Croydon getting a pasting, the thud of anti-aircraft guns reverberating around London. Fortunately, the city had been spared the fate of Warsaw and Rotterdam — for now. It would surely, eventually, come.

Despite telling Imogen, who visited every few days, that he was eager to be back in action, Jack dreaded returning to sea. He was issued with crutches to begin the clumsy business of trying to walk again. Tentatively at first, up and down the ward to the ironic cheers of other patients, then into the garden. Although his body was healing, he knew his mind was not. Jack felt sure Nurse Dobson knew it too. He had grown close to the nurse who put up with his moods and his mares, both night and day.

'I was actually thinking of requesting a transfer to the Cape,' he confided as they took a breather from leg exercises on a garden bench.

'Why there?' she asked. 'It's terribly far from your family.'

'My father is serving at the Cape station. He's helping to set up a South African force to deal with Jerry in the South Atlantic. There's a big Royal Navy base at Simon's Town too. Plenty of opportunities.'

'You don't need to rush back to the action, you know.'

'It's not that I don't want to. I'm just not sure how I'll react under fire again. Things didn't go so well the last time.'

She took his hand. It was her first non-medical gesture in all the time they'd spent together. Jack wanted to melt against this small, brave, kindly soul. He registered the intoxicating touch of each of her fingers, their soft imprint on the back of his hand.

'Give it time. Don't shy away from the memories. And the fears. Let them breathe. You've still got a while here with us. You're no different, no weaker, no less courageous than the rest. The others just put on a bigger show.'

His eyes brimmed.

'Come on, sailor,' she said matter-of-factly, brushing away a strand of hair that had fallen across his eyes. 'Let's get you back to bed. Too much exercise and you'll be all at sea again.'

That afternoon there was another visitor. He walked carefully between the beds carrying his cap in both hands, and seemed to be trying to silence his footsteps.

'Healy,' said Jack, surprised, 'good of you to come!'

'Oh, it's nothing, sir,' said Healy. 'Me mum lives close by and I've got some leave. Just wanted to pop in and see how you was getting on.'

'Please, have a seat. I'm bearing up, thank you. Nearly there. A few more weeks and I'll be back on some or other bridge causing trouble. And how are you faring?'

'Fine, sir, fine. A bit of confusion after Dunkirk. Took me some time to get over the *Havoc*. But now I'm in Portsmouth. Another destroyer, HMS *Gairloch*. Captain Fitzpatrick.'

'Don't know him. And how is our Captain Murray?'

'Discharged from hospital, sir. Remember how we thought he was a goner when *Havoc* went down? Only minor injuries, thank God. I think he's back at sea already. Not sure what ship.'

'That's good news.' There was an awkward silence. 'Healy, I, I wanted to thank you.'

'Sir?'

'In the water, on the float —'

'Oh, it was nothing. You'd have done the same for me.' The petty officer looked down, running his fingernails along the rim of his cap.

'I just wanted to say that I know what you did when I was … out. I'll be forever grateful.'

'Don't mention it, sir.'

'We're both honorary members of the *Havoc* Swimming Club now.'

'Aye, that we are.'

They both chuckled.

'Healy, tell me, did Chief Driscoll get off?'

'No, sir, I'm afraid not. Not one of the stokers made it out of the engine room. They had no chance.'

'And PO Frye?'

Healy shook his head and looked away.

'Taggart, Wright, Ferguson?'

'Taggart survived, sir, lost an arm, not the others.'

'Young Freddie?'

Healy opened his mouth but didn't know what to say.

Jack turned his head to the wall. He didn't want to risk any more names. Healy stared out of the window at the plane trees. The two men sat in silence for a long while.

'Well, sir, best be getting off. Me mum —'

'Yes, yes, of course. So very good of you to come.'

'I'll pop in again, sir. Best of luck with the leg.'

Three long months later, Jack stepped off the train at South Kensington tube station. He dallied on the platform for a few moments, then pressed on. His mother was waiting for him at the flat, where there'd be a fancy lunch and a loud, short-lived fuss. He needed to steel himself.

Using a walking stick, Jack slowly climbed the stairs to street level and surveyed the familiar intersection. There was some bomb damage further up the road, but for the most part it looked as though life was continuing as normal. 'Blitz spirit', they'd started to call it. He bore left and, as he walked down Old Brompton Road, heard the wailing of air-raid sirens echoing across the city. He hastened his step, the pain shooting up his leg.

Then came the menacing drone of Dornier and Heinkel engines, the thumping of bombs and banging retort of anti-aircraft guns. He tried to run, looking for shelter, but his leg wouldn't allow it. The engines grew louder, filling his head. Explosions over towards Victoria. Now Sloane Square. Dark shapes overhead. He darted into a columned portico, trembling with fear. A bomb scythed through the building at the end of the road, then another to his right, knocking him off his feet. The street shook with thunder.

In a matter of seconds, the planes were gone and the reverberation of their passing subsided. Jack stood up unsteadily. His heart continued to hammer as guns tracked the retreating bombers. Stepping tentatively from the portico, he noticed that his uniform was covered in dust. Bells clanged, smoke filled the street, the air prickled with tension. He hastened towards his mother's flat, hobbling faster now, dreading what he might find.

Turning a corner, he stopped dead.

The opposite side of the square had disappeared. Smoke and dust filled the enormous hole in its western façade. As he drew closer, his eyes registered piles of grey bricks, bits of window frame, part of an intact Doric column. And the wing of his mother's writing chair.

Jack took a few paces towards the hill of rubble, then stopped again. A siren sounded and a truck pulled up. Men in blue overalls climbed out and began cordoning off the area. The air stank of coal gas, ancient dust and annihilation. He tasted it in the back of his throat and needed to retch.

'You know who lived here, Lieutenant?' asked a warden.

'My … mother.' He could hardly articulate the words. 'I did too. Sometimes.'

'Terribly sorry to hear it, sir.'

'Is there any chance…?'

'I'm afraid not, a direct hit. Complete collapse.'

'She might have been out shopping.'

'Let's hope so.'

'May I go closer?'

'No, no, sir, the structure ain't stable. That side wall could collapse at any moment. We'll salvage what we can, when it's safe. Do you have an address or telephone number where we can get hold of you?'

'Yes, an aunt.'

The warden wrote the details in a notebook and joined his team at the edge of the rubble. Jack watched as the men started to remove debris. He felt himself shaking uncontrollably and reached out a hand to steady himself on an iron railing.

'Sir, are you all right?' The warden was coming back.

He forced himself to turn around and walk away. *One foot in front of the other. Breathe deeply. One foot. In front. Of the other.*

Jack's mother had not been out shopping. The next morning, he visited Aunt Jane at her home in Knightsbridge where they sat in the drawing room having tea and shortbread and discussing the funeral arrangements.

'Imogen is due back shortly from the Peak District, I believe,' said Jack, trying to fill the ticking silence.

'Yes. I can't think why she'd want to go hiking, of all things. All that mud and fresh air.'

'You know how Imogen loves the outdoors, Aunt Jane.'

'Annabel and I weren't ever like that. I can't for the life of me think where she gets it from.'

Jack had never been close to his aunt. No society too high, no champagne too expensive. Just like Mama. But, he thought, he was being too cold. Guiltily, he knew he should have tried harder to understand his mother's lifestyle, why she craved the reassurance her coterie provided. Now it was too late.

He heard the doorbell and a sobbing Imogen burst into the room. She threw her arms around him, burying her head in his neck.

'Oh God, Jack, oh God!'

'I know, Immie…'

'Did she… Did Mama —'

'No, it was instant. A direct hit. The whole building was destroyed.'

'Oh Jack! Have you let Father know?'

'I sent a telegram, darling,' said Aunt Jane.

'And Harry?'

'We've notified the Admiralty,' said Jack. 'They'll contact his ship.'

'There's nothing here for me now, Jack,' his sister said. 'I don't want to stay in London. I don't want to go to the house — I'd just rattle around with the servants in Hampshire. And Cambridge is out of the question. I was never really convinced anyway. Just trying to copy you, I suppose. Now the thought of reading Classics seems absurd.'

'Are you sure?' said Aunt Jane.

'I'm not sure about anything.'

'Don't make hasty decisions, Immie,' said Jack. 'You're still in shock. We both are.'

'Well, I already have. I think I want to be with Papa right now. In the Cape.'

Jack was stunned.

'You told me *you* were thinking about asking for a transfer to the Cape —'

'Yes, I know … but don't rush into it. Don't rush into anything —'

'As soon as the funeral is over, I'm going to look into getting on a ship and sailing away from all of this.'

'Imogen, there's a war on!' said Aunt Jane. 'There are U-boats crawling about the Atlantic. You can't just *hop* on a ship.'

'Papa's a ruddy admiral, Auntie. Besides, there are convoys leaving for the Cape all the time.'

'Think it over,' said Jack. 'Especially Cambridge. Please. You're a bright young lady. Don't throw it all away.'

'I hardly think the Cape is synonymous with "throwing it all away". It's not forever. And I need Papa.'

'Yes,' he said. 'I suppose you always were a daddy's girl.'

She started crying again. Jack pressed his sister to his chest, feeling her tears through his cotton shirt. *The Cape*, he thought. *The very bottom of Africa, so far from all this.*

That evening, he asked the concierge of the room he'd taken in Bayswater for a pen and paper. He wrote one letter to the Admiralty requesting a transfer to the Cape, listing a string of reasons he didn't think would hold much water. Mentioning that he'd like to be involved in his father's project of setting up a seaward defence force in South Africa might carry some weight. The name Rear Admiral Douglas Horatio Pembroke DSO probably more so. The second letter was addressed to his father, in which he expressed the wish for a posting to the Cape and for the family, such as it was, to be reunited. He mentioned nothing about his own state of mind.

The days dragged by as he waited for a reply. Imogen was at the house in Hampshire, packing up and preparing for her voyage. Jack had no wish to socialise and his time was filled with reading, brooding and grieving. Fortunately, the room in Bayswater was close to the tube station, which provided air-raid shelter. Most nights he found himself on a cramped, fetid platform, far below ground. Posters advertising day trips to the seaside stood in stark contrast to the scene before him. The air-raid crowd seemed like a perversion of a day-tripping party, decamped in a cold, damp hole in the earth. He sat amid the throng, listening to the crump of bombs as dust filtered down from the roof and children whimpered in their sleep like frightened animals. He couldn't wait to leave the city.

By day, he went walking to exercise his leg, as Nurse Dobson had ordered. The evenings were still long and the autumn weather balmy. Wandering through the West End, he marvelled at how Londoners were getting on with things. *Arsenic and Old Lace* and *Blithe Spirit* were still playing to full houses with queues extending around the block. The picture houses and pubs were crammed. Somehow, Londoners kept on keeping on despite the aerial visitations, but he found no comfort in their stoicism.

One evening, while Jack was out walking along Bayswater Road, the Hyde Park ack-ack battery began spitting fire at the sky. Low cloud flickered with flashes. From downriver came the booming of faraway thunder; the East End sky was soon glowing red. Then came the sinister droning of aero engines. His stomach tightened as he quickened his pace, trying to run. *Not again.*

He spotted a parachute mine drifting over the Serpentine as bombs began to fall. Incendiaries thudded onto roofs, igniting deadly blooms. He stumbled on. The guns answered with their guard-dog barking. Shrapnel clattered down. Faster. Brightly coloured flames exploded as something large and chemical ignited south of the river. His leg throbbed. Black smoke rolled across London like a perverted cold front. Turning into Queensway, he scrambled down the steps into the underground shelter. Finding a corner, he dropped his stick and sank to the platform floor, arms wrapped around his knees, his body drenched with sweat.

At last, a summons arrived to report to the Admiralty. Jack shaved carefully, put on his best Number One uniform with gloves and a clean collar, and took a taxi to Horse Guards Parade. He arrived early and had to wait two hours in a noisy corridor. Typewriters chattered and telephones tinkled insistently. He fiddled with his hat, ran his fingers absentmindedly over the scar on his temple and tapped a foot tattoo.

'Sub-Lieutenant Pembroke, you can come through,' said a stern-looking Wren. 'The Commander will see you now.'

Jack stood up, straightened his jacket, picked up his walking stick and strode stiffly into the office. A grey-haired officer, seemingly past retirement age, looked up from a pile of documents.

'Ah, Pembroke, HMS *Havoc*, have a seat.'

'Thank you, sir.'

There was silence as the commander flipped through a sheaf of papers. Pewter eyes, a blank expression that gave nothing away.

'Captain Murray writes here that you did well at Dunkirk.'

'Everyone on *Havoc* did well, sir.'

'And now you desire a transfer to the Cape.' He looked up, eyes boring into Jack.

'Yes, sir. My father is there, Admiral Pembroke. My mother has recently been killed in the bombing and my sister has already taken ship for Cape Town.'

'I am sorry for your loss. However, your request is quite, ah, irregular, Pembroke.'

'Yes, I am aware of that, sir.'

'We need men like you here at the moment.'

'I understand, sir.'

There was a long pause. The commander looked at the young sub-lieutenant, as though searching for something, then turned over a page in the file. 'The Cape will become important as the sea war expands,' he said. 'We expect U-boats in the South Atlantic any time now. And of course there are German raiders and the odd pocket battleship at large, which are damn hard to catch.'

'What sort of positions might there be available at the Cape, sir?'

'Actually, they are rather short-staffed. There are quite a few positions.'

'I see.'

'We have, upon careful consideration, decided to agree to your transfer request.'

'Thank you very much, sir!' Jack's surprise and relief were etched on his face.

'Our headquarters down there will need some good naval minds in the coming months.'

'I'd like to be involved in planning and strategy. I'd like that very much —'

'And then there's minesweeping. I see you were on sweepers before you joined HMS *Havoc*.'

'Yes, sir. I asked for a transfer because —'

'You did a sweeping course at Devonport after your officer training at *King Alfred*. You might be just the man they need. The South African coastline is a long one and if raiders start laying mines, there could be hell to pay.'

'I'd prefer something at HQ, but whatever you say, sir.'

'It's not what *I* say, Pembroke. Let's see what the chaps at the Cape decide. Your convoy leaves on Monday, from Liverpool. Wren Harbison has the details. Speak to her on your way out.'

'Thank you, sir!' He stood up, came to attention and turned towards the door.

'Oh, one more thing. Before you set sail, you might want to see a tailor.'

Jack looked puzzled.

'You'll need another gold stripe on that sleeve of yours. Your promotion to full lieutenant has come through.' There was an impish grin on the commander's face. 'Come on, man, smile!'

'Gosh, sir, thank you very much.' Jack forced a smile and they shook hands.

On the lawn outside he looked up at the charcoal sky. Promotion. For what?

He leant on his walking stick and stared at the trees raining yellow leaves with each gust of wind. The air had acquired a chilly bite of late. In the park, deckchairs stood abandoned. He felt anger that sought in vain for a target, and something akin to shame. Shadows were lengthening and pedestrians hurried for home. Soon, blackout curtains would be drawn as sirens wailed across the city. Searchlights would begin to probe the dusk, followed by the hammering of artillery, starting in the east, and building like a thunderstorm across London.

It slowly sank in that he was, in fact, going to the Cape. As a full lieutenant. He was leaving all this behind. It felt to Jack just then as though a tremendous weight was beginning to lift. With a bit of luck, a change of heart and a change of hemisphere, he might well be able to start again.

CHAPTER 3

The mist formed gossamer wisps on the ocean. In the dawn light, Lieutenant Jack Pembroke watched Table Mountain rising from the deep. The sandstone cliffs glowed pastel pink and a small hat of cloud sat atop the mount. It was one of the most beautiful things he'd ever seen.

His journey to the Cape had passed in a daze. There'd been the overnight troop train to a Liverpool shrouded in fog. The clock tower, a tolling bell, rows of cranes and a great ocean liner sliding out of the harbour to the plaintive crying of black-backed gulls. The twin spires of the Liver Building swallowed by mist, followed by the Bar light vessel at the entrance to the Mersey. A fast beat to open sea, a U-boat scare that came to nothing and then every day warmer as they sailed down the Atlantic into the tropics, every day more easing of the tension, a brightening of the sky.

Now three minesweepers were leading their convoy into Table Bay. The puffing tubs looked like floating kettles. Behind them came a column of ships — merchantmen, troopers, destroyers and a battleship at the rear. The decks of the liner were crowded with soldiers, all staring at the mountain in hushed awe.

The city slowly took shape. Jack could make out a downtown district with a few tall buildings, the slopes around it packed with homes leading up to a wall of rocky crags. Devil's Peak to the left, Lion's Head to the right, said his pocket guidebook. The foreshore zone around the newly built harbour was a wasteland lined with cranes. To the right, the Victoria and

Alfred Basin was dominated by concrete grain silos and, behind them, a power station.

He looked at the minesweepers, dragging the fleet behind them like toddlers leading a coach-and-four. They appeared vaguely comical. On their afterdecks, he could make out scruffy sailors, half of them brown-skinned, some with their shirts off. They looked more like fishermen than naval ratings. Things were obviously quite different here in the Union.

Half an hour later, the sweepers turned away with a few gruff blasts on their horns. Soldiers lining the rail let out an ironic cheer and waved them off.

'There goes the mighty South African Navy!' shouted one of the pongos. A group of jokers began singing, 'Rule South Africa, South Africa rules the waves.'

The defensive boom at the entrance to Duncan Dock was opened and the liner glided into port. As a cluster of tugs ushered her to a berth at the western end of the basin, Jack returned to his cabin and packed the last of his things. A seaman helped him with his duffel bag as he walked gingerly down the gangway, nursing his stiff leg. The troops had been ordered to remain on board, so it wasn't difficult to find his contact among those waiting on the quay.

'Lieutenant Pembroke?' asked a rosy-cheeked sailor, saluting smartly.

'Yes, that's me.'

'I'm Leading Seaman Aucamp, sir,' he said in a thick South African accent. 'Welcome to Cape Town. May I take your bags?'

'Thank you, I'll carry my sword.'

'There's a car waiting. I've been asked to take you to Captain Anderson at HQ.'

Jack got in the back of a dark-blue Ford and they headed uptown over railway tracks and across the barren foreshore to Adderley Street. On the left stood a large railway station with a steam locomotive puffing inside. The buildings were grander than he had expected.

They turned left and drove past a parade ground. Behind a row of palm trees he could see the city hall, an elegant pile in yellow sandstone framed by Table Mountain.

'What an attractive town,' he said.

'Yes it is, sir. And up ahead is the old Castle of Good Hope.'

Through the split windscreen Jack could see the dark battlements of the Dutch fort, South African and British flags fluttering above the entrance. Cannons cemented into the pavement served as bollards beside a moat. His father always boasted that when the British took the fort without a fight during the Napoleonic Wars, one of their Pembroke ancestors had somehow been involved.

The two men got out and walked towards the gates. There was a loud bang and Jack flinched. Pigeons filled the air with clattering wings. He heard the throb of bomber engines, the wail of a Stuka. His body went weak. The leading seaman had come to attention beside him. Baffled and unnerved, Jack did the same, fighting the urge to run. All across the parade ground and in the streets, pedestrians and motorcars came to a halt.

'Noonday gun, sir,' whispered Aucamp. 'Two-minute silence for those who gave their lives in the last war, and for those serving in this one.'

After the eerie quiet, engines and voices resumed their murmur. Jack and Aucamp proceeded to the entrance and showed their identity papers to the sentry. It was a hot summer's day and Jack was already perspiring heavily.

Aucamp led him through the portcullis and across a large quadrangle.

'Please wait here, sir. I'll see if the Captain is available to see you.'

After a few minutes, Jack was escorted into an office.

'Ah, Lieutenant Pembroke, good to meet you. Your father has told me lots about you.' Captain Anderson was energetic with a no-nonsense manner. 'Cigarette?' He held out a tin with a bearded Jack Tar in a life ring on the lid.

'No thank you, sir.'

'Quite right, beastly things,' Anderson said, lighting up and drawing hard on his Player's. 'I won't beat about the bush. We've got our hands full: convoys, commissioning new ships, converting whale catchers, you name it. Then there's the business of getting the other South African harbours up to speed. So we could do with a chap like you on our logistics staff here at the Castle, especially someone with sea time and combat experience. You were minesweeping in the Channel last year, I'm told. You know the drill when the balloon goes up better than anyone around here. It would be a desk job, but you'd be an asset to our team.'

'Thank you very much, sir.'

'Well, don't get ahead of yourself, Lieutenant. This might, as it turns out, *not* be the job for you. Your father has something else up his sleeve. He wants you to go through to the naval base in Simon's Town. He'll give you the lowdown. Leading Seaman Aucamp will drop you at the station.'

An hour later, Jack's train clattered out of Cape Town. He sat watching the mountain as the train wound its way through the suburbs that clung to its lower slopes. Woodstock, Salt River, Rondebosch. Then the famous cricket and rugby grounds at

Newlands.

As he stared out the window, Jack's mind was elsewhere, worrying about what his father might be cooking up. The old man always had 'a plan' and it usually involved his own needs rather than anyone else's, even his children's. What did Jack want? A logistics job at the Castle sounded just about right. Jack would have to resist the great admiral or be smothered by his enthusiasm, or his bullying, or whatever one might call his father's overbearing manner.

The train pulled into Muizenberg — site of a British-Dutch battle in 1795, according to Jack's guidebook — and halted for a few minutes. He got out to stretch his legs. The station building was a grand affair with a wooden clock tower, its walls plastered with red-and-yellow posters that shouted, 'Zip your lips! Don't talk about ships!' Below him lay an endless beach dotted with umbrellas. Rows of colourful bathing huts stood on either side of a pavilion. Children on summer holidays thronged the shoreline; an ice-cream seller tinkled his bell. It was a far cry from good old rainy Brighton. There were even people riding long wooden boards in the waves — it looked like rather good fun. Hardly a country at war.

'All aboard, *alle stasies*, all stations!' A shrill whistle and the sound of train doors banging.

Jack climbed back on board and changed his seat to the left-hand side of the carriage. The railway line followed the shore, often only yards from the boisterous waters of False Bay. They passed St James Beach with a luminous green tidal pool and more coloured beach huts. The shouting of children and hoot of the train filled him with unexpected pleasure as they rumbled through Kalk Bay with its Cornish-looking harbour jammed with fishing boats. The train ran along the back of a wide white beach at Fish Hoek, also lined with bathers at its southern end.

A loudspeaker on the station platform announced that the train would go no further. Due to yesterday's gale, the line was blocked with sand at Glencairn. There was a bus laid on for those with permits who wished to proceed to Simon's Town. Jack gathered his luggage and was helped by another passenger onto the platform. Although he no longer needed a stick, his leg still gave him trouble when stepping down, and he winced as he steadied himself against the carriage.

'Lieutenant Pembroke?' A smartly turned-out Wren stood before him. She was blonde and wore a white shirt, black tie and blue skirt.

'That's me, Wren…'

'Monroe, sir, Janet Monroe.' She saluted.

'How did you know it was me?'

'You look like your dad, sir. Just a bit taller and with more hair. I'm his driver. I was told to pick you up at the station, but then I heard that the line was buggered.'

'Buggered?'

'Beg pardon, sir, covered. With sand. Damn southeaster. I mean, southeaster.'

He smiled. 'I can see you've spent too much time with my father.'

She beamed, showing off both dimples. His father always did have a good eye, Jack thought. Monroe helped him pile his luggage on the seats of the Plymouth and he climbed in the back, keeping his leg straight.

'Dicky leg,' he said.

'I know, sir, HMS *Havoc*. Must've been awful.'

'Doesn't my father know about loose lips sinking ships, Wren Monroe?'

'Oh, he trusts me, sir. And that one's already sunk.'

The black Plymouth followed the coast road south, beside the railway line. When they came to the Glencairn boom, Monroe flashed her ID at the military police, stating that she was collecting Lieutenant Pembroke and taking him to the naval base.

'War footing and all,' she said. 'No one without a permit is allowed to enter the naval zone. Simon's Town has suddenly become *very* important. It wasn't like that until recently. My family used to come here to swim.'

'What are they worried about: spies and secret agents?' Jack smiled.

'Don't joke. A lot of the Afrikaner population is not too keen on the war. Some even support Hitler. You never know what information they could be passing to the Germans. So many warships are docking in Simon's Town these days. We even had *Hermes* in here after her collision with *Corfu*. Our dockyard chaps worked round the clock to patch her up. Imagine having a ruddy great aircraft carrier in Simon's Town's dry dock. She looked a terrible sight with her crumpled snout.'

'Bows, Wren Monroe.'

'Snout, sir.'

'Oh God, it's the Admiral's influence.'

She grinned at him in the rear-view mirror.

In Glencairn, Jack noticed labourers on the tracks with spades. 'Often happens,' said Monroe, as they passed the men. 'We have ghastly gales in the summer months. They last for days and can make life pretty miserable. If you want to go swimming when there's a blow, it's only Seaforth or Boulders Beach that are any good. Both of them are a shortish walk from your dad's house.'

They rounded a promontory and Jack had his first view of Simon's Town. He asked Monroe to pull over and got out. Wren Monroe came to join him on the grassy verge. It was an idyllic afternoon — hot, with a blue-domed sky and a few cat's paws stealing across the water between them and a lighthouse in the middle of the bay.

Over to the right lay the harbour, with the town extending up the slope behind it in tiers. A large scar on the mountain marked the site of a quarry. The harbour was crammed with vessels and the roadstead filled with anchored ships of every size, including two destroyers, plenty of lighters and a Mersey-class cruiser dating back to the 1880s.

'She's a beautiful old steamship, isn't she?' said Monroe, seeing his gaze. 'No longer HMS *Thames*. She was bought out of the service back in the Twenties, renamed the SATS *General Botha* and now serves as a training ship for South African cadets.'

'You're a mine of information, Wren Monroe.'

'A gold mine, not a coal mine, I hope.'

'You have a lot of those around here, don't you?'

'Not in Simon's Town. But yes, we do. Both.'

They drove on, past a gun battery bristling with heavy-calibre and anti-aircraft pieces.

'The nine-inch guns of Scala Battery are up on the hill behind you, sir, and the railway station is on the left, last stop before Antarctica. That's Admiralty House coming up, also on your left, behind the sentries and the grand gates. Your dad prefers to stay in a rented villa outside town. He only comes to the house for functions and meetings. As you know, he's not big on pomp and ceremony.'

They passed the gracious eighteenth-century house overlooking its own private beach and continued through town along St Georges Street. To Jack, the buildings appeared to have been transplanted straight from any naval port in Britain. There were Victorian homes, English churches, traditional pubs, Royal Navy administrative buildings and Jack Tars thronging the streets. A southern Portsmouth.

'Just like home, with a bit more sunshine and a lot less Luftwaffe,' he said.

'Yes, this must be the most British town in Africa. At any one time there are literally thousands of chaps off the Royal Navy ships enjoying a bit of R & R. You'll see, the whole place is set up to cater for them: NAAFI shops, dances, drinking holes, bingo halls, you name it.'

'Sounds like hell.'

'On the contrary, sir. It's actually rather a lot of fun.'

They drove past Jubilee Square, the entrance to East Dockyard and onward out of town.

'Boulders Beach is down that lane,' Monroe said. 'Very pretty. And coming up is Murdock Valley. The farms up on the slope supply our ships with fruit and veg.'

After a few minutes, the Plymouth turned left onto a gravel track that led to a jumble of enormous granite boulders.

'This is Rocklands Cove. Also a nice little bathing beach when the wind isn't too strong. Your dad has a lovely house just above it.'

They drove through a dense grove of trees and arrived at a white wall. The sentry opened a gate and the Plymouth rolled across the grass, coming to a halt under a loquat tree. The lawn gave way to low scrub and a crescent beach.

Jack's father strode towards them. Lean, straight-backed and energetic, despite his advanced years — the 'pocket-rocket admiral', they called him. Jack felt a surge of affection. They shook hands firmly, their eyes locked.

The admiral put a hand on his shoulder. 'Jack, my boy, at last! It's been so long. How are you, dear lad? I've missed you very, very much.'

'Me too, Father.' Jack's eyes filled with tears. He leant forward to give his father a hug, then stiffened.

'Leave your luggage, Jack. It will be collected. Come inside.' The admiral turned to Monroe. 'Janet, would you like to stay for supper?'

'No thank you, sir. I'd best be getting back.'

Father and son walked around the side of the house facing the ocean. False Bay stretched out in deepening shades of blue with a distant dado line of encircling mountains. Cormorants by the hundred sat on the rocks below the house, kelp beds swirling around them to the gentle surge.

'An uneventful trip, Jack?'

'A safe one, at least. We had some bother with U-boats north of the Azores, but then a fast run down the Atlantic.'

'A big convoy.'

'Huge. I was glad to be an officer. Squaddies crammed the decks, thousands upon thousands of them. It was stifling in the tropics, hardly any water to wash, no place to string a hammock, terrible food, frequent fisticuffs. We even had a riot at one point. One chap committed suicide. Awful business.'

'Yes, I was following your progress. The troops and materiel are badly needed in Egypt. They're going to have to crack on. Mussolini has been stopped for the moment, but Hitler is about to step in. He's earmarked Rommel to lead his desert force, so we might be in for a spot of bother.'

As they climbed the steps, Imogen burst through the veranda doors. 'You're finally here!' she cried, throwing her arms around Jack.

'My, how you've grown!' he said.

'I'm eighteen, Jackie boy. You can stop saying that now.' She cuffed him on the shoulder.

'Must I? You'll always be my baby sis.'

She giggled. 'Six years my senior and still my junior in maturity.'

They stood arm in arm on the veranda. A servant brought out a tray of glasses and a jug of lemonade, placing them on the table.

'How are you getting on, Immie?' Jack asked.

'Bearing up, I guess. The sadness comes and goes, sort of in waves. But the Cape is marvellous. You'll see. And you, how are you bearing up?'

'Also in waves. Mother and *Havoc*. They vie for attention, mostly at night when things creep up on me.'

'Come on, let's show Jack around Milkwood House,' said their father, briskly changing the subject and leading them through the French doors into the lounge. Father and daughter walked him through the Victorian house with its cosy lounge and fireplace, long dining room, four bedrooms, garage for boats and cars, and cellar for wine and beach paraphernalia. The veranda was enclosed at the south end and had a big leather sofa with the handsomest of views. Milkwood's garden started out formally, with well-tended flower beds around the house and a croquet lawn, but grew more rambling as it stretched down to the shore. It was a place of utter peace. To Jack, the war seemed a million miles away.

'Rachel has made up a bed for you in the guest room.'

'Thank you, Father, but shouldn't I be getting back to Captain Anderson?'

'Don't worry about Michael. You can report to the Castle tomorrow. There are things I'd like to discuss with you. Did you bring bathing trunks?'

'Yes, I did.'

'Good. Unpack, go and have a swim. Then meet me on the veranda for a drink.'

Half an hour later, Jack walked down a stone path through scrubby vegetation, under milkwood boughs, over rocks and onto the beach. He laid out his towel, took off his sunglasses and walked to the water's edge.

'Wait for me!' His sister, clad in a red bathing suit, came jogging down the path. He stood knee-deep, waiting for her to join him.

'The water's so warm,' he said.

'Yes it is, on this side of the mountain. It's the current or the wind or something. But on the Cape Town side of the peninsula it'll freeze your toes off.'

Jack thought of *Havoc*, her hull pointing at the sky like an accusing finger. He shivered. The sea darkened.

'Are you all right?' asked Imogen.

'Yes, sorry. Quite all right.'

'You went pale for a moment there.' Reaching out a hand, she touched his cheek. He flinched.

'It's nothing.'

'Jack?'

'Just flashbacks. Nothing to worry about. Perfectly normal.'

'Jack!'

'Imogen, please.' He stared at the horizon.

'Talk to me.'

'It's not shell shock or anything as dramatic as that. Probably just common fear.' There was a long silence. He turned to look at his sister. 'To be quite honest, I don't know how I'll react in combat again. I was incapacitated, a block of wood. Frozen with terror.'

'I'm sure everyone's like that the first time.'

'No, I'm an officer. I have to set an example. And there's Mother as well. I was so cold towards her. There was so much that was never said.'

Imogen put her arms around him. His body shook. 'It's going to be all right,' she whispered. 'Everything is different here. England is behind us.'

'Is it really?'

'"Somewhere, over the rainbow",' Imogen sang teasingly as she ruffled his hair. 'Remember, Soho, last year.'

'Yes, damn good film.'

'"Someday I'll wish upon a star, wake up where the clouds are far behind me." The clouds *are* behind you, Jack. You've got to believe that.'

'Clouds can follow you.'

'No, Jack. You left them at the Equator. It's all different down here. Upside down. New. It's like we've flipped the egg timer.'

He looked into his sister's eyes. Not a girl anymore. A strong Pembroke woman.

'Come on, I'll race you to Orange Rock.' She plunged in and struck out for a boulder fifty yards off the beach. He dived in after her, powering through the water with easy strokes and beating his sister by half an arm. They pulled themselves onto the rock. The two siblings lay there like seals, panting from the exertion.

'We're both unfit,' she said. 'With your leg, you can be forgiven. But I've been here long enough not to have any excuses. Rachel's cooking is just too delicious, and there's no rationing in South Africa. Not yet, anyway.'

'The good life?'

'Yes, just for a bit. It's summer hols here, so everything closes down. I suppose I'll do a secretarial course or something when the wheels start to turn again, but there's no rush.'

'How about the university here in Cape Town? It's not exactly Cambridge, but —'

'No, I think I've put those particular aspirations behind me. For now, at least.'

They lay on the rock in companionable silence. The sun was going down over Simonsberg and shadows crept out from the western rim of the bay. A yacht made for home, its sails glowing in the last rays of sunlight. Milkwood House sat on its own behind the trees and Jack could see one or two other houses further up the slope, but the town was obscured behind a headland to the north.

That evening, Jack and his father sat on the veranda, each with a glass of whisky. The aroma of lamb stew wafted from the kitchen.

'Rachel is a marvel,' said the admiral. 'Cape Coloured. Local dishes that have your mouth watering. We'll have to take her back to England with us after the war.'

'So you'll go back?'

'Actually, I'm not certain. What with your mother's passing… This is my third stint at the Cape, you know, and I can see myself staying on after hostilities are over. Besides, I have, technically, retired.'

'And the estate?'

'I'm sure you and Imogen will go back. And Harry won't come out here. He'll need to climb the ladder back in Britain if he wants to reach flag rank one day.'

'He might not want to —'

'No, Jack, it's you who doesn't want to.'

'It's not cut and dried,' Jack snapped. His father always managed to rile him when they discussed his future plans, or the navy, or the 'great Pembroke tradition'. He wanted to run a thousand miles from all that pompous expectation.

'You've always wavered; at school, at Oxford. What is a bloody PPE anyway, Piss-Pot Economics? Your stint at *The Times*. Wanting to come out here to do "logistics". That's got no bite, Jack, no fire. Logistics is for old men, a pen-pusher's job. Leave it for beached sailors like me. Get stuck in, my boy. Think of the family. Your ancestors all found glory in the service.'

'Perhaps we should leave that to Harry.' Jack's voice was deflated. 'I'm not certain my heart is in it.'

'I know you had a nasty scrape at Dunkirk. Lost your ship under you. That's bound to shake one up. And we have all lost Annabel.' The admiral paused. 'But we have something for you here, and I think it's just right. You've had time on minesweepers, you know the ropes. You have seniority and you've seen action.'

'I was only on sweepers for a few months before transferring. It wasn't for me.'

'Just listen to what I have to say. We've got a busy minesweeper fleet in Cape Town keeping the passages clear. The situation in Simon's Town has been a bit ad hoc until now. But we've had four whale catchers converted for sweeping duty. The South African railway workshops have just completed their refits and they're about to come on line. The whalers were built for the Antarctic — tough, sturdy craft. One of the skippers has been transferred up north to the Med,so—'

'I don't —'

'Please, just give it some thought.'

'*Kos is op die tafel*, food is on the table, Master,' called Rachel from the hall.

'*Baie dankie*, Rachel, we're coming,' replied the admiral.

Jack raised his eyebrows.

'Imogen and I are trying to learn a bit of Afrikaans. Rachel thinks it's hilarious. Weeps with laughter when she hears our accents. Not very professional, but she is a dear.'

Over dinner — a waterblommetjie lamb bredie that Jack found delicious — the admiral talked about his work at the Cape. 'I was asked to help set up what is known as a Seaward Defence Force. No one wants to call it a "navy" per se, as that would put a lot of noses out of joint. It's not Royal Navy, nor is it Royal Navy Volunteer Reserve. It's a force manned by locals whose task it is to protect the coastline and South African waters.'

'Do you have a title?' asked Jack.

'Yes, Prime Minister Smuts has named me Director of Seaward Defence, whatever the hell that means. Basically, I've ended up being a bureaucrat, diplomat extraordinaire, political nappy changer and chief thumb twiddler.'

'Papa is just feeling sorry for himself,' said Imogen. 'Don't believe a word he says.'

'If only I were back on the bridge of a ship. Any bloody ship, even a tug. Our head office is at the Castle. I was there full time for a year. Now my deputy, Captain Anderson, is holding the reins. Janet — Wren Monroe — drives me through to the city two or three times a week. And I have an office here in Simon's Town, so I can be close to the Royal Navy. It's a balancing act.'

'Well, you always enjoyed the circus when we were children…' said Imogen.

'Apart from turning trawlers and whalers into minesweepers and anti-submarine vessels, there's been a mountain of other tasks. Converting armed merchant cruisers, setting up signal stations and commissioning small craft for harbour patrols. Installing lookout posts and gun batteries along the coast ... the list goes on and on.'

'You never were big on sleep,' said Jack.

'Yes, but some would be nice.'

After Rachel's famous melktert, Imogen kissed both men goodnight. Father and son retired to the veranda for a nightcap.

'At the moment, our main challenge is to get the minesweeping component functioning properly,' said the admiral. 'Then we can start paying more attention to anti-submarine measures. Thank goodness Jerry hasn't yet deployed U-boats off the Cape.'

'Tell me about the minesweepers.'

'Contact mines laid by raiders are our primary concern.'

'Raiders?'

'Yes, we fear there might be one operating in our waters as we speak. And more to come. Powerful, well-armed ships disguised as merchantmen.'

'Not something one would want to meet in a minesweeper.'

'No, you'd want to get the hell out of there, fast.'

'Who crews the sweepers?'

'Some of the skippers are trawler men who can, because of their jobs, easily handle sweeping gear. We've got a few other sources, such as the South African division of the RNVR. They're basically weekend sailors who received training a couple of nights a week before the war, but there hasn't been much take-up from them.'

'So who's left for you to call on?'

'There are the *General Botha* lads, who've all had a sound training for the Mercantile Marine. They're a good source of officer timber.'

'And fishermen?'

'Yes, of course. You probably know that colour is a stumbling block here, but I've insisted that we recruit local hands, and on the same pay as their white counterparts. They are the traditional fishermen of the Cape. Given our time and training constraints, they're obvious candidates.'

'And the ships themselves?'

'We've been requisitioning Irvin & Johnson trawlers and Norwegian whalers as they return from the Antarctic. I've had some delicate negotiations with ship owners and the Norwegian government. The four newest whale catchers will operate out of Simon's Town. It'll be a versatile unit "without portfolio", so to speak.'

'Why's that?'

'Well, if a new minefield is discovered far from any port, I don't want to have to cobble together an ad hoc group from various units. In any case, this would weaken the port flotillas at precisely the moment an enemy is in our waters. The two old ducks under Royal Navy control, *Kirstenbosch* and *Immortal*, have been doing the False Bay channel sweep up till now and will keep at it. I want you to take over the roving flotilla.'

'Father, I can't. It's too soon and, quite frankly, I'm not up to it.'

'Sleep on it, son.'

'Sleeping hasn't exactly been a strong point of late.'

'Just sleep on it, damn it, Jack!' The admiral smiled, reached over and put a hand on his son's shoulder. He stood up, downed his whisky in one gulp and swept his eyes once around the bay as if searching for enemy craft. Then he strode to his bedroom at the north end of the veranda.

Jack sat a while longer, staring at the bay and fuming at his father. The admiral always got his own way, but not this time. As Imogen had said: everything was different down here. After a few minutes, he started becoming aware of the night sounds. The whooshing of the southeaster in the loquat tree, the insistent trilling of crickets. Was that an owl hooting? He must get hold of a South African bird book. The sound of the ocean's breathing against the shore began to work like a balm on his troubled thoughts. In the morning, he would firmly refuse his father's offer, return to the Castle and request a position under Captain Anderson.

Jack's mind was made up.

CHAPTER 4

Kapitän zur See Emil Falk stood at the guardrail and watched the last of his men climbing the gangplank. The captain was a forbidding figure: tall and straight-backed, his grey goatee neatly trimmed, his eyes a disquieting shade of cyan. A piercing wind from the north swept through Kiel, and Falk turned his leather collar against the elements. Winter still held the town in its grip. His eyes scanned the harbour: its sleek destroyers and cruisers, the low dockyard warehouses and buildings of German naval headquarters. Would he and his men ever find sanctuary here again?

Sealed orders were lying on his bunk, to be opened only once at sea. They would provide details of the months to come, the life of subterfuge they would lead on the high seas until, one day, they'd return triumphant to this port, or come to rest on the floor of some foreign ocean. Already he knew the bare bones of the cruise ahead. The ship had been inspected by Großadmiral Raeder himself, who'd expressed great hopes for the voyage. The grim admiral told Falk that the *Hilfskreuzer* would strike a mighty blow at Africa's soft underbelly.

Standing on the bridge wing, he ran his eye over *Sturmvogel*. She was almost ready for sea. The long weeks of working-up exercises in the Baltic were finally over. How many times had he forced his men to scramble to battle stations? Again and again, they'd practised life-saving, damage control, night shooting, fuelling at sea and firing dummy torpedoes at the cruiser *Nürnberg*. Falk had driven his crew hard and they had responded well. He'd weeded out the men he thought physically or psychologically unfit for a long raiding voyage. Now it was time to launch his mission.

With her black hull and cream-coloured superstructure, *Sturmvogel* looked out of place among the grey battlewagons. Built just before the war as a fast cargo ship, she had the latest equipment. Converted in Kiel to serve as a commerce raider, she'd been transformed into a wolf in sheep's clothing. At a casual glance, she looked like an ordinary 10,000-ton merchant ship with a main superstructure grouped amidships, blunt prow and cruiser stern. However, *Sturmvogel* concealed awesome firepower. Her main armament comprised eight 5.9-inch guns — some masquerading as deck housing or machinery, others hidden behind steel shutters in the ship's side that could be raised by counterweights at a moment's notice.

The *Sturmvogel* also carried an assortment of hidden twenty mm guns and a twin thirty-seven mm right aft. There were two twenty-one-inch torpedo tubes hidden behind painted canvas on either side of the aft deck. She carried 350 mines mounted on trolleys below deck and had a miniature railway to bring them to the poop where they could be dropped over the side. The *Hilfskreuzer* also had two motorboats and one Heinkel He 114 floatplane with British markings to act as a scout.

Sturmvogel was a formidable man-of-war and could take on anything up to, and perhaps including, a British cruiser. Her complement was 266 men, with a surplus to be used as prize crews for captured ships. They were a mix of reservists and recruits, stiffened by veteran senior ratings and active-list officers. Falk was satisfied with the blend of youth and experience.

Her tactics would entail stealth, deception and surprise. Using a veritable box of tricks that included fake ventilators, collapsible deckhouses, telescopic funnels, masts that could be raised or lowered and myriad paint jobs, her appearance could be completely transformed while at sea. She even had a smoke-making device able to create the illusion that she was a coal-burner. One day the raider might be masquerading as a Japanese tramp steamer, the next as the smart flagship of a Swedish line.

Falk looked northeast towards the harbour entrance, his brow creased in concentration. Over the coming months, *Sturmvogel* would be a little outpost of Germany roaming the globe on a quest to confuse, terrorise and destroy. The captain's own reservations about the mission, the greater objectives and about the sea war itself, were put to the back of his mind. His duty was to his men and to the mission at hand. It was time.

The ship was coming alive. Deep inside her, Falk could hear whirring fans, the whine of dynamos and bustle of sailors preparing for sea. He took the stairs two at a time from the bridge, down past the doctor's surgery to the wardroom. When he entered, chairs scraped as sixteen officers stood to attention, their eyes eager, the atmosphere charged with nervous electricity. The wardroom ran the full width of the ship, with the dining area separated by a chintz curtain, a stove in the corner glowing a homely orange. There was a green fitted carpet, wood panelling and elegant furniture — reminders of her peacetime incarnation.

'At ease, gentlemen, please be seated.' Falk placed his cap on the polished table with the gold braid facing his officers. He glanced briefly at the painting of *Sturmvogel* in her pre-war livery, sailing on an unnaturally blue sea. 'I will not keep you long,' he said. 'There is much work to be done.' Falk wore the air of casual power. He remained standing, perfectly at ease, but to his men he appeared to be only half there. His mind, it seemed, had already bade the land farewell.

Falk looked around at the seated group. For the most part, he'd been given good, seasoned officers. Korvettenkapitän Adler was career navy, an excellent Number One and a fervent Nazi. Strong, reliable; a rock he could depend on. Oberleutnant Bauer, his second officer, was a fine navigator, but perhaps too much of a thinker, a dreamer. The rest of the men were a mixed but solid lot. The younger officers did not have much sea time to their names, but were competent enough, disciplined and keen.

Two older lieutenants, Lange and Richter, sat to one side and looked ill at ease. Softer men. These were his boarding officers and would, if needed, sail prize ships back to Germany. Both of them were ex-merchant marine and appeared uncomfortable in this rigidly naval environment. That would have to change.

'All our stores are now on board and properly stowed, thanks to all of you. But especially thanks to Korvettenkapitän Adler. *Sturmvogel* is ready. I cannot tell you much about the voyage ahead. It is, like our very existence, top secret. Even I know only the broad outlines, but once we are at sea and I have opened my orders, I will inform you. Rest assured, given the provisions, stores and preparations, this looks to be a very long cruise. But this you will have already surmised.'

The raider's fuel capacity and water tanks had been vastly increased, and she carried enough provisions to remain at sea for up to a year without being replenished. This meant everything from summer and winter clothing — pith helmets and fur-lined watch coats — to pencils, light bulbs, pigs, razors, soap and zinc oxide. She carried 35 tons of meat, 29 tons of potatoes, 60 tons of flour, 3 tons of coffee, 12,000 cans of milk, 1.2 million cigarettes, 100,000 litres of beer, 25,000 chocolate bars, 99 movies and 530 records.

'Tonight, we will sail on the tide.' There were a few murmurs. 'Tomorrow, we will pass through the Skagerrak. In the coming days we will continue to do exercises. I want to keep the men sharp. We need the best lookouts possible, especially in the first week. The breakout will be a dangerous time, sailing through the enemy's most heavily defended waters. Keen eyes might mean the difference between life and death.

'All right, gentlemen, we will talk again once we are at sea. Korvettenkapitän Adler will inform you of your watch-keeping duties. Carry on.'

Falk climbed the stairs and stepped into the broad wheelhouse, ignoring the salutes. He strode to the bridge wing and looked down at the bustle on the quay. The deck was vibrating beneath his feet, the great seabird slowly waking. His coxswain was at the wheel, a young seaman at the telegraph, both awaiting his orders. PO Schneider and the signalman stood watching their captain. The lookouts on each wing were already drenched to the skin.

A telegraphist stepped from the wireless room onto the bridge, came to attention and said: 'Message from harbour control, Kapitän: "Proceed when ready."'

'Thank you. Stand by.'

The telegraph jangled. Far below in the engine room, Chief Engineer Fuchs looked up at the repeater dial, smiled ruefully and gave a thumbs-up to his men.

'Let go forward.' Falk could see Bauer on the forecastle, gesticulating as mooring lines were hauled aboard. Two officious tugs had sidled up to *Sturmvogel* and were boiling around the raider's bow and stern. 'Let go aft. Dead slow ahead.'

The telegraph clanged again and the ship's vibration increased. A pencil rolled across the Kieler Bucht chart and came to rest against a pair of brass dividers. Adler appeared on the bridge in wet oilskins. 'Ship secured for sea, Kapitän.'

'Very good, close up the hands at battle stations and make sure we are properly darkened. Then I want you to set the watch below to alter the ship's appearance. As discussed, by first light we will be the Russian auxiliary cruiser *Natalya*.'

'Of course, Kapitän.'

'*Steuermann*, make for the boom gate,' said Falk. 'When we are through, bring her around to the northeast.'

'Aye, sir,' said the tall coxswain, bending over his wheel.

The boom-defence vessel drew aside the barrier like a doorman, let out a mournful blast, then pulled the gate closed behind them. Falk imagined he could hear the scraping of a key in the lock. There was no going back. Perhaps this was indeed a *Himmelfahrtskommando* — a suicide mission. Despair swept through him like an Arctic squall. To war, again. For a moment, he held a golden image of Katja and his three little daughters in his mind, then banged that door closed too.

Behind him, as night pressed in, Kiel Harbour was sunk in gloom. There was not a glimmer of light from the town under the enforced blackout.

Falk retired to his cabin and opened the sealed orders. He noticed the tremble in his hands, the age-old apprehension and foreboding, but also the thrill. The raider's main operational area would be the South Atlantic, extending into the south-western Indian Ocean. Falk had visited South Africa in 1930 on the cruiser *Emden* and had fond memories of the country. Cape Town had seemed to him a handsome, sleepy city and the Afrikaner inhabitants in particular had made the crew feel welcome in their homes. It would be strange to return as an enemy. Or perhaps only an enemy to some, not all, South Africans.

Free of the shelter of Kiel, *Sturmvogel* began corkscrewing into an awkward sea. The ship creaked and groaned, tossing back and forth, trying to find comfort again in her uneven home. Like a clumsy dance partner, she seemed to wrongly anticipate all the steps. The first cases of seasickness were immediate, and dramatic. A handful of ashen-faced sailors took to their bunks.

Falk returned to the wheelhouse. A telegraphist entered from the wireless room. 'Coded message from *OKM*, sir. It's from Großadmiral Raeder!' There was a hush on the bridge as every ear strained to hear.

'Yes, what is it?' Falk snapped.

'The Großadmiral informs you that the Führer himself wishes the *Hilfskreuzer Sturmvogel* happy hunting and a safe return to the fatherland.'

Lieutenant-Commander Adler sprang to attention and made a Nazi salute: '*Heil* Hitler! This is a great honour, Kapitän.'

The telegraphist handed the slip of paper to his captain. Falk stared at it for a long time, his face set in a frown, his eyes not registering the words. There was silence on the bridge, as though each man were holding his breath.

Falk scrunched the paper into a ball and threw it to the deck. 'Double the lookouts. I'll be in my sea cabin.' He strode angrily from the wheelhouse.

CHAPTER 5

Sleep would not come to Jack. Perhaps it was still, despite his changed situation, the dread of what slumber might usher in. The ghostly night-time consorts. Even the gentle shushing of the sea stroking the beach could not lull him to sleep. Getting out of bed, Jack pulled on a dressing gown and slippers. He padded down the passageway, pausing beneath the reproduction of a portrait of one of his forebears in dress uniform: a chest full of medals, an outthrust chin, one hand resting on a sword. Another formidable Pembroke.

Jack let himself out quietly through the French doors. His father's snoring was audible from the end of the veranda. A three-quarter moon hung above the Hottentots Holland Mountains, casting a trail of glittering light across the bay. He took the path to the beach. The chirruping of crickets filled the air as he passed beneath the milkwoods, then out into the moonlight and over the rocks. Kicking off his slippers, he walked down the beach. Warm water caressed his feet. False Bay's mountainous rim was dark and mysterious.

He was weighing his father's proposal against his fears. Did he have the nerve to captain a ship, even if she was a small one, let alone lead a flotilla? He certainly didn't have his father's temperament, or his conviction. His arrogance. Could there be a way to make this work?

Having a command of his own was certainly tempting. In the months before Dunkirk, it was exactly what he'd wished for. Now the dream had been poisoned by something inside him that he found both frightening and unfathomable.

He caught sight of a shadow coming round the headland from the north. It was obscured by the backdrop of dark mountains, but there was definitely something there, and it was moving fast. He narrowed his eyes and waited, feeling a strange excitement. It was a ship coming out of Simon's Town harbour, knifing through the swell, showing no lights. Leaving for patrol — perhaps an enemy vessel had been reported. Each time she dipped into a trough, he could make out the moustache of her bow wave. After a while, he heard the low thrumming of turbines. A midnight creature of the deep.

As the ship crossed the path of the moon, he saw her silhouette. A Royal Navy destroyer, long and sleek; an iron arrow, all power and grace. A thing of beauty. On the bridge, he thought he could just make out a couple of heads, staring ahead at the wide mouth to False Bay, opening to the South Atlantic. His heart beat faster.

'Damn,' he said softly. 'Damn and blast.'

The drama of it; the necessity of it. Taking the fight to the enemy in the southern oceans. A chance to hit back after all they had taken from him. Mama. *Havoc.* Hate and anger, infused with the conviction he'd felt at the beginning of the war, flooded through him.

He picked up a pebble, cupped it between forefinger and thumb, and sent it skipping across the water. The stone kisses spread circles through the quiet shallows of the cove. A long line of Pembroke captains stretched back into the fog of British history.

Maybe, he thought, *just maybe.*

'You slept late, like your sister.' His father was buttering a piece of toast over a copy of the *Cape Times* as Jack stepped onto the veranda. The morning was already hot.

'I couldn't get to sleep for ages. When I did, I was out like a light. The sleep of the dead.'

'Good, Milkwood does that to you. It's the most restful house I've ever lived in, just like a ship at anchor. Pour yourself a cup of tea.'

Jack sat down and watched his father struggling to come to grips with a grapefruit using a knife and fork.

'Father.'

'Yes, Jack?' Hearing his son's tone, the admiral put the implements down.

'I *did* give it a lot of thought. Last night. What you said.'

'And?'

'And I think I'd like to give it a bash.'

'Excellent news, son! We should have something a bit stiffer than tea.'

'I'm not sure that I won't make a hash of it…'

'Of course, doubts are to be expected, my boy. Two terrible knocks, one after the other, and your injuries. But a command of your own! To be quite honest, I think it's just the ticket. Gives one focus. Direction.'

'This is a different war, Father. At Dunkirk I saw —'

'No, it's not different.'

Jack sighed. There was no point arguing with the admiral. 'So what comes next?'

'You'll need to report to SNO Simon's Town, Commodore O'Reilly. He can be prickly. We trod on each other's toes at the beginning. Your flotilla is South African, part of the Seaward Defence Force, but you'll be operating out of Simon's Town, which is Royal Navy. So best to keep relations cordial. O'Reilly can give you the nuts and bolts. Later, I'll fill you in on the broader picture. Let me give O'Reilly a bell and see if we can't set up a meeting this morning. Wear your best uniform. Get

Rachel to give it an iron. O'Reilly is a stickler on that front, *very* pusser.'

Jack poured more tea for both of them.

'You know, when war broke out, South Africa had no navy to speak of,' said the admiral. 'I met with Smuts, Pirow, Royal Navy bigwigs, politicians. It was uphill all the way. South Africa is … complicated. I've had to use all my diplomacy skills—'

'Rudimentary at best.'

The admiral chuckled. 'I'll have you know I've bitten my tongue raw since I've been here. You'd be very proud.'

'You haven't considered extending this to family matters?'

'With your dear mother, yes. With my children, no.'

'So, why *is* the politics so complicated?'

'Too many cooks. The creation of a Seaward Defence Force is a way of placating all sides. Not quite a South African navy, but enough autonomy to mollify the nationalist elements in government. "It's the thin end of the wedge," says O'Reilly. He may be right. Perhaps it will mean the Royal Navy eventually gets booted out of Simon's Town, but so be it. Right now, there's a war to be won.'

'I can see the South African position,' said Jack. 'Here they have the British running a naval base right under their noses.'

'And the Royal Navy tries to dictate what they can and can't do in their own territorial waters. I'm left in the middle treading on eggshells. The British attitude, especially emanating from Admiralty House, has been snobbish and insular.'

'The "Britannia Rules the Waves" mentality?'

'Precisely. Let's just say that the Royal Navy clique hasn't exactly endeared itself to the general public. Make sure you don't slip into that trap, Jack. You need to remain light-footed.

In South Africa, things are always more byzantine than they seem.'

'I'll be on the lookout and keep my distance at first.'

'Yes, you get the picture. As you can imagine, I don't always agree with my admiralty colleagues, least of all O'Reilly. He's an inflexible, old-school prig. Anglo-Irish. We've come to a sort of compromise. The Royal Navy looks after the bigger picture of the high seas. My South African force deals with local minesweeping and the like. But, as you can imagine, there are two heads of command at the Cape and I need to be very careful how I deal with the SNO. The reason I'm in Simon's Town — instead of at the Castle — is to have my finger on the Royal Navy pulse. I want to be able to sit down with O'Reilly, every day if necessary, to oil this "alliance".'

'Or pour oil on the water?'

'Too true. It's also why I wanted you, as a representative of the Royal Navy, to command a flotilla that in a way straddles the two forces.'

'You're not hanging me out to dry, are you, Father?'

'Not at all! I'm convinced some of my diplomatic blood has found its way into your veins. Surely?'

'No, not surely. But I'll try my best.'

Two hours later, Wren Monroe drove Jack into town and dropped him off beside the church in Court Road.

'Pretty building,' he said.

'Yes, sir. St Francis of Assisi. Anglican. I can bring you on Sunday.'

'Very kind, Monroe, but no thanks. Right, where do I go?'

'Double-storey house behind you with the green veranda and mast. Through the gate with the anchors and to your right. And sir —'

'Yes, Monroe?'

'Straighten your tie.'

'Ah, thank you.'

The sentry saluted, checked Jack's papers and directed him down a path, through a green door. After a few minutes, he was ushered into a large office. Sash windows offered a fine view of the anchorage. A tall, grey-haired man in his fifties with a long, craggy face sat behind the desk. Jack snapped to attention.

'There you are. Another Pembroke to make my life difficult. Have a seat.'

'Thank you, sir.'

'A good voyage?'

'Yes, sir.'

There was a long pause.

'Minesweepers, I'm told?'

'In the Channel, sir. Before Dunkirk.'

'And now your father thinks it's a good idea that you come and meddle here.' The commodore's eyes were icy.

'Not at all, sir. It's just that —'

'To be quite honest, I don't like having ships in Simon's Town that aren't under my direct command. It's going to cause trouble. As far as I'm concerned, the creation of a separate force is a blatant attempt to wrest control away from this command.'

'I understand your concerns, sir.'

'No, you do not, Lieutenant.' O'Reilly raised his voice. 'And now I've got the admiral's son in my harbour. Rum job, but I suppose we'll have to try to make the best of it.'

'Sir, I'll do whatever is needed. I am Royal Navy, after all.'

'Very well, let's get straight to business. Your flotilla is made up of four ships: *Southern Belle*, *Southern Gannet*, *Southern Wayfarer* and *Southern Star.* They've been taken over from Thor Whaling Company and refitted for minesweeping. About 140 feet long, 400 tons, 1,300 horsepower with a top speed of 16 knots and a range of nearly 4,000 miles. Oil-fired, so they don't need experienced stokers. Triple expansion three-cylinder steam engines powering a single prop. They were built between 1935 and '37. Useful little vessels.'

'Wet ships, sir?'

'Very. With no bilge keel to stop the rolling, and a jolly low freeboard, they're like half-tide rocks. Pack your sou'wester.'

'What armaments do they carry, sir?'

'A twelve-pounder on the fo'c'sle where the whale harpoon used to sit. Two Lewis machine guns either side of the bridge — 1918 vintage, I'm afraid, and prone to jamming — and a single-barrel pom-pom aft. Not that we're expecting enemy aircraft, but it's a handy all-round weapon.'

'What about U-boats, sir?'

'No depth charges fitted as yet. Anti-submarine work will grow in importance. For now, we need to concentrate on sweeping. We know that mine-laying raiders are at large in the Atlantic and they're our main headache at the moment. Questions?'

'Which one will be my ship, sir?'

'HMSAS *Southern Gannet.* Her skipper has been posted to the Med to replace a captain killed on one of the South African sweepers operating out of Alexandria.'

'Can you tell me anything about the flotilla's other three skippers, sir?'

'Yes, Alstad is Norwegian, ex-whaler, very experienced. Wilson is local RNVR — a good man, Sunday yachtsman, knows his way around boats. Du Toit is a product of the

General Botha. You know about her? She's moored behind me in the roads.'

'The old *Thames*. I've heard good things about the chaps who've come through that system.'

'Yes, *Southern Gannet*'s first officer, Smit, is also a *Botha* boy.'

'Operationally, sir, what are my duties?'

'Yours will be a standing tactical unit. Admiral Pembroke can fill you in on the details. For the first couple of weeks you'll work up the flotilla in False Bay. Some of your men have had sea time, but most are pretty raw. You'll have your hands full. Some of your training will involve sweeping the False Bay channel, as well as gunnery and honing your crews in these relatively protected waters. I'll be able to watch you from right here.'

Jack noticed a telescope on a tripod in the corner of the office. He would be in the eyes at all times.

'And accommodation, sir?'

'You won't be staying with the Admiral?' O'Reilly sounded surprised.

'Er, no, sir. It's out of town, and I'd like to be near the ship.'

'I hear what you're saying.' The commodore smiled. 'Simon's Town is chock-a-block at the moment. All the usual naval accommodation is full. We've even got men bunking in the rafters of the old sail loft. Bloody sardines. But if you're a permanent fixture, we can organise something, billet you with one of the townsfolk. I'll put someone onto it.'

'I'd appreciate that, sir.'

'All right, Lieutenant, I need to get back to work. There's a war on, you know. Best of luck.'

Back at Milkwood, Jack received a call from the commodore's office to say that a billet had been found in the home of a Miss

Retief. He was given the address, Belleview House on York Street. A driver would collect him.

Jack gathered his things, said goodbye to Rachel and asked her to tell his father he'd found accommodation and would be joining his ship shortly. She handed him a paper bag.

'*Koeksisters*,' she said.

'What's that?'

'They're sort of fried dough things twisted like rope and covered in syrup.'

While being driven back to town, he reached into the bag, pulled out one of the strange doughnuts and took a bite. It had a golden crust. The sweet, syrupy centre exploded in his mouth. 'Good God, that's delicious,' he muttered.

'Beg pardon, sir?'

'No, nothing, sailor, just this cake-sister thing.'

'*Koeksister*, excellent isn't it, sir?'

The Chevy drove through town, turned left into Arsenal Way and wound up the hill. York Street ended at a farm gate, with 'Belleview' daubed in whitewash on a boulder. The AB got out and opened the rickety gate. They drove up a sand road lined with pomegranate trees and came to a drystone wall.

'Hello, Jack!' came a voice with a heavy Afrikaans accent. A woman wearing a straw hat and a purple smock was standing on a garden terrace above the driveway. She wore gloves and a basket lay on the ground beside her.

'Oh hello, Miss Retief, how do you do?'

'I'll be down in a minute. Just picking something for lunch. Get your man to put your bags under the fig tree.'

He opened the wooden gate and entered an enchanting garden. The lawn was enclosed on three sides by the stone wall, a semi-detached cottage and the main house, which appeared to be the highest building on the mountain slope.

Belleview itself looked very old, the garden cottage a more recent addition.

The fourth side was open to the harbour and bay, spread out far below. There were three trees down the centre of the garden: a fig tree, and a pomegranate and custard apple with a hammock strung between them. On terraces above and below the house he could see olive, apple and lemon trees, as well as a few vines. It reminded him of Provence, where the family had spent holidays, or Greece, which he'd visited with a bunch of his Oxford pals.

Jack thanked the able seaman and dismissed him.

Miss Retief appeared from a gate beside the cottage. Pulling off her gloves, she shook his hand. Dark brown eyes, a hunched posture and a deeply lined face. Her handshake was firm.

'Come inside, Jack. You're fresh from England, aren't you?'

'Yes, I've just arrived. The Cape is so beautiful. And so is your home.'

'You might not be quite so enamoured after a five-day southeaster, but yes, it is. Actually, we're quite protected from the wind up here. The first settlers knew where to situate their houses.'

Miss Retief led him into the garden cottage through French doors with internal shutters. 'This is your place. It was built in the nineteenth century for a spinster aunt of the former owners. It's small but has all the basics.'

The cottage was one long room with a single bed in the corner, an armchair, dresser, table and a tiny kitchen with kettle, sink and hotplate. The bathroom was off the kitchen. There were green sea urchins on a string; an abalone shell served as an ashtray. It was comfortable and spotlessly clean.

Through a square window he could see the mountain rising steeply behind the cottage.

'This will do perfectly, Miss Retief.'

'Good. Come through to the house and I'll make us some *moer* coffee.'

He didn't know what 'moer' meant, but it sounded like trouble.

Jack followed Miss Retief through a side door into a dark dining room filled with antiques. The walls were hung with dramatic modern paintings, some of them quite risqué to Jack's eye. Miss Retief banged about in the kitchen, then emerged bearing a tray with steaming mugs. She gestured for Jack to sit down at the table with her.

'Have a rusk. It's like a biscuit. You dip it in the coffee.'

'Do you make them yourself?'

'*Ja*, I'm fairly self-sufficient up here. I have a *bakoond* round the side of the house to bake bread. A neighbour down the road has a few cows, so milk is not a problem, and Belleview sits on quite a large property with a vegetable garden and fruit trees. I have some chickens at the back too, and a tortoise, but Ignatius is not for eating.'

'If there's war rationing, you'll be well sorted.'

'*Ja*, I suppose so. We both will be.' She smiled. 'If you need groceries, there's Runciman's Store on St Georges Street. For entertainment, there's the Criterion Cinema. The programme changes regularly. Lots of cowboy films without much substance, I'm afraid.'

Copying his landlady, Jack dunked one end of the rusk in his coffee, held it there for a few moments and then bit into it. The 'biscuit' was rather good. The coffee was the strongest he'd ever tasted.

'Are you retired, Miss Retief?'

'*Ag*, I've never really had a proper job, unless teaching a bit of art to children can be considered a job. No, Jack, I'm a painter, oils mostly, sometimes watercolours. Impressionist in my youth … aren't we all? Now more expressionist. Landscapes, nudes, whatever takes my fancy. Still lifes too, although they never seem to sit still.'

'Are these some of yours?'

'Yes, not to your taste?'

'No, no, I do like them.' Jack blushed. 'I just don't know much about art.'

'We can change that, Lieutenant.' She had a mischievous grin. 'Now then, we must let you unpack. I suppose you'll be coming and going, but your rent does cover one meal a day. I think it's best if you sort yourself out for breakfast and lunch, then join me for supper. When you're not at sea, that is. Simple, basic *boerekos* — farm cooking. Nothing fancy here. Let me know by midday if you'll be joining me.'

'You're very kind, thank you.'

'There's no telephone in your place, but I can take messages for you.'

Jack returned to the cottage, unpacked his clothes, placed his handful of books on the shelf and hung his sword from a hook on the wall. He changed into slacks and a short-sleeved shirt and went to sit on a deckchair at the edge of the garden. This might be his last day of rest in a long time. A flock of guinea fowl trotted officiously across the lawn; a southern boubou with a pretty cinnamon belly hopped from branch to branch emitting a piercing whistle.

He scanned the town with his binoculars. Up to the left, he could make out the 9.2-inch guns that commanded the anchorage. Along the coast to the north and south he could see smaller-calibre emplacements and anti-aircraft guns. Simon's Town was a veritable fortress.

Looking closer at the harbour, he watched the bustle down there, at this fulcrum of the southern oceans. A dazzle-camouflaged cruiser was being manoeuvred into the dry dock by three tugs. Lighters dotted the bay and two large gooseneck cranes stood on the harbour wall. In the far corner of the basin, moored beside the eastern breakwater, he could see four grey dots. In comparison to the other warships, they looked insignificant. Supernumeraries. He felt a quickening of his pulse at the sudden realisation that one of those dots was his.

CHAPTER 6

Seaman Paul Brooke struggled under the weight of his canvas duffel bag. The young sailor was short and overweight, his face sprinkled with freckles. Despite an attempt at shaving, there was still no need to wield a blade across his downy cheeks. He looked, and was, too young to be going to war. Brooke tottered along the pier until he came to a stubby craft with the number T65 painted in black on her bows. His new home: HMSAS *Southern Gannet.* He took a nervous step onto the gangplank and nearly lost his balance as the duffel bag threatened to topple him into the oily water.

It had been a long journey to get here. Three months earlier, he'd taken the train from his home in Johannesburg to the Cape. Patriotic duty had not come into his decision. Brooke was after adventure and the chance to leave school before matriculating. He'd visited the Joburg recruitment centre at the Union Grounds near Hillbrow, where there were huts for each arm of the service. After having tried and failed to join the army, medical corps and air force (barred from all three for being underage, at sixteen), he set his sights on the navy hut. Brooke waited until after lunch, when the warrant officer in charge of recruiting was enjoying the warm afterglow of a few constitutional Lion lagers. The man forgot to ask for Brooke's birth certificate and his age was duly recorded as eighteen.

Despite his single mother's vocal protestations, he'd left for Cape Town to begin basic training at the former Grand Prix racing track at Pollsmoor. After medical inspection — no fallen arches, a heart that beat a more or less regular tattoo, and hernias that jumped when he coughed — Brooke was declared fit to join the Seaward Defence Force. He was issued with a kit bag and naval gear, including a white dickey shirt and large bell-bottomed trousers with seven creases representing the seven seas.

Turning out for the first time, his intake was informed by a terrifying RN petty officer that they were the most disgraceful, untidy, useless bastards he'd ever clapped eyes on. The smallest of his intake, Brooke was singled out for particular attention. The bow on his cap tally was always askew, his boots were filthy and his attitude needed an about face if he didn't want to be flogged round the fleet.

Brooke had to learn his port from his starboard, how to salute navy style and how to 'box the compass' by naming all thirty-two points in proper order. During rope work, he managed to get himself tied up in complicated knots, hitches and splices that he couldn't imagine he'd ever need to use. Walls became bulkheads, ceilings became deckheads, doors and stairs were now hatches and companionways. It was all so confusing.

Each morning after divisions, his intake would march around the parade ground to the strains of 'Heart of Oak', as played by the Royal Marines band on a scratchy seventy-eight rpm record attached to a loudspeaker. There were seamanship and gunnery classes, signals and semaphore, shooting at the Woltemade rifle range and endless hours of drill.

'I taught the scum of Britain, now I teach the scum of South Africa,' yelled the rotund instructor. 'Ordinary Seaman Brooke, you're a lazy, lily-livered layabout! Around the main mast, *at the double*!' In fact, everything was done at the double: there was no such thing as walking in Pollsmoor.

Best of all were the sailing days at Granger Bay, where the Seaward Defence Force had a boatshed with two twenty-seven-foot whalers fitted with oars and sails. Chief Thomas took them out and kept up an unbroken stream of sarcastic advice without ever raising his heavily accented Welsh voice, despite many a near ramming, broaching or capsize.

Brooke emerged from three months' training as a 'tiddly' sailor. He'd learnt to bleach his collar the light blue of a real saltwater seaman, crease his trouser legs to look like a concertina and copy the old trick of sewing pennies into the inside of his collar to keep it in place when the wind was up. In his mind, he was more than ready to join the proper navy.

Two weeks' leave over Christmas saw him returning home to surprise his mother in his smart uniform with its distinctive red diamond on each sleeve, announcing his willingness to serve outside the Union if needed. There was an endless round of tea parties organised by his mother, visits to distant relatives and a day watching cricket at the Wanderers with old school friends. All the while he was thinking nervously, excitedly, about what lay in store when he 'joined the fleet'.

Soon it was time to return to the Cape. His mother saw him off at Benoni Station, where he was the only person in uniform on the platform. A group of Afrikaans boys eyed him aggressively.

'England's fokkin' war!' one of them hissed and spat on the platform.

Just in time, a guard blew loudly on his whistle. 'All aboard!'

Brooke hugged his mother. Avoiding her tears, he hoisted his duffel bag and stepped onto the train. Joburg's yellow mine dumps soon receded and the Highveld, luxuriantly green from summer rains, rattled past, followed by the arid wastes of the Karoo. There were other sailors on board and, although he was unused to alcohol, he had a few beers with the men, who all seemed so much older than him, but were, in fact, mostly still teenagers.

Next morning, the train steamed through the vineyard-clad valleys of Worcester and finally arrived at Cape Town station. A square-faced petty officer stood on the platform with a clipboard. Brooke joined a group of seamen gathered around him. Names and units were read out and sailors sent in different directions.

'Ordinary Seaman Brooke?'

'Yes, PO!'

'You're assigned to HMSAS *Southern Gannet*, based in Simon's Town.' The petty officer handed him a slip of paper. 'We've got transport for you. Out the main entrance, turn right and look for the half-ton truck. Report to Minesweeping Headquarters, East Dockyard. Then go and see the paymaster: you're on thirty pence a day. Got it?'

And so began Paul Brooke's war.

'Leave your bag here and report to the Jimmy with your draft chit,' said a gruff quartermaster. 'He's in the wardroom. Starboard side, second door.'

Who on earth is 'the Jimmy'? Brooke peered into the entrance and saw a sub-lieutenant writing at a desk. The wardroom had dark leather furniture, a worn carpet, a dartboard and a well-polished dining table. A faded Van Gogh reproduction hung from the bulkhead and a bowl of rather incongruous flowers stood on the table. The officer was impeccably turned out in his white summer uniform with shorts.

Brooke suddenly felt anxious about his badly ironed dickey shirt. He stepped into the doorway and stood at attention. 'Seaman Brooke reporting for duty, sir.'

The sub didn't look up. The young sailor was nonplussed. Had the officer heard him? Should he sneak away and come back later?

'Seaman Brooke reporting for duty, sir!' he said more loudly.

'What the hell?' cursed Smit, not lifting his eyes from the page.

'Seaman Broo—' he said nervously.

'Yes, damn it, can't you see I'm busy?'

'Sorry, sir, I was told to report to Jimmy.'

'Oh, for crying out loud! Go and see the cox'n.'

'Thank you, sir. Where will I find —'

'How should I bloody well know? Do I look omniscient?'

'Yes, sir. I mean, no, sir.'

Brooke returned to the quartermaster. 'I got a right royal bollocking from that subby. He said I should report to the cox'n.'

'Oh, the Jimmy's a bastard all right. Strong arm, limp wrist, if you get my drift. He's heavy with dishing out punishment. Stay clear of him. He might enjoy a little squeaker like you.'

'The cox'n —'

'*Ja*, aft. PO February. Follow your nose. Next to the galley.'

Seaman Brooke walked down the ship's waist, hurrying past Sub-Lieutenant Smit's open door, until he reached the petty officers' mess. He wrapped his knuckles on the bulkhead and called, 'PO February, are you there?'

'Yes,' came a sleepy voice. 'Come in.'

Brooke tentatively drew back the curtain and stepped into the mess. A petty officer in a rumpled white shirt and blue trousers came slowly upright in his bunk, dragging sleep from his face with a tired hand. February was a burly fellow with a dark complexion, gentle features and a high forehead.

'Sorry to disturb, PO. Seaman Brooke reporting for duty.'

February yawned and stretched. 'All right, I suppose I'd better show you the ropes. Ever been to sea before, er, Brooke, was it?'

'Yes, PO. No, PO. I just finished basics.'

'*Jislaaik*, another one. Lots to learn then, sailor. First of all, let's get you set up in the mess. You'll be starboard watch.'

They walked to the main deck, collecting Brooke's duffel bag at the gangway. Coming to an open hatch, February stepped over the coaming and onto a steel ladder. Brooke followed him down into the dimly lit, badly ventilated cavern that was the seamen's mess. No one was home. The claustrophobic space was stiflingly hot and stank of mouldy clothing, unwashed bodies and the residual smell of whale. A mound of dirty socks and underwear was piled on a pillow.

Two tiers of wooden bunks lined the bulkheads, each with a couple of blankets on a rough coir mattress. Above one of the bunks was a pin-up of a balloon-breasted nude wearing a sailor's cap. Down the middle of the mess stood wooden benches and a narrow table with foul-weather fiddles to keep the crockery from going walkabout in heavy seas. A trapdoor in the deck led to the ammunition store and bosun's store filled with everything from spare cordage and wire to cotton waste and marlin spikes.

'This is your locker,' said PO February. It looked large enough to take about half the kit in his duffel bag. 'No locks in the mess, not even on the lockers. No one steals on this ship. We borrow. That's the only free dossing place: top bunk, for'ard, starboard side. Hang on tight in rough seas or you might come unstuck and land on top of the bloke below.'

'Thank you, PO.'

'You'll be part of the duty watch tonight. It'll give you a chance to settle in and meet your messmates. When your watch is on duty in harbour, you'll do a stint of gangway duty on alternate nights.'

'When will we be going to sea, PO?'

'We don't know yet. The new skipper's coming aboard any day now, so be prepared. He's a Limey, father's an admiral *nogal*. We're gonna have a toff on our hands. Oh, and change into overalls. You don't want to muck up your nice uniform.' The coxswain turned to the ladder, intent on getting some more shut-eye.

'By the way, PO, what's a Jimmy?' asked Brooke.

'It's the First Lieutenant. And stay on the right side of that one. Not a bad person, just a bit mixed up.' With that, the coxswain disappeared through the hatch and Brooke was left alone. The teenager suddenly felt overwhelmed and more than a little despondent. He was shocked at the cramped nature of his living quarters: the mess was a long way from the spit and polish of Pollsmoor. He was surprised to find himself aching for home.

It was already late afternoon by the time he'd unpacked and sorted himself out. Brooke sat on his bunk writing a letter to his mother, telling her about the train journey and his new ship. The duty watch began to filter down the ladder. All of them seemed much older than Brooke, although none had turned twenty-one yet.

'So, we've got a new one, hey,' said Seaman Potgieter, a large Afrikaner with a broken nose, tattoos and an uncanny knack for knowing how to start a fight in almost any situation. 'Fokkin' hell, look at him, he's just a baby! Do you think he's out of nappies yet, *ous*?'

There were a few indulgent sniggers. No one wanted to provoke Potgieter. Brooke raised his chin and reached out a nervous hand. 'Paul Brooke, pleased to meet you.'

'Pickles Brooke with the tiny pickle!' squealed Potgieter, imitating a girl's voice. The man slapped his hand and snorted. 'This is not the Royal Fucking Navy, boykie.' Then the sailor lost interest, and sat down at the table with a comic. Brooke made sure he found a place at the opposite end. As the rest of the crew came down the ladder, he introduced himself. They seemed like a rough lot to Brooke, a mix of Afrikaans- and English-speaking, with a few ratings of colour.

'Don't mind Potgieter,' said a tall blond seaman. 'He can be a bit of a wanker, but you want him on your side in a scrap. I'm Roger, by the way. Roger Fitzpatrick. They call me Lofty.'

'Hello, Lofty. What's your station?'

'When we're not sweeping, I'm on the pom-pom. And you?'

'Dunno yet.'

'Good, we need a loader. Come with me.'

They climbed to the upper deck and went aft, where Lofty showed Brooke his number-two position on the gun. 'This is how you load the pom-pom belts. When firing, hot oil spits off the barrel, so no fancy clothing. Make sure your hand doesn't get caught in the mechanism: instant mincemeat. Got it?'

'Aye, Lofty, got it.'

After supper, Brooke had a hasty scrub in the forecastle's wash closet, then kicked off his boots, climbed out of his overalls and onto the top bunk. Even though he was exhausted, he lay awake thinking about his mother and the green mealie fields near his home. It all seemed unimaginably distant from this nautical world. How was he ever going to fit in? And what of the German Navy lying in wait over the horizon?

Briefcase in hand, Jack walked down Belleview's driveway dressed in his whites. It was another hot summer's day and the pincushion proteas lining his path were loud with the twitter of sunbirds. As he walked, he watched the naval base unfurl below him, his nerves jangling at the thought of the meeting to come.

After passing the Admiralty's tennis courts, he descended a flight of stone steps and emerged onto St Georges Street. The town was jammed with dockyard labourers arriving for work and military transport rumbling towards the base. At every turn he could hear Geordie, Scouse, Yorkie and Taffy accents.

He walked past the United Services Institute building, where ratings found lodging while their ships were in harbour. Bed and breakfast was only sixpence, but the sailors had to endure Mr Barralet's sermons about the demon liquor. Jack noticed a Great Dane asleep in the doorway, snoring loudly. Any sailor trying to enter would have to climb over the enormous hound.

A smart platoon of naval cadets marched into the Victorian gates of West Dockyard, where he saw a Fairey Fox floatplane parked outside a hangar. He passed the British Hotel, the bakery, an off-licence and a row of small palm trees which Wren Monroe had said were planted six years earlier to mark the silver jubilee of King George V and Queen Mary.

Jack flashed his identity card and entered East Dockyard, past the muster-bell tower and down Approach Road via the zigzag air-raid shelter. To his right, a recreation hall with a scale model of HMS *Victory* beside the entrance, to his left, a graving dock, the walls of which were painted with the crests of ships that had undergone repairs there. He picked out the golden sailor's head with winged tin hat of HMS *Hermes*, freshly daubed on the sandstone. On the bluff he noticed a Martello tower with wide gun slits, a relic of Napoleonic times when the French were foe. Or more explicitly foe.

Jack found that his heart was beating faster and his leg had begun to ache. He paused for a moment to catch his breath and gather his thoughts. A group of labourers looked queerly at him as they strolled by; one muttered something in Afrikaans that caused a snigger. What did they see? Was it that obvious? Jack hurried on.

Coming round a corner, he spotted *Southern Gannet* and stopped in his tracks. His heart sank. She was even smaller than he'd expected, more overgrown fishing smack than warship, an ugly duckling if ever there was one. What had he been thinking? He'd made a terrible mistake.

Jack took a deep breath and, despite a sense of deepening despair, set off towards the *Gannet*. His professional eye quickly took in her features. A stubby vessel with a bulbous forecastle, box-like bridge and tall, upright funnel, two masts and a poop deck jumbled with minesweeping equipment. The sparkle of a welding torch showed that someone was putting the finishing touches to the sweeping gear. The twelve-pounder was trained haphazardly to port, and seamen were sloshing paint on the barrel. A shirtless sailor lay sunbathing on the boat deck. For a moment, Jack was incensed.

He reached the steep brow. At the inboard end, he could see a sentry picking his nose. The seaman caught sight of him, registered the two gold stripes and scurried to the bridge. Jack paused to give the sailor a chance to announce his arrival. There was the sound of clattering footsteps. With a sinking heart, he stepped onto the gangway.

Jack winced as a stab of pain shot up his leg — the break had mended but the leg remembered. He walked stiffly down the plank, saluting the ensign at the mizzenmast as he stepped aboard.

The sentry came to attention and saluted — sloppily, to Jack's *King Alfred* eye.

'Where can I find your First Lieutenant?'

'Up on the bridge, sir. Do you —'

'I'll find my way.'

He brushed past the sailor, climbed the steel ladder and stepped onto the open bridge. A neatly turned-out officer standing beside the binnacle saluted smartly. Tall, darkly suntanned, grey at the temples, thin lips, old for his rank.

'Welcome aboard, sir. I'm Sub-Lieutenant Robert Smit.'

'Thank you, Number One,' Jack said, putting down his briefcase. It was a cool greeting, the two officers weighing each other up.

'May I have your luggage brought aboard, sir?'

'I'll send for it later. I've taken a room in town. Would you be so kind as to show me around the ship?'

Smit looked startled. 'We weren't expecting you so soon, sir. *Gannet* is just back from refit and things are a bit of a shambles. Dockyard workers are still all over her like a rash.'

'Doesn't matter, it's not an inspection, Number One. We'll have things shipshape soon enough. I'd just like to get a feel for her.'

'As you wish, sir,' Smit said formally. 'I'll lead the way.'

They climbed down the ladder and stepped onto the forecastle where the orange-white-and-blue fluttered from the jackstaff. 'Our fo'c'sle has been strengthened to support the twelve-pounder, sir. Below the gun we've got showers, heads, a paint locker, chain store and a small cabin for the steward and cook. Under our feet is the seaman's mess and below that, ammunition and bosun's stores. One Carley float up here and one aft.'

Jack saw oil-soaked men in the water, the gunwales of the float awash. The wail of a Stuka's siren and stutter of machine guns. The screaming. He looked away and closed his eyes.

'This way, sir. Sir?'

'Carry on, Number One.'

They walked back down the sloping deck past a large winch. Smit opened a door below the bridge. 'This is your cabin.'

It was a cramped space with a narrow bunk, table and chair. Through the scuttle he could see two whale catchers on the far side of the basin. A portly ginger cat was asleep on the bed.

'Ah, sorry about that, sir. Fido is the ship's cat. She thinks she's in charge and no one has the heart to tell her otherwise.'

'Leave her be. I don't mind sharing. But Fido isn't a cat's name, is it?'

'It's the cook's idea of a joke. He started feeding her and now she's a fixture. You'll find that she's quite bossy, but we put up with her.'

They continued aft past the wireless cabin. Jack stuck his head through the door: a small bunk doubled as a seat beside a shelf crammed with transmitters and receivers, a battery compartment below and charging box above. Porcelain insulators and connections led to the radio aerial rigged between *Gannet*'s two masts.

The men proceeded along the main deck, poking their heads into the wardroom and officers' cabin. To Jack, the two feet of freeboard in the waist looked less than adequate for the Cape of Storms. They stepped through an open doorway to find three men playing a round of Crown and Anchor. The ashtray between them overflowed with cigarette butts and the cabin was thick with smoke. One of the men glanced up and stood quickly to attention. The other two followed suit.

'At ease, gentlemen, I'm just being shown around by Sub-Lieutenant Smit.'

'This is your new Captain, Lieutenant Pembroke,' said Smit. 'Sir, this is PO Joubert, guns, PO February, coxswain, and PO Cummins, bosun.'

'Pleased to meet you all. Don't let me disturb the card game. I'll chat to you all properly later. Carry on.'

He stepped out and turned right. The open barn door leaking a strong smell of boiled cabbage was unmistakably the galley. A shirtless Porky Louw was not looking his neatest, a soiled seaman's cap pushed far back from his crimson face. He wore stained blue serge trousers and the filthiest apron Jack had ever seen. The cook bent over a coal-fired stove, sweating profusely and cursing in the choicest manner about something that had burnt. Jack put a finger to his lips and they moved on.

'Below us is the engine room and above us on the boat deck is a lifeboat and our secondary armament, a single-barrel, two-pounder pom-pom. Up there, you'll also find an ice-box. But it's rather dodgy and leaks like a sieve. Right aft, we've got our minesweeping gear.'

Jack ran his eye over the Oropesa floats, coiled lines and vanes. It looked a mess, but the gear was in good nick. The two officers climbed through a hatch and down a ladder into the engine room. There, a bald man in a dirty boiler suit with a sweaty cloth around his neck was making notes on a clipboard. He was even older than Smit, probably in his forties, thickset with wildly bushy eyebrows.

'This is the Chief ERA, McEwan, our miracle worker,' said Smit.

'Oh, 'ullo, sir, welcome aboard the *Jolly Roger*,' the chief boomed in a thick Scottish brogue. He was accustomed to shouting above the din of the engine and, after two decades at sea, was hard of hearing. He held out a big, oil-stained hand. Smit took a step back, a look of distaste on his face.

'Where do you hail from, Chief?' asked Jack, shaking the man's paw.

'Begging your pardon, sir?' The CPO leaned forward, cupping his ear.

'Where are you from?'

'Dundee, originally.'

'Goodness, is every engineer in the whole ruddy navy from Scotland?'

'Probably, sir, but I've been on Norwegian whale catchers half ma life. Antarctic run. Settled in the Cape with the wife back in the twenties.'

'Any children?'

'Nah, not blessed with bairns, sir.' He grinned, showing a lot of gold.

'You happy with the engine?'

'It's not too terrible, actually. Seen worse. Mooch bloody worse.'

'What can you get out of her, at a push?'

'Och, fifteen knots. Maybe sixteen, absolute tops.'

'Good, I'll take seventeen. We might be needing it.'

The two officers returned to the wardroom and took a seat at the table. The steward, AB Hendricks, had set out a tray with two mugs of tea.

'Right, Number One, let's get down to brass tacks.' Jack opened his briefcase and took out a buff folder. 'I'd like to see all recent signals, the log book, punishment book, and I need a report by tomorrow morning on the refit. Especially anything that still needs to be done. I also want to see a list of ammunition and stores, as well as the new watch bill.'

'Of course, Captain.'

'What can you tell me about the crew?'

'Well, we are three officers — Sub-Lieutenant Van Zyl is still on leave. One chief petty officer and three POs, who you've just met. There are three killicks: Baker is leading stoker, Thomas is telegraphist and Leading Signalman Gilbert is our Bunts. Two able seamen — Hendricks the steward and Louw in the galley. Twelve seamen in the for'ard mess, mostly young and raw. For many, this is their first ship. One or two Cape Coloured fishermen among them, who supposedly know their way around boats.'

'Good.'

'Not that I agree with having men of colour on board.'

'Oh?'

'We do things differently here in the Union. Segregation has been shown to work. I think —'

'I didn't ask for your opinion, Number One. If the man is a good sailor, I really don't care what colour he is.'

'It's not —'

'And see to it that a sturdy chair is bolted to the deck on the bridge. I don't expect to be spending much time in my cabin when we're at sea.'

Smit looked as though he was struggling to bite his tongue.

'Another thing, Number One. I want to meet the other three captains. Ask them to be in *Gannet*'s wardroom at 14:00.' Jack felt the first tentacles of a headache. He pressed his temple with a thumb.

'Are you all right, sir? A glass of water or an aspirin, perhaps?' To Jack, it sounded condescending.

'I'm absolutely fine!' he snapped. 'Thank you, Number One, that will be all.'

CHAPTER 7

The men came to attention as Jack stepped across the coaming. He shook hands with each. Alstad, Wilson, Du Toit. 'Please, have a seat, gents.'

Chairs scraped around the heavy wooden table.

'I wanted the opportunity to meet all of you, put faces to names.' Jack could hear the nervousness in his own voice. Alstad, the tall, thickset Norwegian, was old enough to be his father. Wilson was a refined, affable-looking local chap and Du Toit a stocky Afrikaner with a tough demeanour.

Jack coughed to clear his throat and his thoughts. Hendricks appeared with a bottle of gin and set out four glasses.

'Shall I pour, sir?' asked Du Toit.

'Yes, thank you. Over the coming days, we'll be working up the flotilla. I understand you've all had some experience with sweeping.'

'I've had very little, sir,' said Wilson.

'Well, you'll just have to get up to speed.'

'Yes, sir.' Wilson looked down at his drink.

'We need to galvanise the flotilla into a team. We'll soon be working in rough offshore conditions. I think we should start by doing practice sweeps close inshore, then join *Kirstenbosch* and *Immortal* on the False Bay channel. There will also be live-fire practice, both surface and air. I will be pushing you hard. You will be pushing your men hard.'

There was an uncomfortable silence.

'How long do we have, sir?' asked Alstad.

'Not long. Commodore O'Reilly has given us ten days. Intelligence reports that a German raider is probably coming our way. She could be in our waters any day now and will more than likely want to lay mines off the Cape. We must be ready to sweep before she gets here.'

'And if we encounter her, sir?' asked Wilson. Was there a hint of fear in his lieutenant's eye?

'Extremely unlikely. We'd leave her to the big boys and the air force.' Jack watched Wilson take a gulp of his gin. 'The flotilla will be under the eyes of the Commodore, who's none too happy about a rebellious pod like ours in his midst. So best foot forward, especially when we're in Simon's Bay.' He could hear that his tone sounded cold; he needed to be more engaging.

'Where will we do the practice sweeps, sir?' asked Du Toit.

'Where do you suggest, Du Toit?'

'Well, sir, there's regular live-fire practice at Lower North Battery these days, and lots of traffic close in. So perhaps further along the coast in the sheltered waters off Glencairn and Fish Hoek.'

'Agreed.'

They spent half an hour talking through the details of the coming week and drank a second round before the skippers took their leave.

That evening, Jack sat on a deckchair at the edge of Belleview's garden. He cradled binoculars and Miss Retief's bird book in his lap. Was that a malachite sunbird drinking nectar from the orange flowers? Its feathers were the most handsome, iridescent green…

The view reminded him of Cap Ferrat and the villa his family had rented during his last summer of school. He and Harry had shared an attic room overlooking the bay with spectacular views of Villefranche across the water, little Imogen next door and their parents downstairs. The cascading bougainvillea and scented pine trees, the shrill singing of the cicadas, the path to a tiny beach that they treated as their own. It was the last time the whole family had gone on holiday together, before the clouds had gathered between their parents; when everything was still whole, or seemed so at least.

From the slopes behind the house, Jack could hear the baritone barking of a troop of baboons heading for their night-time perches on the crags. The eddying sound of a muezzin calling from a mosque drifted up the slope as he scanned the bay. The four grey dots in the back corner of the harbour had acquired shape and texture. He could put faces to each of them now.

But what to make of the *Gannet*? He knew the first meeting with his captains had not gone well. He'd come across as too stuffy and his plummy accent didn't help, nor did having an admiral for a father. Back at *King Alfred*, the instructors had advised midshipmen in training to start as they meant to carry on. Show your crew that you'll brook no nonsense: Bristol fashion or the high jump. But was that the right way to do things out here in the Union? Perhaps he should ask his father. Then again, perhaps not.

Jack felt more exposed than ever before in his life. Everything he said and did was being watched, judged. He needed to take charge, be firm in his decisions. Confident, impartial. Discipline was never going to be up to *Havoc*'s standards, and he had to measure how far below that benchmark to set it. He thought about *Gannet*'s punishment book, crammed with recent offences: neglect of duty, late returning from leave, insubordination, drunkenness, fighting. Ratings of colour bore the brunt of the sanctions, and Smit's signature was beneath most of them.

Jack glanced over to where Miss Retief's two cats, Smuts and Hertzog, were playing on the lawn. Hertzog, the black one, was trying to stalk a recumbent Smuts, the white one. At the last moment, Smuts whipped around to face the threat. A riot of wrestling ensued in the long grass. *Ah, politics*, he thought, and smiled at the young toms.

Tomorrow, he would face the crew and begin his new command. And take his first ship to sea.

Jack strode down the gangplank the next morning. The shrill call of a bosun's pipe rose, dipped and was cut dead. As he stepped aboard, his hand snapped to a salute. He saw Smit standing smartly at the salute beside *Gannet*'s burly coxswain, Cummins next to him doing the piping. To his right, he could see a line of sailors at attention. Smit stepped forward. 'I'd like to officially welcome you aboard, sir.'

'Thank you, Number One.' Jack could hear that his voice sounded nervous, high-pitched. 'I will address the crew in a few minutes. Please have them fall in on the main deck.'

Jack ducked into his cabin and took off his cap. He was sweating and his heart was racing. Deep breaths. *My ship, my command, my men.* It suddenly felt like too much. He took a moment to compose himself, then stepped out.

Almost the entire crew — he counted twenty-two heads — were mustered. The second officer had still not returned from leave, and they might have to sail without him. Most of the men wore working rig: blue overalls and boots. Young, open-faced sailors inquisitive about their new captain. Most, such as Seaman Brooke, were new recruits and had only arrived in the last couple of days. The more experienced sailors wore knives in handmade leather sheaths and eyed Jack with what seemed like disdainful curiosity. English, Afrikaans and men of colour;

old salts and schoolboys. How long would it take to mould them into a fighting unit? He had ten days. Impossible.

Jack had hardly slept and his mouth was dry. In his pocket were handwritten notes, prompts. His fist closed around the paper, crunching it into a ball. He cleared his throat. 'Good morning, Gannets.' The faces staring up at him appeared surly, resentful even. 'I am Lieutenant Pembroke, your new captain. Over the coming days, I will get to know each of you better. For now, I'd just like to introduce myself and remind you how critically important our job is. The British Empire, the very outcome of this war, depends on protecting our harbours.'

Just then, there was a clattering at the brow. Jack paused and turned to see a young sub-lieutenant scurrying down the gangplank. 'That will be Van Zyl, sir,' whispered Smit with distaste. 'Punctuality is not his strong suit.'

'Send him to my cabin, Number One.' Jack turned back to the mustered men. Their faces remained impassive. 'With the Mediterranean effectively closed to Allied shipping,' he continued, 'it is no exaggeration to say that the campaigns in North Africa and the Middle East could be won in South African waters. HMSAS *Southern Gannet* will play her part. I want no passengers or bad hats.

'This morning we will take on stores and ammunition. This afternoon we will take *Gannet* for a turn around the bay. In the coming days, we will train with the rest of the flotilla and become a fighting unit that we can all be proud of. You will do your bit, I will do mine. Thank you, that is all.'

'Ship's company, attention!' bellowed February. 'Ship's company, dismissed!'

The errant sub-lieutenant was standing at attention beside Pembroke's door.

'At ease, Van Zyl, step inside.'

Jack took a seat behind his desk. He didn't offer the panting sub a chair. The young man before him was short with a cherubic face and unkempt blond hair. His shirt wasn't properly ironed, his morning shave slapdash.

'You're late. Not a very good first impression, is it?'

'I'm very sorry, sir.' His accent was thickly Afrikaans. 'I had leave and thought I'd be back in Simon's Town with lots of time this morning. The train —'

'Don't tell me, sand on the tracks.'

'Yes, sir.' The young man looked crestfallen.

'In future, if there's any doubt about the South African Railways, make sure you're back the night before, understood?'

'Yes, Captain.'

'Number One will fill you in. I expect punctuality and a better turnout from you in future. I don't need to tell you that officers must set an example.'

Van Zyl flushed bright pink.

'Dismissed.'

Throughout the morning, there was an industrious hum about the ship as officers and ratings went about their duties. While throbbing hoses pumped fresh water and oil into the minesweeper's bunkers, ammunition was loaded and stowed in the correct compartments, from heavy twelve-pounder shells to boxes of machine-gun ammunition. Space had to be found for extra canvas, rope and wire hawsers. Everything from jars of jam and loaves of bread to tinned milk and cigarette cartons poured down the gangway.

The ship's tannoy squealed to the bosun's call, then the voice of the quartermaster announced: 'Sea-duty men close up. Hands to stations for leaving harbour in fifteen minutes.'

It was time. Jack pushed back his chair, stood up and reached for his cap. He looked at himself in the mirror, tucking away a wayward lock of chestnut hair. Creased brow, steel-blue eyes that appeared permanently troubled. The scar on his temple was livid, almost purple. He had the square Pembroke jaw, but where was the legendary Pembroke confidence, the fire and brimstone? Now would be a good time for it to reveal itself.

'Both watches will be needed,' crackled the quartermaster. 'Quarterdeck men to the quarterdeck. Fo'c'sle men to the fo'c'sle.'

That would be Smit's doing, Jack thought: best have both watches ready with a nervous, untried captain. Who knew what kind of hash he might make of it? In truth, Jack had been dreading the prospect of taking *Southern Gannet* out for the first time — through the heart of the harbour, with the eyes of a dozen captains on him. It was like being in the centre of a colosseum. One mistake and he could be the laughing stock of the fleet.

There was a knock at the door. It was Thomas, the leading seaman telegraphist. 'Yes, Sparks, what is it?'

'From the tower, sir. Proceed when ready.'

'Very good, tell the First Lieutenant I'll be up in a minute.'

Jack climbed to the open bridge and took up position beside the binnacle. *Gannet*'s deck vibrated gently. February stood at the wheel below, awaiting orders. Sub-Lieutenant Smit, the Leading Signalman and a lookout stood on either side of him. Van Zyl was on the main deck, peering over the side. Cummins had gone aft to the boat deck, ready to relay instructions and keep an eye on the stern mooring party. Jack took a moment to compose his thoughts, making sure he remembered every step of the manoeuvre. Once *Gannet*'s 400 tons were in forward motion, he'd better know exactly what to do with them, especially in such a confined space.

'Stand by wires and fenders!'

'All singled up, sir,' said Smit.

'Ring stand-by,' said the captain. A bell jangled in the engine room. The deck began to quiver more purposefully. Jack imagined CPO McEwan and his men far below in their dark cavern of steam, dials and gauges. A plume of black smoke belched from the funnel and wafted across the harbour.

'Ready to proceed, sir,' said Smit.

'Thank you. We'll go astern on the aft spring and let the bows swing out. Cast off all other lines, Number One, and slow astern.'

'Aye, Captain.' The orders were relayed.

Trying to appear calm, Jack stepped to the side of the bridge and saw a couple of bored dockworkers release the spliced eyes from the quayside bollards. The lines splashed into the water and were slurped aboard. He watched the tightening of the aft spring wire, leading from the stern to a bollard on the quay abeam of the bridge. An oily patch of water opened between himself and the land. Painstakingly slowly, the bows swung away from the berth. He held his breath, as though willing the ship's head around. Now she was facing the harbour entrance. Ready.

'Stop engine.' The ship fell silent, save for a low pulsing. 'Bosun, let go spring! Slow ahead.' Water frothed beneath the poop as her propeller began to find purchase. The stern swung round, pushed by the southeaster. Jack gripped the rail. His head throbbed as if it had its own propeller. *Stay composed*, he told himself, *deep breaths*. *Southern Wayfarer* and *Southern Star* to starboard, *Southern Belle* to port. All idle eyes were on their sister ship. The stern kept swinging, helped by the wind. In a moment of terrifying clarity, Jack realised his ship was going to hit *Belle*.

'Hard aport, Cox'n! Full ahead!' he shouted into the voice pipe. In his head he heard the advice of his old instructor at *King Alfred*: 'When in doubt, full head. At least you'll have way on to manoeuvre.' But perhaps full astern might have been better in this instance.

'Full ahead, sir?' came a querulous voice from below.

'Yes, damn it, do as I say!'

'Fenders, port quarter, look lively there!' came a shout from Van Zyl as seamen ran to the stern carrying extra fenders.

Jack clenched his fists behind his back and forced himself to stroll to the starboard rail and sweep his eyes across the harbour. Concerned faces watched from the quayside and nearby ships. He heard shouting. Damn and blast. Heads appeared from scuttles to stare. When he returned to the port wing he could see that they weren't going to make it. Wide-eyed sailors on *Southern Belle* were scrambling for their own fenders to soften the impact. He waited for the agonising crunch, fingernails biting into his hands behind his back.

Gannet was gaining speed, her stern still slewing to connect with her sister. Jack turned away, unable to look. He braced himself for impact. Any moment now…

'Cleared, with a foot to spare, sir!' said a breathless Van Zyl, heaving himself up onto the bridge.

'What are you smiling at, Sub?' asked Jack, not disguising the rage in his voice. He felt the humiliation of his mistake keenly and thought Van Zyl was mocking him.

'Audacious sailing, sir!'

'Shut up and get back to the quarterdeck!'

'Yes, sir.' Van Zyl's puppy-dog face looked hurt as he left the bridge. Jack's mind was in a mild state of panic. Meanwhile, Smit stood to one side, surveying the scene with what looked like a smirk.

'Slow ahead.' Jack forced himself to breathe normally. 'Wheel amidships, steer two-nine-oh.'

PO Joubert, the gunner, already had the mooring lines neatly coiled down. His team had fallen in on the forecastle for leaving harbour. To starboard lay a big, County-class cruiser. Men stood at the rail, watching the clumsy sweeper chugging across the basin. Jack was sure they were laughing at him.

'Attention on the upper deck, face to starboard and salute!' came the voice over the tannoy. Thank goodness, he'd forgotten to give the order. At least others were on their toes — while he had yet to find his own feet. The bosun's pipe sounded its shrill call and the men on the forecastle came to attention. Jack and Smit saluted smartly. The cruiser replied with the blare of a bugle, which echoed across the basin, followed by the 'carry on' from the bosun's call on the sweeper.

Southern Gannet passed through the defence boom at the bullnose and suddenly they were in open water. Air, sky, sea room. Jack let out a deep sigh. Ahead and to port, the anchorage was cluttered. 'Starboard thirty,' he said. 'Fall out harbour stations. Starboard watch to defence stations.'

Van Zyl reappeared on the bridge and saluted stiffly. 'All secured for'ard and aft, Captain.'

'Thank you, Sub.' Jack did not meet his eye. 'Smit, set a course northeast, half ahead. Van Zyl, enter in the log, "Slipped and under way at 14:00."' Jack climbed into the tall chair on the port side of the bridge. The back of his shirt was soaked with sweat. He was exhausted, shaky. How had a simple manoeuvre managed to make itself so complicated and take so much out of him?

Clearing Selborne Lighthouse at the end of the harbour wall, the ship began to heave. There was a short swell from the southeast, creating an awkward motion. Jack ordered the coxswain to alter course to take the sea on the nose. He heard someone retching on the fo'c'sle. Good grief, as green as that. This was practically a lake.

HMSAS *Southern Gannet* cruised down the western flank of the bay towards Castle Rock. They sailed past Milkwood House, all on its own above a deserted beach. Through his powerful Barr & Stroud binoculars, Jack could see a rowing boat drawn up on the sand. Then he noticed a tiny figure on the veranda. His father was watching them through his binoculars.

CHAPTER 8

Soon after leaving Kiel, *Sturmvogel* took on the guise of the *Natalya.* Amidships on each side appeared a red field with a white edge, and on this, painted in white, the letters 'USSR'. A red star was emblazoned on Number Two hatch. The crew's uniforms also acquired a suitably Soviet look. All through the night, *Sturmvogel* sailed through a choppy sea to Langeland, passing in and out of squalls that reduced visibility to less than 100 yards. She cruised through the Kattegat, giving Skagen a wide berth, turned west into the Skagerrak and then northwest along the Norwegian coast. The visibility was poor, and her passage did not raise any suspicion from Germany's three Scandinavian neighbours, or the fishing boats and patrolling British submarines.

Kapitän Emil Falk sat in an armchair in his sea cabin behind the bridge, smoking his pipe and studying the orders in detail. They were much as he'd anticipated: to cause as great a disturbance as possible in far-flung corners of the Atlantic and Indian oceans, drawing enemy warships away, sinking merchantmen, forcing the use of convoys — often rerouted on long detours — and scaring away neutral shipping. If a heavy cruiser of the Royal Navy spent weeks searching for him as far south as Gough Island or even the Antarctic, it would be removed from the Mediterranean or North Atlantic. To this end, it was more important to prolong the life of his *Hilfskreuzer*, keeping the enemy tied up over an extended period, than to sink large numbers of ships on a short, daring raid.

Falk's first objective was to strike at the Freetown to Cape Town route, then head south to lay mines off the Cape of Good Hope. If defences grew too strong, he would shift operations to the central Indian Ocean or even Australia. The Southern Ocean was designated as a refuge area. Refuelling zones had been earmarked where he could rendezvous with other raiders or the U-boats that were due to be sent south in the coming months. But the bottleneck of shipping around the southern tip of Africa was his primary objective.

Now, having reached the North Sea proper, it was time to change *Sturmvogel*'s disguise again. In a matter of hours, she'd become the SS *Kronan* of Sweden. With the aid of canvas and boards, her superstructure acquired a new outline. Her funnel, now blue, wore a bright red 'K' and a large Swedish flag was painted on each flank, proclaiming her neutrality.

Turning west, *Sturmvogel* aimed for the ice-free passage of the Denmark Strait between Greenland and Iceland. The weather remained foul, the raider's logbook recording persistent gales, fog banks and the occasional blizzard. Icicles hung from the rigging; the lookouts called regular sightings of ice floes. The stench of sweat and tobacco smoke, damp clothing and vomit, filled the mess decks. In spite of this, no door or hatch to the upper deck was left open for longer than was absolutely necessary because of the cold.

Falk stepped from his cabin and surveyed the scene. His tall coxswain was at the wheel, glancing every now and then at the compass as he eased the raider up and over the hillocks of a large swell. Lookouts on the bridge wings were bundled up in every item of warm clothing they could find — wool underpants, union suit, wool shirt, sweater, leather jacket, watch coat and leather overcoat.

Up in the foremast crow's nest, Falk could see an oil-skinned figure scanning the sea ahead with his big Zeiss binoculars. The rain had turned to sleet once again. The lookout would be having a ghastly time of it. Falk walked to the wooden chair bolted to the port side of the wheelhouse and lifted himself into its hard embrace. Another day, another gale. He longed to turn south and be done with this atrocious winter.

The Denmark Strait was only partly clear, and lookouts had to remain on high alert for icebergs. Keeping well to the north of Iceland, Falk took the raider perilously close to the Greenland ice sheet. The short, grey days and long, black nights were ideal for *Sturmvogel*'s stealthy purpose. She avoided all shipping and turned sharply away from any stain of smoke on the horizon, sure to denote a convoy or patrolling warship.

One bleak Tuesday morning, they broke out into the North Atlantic and were free to roam. Falk stood on the bridge gazing at the vast Atlantic steppes, rising and falling like liquid tectonic plates. His breath left his mouth in gouts of steam. Finally, he had enough legroom to choose his course. Although the great Atlantic battleground lay before him, his orders urged him to refrain from sinking any ships until he arrived in the tropics. *SKL* did not want the mission jeopardised before *Sturmvogel* had reached a position where she could cause the most surprise and disruption.

The wind blew hard from the northwest and the glass began falling sharply. As a greenhorn helmsman tried to keep the raider on course, wind moaned through the rigging and the ship was filled with the sound of rattling and banging. Below, Seaman Waldo Meyer was trying and failing to eat his supper of thick sausage slices and sauerkraut. He sat on a bench at one of the long, scrubbed-deal tables that ran fore and aft. But the ship, his food and the table all seemed to have acquired minds of their own. As *Sturmvogel* launched herself off the top of a wave, everything in the ship appeared, for a moment, to be airborne. Stomachs lurched. Some sailors lost the fight and brought up their food.

The whooshing of the gale, growling of the sea, bass drumming and percussion of the ship increased with each hour. Loose gear tumbled across the decks, rigging clanked, sick sailors groaned in their bunks; lifeboats jumped their chocks and were battered to bits. More terrifyingly, the mines threatened to carry away their securing lines and turn the lower deck into a deadly ten-pin bowling alley. Engineers were dispatched to double the lashings.

On the starboard bridge lookout, Seaman Meyer stared at the tormented ocean. One moment he was in the belly of a trough surrounded by liquid mountains, the next he was flying above a crest surveying dark valleys. Cleaning his spectacles on a salty handkerchief, he thought the scene might well be beautiful if it weren't so threatening. A schoolteacher had told him about the Romantics and their ideas. Meyer tried to find a way of seeing the *Sturm und Drang* of this sea, this sky, as uplifting — something Friedrich could perhaps have captured in paint. But for Meyer at this moment, the Romantic sublime was, simply, terrifying.

It was freezing in the wheelhouse and all watched the moving mountains with exhausted, fearful eyes. Green seas broke over the raider, inundating her decks with frothing white water. At times, the great propeller thrashed uselessly at the air. The shaft, freed of its sea load, shook the raider from end to end. At other times, it bit deep into the ocean as *Sturmvogel*'s poop deck was swamped. She took the swells on her starboard quarter, lumbering along in a dreadful twisting motion and yawing onto her beam ends. Each swell tossed the raider forward with a mighty shove, then she would rear up and slide back into the trough with a stomach-turning plunge.

The men felt they were in a never-ending boxing match, with cracked ribs, sprains and bruises to show for it. Even the most sea-hardened among them were worn down by the constant physical effort required to counter the movement of the ship. As *Sturmvogel* continued to slam her way west and south, the air remained thick with spray and sleet. Bauer found precise navigation impossible. The raider groped through an Atlantic wilderness with only the compass to give direction, and dead reckoning a loose purchase on the world.

At last, the weather began to ease. Falk needed sleep. How long had he been sitting in this upright chair? He knew he could not go on for very much longer.

'Adler, I will be in my sea cabin. Call me for anything. Anything at all.'

'Yes, Kapitän, of course.' Falk could hear the resentment in his first officer's voice. What would he need to do to bend the man? Perhaps Adler felt that he was not trusted to take command during the storm. Well, perhaps he wasn't.

Falk pulled off his boots and lay down on the narrow bunk. Despite his exhaustion, sleep would not come. He thought of his home, in the outskirts of Lübeck, with its rambling garden. Within the safety of its walls, his beautiful wife and precious daughters. His four blonde treasures: the only reason to live. Perhaps the only reason to die. Would he ever see them again?

He pictured a chart marked with the ship's slow progress down the Atlantic. The furtive zigs and zags out of the Kattegat and across the North Sea; the painful vigilance, the tension and sleepless nights that those pencil marks could not record. They had come through the worst of it. The weather was certainly improving: *Sturmvogel* would soon find herself far from convoy routes and the easy reach of British warships. Then, Falk would become the hunter. There'd be plenty of targets in the south, where ships still sailed unescorted, but he must never forget that he was also, always, one of the hunted. Sooner or later, he'd no doubt encounter an enemy ship that would whistle up a squadron of cruisers ... and the trap would snap closed. He had to thread the eye of the needle, strike hard and disappear. He had to plan for every eventuality, seek every deception and disguise, take every precaution. The lives of 265 good men were in his hands. He ran a hand across his heavy eyes. Sleep, he must find sleep.

Adler paced the bridge, his pedantic eye finding fault where it could. The helmsman strayed slightly from the course and received a tongue-lashing. Signalman Weber had dirt on his collar and was a discredit both to the Kriegsmarine and his race. The bridge lookouts dared not glance away from their arcs of view, not even for a moment.

Up in the crow's nest, Seaman Meyer was trying to keep warm. His legs were cramped, aching from pins and needles. Ice had formed on his coat and hat, on his eyelashes and eyebrows too. His breath froze with each gasp. Far below him, the deck swayed drunkenly as hills of water exploded over the bows. Meyer kept scanning the ocean ahead, a regular, monotonous sweep of his binoculars.

Then he spotted something on the horizon that set his heart racing. A tendril of smoke, perhaps. Or a figment of his imagination?

The bridge telephone trilled and Adler pounced on it before the second ring.

'Yes, what is it?' he barked.

'Smoke, sir, I think. Bearing port three-oh.'

'What do you mean you think? What is your name?'

'Seemann Meyer, sir,' came the quaking voice.

'Keep it in sight. Keep me informed. You'd better not be making a mistake.'

Adler stepped out of the wheelhouse and tapped on the captain's sea-cabin door.

'Yes?' came a muffled voice.

'Suspected smoke in the southwest, sir.'

'I'll be there directly.'

Meyer kept his binoculars trained on the tiny brown stain and the telephone to his ear.

'Report everything you can see,' said Adler into the mouthpiece. 'Warships have bigger, tripod masts. Can you make out any funnels yet?'

'No, sir. But it's definitely a ship. Merchant, not navy, I think.'

Falk stepped onto the bridge. He took one look at the situation and ordered the ship to turn away to the north, ringing down 'full ahead'.

'But Kapitän!' exclaimed Adler. 'She is alone. This is our first chance to strike the enemy.'

'Korvettenkapitän Adler, we are not yet in the tropics. For now, our objective is to proceed unnoticed. I do not want to jeopardise the mission.'

'With all due respect, sir, we are far enough south, surely. If there's a target, unescorted, I can't see —'

'Listen to me, Adler, I am responsible for this ship. Not you. One day, you may well have your own command. Maybe even on this voyage, if I am wounded or killed. Until such time, it is *my* decision when, where, how and what to attack.'

'But sir, a sitting duck —'

'Adler, I have spoken.'

'But to turn and run, sir?'

'Run? Run! What exactly are you suggesting?' The captain contained his fury in soft, precise speech.

'It's just that…' The first lieutenant saw the look in Falk's eyes.

'Hiding and circumspection must be our tactics. Whether you like it or not, Korvettenkapitän. Perhaps this clandestine warfare is not for you.'

CHAPTER 9

Cummins stuck his head through the mess-deck hatch and called:

'Wakey, wakey, wakey, rise and shine,
You've had your time and now you're mine,
Let go of your cocks and grab hold of your socks,
Wakey, wakey, wakey, lash up and stow...'

Pickles Brooke opened his eyes and looked around. Eleven messmates lay in the bunks beside him. Outside, he could hear bugle calls from the bigger ships. It was 05:30 in Britain's largest naval base in the southern hemisphere. Time to get up.

Later, while scrubbing the upper deck, he noticed wisps of smoke beginning to trail from galley funnels as the smell of frying bacon and sausages drifted across the basin. Later still, the preparatory flag climbed the gaff of the port's signal tower: two minutes to Colours. Across the harbour and out in the roadstead, signalmen waited to hoist their white ensigns.

At the appointed moment, a young bugler beside the tower raised his instrument. East Dockyard's officer of the day roared out: 'Make it so!' The flag travelled jauntily up the mast, matched by those of nearby ships, and the bugle's call echoed around the basin. From every tannoy on every ship came the order: 'Attention on the upper deck. Face aft and salute.'

Jack looked out of his scuttle and watched the South African flag being raised on the forecastle. Another naval day at the southern tip of Africa had officially begun. He hoped this day would be better.

'Bunts!'

'Yes, sir.' The wide-eyed signalman scrambled up the ladder to the bridge.

'Are you fast?' asked Jack as he scanned the flotilla cruising astern of *Gannet.*

'Um, sir, I only completed my Signal School course last week, sir.'

'But are you fast?'

'Er, no, sir. If they start slapping out signals, I've got no blimming hope. Beg pardon, sir.'

Jack sighed. 'All right, Bunts, I can read pretty well. Get your Aldis lamp. Make to flotilla: "Prepare for starboard-side sweep."'

Gilbert rested the signal lamp on his forearm with the V-sight framing the second ship. He began pressing the trigger, sending a series of bright dots and dashes. The flickering light was accompanied by loud clicking. Soon, the other three sweepers replied and Bunts reported their winking acknowledgements.

'The signalman on *Southern Belle* looks lively. I suggest you buy him a pint and quiz him, Bunts.'

'Sir?'

'Ask him to teach you some Morse shorthand. It'll make your life a lot easier. Like "u r" for "you are" and "stn" for "station". You'll get the hang of it in no time. And Bunts…'

'Captain?'

'Never ever guess at a word. Always ask for it to be repeated. Lives depend on signals. Our lives might depend on you.'

'Yes, sir. Thank you, sir.' Gilbert's cheeks flushed.

'Number One, get the sweep ready. I don't want us to embarrass ourselves again.'

Jack looked astern. *Belle* and *Star* were following neatly in his wake; *Wayfarer* was off to starboard and well adrift of the flotilla.

'Bunts, make to *Wayfarer*: "The train to Cape Town is now departing from platform one."'

The signal flashed.

'Forgot my lunchbox, will join shortly, tie someone to the tracks,' came the cheeky reply from *Wayfarer*'s bridge.

The captains of the three trailing vessels called down their voice pipes every few minutes, making small increases and decreases to the revolutions to keep precise station. They all knew the flotilla was being watched from the naval base. Perhaps they were, at that very moment, in the crosshairs of the commodore's telescope.

'Hoist the sweeping signal,' said Jack.

Bunts clipped on the flags and hauled them aloft. The minesweepers responded, falling astern so that each ship was 130 degrees on the other's starboard quarter, 200 yards apart. Jack checked their spacing with a Stuart distance meter. Wilson was finally on station and his team looked ready on *Wayfarer*'s quarterdeck.

'All right, Bunts, hoist "out sweeps".'

There was a bustle of activity on *Gannet*'s poop as the gear was made ready. Jack picked up the speaking trumpet and called out: 'Let go sweep!'

The otter, kite and Oropesa float — which looked like a mini Zeppelin — were lowered over the side and bobbed astern. The wire was slowly paid out on the winch, PO Cummins making a whirling motion with a hand above his head. With a thumbs-up, the sweep was set.

Jack looked astern. The Oropesa float bobbed along on the ship's quarter, its red flag fluttering. Suspended underwater below it was the otter, an oblong frame with vanes that kept the sweep wire submerged. Nearer the ship was a similar vaned device, the kite. Between them was strung the sweep wire, hardened with serrated steel. Acting like a knife, it was able to cut through a mine's mooring cable, forcing it to the surface. For more robust mine cables that resisted the steel wire, there was a cutter at the outer end of the sweep. When a mine cable slid into the cutter, its jaws closed automatically and severed the mooring.

Once *Gannet*'s sweep was set, each succeeding ship took up station close to the Oropesa in front of it, thereby travelling through already swept water. This way, they were able to clear a path about half a mile wide. The pennants from each yardarm came down one after the other — *Wayfarer*'s a lot slower than the rest — and they were soon settled into the sweep. He would have to have a word with Wilson.

Jack admired the elegance of this great contraption, the ingenious manner in which a piece of ocean could be scoured and made clean again. It was a fiendishly effective way to neutralise Hitler's pods of death.

What Jack didn't know was that the smooth progress of the sweep belied a chaotic situation on the bridge of *Southern Wayfarer*. Wilson was trying to find his way as best he could. He had a general idea of what was expected, but the finer details remained hazy. What should he do, for instance, if his kite fouled a mine? And what was the best way to execute a 180-degree turn while towing sweep gear?

Wayfarer was light in the bows and the thrust of her propeller made the whale catcher veer slightly to port. After an hour at the helm, the coxswain had been replaced by a less experienced hand. Too late, Wilson spotted the mass of floating kelp. The quartermaster responded by turning to port instead of starboard, the kelp snagged the Oropesa, and the helmsman put on even more port rudder to compensate. The vessel slewed around and collided with *Star*'s Oropesa.

'What on earth?' cried Jack. 'Those bloody fools! Signal "Stop engines."' The four ships came to a halt, two of them drifting closer together as their crews tried to disentangle the mess.

'In sweeps!' Jack shouted angrily. A signal fluttered to *Gannet*'s yardarm and was repeated through the flotilla. Drum winches began hauling in the gear, each bosun carefully watching the wire as it spooled over the glistening sheaves. It had been a bad showing.

On entering harbour, Jack noticed that some of the men on the forecastle were not in the correct rig. 'A word, if you please, Smit.' He could barely contain his rage. 'I don't mind too much if the hands dress like a vaudeville act when we're at sea. But I will *not* have anything other than Bristol fashion when we enter and leave port. Is that understood?'

'But, sir, that's not my —'

'Just see to it, damn it!'

The flotilla motored line astern across the basin. Ratings had fallen in fore and aft, the ropes and wires laid out ready for making fast. Seaman Cloete stood on *Gannet*'s forecastle, a heaving line in his hand.

'Starboard ten, slow astern.'

Cloete's arm bent back and with a bowling action sent the heaving line towards the waiting dockhands. It splashed into the dirty water. He quickly hauled it in and tried again. Dismayed, Jack watched his men fumbling with the fenders. Keystone cops. At last, the head rope was dragged across. Jack looked aft to where the stern party casually secured the lines, chatting happily among themselves as they worked. Sloppily done, all of it.

Gannet edged towards the quay.

'Stop engine.'

'Signal from tower, sir,' said the signalman. 'Captain of HMSAS *Southern Gannet* to report to SNO Simon's Town, immediate.'

'Thank you, Sparks, you've just made my day.'

Fenders squealed as the springs were passed across and secured to the bollards. As *Gannet* came to rest, Jack let out a frustrated sigh.

'All secure fore and aft, sir,' said Smit dryly.

'Ring off main engine. I'm going ashore, Number One. Take over.'

'Aye, Captain.'

'I'm told you nearly sank the dock when slipping yesterday.' Commodore O'Reilly sat with his back to Jack, surveying the anchorage. 'Apparently half the harbour had their eyes out on stalks. Lucky you didn't hole *Dorsetshire*. Which wouldn't have been such a bad thing, actually. Her captain has been an absolute pain in the arse with his demands.'

'I'm, I'm sorry, sir. It was my first time and I misjudged the wind.'

O'Reilly swung round in his chair, bringing his hard blue eyes to bear. 'Damn it all, Lieutenant, let your Number One take her out the first time if you're not confident. And as for the shambolic display of sweeping I've just witnessed! Your flotilla is a laughing stock. The Admiral's son all tied up in knots. It makes good theatre, but it's not bloody good enough in my naval base.'

'I sincerely apologise, sir.'

'You know I'm not happy with this separation of powers. I've warned you already. We don't need a supernumerary force here. I'm going to put in a request to C-in-C South Atlantic that your flotilla be moved to Cape Town Harbour. Frankly, Pembroke, I don't want you here and I don't give a fig who your father is! You're dismissed.'

That evening, Jack sat glumly at the dining-room table in Milkwood House. His father was at the head; Imogen had gone up the line to Cape Town with friends. Rachel placed steaming dishes of Cape Malay chicken, yellow rice and pumpkin fritters on the table.

'How are things going with your flotilla?' asked the admiral, serving himself.

'Not well, I'm afraid. Not well at all. O'Reilly read me the riot act. He wants us moved to Cape Town.'

'That won't happen. He doesn't have the authority. These things are as much political as military.'

'It was a fiasco on the water today. These South African chaps don't seem up to the job.'

'Rome wasn't built in a day, son.'

'My skippers are barely capable of accurate station-keeping, discipline is not what it should be and punishment haphazard. So many of the men are new recruits.'

'You can mould them. Your flotilla is brand new — it will find its feet. The other South African sweepers are doing good work.'

'We're going to need more time for training.'

'There isn't time. The latest reports suggest that one of the German raiders we've been worried about may get here sooner than we thought.'

'That is not good news.' Jack's heart sank; they were not even close to being ready. 'Not good at all.'

'You'll be fine. In the last war —'

'Father, don't you understand: this is not the last war! I saw the German military machine at Dunkirk. It tore through us like wildfire. It was … unstoppable.' His eyes were pleading. For once, his father seemed at a loss for words.

There was a long, uneasy silence. 'How are things in the upper echelons of power?' asked Jack at last, wanting to change the subject.

'Not good either, I'm afraid.'

'The dockyard looks terribly busy.'

'Yes, we're fitting out armed merchant cruisers to fill in the gaps in our cruiser fleet. The dockyard has done an overhaul of the Union-Castle mail ship *Carnarvon Castle*.' They were on more comfortable ground.

'I heard she'd been in a scrap.'

'Quite so. She bumped into the German raider *Thor* and had a five-hour running battle with her. She suffered heavily. Unfortunately, *Thor* got away and is probably heading back to Germany, but now there's this other bally ship, provisionally designated Raider X, coming our way.'

Jack helped himself to another spoon of curried chicken. The admiral continued: 'As we sit here, there are more than 400 ships on my tracking chart either approaching or leaving the Cape, including two troop convoys with the *Aquitania* among them due into Table Bay. You can imagine how this keeps me up at night.'

Later, Jack lay on his bed at Belleview, staring at the ceiling. His mind replayed the day's sweeping, the mistakes and shortcomings, the gaps in his knowledge, the lack of experience in his crew. And his father's ominous words about Raider X. When those worries were exhausted, the old faithfuls returned. Doomed men on a beach, the banshee howl of Stukas, icy water filling the ship and closing over his head. He twisted and writhed his way through the semi-conscious compartments of his mind, not one of them watertight, not one offering solace.

A day of live-fire practice. The flotilla was cruising southeast of Whittle Rock in a lumpy sea. The machine guns mounted on either side of the wheelhouse were manned by Behardien and Potgieter.

'Ask PO Joubert to fire a star shell so we can all have a crack at it,' said Jack.

'Aye, sir,' replied the signalman.

There was a popping sound, and an incandescent white light burst high on their starboard beam. Seaman Behardien on the starboard wing cocked the Lewis gun and let out a rippling burst. Tracer climbed away from the ship in a wayward arc, well below the target. He fired another burst. Too low again. Red streaks from the other ships rose towards the star shell, all of them wide.

'Terrible shooting! Another star shell if you please, port side this time.'

The second Lewis opened up with an erratic burst that started too low and ended up spraying high over the target. Then the gun jammed. 'Bugger, it's those weak springs!' cursed Potgieter.

'What's the bloody matter?' shouted PO Joubert, red in the face with frustration.

'Don't know, PO. I'll have to strip it and have a look. Again.'

'I'll have your fucking guts for garters. That gun has been playing up for weeks. You will not leave this ship until it's fixed.'

Smit glanced to the north and said to Jack: 'Almost time for the aircraft, sir.'

'Very well, tell the lookouts to keep their eyes peeled.'

Four men in tin hats stood at the twelve-pounder on the bandstand. One was on the training wheel, another on the laying wheel, a third stood against the shield peering ahead and a fourth was poised with a shell. The magazine lay deep in the hull from where a rating passed shells through a hatch to a man in the mess, who in turn handed it up to the deck.

'Target bearing green three-oh, low!' came a lookout's cry. 'Five miles out.' The barrel swung smartly onto the bearing. Aft, the pom-pom did the same. Gloved hands fed a shell into the twelve-pounder's breech, which clanged shut. The officers on the bridge trained their binoculars on the Fairey Battle. Approaching slowly, the single-engine bomber towed a drogue target 100 yards behind it.

'Open fire when ready,' said Jack. Smit relayed the order.

Crack! A tongue of flame. Black smoke poured downwind from the gun. Deep in the hull, the stokers flinched as the ship jolted. The shell burst just below the plane. Its pilot jinked in fright. Then the three following sweepers fired, all missing by a wide margin.

'Message from aircraft, Captain: "Please be advised that I am pulling the target, not pushing it."'

The gun barked again. Jack inhaled the cordite and found that he'd broken out in a sweat. Each bang was a blow inside his skull. Constriction in his chest. Soldiers on the beach. Ears primed for the Valkyries' scream. The other ships fired next.

With each thud, he winced. A puff of cloud below the target, three above. Then more puffs, raggedly straddling the drogue.

'Sparks,' he called into the voice pipe, trying to keep an even tone, 'radio the pilot and ask if he would be so kind as to pass down our flank a couple more times, close in. It'll give the pom-poms a chance.'

'Aye, sir.'

Van Zyl looked curiously at his captain, noticing the strain on the man's face.

As the plane came in low from the stern, the pom-poms on all four ships opened up, their two-pounder shells groping for the drogue. Jack gritted his teeth, fighting the urge to put his hands over his ears. *Thump, thump, thump.* It made his skin crawl. The sound of hate.

'All right, all right, that will do.' His voice was barely audible. Smit peered at him, alarmed by his captain's pale face and obvious distress. 'Please thank the pilot, Number One. I'll be in my cabin. Take us back to Simon's Town, if you please.' His limbs were trembling so much that he had to take care on the ladder. Once in his cabin, he sat down heavily on the bunk. His head throbbed with the opening salvos of a migraine.

The following day was scheduled for gunnery again. Jack had to steel himself for more firing and the persistent bark of memory. This time, the tug HMS *St Dogmael* towed a floating target, and the twelve-pounder crews were given time to get their eye in, scoring repeated hits. Jack tried to dissociate the gunfire from his flashbacks by focusing on his men. It required a Herculean effort that left him utterly drained by the end of the shoot.

The next day it was back to sweeping. Returning to Simon's Town in the afternoon, just when the men were looking forward to a run ashore, Jack ordered a switching of roles: seamen to the engine room as makeshift stokers, Porky the cook and February to the twelve-pounder, stokers ordered to launch the ship's boat. The result was utter chaos, the crew's mutinous grumbling and swearing audible on the bridge.

'But sir, you're making everyone look like a fool,' complained Smit.

'In action, men are wounded and killed, Number One,' Jack said. 'I want the survivors to know what to do. They don't have to be proficient, but they do need to know the basics. What happens if a shell lands on the bridge and kills the officers?'

'Yes, sir.' Smit's tone was unreadable.

'Out port sweep.' Another day, another practice sweep. *Belle* swung in behind *Gannet* with *Star* after her and *Wayfarer* as tail-end Charlie. They were chugging along at six knots once again, going about the daily round with Oropesa floats bobbing on their quarters like pilot fish. Their ten days of training were almost up. But were they ready?

Jack left Smit on the bridge and walked aft. His men were all at their correct stations. Cummins stood at the sweep winch, a cigarette dangling from the corner of his mouth. His Sunday-picnic air belied the hazards of trailing a sweep in heavy seas. The bosun's time on trawlers stood him in good stead — a man Jack could trust. The PO's job was to make sure that the wire didn't become too slack or too taut. Jack knew from experience that overstrained hawsers were deadly things, able to sever an arm or a head better than the sharpest axe. But judging by the nonchalant ease with which Cummins worked the levers, Jack had nothing to fear. He glanced around the poop deck once more and found himself satisfied.

Each day, Jack had noticed improvement. His flotilla was not yet the finished article — and certainly not ready to meet a warship of Herr Hitler's navy — but he did feel more confident. The ships were now able to hold station while sweeping in rough conditions. Every so often, he would check their positions with his distance meter and found them on station, give or take a few yards. It was much, much better.

By the third live-fire session, the gunners were finding their targets more regularly. When star shells burst over their starboard beam, the amount of accurate tracer fire pouring into the air from four Lewis and four pom-poms was impressive. When they switched to the port side, the accuracy was repeated. *Right, then*, Jack thought — *that's more like it.* Now he just needed to change the men's surly attitude and somehow lift the *Gannet*'s morale.

On Saturday afternoon, there was an officers' tea dance at Admiralty House. Most of the crew were on shore leave and, since Jack had nothing better to do, he decided to go. It was the first event of its kind he'd attended since the sinking of *Havoc.* Parties, drinking and dancing had seemed unthinkable in the intervening months, and alcohol had become medicinal rather than pleasurable.

Returning the sentries' salute, he entered the grand gates, past a fountain and across the lawn, to join the groups gathered under the trees. A Royal Marines band on a raised podium played jazz and dancehall tunes. As always at such events, there was a fair sprinkling of Air Force officers in their light-blue uniforms. Jack bypassed the table with tea, cake and petits fours, and headed straight for a steward serving champagne.

A young woman with wavy blonde hair was also waiting at the drinks table. She wore white gloves and a fitted green dress, with a string of pearls at her throat.

'Lemonade, not bubbles?' he asked, as her drink was poured.

'Yes, I don't drink much.' She had a slight Afrikaans accent. 'Not on a hot summer's day anyway.'

'You should let your hair down a bit.' Something about her made Jack feel rashly brave and out of character.

'This is as down as it gets, Lieutenant —'

'Pembroke. Jack.'

'Marais, Clara,' she said sternly, imitating him.

He blushed, sensing that he was out of his depth. Pale green eyes to match her pale green dress. Full red lips, a high forehead and a petite, curvaceous figure. He soldiered on: 'Do you often come to these things?'

'Occasionally. My brother is a pilot — coastal patrol.'

'And yourself?'

'I'm at UCT, majoring in Afrikaans/Nederlands and French. I want to be a journalist one day.'

'I tried my hand at journalism before the war. Not for the faint-hearted... Would you, ah, care to dance?'

She looked around, perhaps seeking an escape route. None presented itself. 'I was waiting for...' She must have seen a gleam of something like desperation in Jack's eyes. 'Oh, all right, why not?'

A polished wooden dancefloor had been laid out on the lawn. The band was playing a Joe Loss quickstep that had enticed a number of couples onto the floor. *Why does it have to be a quickstep, of all dances?* Jack thought. *Slow, quick, quick, slow*, he rehearsed the steps in his head.

They set off at an easy pace, but even this he found difficult. She felt the tension in his grip. Jack wasn't a good dancer at the best of times. Now, his wounded leg refused to keep up and he narrowly missed Clara's toes on a couple of turns. Inevitably, he achieved a direct hit. 'Ouch!' she said, coming to a halt in the middle of the dancefloor. 'I thought all you Royal Navy chaps were good dancers.'

'I'm awfully sorry, a dicky leg. War wound.'

'That old story. Every sailor in town has a war wound and a chest of apocryphal medals.' She giggled. 'Come on, Lieutenant Pembroke, let's try again.'

Clara was feather-light in Jack's arms, leading him more than he was able to lead her. Desperately seeking the rhythm, he was at the same time entranced to be holding her. When the number ended they stood apart, stiff and awkward.

An airman came over and tapped her on the shoulder. 'May I?'

'Peter, how wonderful, you came!' Clara beamed a smile that left Jack speechless. 'Will you excuse me, Jack? It was nice meeting you.'

He retreated to the drinks table. Her smile had suggested relief at being saved from the dour Englishman with the two left feet. Soon afterwards, the glamorous couple departed, and all colour seemed to drain from the garden. After some desultory conversation with a pod of lieutenants, Jack downed his glass, made his excuses and strode out of the gate, nursing the onset of another migraine.

CHAPTER 10

Commodore O'Reilly had a nasty habit of paying unannounced visits to the ships, especially those undergoing training. One morning, an apparition in white and gold appeared at the brow. The quartermaster turned pale. It was a vision from hell.

The great man was piped aboard, and the banging and crashing below decks betrayed the terror his presence evoked. Jack and Smit were ashore, so Van Zyl was officer of the day. The duty watch hastily assembled on the fo'c'sle to be inspected by the 'Vampire of Snoektown'. One of the commodore's favourite tricks to unsettle a crew was to toss his gold-encrusted cap on the deck and shout, 'That's a grenade: do something!'

This morning was no different, and the men of *Gannet* were paralysed as the cap was flung to the deck. No one dared touch the hallowed object. But then Stoker Hughes leapt forward and kicked it overboard into the oily water. Silence descended on the upper deck. Furious, the commodore stared at his floating cap, then back at Hughes, whose sheepish grin was beginning to falter. The crew looked on, appalled at their messmate's moment of insanity.

'All right, wise arse!' bellowed O'Reilly. 'My cap is now a drowning man and you, sailor, will save him.'

To his credit, Hughes unhesitatingly dived into the filthy water and retrieved the cap. He reappeared on deck and handed it to the commodore.

'Thank you, sailor. Next time it'll be a depth charge.' There was the vaguest suggestion of a smile at the corner of O'Reilly's lips. He turned to the assembled crew and said: 'I will be back. Vigilance at all times, Gannets.' With that, he disappeared up the gangplank to the shriek of a bosun's pipe.

Back on board, having been apprised of the commodore's antics, Jack was going over the defaulters' list. Smit had reported almost all of the transgressions, for the most part petty offences that required light punishment. If it had been him, he'd have settled for a firm dressing-down rather than official sanction. On *Havoc*, punishment was administered and accepted dispassionately; however, on a small ship such as *Gannet* — and from a harsh, unpopular officer like Smit — the effect was detrimental to morale. But, clearly, his first officer needed things done by the book.

The atmosphere on board was becoming increasingly fractious: the men were often sullen, the orders grudgingly obeyed. And Jack knew that Smit was at the heart of the problem. Sooner or later he would have to confront him.

'They're an insolent lot,' Smit burst out when he was asked to explain another offence, penned in his neat, upright handwriting. 'Disrespectful and ill-disciplined. We need to crack the whip, sir.'

'Number One, I hear you. But a ship with too much discipline becomes a less efficient fighting unit. When I ask the men to go beyond the ordinary, to give everything, perhaps even their lives, I want them fully committed to this ship. I need our crew to be of one single mind. Bullying will not get us there. Do you understand?'

'I just —'

'Do you understand?'

'Yes, sir.'

'Let's go easy with the rod, Number One.' Jack attempted to lighten his tone. 'Try to turn a Nelsonic blind eye. These men aren't conscripts and *Gannet* is not a training ground. We can't flog them round the fleet with 100 lashes from each ship anymore.'

'I know sir, but —'

'Understood?'

'Sir!' He came to attention, his jaw set in defiance.

'Thank you, that will be all.'

When Smit had left, Jack turned to the pile of mail on his desk. It was his job to censor letters written by the crew. Although the task was tiresome, it did give some insight into what the men of *Gannet* were thinking and feeling. He opened a letter from Seaman Ellis to his brother, scanning the page until he came to the line: 'The officers on this ship are shit.'

He called out: 'Cox'n, please send Seaman Ellis to me at once.'

'Aye, Captain,' came the call from the wheelhouse.

A few moments later he heard February say, 'Caps off.' Ellis stepped through the doorway and stood to attention. He was a brawny, hirsute, taciturn sailor and Jack knew he wouldn't get far in questioning the man. Perhaps it would be best simply to mete out the punishment.

'So, Ellis, "The officers on this ship are shit." Do you want to explain yourself?'

'Sort of like it's written, sir,' he said, avoiding Jack's eye. 'Except not all of them, like.'

'Yes, go on. There are only three of us.'

'Well, you isn't too bad and Van is actually all right.'

'Van?'

'Sub-Lieutenant Van Zyl, sir.'

'And what is it that renders Sub-Lieutenant Smit, ah, "shit", so to speak?'

'Well, sir, I may have put it a bit harshly, but me and the lads feel very dissatisfied about the boat deck being declared out of bounds when we're at sea. That's the place off-duty men usually gather, and in bad weather we've got nowhere else to go. It's cramped and stuffy in the mess deck and I thought it was very unfair.'

'And that is your considered view?'

'And the lads'.'

'Except you put pen to paper, so you will take the blame.'

'Yes, sir.' His expression was blank.

'Very well, Ellis, let me give this some thought. I'm not at all happy with your disrespectful tone. But, in the meantime, I think it best that we tear this letter up and forget all about it. You've made your point.'

'Yes, sir.' Ellis looked dumbfounded. 'Thank you, sir.'

'Dismissed.'

When the seaman had gone, Jack called his coxswain.

'PO, please pass the word that the boat deck is no longer out of bounds when we're at sea.'

'Aye, Captain.' February returned to the bridge wearing a broad grin.

All too soon, the ten days of training were over. To complete its working-up, the flotilla joined the Simon's Town minesweepers, *Immortal* and *Kirstenbosch*, in their clearing of the False Bay channel. Each morning, they sailed out of the harbour and formed up for a long, southward sweep past Whittle Rock and out to the 100-fathom line.

One morning, Jack was in his cabin eating breakfast before departure, preparing for the day ahead. It would be their first channel sweep without *Immortal* (in harbour for boiler cleaning) or *Kirstenbosch* (engine trouble). The steward knocked softly, placing a pot of tea, a copy of the *Cape Times* and an envelope marked CONFIDENTIAL on his desk. Jack ran his eye over the headlines, then opened the envelope, pulled out a folder and read: 'The Secretary of the Admiralty regrets to announce the loss of the minesweeper HMSAS *Southern Floe*, Skipper Lieutenant JE Lewis, RNVR SA. There was only one survivor. The next of kin have been informed.'

Such bland, empty words to convey the loss of so many sailors. No, not 'loss': the drowning, the violent dismembering, the vaporising of brave souls. Jack could picture every detail. Feeling numb, he walked to the wardroom carrying the folder and informed his two officers. There was stunned silence.

'I knew Lieutenant Lewis well,' said Smit quietly. 'He's from Fish Hoek. We used to swim off the rocks at Sunny Cove.'

Jack read aloud from the folder: 'In January 1941, *Southern Floe* and her sister ship *Southern Sea* reached Tobruk to take over patrol duties along the swept channels and to escort ships through them. On 11 February, *Southern Sea* arrived at the rendezvous position two miles east of Tobruk, but there was no sign of *Southern Floe.* A passing destroyer notified the vessel that they had picked up Stoker CJ Jones, clinging to some wreckage. He was the only survivor.

'Back in Alexandria, Stoker Jones was interviewed by naval intelligence. He said that the sinking happened just after 04:00 on Tuesday last. "There was a massive explosion, the ear-splitting sound of escaping steam and sea rushing in," he reports. "The water carried me upward with a lot of oil and debris. I found myself opposite an open skylight and managed to pull myself through. I broke the surface. It was pitch dark and the ship had gone. There was nothing left. I was one of only nine out of the whole crew. Lieutenant Lewis, our commanding officer, was with us."'

Jack paused. Smit was staring out of the scuttle, his shoulders hunched. '"Lewis called the survivors together and said a short prayer,'" he read on. "'We sang a hymn. Then he wished us good luck. We tried to stay together but drifted apart in the dark. I found a piece of wood and clung onto it. When the sun came up all my shipmates had disappeared. I hung onto the driftwood all day. Eventually I lost consciousness. I came to in the sickbay of an Australian destroyer, HMAS *Voyager*. The captain said they found me at 18:30. A lookout on the fo'c'sle spotted me just as the sun was going down."

'Although it has not been confirmed, it is assumed that *Southern Floe* struck a mine.'

Forming up outside the harbour, the flotilla set its gear and headed south, three cables apart and three black balls at their mastheads to announce wire sweeping. The sea was calm with a light southeaster ruffling the bay's bedclothes. Passing Roman Rock, they spotted a slow vessel escorted by a tug moving up the channel. Van Zyl whistled. 'Take a look at her bows, sir.'

Jack trained his binoculars on the ship. The armed merchant cruiser HMS *Corfu* was limping into Simon's Bay with a gaping hole near her prow. Water sloshed in and out of the gash. The former P&O liner had been involved in the collision with HMS *Hermes* and, after a patch-up job in Sierra Leone, was coming south for more comprehensive repairs.

By noon, the flotilla was off Cape Point. Seaman Pickles Brooke was right aft on lookout duty, humming 'Rule Britannia' as he stood on the quarterdeck beside the voice pipe, ready to notify the bridge of any worthy sighting. He was alert, conscious of the importance of his task. The *Gannet*'s survival might depend on his vigilance. He quartered the horizon, scanning for ship, aircraft or periscope. Each sweeper was on station, following in the wake of the other. Brooke was proud of the flotilla and of the *Gannet.* Despite Potgieter's bullying, he was beginning to feel part of the crew. His flotilla, his ship.

Brooke watched the sweep, watched as 400 fathoms of two-and-a-half-inch wire scythed through the water. The cable vibrated slightly as it sailed along. This contraption of otter, kite, float and cutters was the reason for their existence. He glanced at Cummins at the winch, who gave him a thumbs-up, which he returned with a grateful smile.

Jack was also staring aft. The flotilla was chugging along at a comfortable six knots, four bronze propellers chewing the Atlantic. He was satisfied with their progress. They had all but mastered their craft and were dutifully ploughing the ocean like maritime farmers in nautical tractors. Back and forth, cutting furrows in the sea. The gentlest of corrections on the wheel, just one or two spokes either way to keep an arrow-straight wake. Back and forth on their humble plod so that the more glamorous, more powerful and more important could freely sail the Seven Seas.

They reached the 100-fathom line. It was time to turn the flotilla around and sweep back along a parallel course, widening the safe channel into False Bay. Raising a signal and sounding the siren, *Gannet* cut her speed to dead slow as the other three ships sped up and carved around in a wide arc. Turning while sweeping was a hazardous manoeuvre and Jack watched their progress closely. *Wayfarer*, as always the tail-end Charlie, was going like the clappers. *Gannet* was the pivot around which the little ships danced. Their half circle duly completed, they headed back the way they'd come. The turn had been executed without fuss or foul-up.

'Not too bloody bad,' he muttered.

'Yes, sir, just like a waltz,' said Smit. Jack hadn't realise he'd been heard.

During his off-watch, Brooke retired to his bunk with a *Popeye* comic, the throb of *Gannet*'s engine soon lulling him to sleep. Suddenly, there was a loud bang. He sat bolt upright, knocking his head on the steel plating. His heart was thumping. Something had been dropped on the deck above.

The moment of terror unsettled Brooke and he couldn't get back to sleep. He listened to the water sloshing down the side of the hull, a foot away from his head. Only half an inch of steel separated him from the vast, terrifying, unfathomable deep. If *Gannet* struck a mine, he'd have no chance of getting out of this coffin.

He tormented himself for another five minutes, then picked up his mattress and carried it on deck, laying it behind the funnel where his off-duty mates had done the same. Some were resting against the Carley float, hats tipped over their faces. One had his nose in a *Reader's Digest*. With blue overalls rolled down and lifebelts inflated as pillows, the sailors were catching up on their suntans. Their skin was bronzed, Jantjies a lot darker than Hughes, whose red hair was ruffled by the wind. This was the best place to be if they struck a mine.

From their boat-deck perch they could hear Porky banging about in the galley, aromas of a non-specific stew wafting up to them. The crew continually joked about Porky's food and once again began singing the Vera Lynn hit, adapted for the cook's benefit: 'Whale meat again, don't know where, don't know when.'

A blast sounded from the ship's siren, drowning out their singing. Brooke scrambled to his feet. Mine-warning flags fluttered from all four yardarms and Aldis lamps flashed instructions. *Gannet*'s engine stopped and she wallowed to a halt. Just below the surface, a mine's mooring cable had bypassed the cutters and fouled their otter. Brooke joined the other hands at the rail, staring intently at the bobbing Oropesa. *Gannet* began drifting back towards the mine. There was silence on board as all eyes stared aft.

The sweeper dropped into a trough, jerking the wire and snagging the mine's detonating mechanism. A thunderous crash rent the stillness. Then an eruption of water climbed 300 feet into the air, dragging the float, otter and sweep wire with it. The shock wave struck *Gannet* like a giant hammer. Its breath sucked the air from Brooke's lungs and threw him to the deck. Red-hot splinters clattered against the ship's side like deadly hail, followed by a cascade of water as though they'd entered a rainstorm. Sailors tried to bury themselves in the deck planking as crockery crashed and flakes of paint drifted down from the deckheads.

Jack felt the explosion as though it were inside his chest. The bridge shook and his world appeared to turn turtle. He saw white, then a murky picture began to reassert itself. One of the lookouts was down on his knees with an ugly gash to the forehead. Smit had been hit in the shoulder by shrapnel and his sleeve was red. Jack stood up slowly, his body trembling.

'That was a near thing, sir, almost spilt my tea,' came the calming voice of February up the voice pipe. Jack walked unsteadily to the side of the bridge and looked down. He was partly deafened, registering only muffled sounds from the chaotic scene below. The ship's flank was peppered with holes and the funnel looked like a colander.

'Rig another sweep!' Smit called through the speaking trumpet.

'Thank you,' Jack said shakily. 'Go and get yourself cleaned up. I'll take over.'

'That's all right, sir.' Smit seemed alarmed by his skipper's wild eyes and ashen face. 'Just a scratch. I'll get it patched up later. Have a seat, sir.'

'Th-thank you, Number One.'

Smit noticed that Van Zyl also looked disoriented and thought it best to keep him busy. 'Sub-Lieutenant, go below and see how Chief and his engine are doing. Check the rest of the ship while you're at it. We might have sprung a few leaks.'

Van Zyl shook his head to clear the confusion, then climbed slowly down the ladder. A cursory glance revealed that some loose gear had been blown over the side, but nothing vital. The men stood around looking dazed. 'Come on, lads, clean this mess up,' he said unconvincingly.

Van Zyl climbed into the forecastle mess deck. There were a few smashed items and clothes strewn about. He opened a hatch and descended via the bosun's store into the magazine. Switching on the light, he was relieved to see that, apart from the usual condensation on the bulkheads and deckhead, there were no leaks. The sloshing in the bilges sounded no worse than normal.

The officers' mess also looked a shambles and the cook was cursing the breakages, though not much beyond crockery. The canned food store below the PO's mess also showed no sign of flooding. Van Zyl passed through another hatch and down into the engine room. The heat was a solid force, the bulkheads streaming with condensation; the thud of the engine was deafening. He thanked his lucky stars, yet again, that he didn't have to work down here. Stokers — the black squad — were at their posts, tending the oil fires in front of the boilers. It was a snapshot of Hades. If the ship struck a mine, their only escape was up a narrow steel ladder. They might only have a few seconds to get out. Survival chances were slim. Van

Zyl pictured men frantically groping for the ladder in Stygian darkness as their coffin began to flood. He could hardly think of a more horrifying end. How would they bear the tension when *Gannet* was sweeping a known minefield?

'First Lieutenant's compliments, Chief,' Van Zyl shouted above the roar of the engine. 'He wants to know if the blast caused any damage … and are you all right?'

'A little bit o' banging won't scare us. We popped a couple of rivets, some pipes and fittings shook a bit loose, but nowt to worry about.'

Van Zyl tried to imagine what a mine explosion, even at a fair distance, would sound like in this echo chamber. He saw that one of the stokers was sitting on the deck, twitching and mumbling to himself. Another sat with an arm around him. McEwan noticed Van Zyl's concern.

'Oh, yes, Jantjies got a bit of a fright. Said some very interesting things about his mum, or my mum, or somebody's mum. Or perhaps it was a part of her anatomy. We'll put him in his kip as soon as he's ready to stand.'

'Can I get you anything, Chief?'

'A fanny of tea would be grand for the lads.' McEwan gave an uneven, gold-toothed grin.

'I'll have Porky send it down immediately.' Van Zyl scampered up the ladder as fast as his wobbly legs could carry him.

Och, they're all the same, thought McEwan. *Nice uniforms, no bottle for the ship's bowels.* He sighed and winked at Chief Stoker Levy, who blinked back at him, still too twitchy to control one eyelid at a time.

As they passed Roman Rock and turned towards the harbour, McEwan's voice came up the pipe from the engine room: 'Skipper, perhaps we should have a wee dram of something I've been saving for a rainy day.'

'It's not raining, Chief,' Jack replied.

'Raining bloody shrapnel, sir.'

'Aye, that would be fine, Chief. Once we're alongside, come to my cabin.'

The flotilla tied up and the three officers inspected *Gannet* from prow to stern, assessing the damage, which was mostly superficial. Back in his cabin, Jack sat down to write a damage report. There was a knock at the door.

'So, the Lord hath spared us this time.' McEwan carried a bottle of Glen Grant single malt and two glasses. In their occasional meetings, Jack had come to think of McEwan as someone he could depend on.

'Hello, Chief, yes, just this once,' said Jack. 'Pull up a chair and anchor your arse.'

'Thank you, Cap'n, don't mind if I do.'

'How's the engine after today's bump?'

'Och, she didn't like it, but she'll live.'

'Good.'

McEwan poured a prodigious finger in each glass and held his up to the light. Both men took a sip. There was a long silence.

'You know, Chief, I don't think I understand these South Africans. It's certainly not the Andrew I know.'

'I've been in the country twenty years and I'm still often baffled. Give it time.'

'That's just the thing, we don't have time. The war has come to the Cape. We saw that today. There can't be any more mucking about. Or mucking things up.' Jack took a swig of the golden liquid.

'Oi, sir, don't chug it. Let it roll around your tongue. This isn't a terrible whisky.'

'Sorry. You're right. Damn fine stuff.'

'And Skipper —'

'Yes, Chief?'

'You've got to give yourself time too.'

Jack looked into McEwan's kind, weary eyes. 'Thank you, Guy.'

Jack's head was swimming, but he was grateful for the company. The two sailors sat savouring the whisky and hardly another word passed between them.

CHAPTER 11

The mine had shaken the crew, so Jack thought it a good idea for them to let off some steam. Most were given overnight shore leave, only needing to be back on board by 08:00 the next morning. Both officers were also granted liberty, as Jack wanted a quiet evening on board. Naturally, they all decided to head for Cape Town and make a night of it.

The off-watch hastily dressed in shore-going rig. Stoker Hughes climbed on a bench and called out, 'Hey lads, it's been brought to my attention that Pickles here is a virgin.' This elicited good-humoured jeering. 'So me and Popeye Ellis have decided that tonight is the night to pop his cherry!' Loud cheering. Brooke blushed and tried to push Hughes off the bench. 'Rest assured, lads, we've got a plan. Tomorrow, young Brooke will return with a properly deflowered pickle.'

'Not so fast!' shouted Lofty. 'Listen up, Pickles, if you're going to dip your wick, I think it behoves me to read from this here Bible, the Royal Navy handbook: *With a view to assisting the police in their efforts to trace women who may be spreading venereal disease in the Cape Peninsula, Africa Form 28 is to be rendered by ships whenever a case occurs of a man contracting this disease. The information will not be pursued in a vindictive spirit, but only to prevent their messmates falling victim to the disease.* So, Pickles, if your nob has got nobs on it tomorrow, come and show us, laddie!'

'Where you gonna take him?' shouted Seaman Levy.

'The blue house,' said Hughes, tapping his nose. Mess-deck hands chimed in with lewd comments about the ladies of that notorious den and what they'd do to Brooke once they'd tied him to a bed.

'There's a buxom Xhosa broad that pounds so hard she'll break your back!' cried Cloete, laughing diabolically.

'What about the nanny with the toothy fanny!' called out Ellis.

'*Ag*, don't listen to them, Pickles,' said Seaman Plato quietly. 'We'll get you a *lekker*, sweet girl who knows exactly how to teach a first-timer. She'll kiss you tenderly, just like your mommy … then she'll stick her finger up your arse!' he shouted. The mess deck guffawed, drowning out Brooke's protests.

As Brooke climbed the ladder, Cummins called after him, 'Don't forget your Durex! The Jimmy will be the hell in if you come back with the clap!'

Laughter followed the sailors as they dragged a smiling Brooke along with them. The mine explosion had brought the war to their doorstep and each of them harboured a kernel of fear at what lay in store, but tonight they were going to paint the town.

They stopped for a pint at the Lord Nelson Inn, then pressed on towards the station. 'Gosh, there's that ruddy big dog again,' said Brooke, pointing to a Great Dane crossing the road.

'Ah, pay the hound no heed,' said Hughes. 'He's not a friend of ours. Just Nuisance is his name. Very popular with the ratings, but not the *Gannet*. He's actually been made an able seaman, so he's more or less got the run of the naval base. Nuisance accompanies sailors on the train to town and leads the worse for wear back to their ships. Being a member of the armed forces, he's even entitled to free rail travel.'

'So why don't we like him?' asked Brooke.

'He and Fido don't get along. Nuisance thinks he can board any vessel and demand food. One day he comes swaggering down our gangplank, tongue lolling out, demanding grub from Porky. He spots Fido and starts barking at her. She strides up to him, no fear, reaches up and gives him a wallop on his nose. Claws out, no prisoners, blood on the deck. The dog goes ballistic and Fido retreats to the bridge. It took four of our lads to drag him ashore. So, no more Nuisance on *Gannet*.'

Brooke noticed that the dog was following them to the station, having latched onto a group from HMS *Corfu*. Boarding the train, Nuisance was first through the doors and made himself comfortable on three seats at a sea-facing window. The *Gannet* party managed to find seats, but others had to stand all the way to Cape Town. No one dared suggest that the dog make room for humans.

When they reached the city, the sailors bought a round of Tickey Hock at the railway-station bar, then trooped uptown. Nuisance attached himself to a crowd heading for the NAAFI canteen in the mayor's garden behind the City Hall. Brooke watched as the volunteer cooks and waitresses made a fuss of the sailor dog, arranging a plate of cutlets and a chamber pot filled with lager for him.

A pianist played dance tunes and waitresses doubled as occasional partners. Some Gannets ordered a meal for a few pence, but none plucked up the courage to dance. Instead, Brooke played table tennis with Lofty, others managed to score a free billiard table and a couple joined a game of housey-housey. There was a convoy in port and, with so many soldiers about, the prize money was considerable. But none of the Gannets was lucky and, after a few rounds, they moved on.

Their next port of call was the Grand Hotel on Adderley Street.

'All right, mates, let's hit the upstairs lounge!' shouted Cummins as they entered the lobby.

'Not the bar?' asked Brooke.

'Men only in the bar, stupid,' said Hughes. 'The lounge has got skirt. Or haven't you ever been to one?' Brooke kept his mouth shut. 'Just stick close to me, Pickles.'

The *Gannet* party trooped upstairs, not being too quiet about it. They found tables at the window and Cummins ordered a round of Lion Lagers. 'As promised, lads, first one's on me.'

Some downed their drinks in one gulp, ordering more immediately. Brooke sipped his. A few tried to chat up a group of women at the next table. When *Gannet*'s two sub-lieutenants wandered into the lounge, there was a loud, mildly ironic cheer. 'Come and join us for a wet, sirs!' called Cummins. The officers strolled over.

'Thank you, PO, we'd like that,' said Van Zyl.

Conversation became more formal and stilted, the men wary of Smit. Before long, Van Zyl noticed two attractive women at a nearby table. He caught the eye of the brunette with curls and walked over to introduce himself. 'Hello,' he said. 'I'm Jannie. May my friend and I join you?'

'Um, yes, why not … I'm Sylvia,' said the brunette in an accent Van Zyl could not place. 'And this is Mary.' The blonde with a ponytail and freckles held out her hand.

'*Enchanté*,' said Van Zyl in his best French and turned to wave Smit over. 'This is Sub-Lieutenant Robert Smit, first officer of the good ship HMSAS *Southern Gannet*.'

They pulled up two chairs.

'Your accent is foreign, isn't it?' said Van Zyl.

'German. I'm Austrian. We had to flee after Anschluss.' There was an awkward silence.

'So, what do you girls do when you're not out on the town?' asked Van Zyl.

'Mary works in a gallery, and me, I am studying fine art at Cape Town University,' said Sylvia.

'I don't know much about art, but I know what I like,' said Van Zyl.

'Very corny, Lieutenant,' said Mary with a pained smile. 'I hope your friend here has a better understanding of art.'

'As a matter of fact, I do,' said Smit. 'I like Picasso and the German Expressionists. I find Chagall charming and Bonnard unchallenging, but oh so pretty.'

Van Zyl was even more surprised to find that his senior officer turned out to be a first-rate raconteur and soon had the women laughing at his witticisms. He'd never seen this side of the number one.

For Brooke's group, the evening grew increasingly frayed. Those who'd harboured their three shillings a day moved to the grill room and ordered steak. Brooke joined the bunch who bought fish and chips at the Greek around the corner and ate his supper off newsprint on the pavement.

Then it was time for more drinking. They headed up Adderley Street to the Texas Bar. Banging through the cowboy-style swing doors, they made their way upstairs to a balcony overlooking the street. More quarts of Lion Lager all round. Brooke had begun to make heavy weather and the room appeared to be losing focus. Around him, groups of servicemen were getting louder and rowdier.

A burly Royal Navy sailor off HMS *Milford* came up to Potgieter and asked: 'Say, are you blokes from the Seaweed Defence Force or the real navy?'

Given that the Gannets all wore red diamonds on their sleeves, this was the kind of provocation Potgieter could not resist. The Afrikaner returned his big-dimpled glass to the counter, stood up slowly and said: '*Ekskuus, rooinek, wat het jy gesê?*'

'What are you jabbering on about?'

Brooke noticed that Potgieter's eyes had gone dull. He looked for an exit.

'I asked you to repeat what you said, redneck.'

'So, rock spiders are deaf too —'

Potgieter's fist connected with the sailor's jaw. The Limey was sent sprawling, and, within seconds, other sailors had joined in. Brooke ducked under a table as one seaman was tossed over the balustrade, landing on an Austin parked below and leaving a dent in its roof. Potgieter's oppos managed to extricate him from a scrum of flailing arms and bundled him out the door just before the Shore Patrol showed up.

They found a quieter pub and continued drinking, though Brooke was unsettled by the fight. It was almost time to call it a night. Some of his shipmates aimed to make it back to *Gannet* on the last train; others would catch an early train the next morning after sleeping off their heavy heads at the Soldiers', Sailors' and Airmen's Club on Church Square. But, despite the advanced hour, Ellis and Hughes decided it was an opportune moment for romance.

'What you think lads: time for Pickles to anoint his wick?' said Hughes to the remainder of the band.

'Nah, chaps, perhaps another night,' said Brooke.

'Rubbish, no time like the serpent, I mean present,' said Hughes, taking Brooke by the sleeve and leading him out the pub. 'Strike while the pecker is hot. We may be visiting Davy Jones's locker tomorrow. Cheerio, lads!'

Ellis and Hughes had Brooke by each elbow and guided him unsteadily along Darling Street, past the Castle and into District Six.

'Isn't this a dangerous part of town?' Brooke asked nervously.

'Don't worry, we'll be fine,' said Ellis.

'Gangs and stuff?'

'Just get a move on and keep your bloody voice down,' hissed Hughes. The sailors progressed as swiftly as their waterlogged legs allowed.

Brooke had been terrified when the mine detonated beside *Gannet*, but the prospect of what lay ahead filled him with almost as much dread. He wanted out, but didn't want to appear yellow. After all, the lads were taking the trouble to show him a good time.

Ellis knocked at the side entrance of a dilapidated Victorian building. The door opened a crack, words were whispered, and the sailors were ushered into a dimly lit lounge. An older woman in a black dress offered them drinks, which they declined, then disappeared for a few minutes. Brooke looked sheepishly at his mates, who winked at him, punched his shoulder and offered the kind of encouragement that sounded patently discouraging.

After a few minutes, they heard high heels clopping down the stairs. Brooke's heart beat faster as the door opened and five women walked in. Hughes got unsteadily to his feet and introduced his two friends. Brooke was tongue-tied.

'Go on, mate, choose one,' said Hughes under his breath.

Brooke looked at the row of women. Who to pick? How to decline gracefully? How to encourage the floor to open up and devour him? Reluctantly, he pointed to a short dark-skinned woman with an impish face and blonde wig.

'Good, Jasmine is a very clean girl,' assured the madam. '*Very* clean.'

The young woman led him up the creaking stairs. It felt more like a horror film than a romantic initiation.

'Money first, Mister,' she said matter-of-factly, closing the bedroom door. 'Two pounds gets you everything.' He handed over the grubby blue notes. 'All right, drop your trousers.'

'What?' It sounded like his basic-training medical.

'You heard me. Drop 'em.'

Self-consciously, Brooke undid the fly buttons and let his trousers fall to the floor. Jasmine sank to her knees and carefully examined his genitals for crabs, then pulled back his foreskin to check for any sign of gonorrhoea or syphilis. Satisfied, she handed him a tin of Condy's crystals solution and instructed him to wash his member with it in the basin. By this stage, he was already buttoning up his pants.

'Thank you, Miss. I'm very sorry, not tonight. I've got to get going!' Before she could protest, he was out the door and clattering down the stairs.

At the other end of town, Sub-Lieutenant Smit had found his way to a pub frequented by the city's homosexuals. After a few too many Cape Smoke brandies, he made an advance on a pretty lad at the far end of the bar. The young man was not interested until money had surreptitiously changed hands. Retiring to the alley behind the pub, the pair were in an embrace when a group of off-duty soldiers appeared round the corner.

'Look at that, *ous*, pansies going at it!' yelled one.

'Let's get 'em!'

The younger man managed to escape over a fence. After a short, desperate chase, Smit was caught, held against a wall and given a thorough beating. He returned to Simon's Town on the last train with a bruised face, black eye and cracked rib.

Van Zyl spent the evening with Sylvia and Mary at Delmonico's Restaurant. He found himself increasingly drawn to the young Austrian woman with the bluest eyes he'd ever seen. After the trifle and custard, they sat smoking over cups of coffee. Van Zyl watched, mesmerised, as Sylvia coyly traced a shred of tobacco around her lips, then removed it with her fingertips.

After dinner, they accompanied Mary to the station where she caught the train home to Rondebosch. Van Zyl then walked Sylvia back to her flat through the Company's Gardens, up the avenue of oaks past the cathedral and parliament buildings. He linked arms and Sylvia did not resist.

'That is the National Gallery,' she said, pointing to the white-columned building on their left. 'Have you been inside?'

'Actually, I have. I was only trying to make a silly joke earlier. I love art.'

'You are just saying that, Lieutenant.'

'No, really. I've seen the gallery's Turners and Gainsboroughs, even the Frans Hals. And I'm a big admirer of some of the local works — especially Baines and Bowler.'

'My, my, you do know your stuff.' She smiled her broad, kissable mouth. Van Zyl was at a loss and took a moment to collect himself.

'How did you land up here at the Cape?' he asked, awkwardly.

'At the time of Anschluss, we had to get out of Salzburg. Fast. My *mutter* and me. *Vater* was arrested and sent to a camp. We had in one day to pack what we could and leave. We fled south to Italy and from there to the Cape by ship.'

'And your father?'

'We have not heard from him. It has been months.'

'I'm very sorry.'

She looked up at the dark oak boughs. 'There is nothing we can do. There is nothing any of us can do.'

'We can make war. We can destroy the Nazis.'

'*Ja*, but for us, for my family, that is — how can you say — a *Nachschrift*?'

'Postscript. We say "naskrif" in Afrikaans.'

'*Ja*. My war has already been fought and lost. Our whole family is scattered. Many of them are in camps.'

'But how do you and your mother get by?'

'She works in a Jewish delicatessen on Long Street. Baking was always her hobby, now it is her job. I help out sometimes.'

Van Zyl stopped and took both her hands in his. 'I'm so sorry, Sylvia,' he said again, clumsily. 'It's just that —'

'It is just that it is getting late.' She looked away. '*Mutter* will be waiting up for me. I must be going along.' They walked hand in hand past the Mount Nelson Hotel and up to the small Edwardian block in Gardens.

'*Danke*, Jannie. That was a lovely evening.'

'May I see you again?'

'Let me think it over.' She saw his crestfallen face. 'Of course, you can, *dummer Junge*.' She kissed him lightly on the cheek. The gate clicked and she was gone. He stood for a long time looking up at the dark, immovable shape of Table Mountain, feeling as if the shape of his own life might just have shifted.

CHAPTER 12

Sturmvogel slid across a sea of shimmering silk. The horizon was a hard line of sapphire. Flying fish leaped from the crests and glided through the air beside the raider, dolphins sported with the bows. The day was hot, and the ship's fans tried in vain to stir the dead air between decks. Every hatch and scuttle was wide open, and the pitch in the deck seams melted in the heat.

They were sailing on a south-easterly course, 600 miles west of the Cape Verde islands. The men on the bridge were in their white uniforms at last. Captain Falk gazed down at the main deck where the crew lazed about with their shirts off or in gym kit. They played Skat, Doppelkopf or chequers, read sentimental novels, washed clothes in buckets and mended kit. There were songs and laughter; the sound of an accordion drifted up to the bridge. Falk was always amazed at how a change in the weather could transform the atmosphere on board.

Each afternoon, like clockwork, herds of dark-bellied clouds would gather as rain squalls raced across the water towards them. Clothes were quickly discarded and naked sailors waited expectantly for the clouds to arrive. As warm rain hissed down, they stood open-mouthed, drinking from the sky. Others grabbed cakes of soap for impromptu showers, whooping and shouting as they scrubbed themselves.

'The rain is good for cleaning the superstructure,' said Lieutenant-Commander Adler, looking down from the bridge.

'And good for the men, too,' said second officer Bauer. 'Just look at them.'

'Like children,' sneered Adler.

'Like men without a care,' said Bauer.

'Yes, children.'

Sturmvogel continued slowly south, disguised as the merchant ship *Nagata Maru* of the Kochi Steamer Company Ltd, with a black hull, yellow funnel and large red-sun flag painted on each side. No one on board knew how to write her name in Japanese script on the stern. A Kodak advert on a box of film provided kanji characters that could easily have read 'Brownie camera' or 'colour snapshot'.

Passing a Portuguese fishing boat, they had the chance to test their disguise. A well-to-do couple — Seaman Meyer dressed in a kimono and PO Schneider wearing a homburg and blazer — was accompanied by an 'au pair', a small lad, conspicuously pushing a baby carriage about the forecastle. Only the shortest, darkest men were allowed on deck, their shirt tails flapping and heads wrapped in tenugui, much to the mirth of their crewmates.

No suspicious messages were sent from the fishing boat. Their disguise had passed muster.

'We have entered the African Narrows,' Falk's voice crackled over the ship's PA system one morning. 'Here, the Atlantic is less than 2,000 miles wide — a much smaller area for the British to patrol. We must keep an even more vigilant lookout for enemy aircraft and cruisers. However, two thousand miles is still a lot of ocean for us to hide in, as long as we see them first!'

Every day, the Heinkel floatplane was winched from its hold and launched to fly patrols. After each sortie, it would return having spotted nothing. *Sturmvogel*'s luck was holding.

As they neared the equator, the days grew hotter. The crew followed a dull routine of drills, repairs, painting and the occasional movie to break the tedium. The on-board shoemaker still charged 1.50 marks for a new pair of heels, the barber thirty pfennig for a haircut. The radio continued to blare through the day and the smutty jokes got staler, matched by the deteriorating quality of fresh produce, most of it approaching the putrid stage. Peas, beans, lentils and blood sausage became the usual, monotonous fare.

Then, one sweltering afternoon, alarm bells destroyed the peace. An enemy ship had been sighted. Adler's voice boomed over the tannoy: 'Hands to battle stations, close all watertight doors!' Men swarmed up the steel ladders from the mess decks and sprinted to their posts. The bridge filled with the attack crew. Coxswain Schmitt took the wheel. Nervous energy coursed through the ship as the thudding of watertight doors echoed below. Within three minutes, every man was at his station.

'Number one gun ready…'

'Number two gun ready…'

'Number three gun ready…'

'Torpedo tubes ready…' The reports poured into the bridge.

'Ship closed up, sir,' said Adler.

'Very good, Korvettenkapitän,' said Falk.

Silence descended on the raider, save for the pulsing of her diesel engines. Deep inside *Sturmvogel*, the electricians, engineers, damage-control teams and ammunition handlers stood by their generators, motors, fire extinguishers and hoists. Torpedo men in white denims adjusted the settings on their tubes, and gunners waited beside their 5.9s for the order that would release the shutters and reveal their guns.

The only sound on the bridge was a monotonous voice calling the ranges from gunnery officer Fischer's rangefinder, hidden in a water tank above the wheelhouse. Painstakingly slowly, the ships approached one another. First the merchantman's mast, then her stack and ventilators materialised from the haze. She carried a gun in a tub on her stern, leaving no doubt that she was an enemy.

The merchantmen closed on a converging course — two creatures about to lock horns, the bigger and meeker of the pair oblivious to the danger. Falk studied the ship closely, noting a number of short, heavy-duty derricks.

'Make a signal, Weber,' said the captain. 'Ask her name. Not too fast with your lamp. Remember, you're a merchant seaman who is not good at naval Morse.'

The jerky clatter of the lamp's venetian blinds spelt out the interrogative.

'She's the *Axios*, sir. Greek. She asks who we are.'

'Reply slowly: "*Nagata Maru*, Japan." Buy us time to get closer.' Despite long experience, Falk found his heart racing. He had not seen action since the Great War — half a lifetime ago. The hunt again, and its thrill, its terror. His emotional hatches were battened down, isolating the anxiety within.

Sturmvogel's gunners crouched beside their hidden weapons. Some trembled in fear, others said prayers. Those who'd fought before tried to empty their minds of all except the efficient handling of the gun. Seaman Meyer, sweat pouring from his forehead, eased back the last bolt on the steel shutter that would open to reveal the forward 5.9. It was dark and stifling under the forecastle's low deckhead. His throat was like sandpaper. He stifled a yawn as the minutes leaked by.

Sauer winked at him. Meyer tried to smile. His big messmate stood at the breech with a shell in his arms. The gun layer and trainer, hands on their wheels, stared at the closed shutter, anticipating the rush of air and light that would galvanise the crew into action. Behind them, the ammunition ratings stood beside a hoist that led to the magazine far below, ready to pass shells to Sauer.

'Load high-explosive, delayed-fuse shells!' came the shout.

Sauer fed the projectile into the breech and slammed it shut with a reverberating boom.

'Number One loaded!'

The cry was echoed by other guns as the two ships drew closer.

'All right, Oberleutnant, now!' barked the captain.

Bauer pressed the alarm. Bells rang and the shriek of whistles echoed over the tannoy, piercing every corner of the ship. Metal shutters clanged open, like scales peeling from the ship's eyes, to expose the guns. The hut on the afterdeck collapsed to reveal the grey menace of another 5.9. A German battle ensign raced to the main gaff and streamed its scarlet threat, a bloodstain on the tropical afternoon.

The Morse lamp slapped out an order, naval speed this time. 'Stop your engines. This is a Kriegsmarine ship. Do not try to use your wireless.' The flag signal 'OL, LNU, LUL' — 'heave to or I will fire; you are prohibited from radioing' — jerked into view.

The Greek captain took a moment to get over the shock. Letting the cigar fall from his mouth, he ordered hard astarboard, full ahead.

'They are turning away, Kapitän,' said Bauer.

'One shot across her bows,' ordered Falk.

In the forecastle the tension was broken: 'Fire!'

An ear-splitting crack. The 5.9 hurled itself back on its mounting as a tongue of flame spat from the muzzle. The deck jumped beneath Meyer's feet and the forecastle filled with acrid smoke, making him choke and cough. A column of water climbed out of the ocean fifty yards ahead of *Axios*.

On board the Greek ship, sailing from Durban to Liverpool with a mixed cargo and a few paying passengers, alarm bells clanged unceasingly. One of the passengers, Mrs Kathleen Richardson, shook her six-year-old son awake in a damp cabin on the second deck. He'd been suffering from a summer cold and was groggy. 'Put on your coat and boots, Charlie,' she said. 'Over your pyjamas. And your lifejacket. Quick as you can.'

'What's happening, Mummy?'

'I don't know. Just hurry up, darling.'

Clad in bright-red kapok lifejackets, mother and son made their way quickly to their boat station on the upper deck. A small group of passengers had gathered, awaiting instructions from a panicking crew. Among them was Sophie MacFarlane, travelling alone, returning to England after a spell in Australia working for her uncle's business. She was a striking twenty-two-year-old Bette Davis lookalike with a passion for Hollywood movies, jazz and dancing.

Back on *Sturmvogel*, Adler could barely contain his excitement.

'She is still turning, Kapitän, and increasing speed!'

The freighter listed heavily to port as she lumbered through her turn. The sound of stuttering Morse — an urgent 'QQQQ' denoting enemy raider — poured from *Sturmvogel*'s wireless room.

'Sir, she is sending a distress signal!' shouted Becker, the telegraphist. Falk bent his head to the voice pipe and said, 'Fischer, open fire at once on the wireless room behind the bridge. I want it destroyed.'

The 5.9s spat a salvo of flame. The full broadside caused the raider to lurch sideways as though she herself had been hit. Smoke billowed across the deck as an echelon of 100-pound shells streaked towards the merchantman. The range had closed and they could hardly miss. One projectile dropped short, but the other four slammed into the superstructure. Meanwhile Telegraphist Becker tried to jam the enemy's distress signal by smothering it with a string of banal personal messages: 'We are so happy your pet rabbit has recovered well, hugs and kisses, Pops and Gerty.'

The gunners were reloading, shells and charges fed into the breech blocks. Spinning hands, aim, steady… *Crack!* The 5.9s spoke again. Two shells penetrated the sandbagged wireless stack in an eruption of flame. There, the brave, stubborn leading seaman was blown to pieces, his distress signal having been heard by no one other than the raider.

Pandemonium gripped the *Axios.* Passengers rushed to the opposite side of the ship, fleeing from hurtling debris and shrapnel. Somewhere a woman sobbed. A wounded officer yelled for the crew to help the passengers. Mrs Richardson wrapped Charlie in her arms, folding her coat around the boy as though the dense weave could shield him from flying metal.

A group of sailors was trapped below, their only exit blocked by a curtain of fire. Smoke filled the passageway, choking the life out of them. Just when it seemed certain they would all be burnt to death, one of their number took courage and charged at the flames, bursting through into clean air. He screamed for his shipmates to follow. Some made the leap and emerged only mildly singed, others faltered, fell or waited too long, only to perish in the inferno.

Sturmvogel's guns roared again. A shell exploded on the freighter's bridge, sending splinters tearing through the space and cutting down the captain and his mate. They slumped against each other, their bodies pumped with holes. The explosion set off the distress rockets, which added a perverse carnival atmosphere to the dying ship as they fizzed and spat out of the wheelhouse in all directions.

Another detonation trembled inside the freighter's hull. Its blast sent some of her crew hurtling across the deck. The fire below was growing, eating through the decks and sending out exploratory tentacles of flame.

'Abandon ship!' came the call over the tannoy. It was the third mate, mortally wounded but still able to give orders.

Sailors shouted in a babel of languages. The wide-eyed Chinese cook ran past the passengers carrying a banjo and a carton of cigarettes. A few crew members — one with bleeding hands, another with scorched face — shepherded the women into a lifeboat. The wounded were laid between the thwarts with quiet words of encouragement. Heat from the burning ship seared their throats and smoke stung their eyes. Flames had taken hold of the superstructure. There was little time left.

Another shell burst on the boat deck, killing those manning the falls. One lifeboat plummeted to the water, spilling its occupants. The second was quickly filled with passengers and made a safe descent, little Charlie wide-eyed and whimpering.

'Cease fire,' said Falk. He looked at Adler and saw the bloodlust in his expression. Bauer was pale and motionless.

A third lifeboat was being lowered jerkily, accompanied by desperate shouting and gesticulating. But the last lifeboat had jammed at a stern-down angle and would not be budged. Some of the crew jumped over the side, arrowing into the water like untidy cormorants. By now, the fire had spread throughout the ship, roaring, devouring and belching smoke as it went. With the *Axios* listing more steeply, cargo broke free, destroying anything in its path.

Having taken shelter near the stern, Sophie found herself out of lifeboats, and out of options. The flames drew closer. She would have to jump. The low diving board at the Sydney council pool was the highest she'd ever attempted. Terrified, the young woman took off her shoes, climbed unsteadily onto the guardrail and stared down at the dark water. 'Jump, Missy!' came a shout from below. *Oh God*, she thought, *what a way to go*. She hesitated, her body trembling. 'Quick, Missy, the ship's done for!' She crossed her arms over her chest, closed her eyes and stepped off the rail.

Sophie hit the sea flat on her back, knocking the wind from her lungs, pins and needles of burning pain shooting through her body. The badly tied lifejacket was ripped from her torso. Down and down she went, her dress slowing her progress into the depths. Out of air, she began to choke, and the light appeared to fade. Then, with a force of will, she kicked and swam upwards, swallowing water as she went.

Bursting the surface, she gasped and, as she fought to stay buoyant, her body was wracked with a fit of coughing. The ship stood over her, leaning towards her, reaching down to take her. She spun around in terror and struck out for the nearest lifeboat. One of the derricks wobbled and toppled over, taking a mast with it and dragging a mess of rigging and wireless aerials into the sea behind her.

The doomed ship was settling by the bows. Some sailors had been trapped below by the buckling effect of the explosions and the warping of watertight doors. Arms waved desperately from portholes. Others, who'd managed to get free of the lower decks at the last moment, were now threatened by the great whirlpool that would suck them down with the ship. From the lifeboats, the sailors pulling at the oars stared back at their ship as she settled deeper and the column of smoke grew thicker, taller.

'Korvettenkapitän, go down and see to the recovery of survivors. Scrambling nets over the side. Muster a first-aid party. I want them aboard as quickly as possible. Make sure you pick up every living survivor. We want no witnesses left behind.'

'Yes, sir.'

'And Adler, we treat them with civility. Send the wounded to the surgery and make the rest as comfortable as possible. We are not barbarians.'

'They call us murderers, sir,' said the lieutenant-commander.

'Pirates, perhaps. Privateers more likely. But murderers: no.'

The raider, her engines at dead slow, approached the two lifeboats and groups of bobbing figures. Just then, the smoke on the blazing poop deck cleared for a moment to reveal a handful of sailors clustered around the ancient twelve-pounder. There was an orange flash, a bang and the sound of a shell whining over the raider's bridge.

'*Guter Gott*, the fools!' cried Falk, slamming his fist on the rail. 'Fischer, destroy that gun immediately! Even one lucky hit can send us back to Germany!'

Already *Sturmvogel*'s 5.9s were training onto the enemy's poop deck. There were two quick shots, a pause, then three more. The stern of *Axios* erupted in fragments. When the smoke cleared, there was nothing left of the gun or the crew who'd manned it.

Falk heard the popping sound of lighter armaments. He rushed to the bridge wing and looked aft to see Adler standing beside the twenty mm, directing its fire at survivors. Shells ripped into the first lifeboat, shredding the woodwork. Splashes of blood, an exploding chest, hysterical screaming.

Falk saw a woman hit in the head, removing half her face. She slumped over a little boy. As he struggled out from under her, a shell struck him in the back. His torso disintegrated.

'Stop firing!' cried Falk, pressing the cease-fire lever, its siren blaring through the ship. His face was scarlet with rage. But as survivors dived from the lifeboat, rounds stitched the water, picking off the swimmers.

In the second boat, Sophie was hit by a shell that ricocheted off the water. She felt a sharp pain in her shoulder and noticed, numbly, a large tear of flesh.

'Cease fire, damn you, that's an order!' Falk yelled into the tannoy.

The hammering twenty mm stopped abruptly, casting a shadow of silence over the scene. Bauer stared in shock at the floating bodies, at the red stains spreading around them. The young lieutenant looked ill, unable to fathom the dreadfulness that had just been wrought upon this quiet acre of ocean.

'Commence picking up survivors,' said Falk into the microphone, his voice deadpan. 'Korvettenkapitän Adler, report to the bridge.'

The second lifeboat bumped against the raider's side. Stunned, petrified faces stared up at the black flank of the ship. Some of *Sturmvogel*'s sailors scrambled down the ladders to help the survivors; lines were attached to the wounded. One of the *Axios* crew had lost a leg and was barely conscious. His body left a trail of blood up the ship's side.

Adler entered the captain's sea cabin. 'Have you lost your mind, Korvettenkapitän?' Falk's voice was quiet and controlled. 'Why did you fire on the survivors?'

'But Kapitän, you were doing the same with the 5.9s.'

'I was *not* doing the same. We were being fired on by the enemy ship.'

'I thought —'

'Perhaps you should refrain from thinking. Our nation has gained a reputation. We are portrayed as criminals. As you know, the international press accuses the Kriegsmarine of machine-gunning survivors.'

'Sir, this is a —'

'Adler, listen to me, for neutral countries like the United States, these things are very important. An insane act such as yours can have disastrous consequences. Public opinion out there in the wider world counts, even if it does not count for you.'

'Sir, that is not fair.'

'I decide what is or is not fair on my ship.' The captain was pale with suppressed rage. 'Go to your cabin. I do not want to see you on the bridge again until I say so. Dismissed!'

Falk waited a few moments, then stepped back into the wheelhouse. The *Axios* remained afloat. 'Bauer, she is making far too much smoke. We cannot have ships coming to investigate. Instruct Leutnant Lehmann to fire one torpedo into her amidships,' he said.

There was a thud and a thin shape leapt from the tube on the aft deck. A frothing white path streaked towards the freighter. Moments later, a pillar of water rose from the hull, accompanied by a shattering detonation. When the cascade subsided, it was clear that the back of the freighter was broken. A black wound opened in her flank as *Axios* slowly folded in two. The bows sank quickly; the screech of tortured steel rent the air and its insides tore apart as hundreds of tons of water poured, hissing, into red-hot holds. The stern stood upright, like a monstrous tooth. Trapped air, rushing to escape, blasted off the aft hatches and whistled through the ventilators.

A group of disconsolate survivors stood on *Sturmvogel*'s deck watching the freighter sink. Then the raider got under way again, gliding through a mess of spars and flotsam, an upturned lifeboat, mangled bodies. The sea was stained with coal dust and oil.

'Ring down for full speed,' said Falk.

'Right away, sir,' said Bauer.

'We need to put as much distance between us and the sinking as possible. Her distress signal may have been picked up. I also want us to change our disguise. We were spotted a few days ago by that fishing boat. She could have reported our course, appearance and nationality. The enemy might put two and two together.'

'Yes, Kapitän. And the prisoners?'

'Have them searched for concealed weapons. Collect their money and valuables and give them receipts. Issue dry clothes and tea. Then take them to the aft prison hold. Bedding, eating utensils, soap and shaving equipment for everyone. Forty pfennigs per day per man for use in the canteen.'

'And the women, sir?' asked Bauer.

'Make cabins available for any women, children or officers. If any are badly injured, my own quarters are available. The sea cabin is all I need.'

After giving instructions for transforming the ship, Bauer went to inspect the prisoners. Sophie was sitting on the deck, ashen-faced, holding a wad of bandages to her shoulder. She had lost a lot of blood.

'Miss, if you please, will you come with me?'

She looked up at the blond lieutenant. 'What do you want?' she asked coldly.

'First to the doctor. And then my Kapitän has graciously offered his cabin for the injured. For you.'

'I don't want his hospitality, *thank you*.'

'Miss, your wound, it requires attention. His cabin is just above the surgery. It is more comfortable than being crowded in with the others. And better for your recovery.'

'What do you care about my recovery? Minutes ago, you were machine-gunning us in the water.'

'That was a terrible mistake.'

'Mistake?' she scoffed.

'I am truly sorry, but your ship was firing on us.'

'A mistake,' she said bitterly. 'Never mind, Lieutenant, people like you —' Before she could finish her sentence, she slumped over.

'Karsten, Hemmer, quickly! Help me carry the fräulein to the surgery.'

During the rest of the day and into the night, *Sturmvogel* acquired a second, dummy funnel — a telescopic affair built of wood and tarpaulin. The Greek flag now fluttered from her gaff and a pig pen made of sewn canvas had materialised on the poop. Washing hung from lines strung across the main deck and chickens strutted about like diminutive Napoleons.

That evening, Bauer looked in on the young woman. Sophie was lying in the captain's bunk, her shoulder heavily bandaged and her arm in a sling. Doctor Gerlach had tended to her, removing the shrapnel from her wound. She wore a white officer's shirt that was too big for her tiny frame. Her face was sallow, giving her hazel eyes a compelling, almost unnerving, look.

'The Kapitän asked me to make sure that you are all right,' he lied.

'Under the circumstances, I suppose so.' Her voice was weak. She could not lift her head from the pillow.

'What is your name, please, Fräulein?'

'What's it to you?'

'It is for the record.'

'Macfarlane. Sophie Macfarlane.'

'My name is Friedrich Bauer, second officer. If there is anything you need?'

'Anything?'

'Well, I —'

'Bring back the *Axios*? Grant me my freedom? Save the innocents in the water?'

'Within reason, Fräulein.' He flushed.

'Reason? You have a very particular way with words.'

'I am sorry. My English is not so good.'

'Like so much else in this war, Lieutenant. What happened to my brother, for instance. Shot down over Kent. Not good at all, as a matter of fact.'

'My sympathies, Miss Macfarlane.'

'But your nation is to blame —'

'We all have been drawn into this war. My sister was killed in a raid on Berlin by the RAF. She was an innocent too.'

'Your people sink hospital ships and passenger liners crammed with civilians,' she hissed. 'You lay mines off harbours where anyone, even neutrals, can be hit.'

'This is not true. We are the Kriegsmarine. It is an honourable service.' His voice was soft, pleading.

'You're murderers, the lot of you!'

'This is British propaganda. You must see —'

'How can you call U-boats honourable? A raider such as yours is not *honourable*! Good God, Lieutenant, you delude yourself.'

Bauer could not meet her eyes.

'I would like to sleep now, Lieutenant. Please will you leave.'

'Of course, Miss. There is a sentry outside the door should you require anything.'

She turned her face to the bulkhead and waited for him to go.

CHAPTER 13

Two convoys were due into Cape Town on the same day. The first was from the north and known as a WS — Winston's Special. The second, a large Indian Ocean group, came from the east and included the *Queen Mary* escorted by an eight-inch cruiser and half a dozen destroyers. The Cape Town minesweepers had their hands full with the northern channel, so the Simon's Town flotilla was dispatched to assist with the eastern convoy.

The previous day, a ship had struck a mine at the outer limit of the southern channel, in ninety-five fathoms, but had been able to limp into Cape Town on her own steam. As a result, both channels needed to be extended beyond the 100-fathom line and swept again, ahead of the convoys, in case a raider had slipped in between.

From the *Gannet*'s bridge, Van Zyl scanned the horizon with his binoculars. Fingers of smoke appeared in the late afternoon, marking the van of the convoy. 'Here they come!' he said. 'More than thirty ships, by the look of it.'

He spotted the accompanying aircraft, two Ansons flying a perimeter patrol. At sunset, the planes returned to their base at Youngsfield. Bunts read the interrogative challenge from the leading destroyer, zigzagging ahead of the convoy and showering herself with spray like an elephant. Gilbert's Aldis lamp immediately clicked out the answering identification, wary of a shot across the bows if he wasn't lively about it.

Jack's flotilla took up station due south of False Bay, sweeping a wide path ahead of the convoy. Steaming six abreast, the mass of ships narrowed down to two columns as they prepared to enter the swept channel with destroyers racing up and down the flanks. The cruiser in their midst looked like a large grey wedding cake, bristling with spikes.

Surveying the armada, Jack had the strange sensation that he was dragging the fleet in his wake. They rounded Cape Point and the peninsula presented a magnificent tableau to starboard, the sky above it tinged with pink.

'Looks like a sea monster, doesn't it, sir?' said Van Zyl.

'Yes, it does, rather.'

'The first Portuguese navigators called it Adamastor, a giant in Greek mythology. He was banished to the Cape where his foul temper took the form of stormy weather, preventing sailors from rounding Africa.'

'Appropriate, I'd say.'

'Yes, a Cape of Good Hope but also a Cape of Storms. Beautiful, vindictive.'

'You're a bit of poet, aren't you, Van Zyl?'

'Oh, I never focused properly on my law degree. Kept running off to lectures on literature, art, languages. Anything but jurisprudence.'

'Where did you —'

Bang! The explosion came from dead astern. Incredulous, the officers scrambled to the bridge wing and looked aft. The Norwegian oil tanker began to slew out of formation, belching smoke.

'Good God, U-boat attack!' Jack gasped. 'Sound action stations and cut the sweeps!'

The clanging sounded through the minesweeper and was taken up by the other ships as large red warning flags broke out on the escorts' masts. *Gannet*'s radio crackled into life in the wireless cabin. Sparks leant closer to his set. 'Echo bearing oh-eight-oh degrees, approximately 3,000 yards,' came the voice from one of the destroyers. 'Am attacking.'

A terse voice from the cruiser responded: '*Gannet* to pick up survivors. *Belle* to fall back and provide starboard screen.'

Sparks relayed the messages into the voice pipe.

'Full ahead, hard astarboard!' called Jack as *Gannet* wheeled around and raced towards the tanker.

'Guns' crews closed up, sir,' said Smit.

Jack was breathing shallowly. His body began to quiver; his legs struggled to support him. He was racing from Dunkirk, bound for destruction.

The hunting destroyer over to starboard had been joined by a second escort. There were detonations of white water, and the booming of depth charges echoed across the sea. Jack imagined the black drums sinking silently at ten feet per second, then, at the set depth: eruption. Mushrooms of atomised water hung in the air behind the destroyers. The men on *Gannet* felt the shock wave of each explosion.

Down in the engine room, the grease-streaked faces of the stokers looked fearfully at the chief. A torpedo piercing the thin skin of their hull would mean instant annihilation. 'It's all right,' he mouthed into the roar and gave a thumbs-up.

On the bridge, Jack's mind was paralysed, the cogs of his brain spinning in neutral. He couldn't engage any thought that would produce the necessary action.

'Captain, sir!' Smit stared at him, perplexed. 'Sir!'

'I, I... Number One...' Jack's eyes were wild.

'Don't worry, sir,' said Smit under his breath. 'I've got her.'

'She's going down!' Behardien was shrill, almost screaming from the bridge wing.

'Shut up, sailor!' hissed Smit. 'Look for the periscope, or torpedo tracks. Damn your eyes!'

The convoy steamed on as *Gannet* raced against the tide of ships, closing with the stricken Norwegian. An explosion inside the tanker appeared to lift the bridge clear of the superstructure. Her funnel buckled and collapsed, and an ugly cloud of smoke stood over the ship like a black umbrella. Burning oil spilled from the hole in her side, setting the sea alight.

As her prow settled lower in the water, men scrambled like termites across her decks. A party on the afterdeck struggled with the davits of a lifeboat. Its bows dropped jerkily, then the pulleys jammed. Giving up, the men began to jump into the icy Atlantic and tried to swim clear of the ship as tongues of flaming oil pursued them. Jack could hardly bear to watch.

The tanker moaned as her prow slid below the surface. Rigging and equipment broke free and rumbled across her sloping deck. Smoke billowed from the engine-room skylights. Her bronze propeller stood up out of the ocean, dripping as it still slowly turned, towering over the men in the water.

Gannet was nearly there. Jack could hear shouting and looked on helplessly as sailors swam from the suction that would drag them under. He could taste their fear — or was it his own? Chapman's Peak and the Twelve Apostles, etched against the purple sky like a dragon's back, made an imposing backdrop to the nightmare.

Now *Gannet* slowed her approach. The smoke was black and acrid, stinging their throats. A slick of burning oil caught the first group in the water and set their lifebelts and heads on fire. Water torches, floating pyres. The screaming was barely human. The sound of an abattoir. Asphyxiation, incineration, merciful drowning.

The group that had delayed its jump floated in a pocket of calm. They were cut off. Flames and smoke closed in, corralling the men like sharks around a bait ball. Nothing could save them.

Jack felt rising panic, like a fever taking hold, setting his mind on fire. His mouth was dry; his eyes smarted; his heart raced. Then he heard the strains of 'Show Me the Way to Go Home', reaching him faintly from the pod of doomed men. Something inside him shifted and his vision cleared. 'Full ahead! Hard aport!'

'Captain, no!' cried Smit. 'We will lose the ship!'

'Not if we're quick about it, Number One. Fire parties fore and aft. Prepare the hoses.' He put his mouth to the voice pipe. 'Cox'n, steer for the narrowest band of flames.'

The wall of fire drew nearer.

'Half ahead.' The telegraph clanged and *Gannet* slowed. Jack listened to the roaring of the blaze. 'Dead slow.'

The minesweeper penetrated a wall of fire. Jack's nostrils filled with the stench of oil and burning paint. Hosing parties desperately sprayed her hull. To the trailing vessels of the convoy, it must have appeared as though the little ship had been swallowed by flames.

Within the ring of fire was an eerie scene. *Gannet* crept closer to the group of bobbing men. Some were badly burnt, others were unconscious. The low waist of *Gannet* gave its crew easy access to the survivors. As time was critical, the Norwegians were unceremoniously dragged aboard, then gently laid on the deck. The pitiful figures were caked in oil.

'*Takk … takk for at du kommer tilbake.*'

'Don't mention it.'

'*Takk for —*'

'Shhh, easy there, save your breath, mate.'

The flames closed in and began to lick at the bows. Jack was about to give the order to withdraw when he noticed a young lad floating off to one side. There was a splash. Seaman Hughes — bloody impetuous fool that he was — had dived in with a life ring and struck out towards the boy. A snake of flame stole across the scene to cut the two off. Jack watched, transfixed.

'Captain, we have to go!' cried Smit. '*Gannet* is on fire, port side aft.'

Jack remained silent. His entire being willed salvation.

'Sir!'

'I heard you, Smit.'

Time had run out. He was going to have to leave them. Hughes had reached the boy and was struggling to place the ring around him. Now he was kicking with all his might, back towards the ship, pulling the lad behind him. There was a splash, then another. Two more sailors had dived in. Shouts of encouragement came from the waist. At last, the boy was hauled alongside. Hands reached down to grab him.

'Half astern,' said Jack into the voice pipe. 'Back out the way we came, Cox'n.'

'Aye Captain, back the way we came,' came the laconic voice from below.

Jack stared at the place where the tanker used to be. He noticed a blackened figure sitting on a makeshift raft to starboard, right at the edge of the wall of fire. His heart froze. The raft was already burning and flames lapped at the sailor's clothing. The doomed man slowly raised a hand. A call for help, a farewell? Jack could not take his eyes off the apparition. Then a curtain of fire was drawn between them. *Gannet* cleaved through the flames, further blistering her paintwork as sailors ducked away, trying to find cover from the heat. Moments later, she was past the danger and into open water. Jack sucked clean air into his lungs, trying to banish the image of the burning man.

'Full ahead,' he said between gritted teeth.

Gannet raced to catch up with the convoy. The two columns of ships had increased speed, aiming at the flat-topped mountain. The convoy responded instantly to the commodore's orders for changes of course to throw off the U-boat.

'From Commodore, sir,' said Bunts. 'Alter course to one-one-oh at 21:20.'

'Acknowledge,' said Jack.

The ships executed the turn in succession. After half an hour, the destroyers reported that they had lost contact with the enemy.

'Murdering bastards,' said Jack. 'I'd give my left arm to see a U-boat surface and be obliterated by shellfire.'

'So would I, sir,' said Van Zyl.

'We'd hammer it with everything we've got,' said Smit.

Jack wanted to see bloated Nazi corpses floating in the water. He needed to replace the visions of Dunkirk, the image of the burning man. The hate was so palpable he could almost smell it on himself.

Those not tending to the wounded remained at action stations. Cummins went around the ship with a pail of water and mugs — the attack and the sudden rush of adrenaline had left the men drained, parched. Brooke took a swig from his secreted tin of condensed milk and passed it around the pom-pom crew. The sugar burst seemed to help with the shock.

Gannet did not have a sickbay or medical orderly. The cook had some first-aid training and a box with rudimentary supplies that didn't extend much beyond morphine syringes, dressings and anti-burn jelly. The crew used paraffin to clean the thick, foul-smelling oil from the survivors' bodies as their ship raced ahead of the convoy towards Cape Town. By the time the blackened minesweeper reached Green Point, all the tubes of anti-burn jelly had been exhausted.

As they were about to enter harbour, the bridge of the cruiser flashed a message. 'From flag, sir,' said Bunts. '"A damn foolish thing you did, *Gannet.* You deserve to be court-martialled. And jolly well done!"'

Smit and Van Zyl turned to their captain, who was staring ahead as though he hadn't heard.

'Sir, did you —'

'Yes, thank you, Smit,' Jack snapped. 'Prepare for harbour stations.'

Gannet swung round the Elbow, passed the entrance boom, glided through the still waters of Victoria Basin and tied up at Alfred Basin's North Quay. Hospital orderlies hastened aboard with stretchers and carried the wounded to a row of ambulances parked on the wharf.

It was late and most of the crew retired to their bunks, feeling utterly spent. They knew that the next day would be filled with repairs and repainting their scalded ship. Brooke stared at the deckhead above his bunk, still registering the aftermath of the shock, the horror of what he had seen. He would write a letter to his mum. He would tell her everything.

Jack, too, could not sleep. His men had done well; they had shown bravery and selflessness. But the smells and sounds of the doomed tanker filled his mind. The drowning Norwegians, the burning man; the images kept replaying themselves, against his will. Getting out of bed, he switched on the lamp, pulled a flask of whisky from his drawer and poured a tumbler. The Nazis were here. He had travelled 10,000 miles, and they had followed him. There was nowhere to run.

Jack worked his way steadily through the flask and started on a bottle. The first flush of dawn ushered him into a comatose sleep.

CHAPTER 14

By late afternoon the next day, *Gannet* was looking more respectable and Jack wanted to let the men have a night on the town. He decided that he, too, would step ashore after taking a nap to freshen up and recover from his hangover. Perhaps the charms of Cape Town might distract him from the pictures running through his head in every idle moment. Smit would remain on board as officer of the watch. The first lieutenant's last venture ashore had resulted in a brawl of some sort. Smit had not wanted to speak about it. Jack worried about his number one, sensing the man's predicament. But, whatever his private struggles, Smit persisted in making himself unlikeable on *Gannet*.

Most of the crew were granted overnight passes. Brooke took a cold-water basin bath in *Gannet*'s washroom using the hard issue soap and had another unnecessary go at shaving. He put on his neatest uniform — shore-going blues that had been pressed between the mattress and wooden boards of his bunk — and joined the rest of the liberty watch on the wharf. He hoped the blue house was not on tonight's menu.

To Brooke, it appeared as though his oppos had wilfully put the horror of the sinking behind them and were determined to make a night of it. He joined a group heading along the wharf to the Harbour Café, where they bought steak-and-kidney pies and bottles of Coca-Cola. The sailors sat on a row of benches and ate their pies, looking out at the Fairmile motor launches under construction in Quay Four's boatyard.

'Handsome little boats, aren't they?' said Levy.

'And fast, too,' said Plato. 'Way, way faster than the *Gannet*.'

'Would you swap?'

'Not on your nelly,' said Plato.

'Me neither, the old bird's just fine,' cut in Ellis. 'Although Smit and the skipper need a peg or two taken out from under them. Then everything will be hunky-dory.'

'I'm not sure you're right about the skipper, Popeye,' said Behardien. 'You should of seen him last night on the bridge, taking us into those flames. I think he might be okay.'

'Jury's out, mate. Come on, let's hit the town.'

The sailors strode past the warehouse that acted as Seaward Defence Force base to the dockyard gates, where they caught the harbour bus to Cape Town station. From there, they strolled up to the City Hall, which was playing host to an evening concert for the troops.

As they took their seats near the back of the auditorium, Brooke noticed that Just Nuisance had sneaked in and was lying in the aisle near the front. An opera singer in a sequined dress took to the stage, backed by a large female chorus. She began an aria that was apparently not to the dog's liking. In fact, Nuisance reacted in the same manner as he did to the meowing of cats. He began to bark, then stormed the stage, bounding towards the soprano. Sailors pursued him, the chorus hastily exited, and, after a few minutes of pandemonium, the dog was ejected. Once order was restored, the musical programme resumed.

Later that evening, Jack, still feeling the worse for wear, left the ship and also took the bus into town. He thought he'd try to see a show recommended by Lieutenant Wilson, so he found his way to the Alhambra Theatre, a grand building with an ornate, faux Moorish façade adorned with arches and spiral columns. Waiting in the crowded foyer for the doors to open, he glanced across and noticed a lighthouse of blonde hair coming through the entrance.

Clara looked ravishing in a knee-length white skirt and tight-fitting black jacket with box shoulders. She was on the arm of an air-force officer. Despite the high-ranking obstacle, Jack decided to go over and at least say hello.

'Good evening, Clara, we shouldn't keep meeting like this,' he said, coming up behind her, and trying to sound as casual as his beating heart would allow.

'Oh, it's you, Lieutenant,' she said, turning around. Was her expression mildly annoyed or mildly surprised?

'This is my brother, Pierre. And this is … I'm sorry, I've forgotten your name.'

'Jack Pembroke, pleased to meet you.' The two men shook hands.

'Jack and I met at Admiralty House. I went with Henry. The lieutenant here very kindly stood on my toes.'

Jack blushed. 'I felt wretched about that. I was mortified —'

'I'm teasing you, Lieutenant. Don't look so serious.'

'We'd better go in,' said Pierre, as the doors opened. 'Why don't you come and sit with us?' Jack noticed Clara squeeze her brother's arm.

'Oh no, don't worry,' said Jack. 'There's booked seating anyway.'

'Nonsense.' Pierre was smiling. 'It won't be full. Come on.'

'All right, then, that's very kind of you.'

He saw the resigned look on Clara's face and felt a stab of embarrassment. But this might be his only chance. He would blunder on and see where things led. Perhaps this time he would land on both feet, and miss both of hers.

They entered the auditorium with its twinkling ceiling lights and plush curtains. Clara sat between them. Jack paged through the programme: Cape Command presents *Fortress Cavalcade*, the greatest revue ever staged by the services. He ran his eye down a dizzying array of acts, including a native war dance, a Malay choir singing '*Daar Kom die Alibama*', a scene from *The Mikado*, a Warsaw Concerto and plenty of massed bands — oh dear, not his thing at all, but he was glad he'd come. It meant he could sit next to Clara Marais, even if she didn't necessarily want to sit next to him.

It was a long programme, most of it tiresome. During the acts, he couldn't help stealing glances at the beauty beside him; between acts, he tried to pass witty comments. She smiled politely, probably to humour him. At the end of the show, after singing '*Die Stem*' and 'God Save the King', he and Clara waited in the foyer for Pierre, who'd gone to chat to some airmen.

Jack seized the moment. 'I'm afraid I didn't make a very good first impression…' he began. He noticed with alarm that Pierre was already saying goodnight to the group. After everything he'd recently experienced, there seemed less time or space for his usual diffidence.

'Not at all, I was only —'

'Look, Clara, I just wanted to tell you that I think you're smashing. And I'd love to invite you out sometime.' His heart was pounding.

'Lieutenant —'

'Jack.'

'Jack.' She smiled. 'What did you have in mind, another dance?'

'Well, yes, actually, maybe. I could bring my dancing shoes this time, leave the Dunkirk clodhoppers at home.'

'You were at Dunkirk?' She raised her eyebrows.

'Briefly. We lost our ship on the way home. HMS *Havoc*.'

He looked away, but Clara had seen the earnestness in his eyes. 'All right, then,' she said, 'if you're so jolly insistent.' She smiled, revealing her dimples. 'Let me give you my telephone number.'

'Splendid.'

'Do you have a pen?'

'No need, I'll remember it.'

'Till your dying day?' She chuckled.

'As a matter of fact, probably yes.'

CHAPTER 15

It was a warm, windless evening at Milkwood House. Rachel had laid a table on the croquet lawn, and the admiral sat between his two children enjoying a traditional bobotie.

'The sinking of that Norwegian tanker of yours has just been recorded as "non-sub", Jack,' said the admiral, spooning Mrs Ball's chutney onto his plate.

'But Father, the destroyers got a firm fix on their asdics.'

'You're wrong. There have been no other reports of U-boat activity in South African waters. No signals, no radio chatter, no attacks. Perhaps the asdics picked up a whale or a shoal of fish. Your "submarine" must have been a mine.'

'But we'd just swept that channel. It was clean as a whistle.'

'No, it wasn't, Jack.'

Imogen passed around bowls of banana slices and coconut flakes, letting the naval talk wash over her, as she'd always done.

'It seems that in deep water some of these German mines have a habit of dipping, especially if there's a big swell or strong current,' said the admiral. 'So you're bound to miss one every now and then. It could also have been a drifter that broke free.'

'I find that hard to believe.'

'It's the most plausible explanation, Jack. The Cape Town flotilla bagged a mine at the very end of the cleared channel this morning. We're convinced no ship could have laid it since the last sweep.'

'In that case, we'd better employ an A-sweep in deeper water and use a lot more kite wire, just to be safe.'

'Do that. Deep-water sweeping is so much more tricky … and slow.'

'Our dan buoys marking the cleared channel get dragged all over the show by the current. Also, the time and effort it takes to haul in 600 feet of mooring wire at each buoy becomes so onerous as to negate the whole bally exercise.'

'I hear you, but sweep you must.'

'If it really was a mine, that means a German ship has been working the swept channel recently.'

'Ship, or ships,' said the admiral. 'It could be an old mine, but I'm sure there's at least one raider in our theatre. We're flying daily patrols with Ansons and our new, longer-range Marylands. Simon's Town has released three cruisers, one AMC, an aircraft carrier — *Hermes* — and five destroyers to join the search.'

'That's quite the armada. Good intelligence?'

'Yes. Just to add to the headache, we've reason to believe that the pocket battleship *Admiral Scheer* is back in the South Atlantic. As you know, her eleven-inch guns are more than a match for any single ship we have at our disposal. She's been giving our Indian Ocean units the runaround, sank a number of ships, and is now at large in our neighbourhood.'

'The anchorages are so vulnerable.'

'Exactly. And Cape Town is terribly congested at the moment. If a pocket battleship, raider or U-boat made a night attack, we'd be in deep trouble. Duncan Dock has eighteen berths, but it's a shambles when we have a big convoy in Table Bay. We can double-bank them in the harbour if we have enough warning, but it could take two days to pack them all in.'

'So, what are the alternatives?'

'Well, Jack, as a matter of fact, one of them might involve you. We've decided to prepare Saldanha Bay, sixty-five miles north of Cape Town, as a defended port that can take the convoy overflow. It's perfect as a relief anchorage — a natural harbour that can be made submarine- and raider-proof. The problem has always been potable water. It's semi-desert up there. So the sappers are going to build a twenty-seven-mile pipeline to bring a million gallons of water a day from the Berg River. That set-up should be operational next year.'

'More bobotie, anyone?' asked Imogen. Both men nodded and she served them, rolling her eyes, which neither noticed.

'How do I fit in?' asked Jack.

'I'd like you to take *Gannet* up to Saldanha and chart a permanent swept channel. While you're there, I want you to draft a provisional report on the defences needed to make the anchorage secure. Naval guns, anti-submarine netting, boom defences: let me have a wish list. I like the look of Saldanha. It's actually a better natural anchorage than either Cape Town or Simon's Town.'

'Has there been any raider activity up the West Coast?'

'Almost certainly. We had a report last week about a farmer, a Mr van der Merwe, who found a strange metal container on the beach near Paternoster. Using an ad hoc pulley system, he and his son managed to load the thing onto a cart. At this point, he noticed that the container was leaking something that looked like brown tar. Curious, the idiot lit it with a match. The substance began to spit and fizzle. The two clowns beat a hasty retreat.'

'TNT?'

'Spot on. Fortunately for them, it had been softened by the sun and didn't explode. But it blazed to a height of 200 feet, causing consternation on the farm and in the nearby village, as you might imagine. A local policeman was called, but he wasn't interested, so they rolled the object into the bushes.'

'Astonishing. You wouldn't think there was a war on.'

'I got wind of all this and sent a team to investigate on Monday. They discovered that the farmer had dismantled the primer with a tin opener and, to roll it more easily, he'd cut off the horns with a hammer and chisel.'

'He must have a whole regiment of guardian angels,' said Imogen, catching the coattails of the conversation.

'Just so, my dear. Mr van der Merwe was persuaded to hand over the mine's mechanism, which he had in his barn. He told our chaps he thought it was a new kind of boiler being used for wireless telegraphy. I mean, I ask you!'

Rachel cleared the plates and returned with a dish of crème caramel and a tub of clotted cream. The three served themselves, then sat contemplating the bay below them. Wind tousled the fronds of the wild date palms. Guinea fowl clattered in their treetop roosts, probably disturbed by a mongoose, or perhaps even a leopard. A ripe moon rose from the Hottentots Holland Mountains.

'Father, there's something I'd like to discuss,' said Jack after a while.

'Yes?'

'It's rather tricky.'

'Go on.'

'I think I need to replace my number one, Smit. We don't see eye to eye and he's appalling with the crew. He's the weakest link on *Gannet*.'

'I strongly advise against it, Jack. You don't want to be seen as that sort of captain.'

'But I don't trust his judgement. The men can't stand him.'

'Jack, you're already treading on thin ice with O'Reilly. The fact that you're my son and seen to be benefitting from family connections —'

'I've had more minesweeping and combat experience —'

'You don't need to convince me. But if you start rocking the boat… If you start trying to get rid of officers… It's not going to look good for either of us. Try to find this man's strong points. Talk to him, man to man. The best officers are those who can render the bad eggs useful to the navy.'

Jack knew his father was right. Although the crew loathed Smit, Jack did feel some sympathy for him. His first lieutenant had an inner battle going on that he could only partially understand. Somehow, Jack needed to find a way to work with or around his number one, temper his antagonism towards the men, make him feel part of the ship's company. As if Jack's own uncertainties were not enough.

Gannet sailed up the west coast towards Saldanha in a following sea. It was a mild autumn day, so February called Brooke to the wheel and gave the lad his first steering lesson.

'Grip the spokes firmly, legs apart, balance yourself for the roll of the ship.'

Brooke took the wheel, feeling the vibration of the vessel through his feet. He stared over the prow at the ocean ahead. *Gannet* was in his hands: it was a thrilling sensation. A swell lifted her quarter, the sweeper slewed to starboard, and Brooke turned the spokes.

'Easy does it,' said February. 'Don't overcorrect her. Remember to use just enough helm to hold the lubber's line on the set course. Keep your stern wake in mind: it must be as straight as possible. There you go, nicely done.'

Brooke looked down at the floating card under the binnacle's brass hood: 330 degrees. On course. The creaking of the wheel, the quiet ticking of the compass and a wide blue sea before him. 'I could get used to this, PO,' said Brooke.

After half an hour, February took the helm again. They passed Yzerfontein and laid a course for Vondeling Island. *Gannet* motored past South Head and swung around Marcus Island into Saldanha Bay. Over to port, Jack could make out a railway station and a couple of small-boat jetties; beyond them lay the village of Saldanha, a cluster of whitewashed cottages and a fishmeal factory. Jack swept his binoculars around the bay. *What a handsome anchorage*, he thought — fifty ships or more could be accommodated in its tranquil waters. A Scapa Flow of the south.

'Do you see that wreck on the far shore, sir?' asked Van Zyl.

'Yes, looks old.'

'It's the *Präsident.* German — she was a tender to the cruiser *Königsberg* in the last war.'

'My father has told me about the *Königsberg*, sunk by British monitors in the Rufiji River. He served out here back then and had a hand in it.'

'The *Präsident* was captured and towed from Dar es Salaam to Saldanha by a South African tug. She broke adrift in a storm and ran aground.'

'Well, I never. A memento of the Rufiji battle here at the Cape.'

'And over to starboard is Donkergat, just around that headland. It's a whaling station.'

'Alstad was based there before the war, wasn't he?'

'Aye, sir.'

'This place has many fine anchorages.'

'Yes, but fresh water has always been the problem,' said Van Zyl.

'I'm told the alternatives are rainwater, a brackish well in Hoedjes Bay, or water bought from the railway tank.'

'And there's a small freshwater spring higher up the lagoon at Oostewal,' said Van Zyl. 'It's on the chart. We might need to pay the farmer a visit if we get thirsty. Until the pipeline is completed, a stopgap measure for visiting ships might be to bring water barges up from Cape Town.'

'Good idea, Sub, I'll include it in my report.'

Gannet reached the northwest corner of the bay and dropped anchor. Over the next few days, they surveyed Saldanha's waters and marked out a swept channel with buoys. Jack was rowed ashore at North Head, Danger Bay, South Head and Plankies Bay to find suitable sites for gun emplacements. In the evenings, he sat with his two officers in the wardroom, a chart spread out on the table and held down by an ashtray and a copy of *For Whom the Bell Tolls*.

'I suggest that mines be laid here.' Jack ran his finger across the strait. 'In fact, the best would be a controlled minefield between Hoedjes Point and Marcus Island, and another one between Marcus Island and Eland Point. The mines could be remotely detonated if a U-boat tried to enter.'

'How about anti-submarine netting on either side of Marcus Island, and a boom?' said Smit.

'Absolutely,' said Jack. 'The defences will have to be served by a naval station. I suggest here, in North Bay. We'll also need lookout points on both sides of the bay. I'm going to recommend a battery of six-inch guns on Baviaansberg and another in North Bay.' His finger tapped the chart. 'Perhaps a couple of twelve-pounders on this little island too. And a few powerful searchlights.'

'Sir, with all the additional traffic, Saldanha will need a minesweeping and anti-submarine flotilla as well, and an examination vessel,' said Smit.

'Quite right. This is far bigger than I first imagined.'

CHAPTER 16

'Smoke, Kapitän, bearing red three-five,' said Adler.

Falk rubbed his eyes and raised himself stiffly from his upright chair. The strain of sitting there for what seemed like months had taken its toll. His body ached. But adrenaline overrides lethargy: this he knew well. He picked up his binoculars and trained them on the horizon.

'Crow's nest lookout says a merchant ship, sir. Almost converging course, it seems. One funnel, low in the water and slow.'

'Very good. Sound battle stations.'

Bells clanged throughout the ship, accompanied by the drumming of feet, followed soon after by the squeal of ammunition hoists. Coxswain Schmitt's tall frame replaced the quartermaster at the wheel. Sub-Lieutenant Fischer swung his rangefinder onto the freighter and Seaman Hoppe began calling the bearings and ranges. Covers were dragged off the hidden 5.9s, shells rammed into open breeches and spare ammunition stacked in ready-use lockers beside the guns.

'We will approach her quite naturally,' said Falk. 'Port five.'

The helmsman answered, easing the ship's head closer to the oncoming vessel.

'She is doing about eight knots and we are doing twelve, Kapitän,' said Bauer. 'We should be up to her in twenty minutes.'

Resting his elbows on the signal locker, Falk trained his glasses on the freighter. Vertical prow, about 7,000 tons. British by the look of it. Tension mounted on a silent bridge.

Falk could feel sweat trickling down his spine. He wanted, at all costs, to avoid a repeat of the *Axios* fiasco.

Across the water, on the *Kimberley Star*, Captain Evans was also aiming his binoculars at the oncoming ship: Norwegian, a neat, modern freighter. The Welshman turned to look at the chart of the waters off Angola and South West Africa, spread out on the table behind him. On this course, she was probably bound for Cape Town. He had a sudden memory of the family that had hosted him in Constantia: such a heart-warming interlude…

'Sir!' came the high-pitched shout of a lookout.

Captain Evans whipped around and stared in disbelief at the other ship. The Norwegian flag had vanished, replaced by a red ensign bearing the swastika. Shutters clanged open as the raider's full set of teeth was laid bare.

The Welshman ordered hard astarboard full ahead.

'Stop your engines,' came the command from an Aldis lamp on the enemy bridge. 'Do not try to send a wireless signal.' To reinforce the message, a 5.9 barked and a column of water rose ahead of the *Kimberley Star*.

'I have stopped my engine,' came the reply from the freighter. The signal flags 'OMR' — 'I am surrendering' — fluttered to the gaff. The British ship blew off steam and slowed to a halt, wallowing in the lumpy swell.

Sturmvogel crept closer at dead slow, her guns trained on the British ship.

Falk noticed Bauer letting out a sigh. Perhaps his second officer was relieved that they had not opened fire. Bauer lacked spine. Perhaps he was more of a liability than Falk had anticipated. He would have to keep an eye on the young man — Bauer with too little bloodlust, Adler with too much.

Falk ordered another signal: 'Abandon your ship. No one is to remain on board.'

The *Kimberley Star* carried a dozen passengers, including a handful of women. Clutching a few hastily grabbed possessions, they were soon being helped into lifeboats. 'Come on, Mrs Farmer,' said a beefy PO Jones. 'In you get. Nuffing to worry about. We'll be picked up in a few minutes.'

He held the octogenarian's trembling hand as she climbed into the lifeboat. The PO got in next to her, tried to make her comfortable and then helped to release the falls. The lifeboat lurched towards the water. The iron side of the ship passed by like an elevator as Mrs Farmer steeled herself to face what lay ahead. A prisoner of the Nazis on an enemy ship thousands of miles from home.

Sailors began rowing them across to the raider, crossing paths with two rakish motor launches from *Sturmvogel*. The leading one was filled with an armed boarding party and a prize captain. Lieutenant Bauer had been instructed to secure the British ship and make sure there hadn't been any acts of sabotage. Later, a prize crew would be sent over with a few prisoners and the *Kimberley Star* would be prepared for her new role.

Flailing oars brought the lifeboats alongside *Sturmvogel*. Above them, the red ensign stood out against a cloudless sky. Seamen hooked onto the dangling blocks, and the boats were hoisted up the ship's side. A group of German sailors, some of them shirtless, watched the prisoners silently as the raider's upper deck drew level. Mrs Farmer was gripped with fear, but raised her chin and refused the hand of a German as she climbed down onto the deck.

Meanwhile, Bauer and his men scrambled up the merchantman's ladder armed with pistols, MP 40 Schmeissers, grenades and a Very pistol. They met no resistance and found no evidence of sabotage. Entering the wheelhouse, Bauer came upon *Kimberley Star*'s captain and chief officer with glasses of whisky in hand. They were the only ones to have remained on board. Bauer treated them courteously, as Falk had ordered. No, the enemy captain was unfortunately not able to furnish Bauer with the ship's naval papers and secret codes as these had been thrown overboard in a weighted sack, as per standard procedure.

Falk studied the freighter through his binoculars. At last, a signal lamp flickered on the enemy's bridge. That would be his second officer. 'Meat carcasses, dairy produce, beer, steel tubing, wheat,' said Signalman Weber.

Falk replied: 'Make to Oberleutnant Bauer: "Fill the boats with fresh provisions and as many crates of beer as you can carry. *Sturmvogel* is thirsty."'

The launch returned to the raider carrying the two prisoners and piled with produce, as well as mailbags, charts, compasses and sacks of magazines and newspapers plundered from the messes and wardroom. The senior officers would go through them carefully, searching for any intelligence that might be useful. Even censored letters sometimes betrayed valuable information.

Captain Evans was led to *Sturmvogel*'s bridge at nominal gunpoint. The short, white-bearded Welshman looked pale, but his eyes flashed defiance. Straightening his rumpled blue uniform, he stepped into the wheelhouse. Falk stood up and proffered his hand. The Welshman hesitated, stuck out his jaw and shook Falk's hand.

'I am Kapitän zur See Emil Falk.' His English was clipped and precise.

'Captain John Evans.'

'I am sorry for taking your ship. But it is duty.'

'I know, Captain.'

'You and your crew will be taken care of. We are not the barbarians of your propaganda.'

'Oh, I don't know about that: Warsaw, Rotterdam, London's nightly blitzing —'

Adler took a step forward. Falk shot him a warning glance.

'German cities are being bombed by the Royal Air Force, Captain,' he said quietly. 'No one is innocent. Not anymore.'

'And the women, the children?' asked Evans bitterly.

Falk chose to ignore him. 'Women and children will be given separate quarters. My men will not discomfort them.'

'What do you intend to do with us?'

'You will find out soon enough. Oberleutnant Bauer will show you to a cabin. That will be all, for now.'

Adler looked away. His captain should not be showing such respect to an enemy of the fatherland.

The two ships continued southwest in close company, the prize crew getting to know their new home and the prisoners theirs. Falk called a meeting of his officers in the wardroom. 'It is my intention,' he said, 'to send the captured ship back, in due course, as a prize. Probably to Bordeaux, but *SKL* will confirm. She will take most of the prisoners with her. I will keep the captain, first mate and chief engineer on *Sturmvogel*.'

'And the injured woman from *Axios*, sir?' asked Bauer.

'They will all go. Why? Do you have a particular interest in the girl?'

'No, sir.' Bauer blushed. The other officers laughed.

Falk held up his hand. 'In the meantime, we will keep the *Kimberley Star* with us and transfer stores. She is carrying a mixed cargo. There is much in her we can make use of to prolong our cruise. I will leave her with just enough fuel and supplies to make it to France.'

After hearing Falk's orders, Bauer needed to see Sophie again — even if she treated him with disdain. He knocked apprehensively at her door and waited for permission to enter. To his surprise, this time she invited him to sit.

'To what do I owe this visit, Lieutenant?'

'Please to call me by my Christian name,' said Bauer. 'Friedrich.'

'Friedrich, then. And you, I suppose, may call me Sophie.'

'How is your shoulder?'

'Oh, it's sore, but healing. I wish you'd stop rocking the ship about so monstrously.'

'There is nothing I can —'

'I know, Friedrich.'

'Ah, a joke.' He smiled for the first time, a smile that betrayed the pain and vulnerability in the young officer. He brushed a piece of blond fringe from his eyes and looked out of the scuttle, unsettled by her scrutiny.

'You mentioned that your sister was killed,' she said, after a long pause.

'There is nothing to say. It is happening everywhere, to everyone. Few families are spared. And your brother, he too.'

'Yes, he was jumped by a Messerschmitt while returning to base. Crash-landed in a field, but didn't manage to get out before his Hurricane blew up.'

'I am sorry.'

'I do believe you are. But there is no end to this. It's sucking us all in, sucking us down. And you are the enemy.'

'You are my enemy too, Sophie,' he said softly. She looked into his troubled eyes. He placed his hand on the bed beside hers.

She looked away. 'Lieutenant, you must go.'

On a day of dead calm, the two ships came together. Heavy rope fenders prevented too much damage to the paintwork as *Sturmvogel* filled up with 150 tons of oil from the prize and transferred most of the prisoners back to the *Kimberley Star.*

'Can't say I'm sorry to see the back of them,' said Falk. 'They have been eating us out of house and home.'

'Yes, sir. Shall I see to the transfer of the girl?' asked Bauer.

'Is she fit to go across?'

'The doctor says she is probably ready. But he is not absolutely certain. She is still very weak.'

Falk smiled. 'Perhaps we should wait for her full recovery. There is no doctor on the prize. We will send her home with the next ship we take.'

'Yes, sir. Thank you.' He blushed at his involuntary gratitude.

Later, the two officers stood on the bridge wing watching the freighter turn and head north. Falk was thinking about a house in Lübeck and its four precious occupants. A house of sunshine. Bauer's mind was on a cabin not very far from the spot they were standing on.

Sturmvogel proceeded towards the African coast. Approaching the mouth of the Orange River, she turned south and Falk called a meeting of his senior officers in the wardroom. 'We have various options,' he said, leaning over a chart of the South African coast. 'We can lay one or two large minefields in a busy shipping lane, for instance off Cape Town, Cape Agulhas or St

Francis. Or we can lay a number of smaller, scattered fields. My preference is for the latter. I think we will cause more disruption to traffic if we spread the mines, laying them in different places at long intervals.'

'I beg to disagree, Kapitän,' said Adler. 'Surely a single, bold approach, getting in close to a harbour and clogging her swept channels, will cause chaos.'

'You may be right, Korvettenkapitän, but from what our intelligence tells us, the enemy's port minesweepers are quite effective. They might be able to clear the channels quickly. Bauer?'

'I agree with you, sir. It might be better not to put all our eggs in one basket, so to speak.'

Adler regarded his junior with barely concealed contempt.

'Right,' said Falk, 'small fields far apart at odd intervals it will be. Let's take a closer look at the charts and decide on locations, depths and patterns for laying.'

Bauer leant over the chart and pointed: 'The profitable zones are here, around the approaches to Saldanha Bay, as well as at the end of Cape Town's swept channels. Also at Cape Agulhas, where shipping rounds the southern tip of Africa. The Agulhas Bank is a shallow area that is perfect for us.'

'Almost all traffic between the Atlantic and Indian Oceans passes through there, sometimes scores of ships a day,' said Falk.

'We'll strike a blow for Rommel and the Afrika Korps, sir,' said Adler.

'The Agulhas Bank is a big triangle — 250 miles long at the top and extending 120 miles into the ocean,' Bauer continued. 'Beyond this zone, the seabed drops away steeply to 1,000 fathoms. And with the powerful Agulhas Current flowing from the east and strong westerly winds, the seas there are very dangerous. Most ships try to stay inshore.'

'So this is where we will trap them.' Falk banged the chart with his fist.

'What about Cape Town?' asked Adler stiffly. 'Surely that is where all the convoys gather?'

'You are right, Adler, we can possibly lay there too.' Falk wanted to placate his tetchy first officer and include him in the plan. 'However, I fear that, close inshore, Cape Town will be well protected. Aircraft, minesweepers, patrols, gun batteries.'

'But what if we lay in deep water at the outer limit of their searched channels?'

'Good idea. It will put strain on our mooring cables, but probably worth a try. And the mines will be much more difficult to sweep. It will give the South Africans a proper headache.'

Bauer pointed to the chart again. 'Sir, I recommend that our first field should be laid here — off Cape Columbine and along the approaches to Saldanha Bay. As you know, *SKL* has received intelligence that this area is being prepared as a convoy assembly point.'

'All right, agreed,' said Falk. 'Columbine to Saldanha is where we will begin.'

CHAPTER 17

After a week in Saldanha, *Gannet* was running low on water. Jack decided to top up their tanks from the spring at Oostewal Farm, just inside the mouth of Langebaan Lagoon. On the Saturday afternoon, when their work for the week was done, they sailed three miles southeast, rounded Schaapen Island and entered the luminous green shallows of the lagoon.

'Black harrier, three o'clock, low!' cried Jack.

'Shall I sound action stations, sir?' asked Van Zyl.

'Don't be ridiculous, Sub.'

'Where away, how does it bear?' asked the smiling Van Zyl.

'Never mind.'

'What exactly is a harrier, sir?'

'A raptor, Sub. A sleek black raptor with white flight feathers.'

'Not really my line. Not the feathered kind at least.'

'Plucked? Sunday roast?'

'Large-chested, blonde.'

'I see. And I can't tempt you?'

'I've never really seen the point in birdwatching, sir.'

'You don't know what you're missing.'

Jack went ashore with the watering party to chat to the farmer. He took Van Zyl along in case translation was needed.

'It's a fine old Cape Dutch house, sir,' said the sub as they were rowed ashore. 'There are a handful of farms around the lagoon that date back to the eighteenth century. Graceful buildings, all of them.'

'You know much about architecture?'

'Not really, sir. Just an admirer. Our ancestral farm is outside Stellenbosch, and I've always loved the old homesteads. Have you seen them, sir? Whitewashed, thatched, gabled.' Van Zyl's tone grew dreamy. 'The way they sit on the land, surrounded by vineyards and orchards…'

The rowing boat bit into the sand and the sailors jumped ashore. Jack and Van Zyl stepped off the prow without getting their shoes wet and went to find the farmer. The man was not at home, but a foreman answered their questions in Afrikaans and gave them permission to fill a few barrels from the spring.

'Please ask him if there's a quiet anchorage where we can let the crew have a run ashore and not be bothered by prying eyes?'

Van Zyl translated. 'Yes, sir, he says just across the lagoon in the lee of Postberg Mountain. Kraal Bay, it's called. Got to watch the tides, though. It gets very shallow. We might touch bottom on the low. He says his boss goes fishing there.'

Late afternoon, *Gannet* nosed around Postberg headland on the incoming tide. Jack stuck to the darker blues of the channel; the bosun was sent to the bows with a lead line. Cummins ran the rope through his fingers, testing the lump at its end. He swung the line back and forth above the water until, with a mighty heave, he sent it arcing ahead where the lead sank to the sandy bottom.

As *Gannet* passed the spot where the rope stood vertically, Cummins bobbed it up and down to make sure it was bottomed properly. Reading the material spliced into the line, his voice called out the sounding, 'By the mark, three!'

The water was pale green and inviting. All the sailors were on deck looking ahead as a lovely bay opened before them, edged by a crescent of white sand.

'By the mark, two!' cried Cummins.

Just twelve feet. It was getting shallow. They would need to drop anchor soon.

'Stop engine.'

Gannet slid through glassy water. Van Zyl had his hand in the air and was being watched by Seaman Cloete on the fo'c'sle.

'Let go,' said Jack. 'Slow astern.'

Van Zyl dropped his arm and the clink of Cloete's hammer knocked off the slip. There was a splash and the loud clatter of anchor chain running out. The dark hook was clearly visible on the sand as *Gannet* drifted astern and came to rest.

'All right, Smit, I think we need only leave here on Monday morning, so we'll have two nights at anchor. The men can let their hair down, go ashore, what have you.'

'Aye, sir, I'll pass the word.'

On Sunday, a game of beach cricket was arranged, port versus starboard watch, which became ever more competitive as the day wore on. It turned out that Ellis had been opening bat for his school in Rhodesia and that Potgieter was a decent pace man with a mean yorker. Although Fitzpatrick was an unreliable runner between the wickets, he proved to be a surprisingly adhesive batsman.

Meanwhile, some sailors caught up on mending clothes and doing their dhobi, others lay on deck reading out-of-date copies of *Huisgenoot* and *The Outspan*. A couple of ratings baited hooks and tried hand-line fishing, but with little success. The lagoon water was warm and everyone took regular dips as the day heated up, except for Brooke, who couldn't swim.

Jack asked for the mast and sail to be rigged on the ship's boat. He packed binoculars and a copy of *The Birds of South Africa* by Austin Roberts, and set off up the lagoon on his own.

The boat was clinker-built with a brown lugsail. As it had no centreboard, and thus couldn't beat effectively, he was lucky with a beam breeze that propelled him southeast along the lagoon shore. Rounding a promontory, he came upon an enchanting spectacle. As far as the eye could reach, thousands of flamingos stained the water pink. He eased the boat among them and they took flight in a rippling ballet of sinuous necks, beating wings and spindly legs.

Turning towards the headland, he grounded the boat on a beach and stepped ashore, lodging the anchor in dry sand. To the south, he could see a cluster of fishermen's cottages and surmised it must be Churchhaven, which he'd spotted on the chart. He climbed a bluff and found a smooth limestone rock for a perch. Porky had made sandwiches and a flask of tea, and Jack whiled away a few happy hours recording more avian life than he usually saw in Hampshire in a year. Along the shore, he spotted pelicans, spoonbills and any number of gulls, ducks, cormorants, plovers and sandpipers. In the vegetation he identified korhaan, marsh harrier, flufftails and sunbirds. At one point, a family of ostriches sauntered past, less than fifty yards from him. He marvelled at their muscular legs and ungainly grace.

When the sun slipped behind the dunes, he sailed back to the ship feeling refreshed and thrilled by the sightings.

'I saw my first ostrich, Van Zyl,' he said as he climbed aboard.

'And we beat starboard watch by nine runs, sir.'

'Jolly good. It seems everyone's had a splendid day.'

'And a special treat for our Sunday dinner, too, sir,' said an ingratiating Smit.

'Oh, what's that, Number One? Another of the cook's spotted dicks?'

'No, sir, penguin eggs. Retrieved from one of the islands in the bay. Porky went looking early this morning and hit the jackpot.'

'Jackass pot,' said Jack.

'Beg pardon, sir?'

'Oh, just the species of penguin, Jackass, so named because of their braying sound. But isn't it illegal to poach their eggs?' asked Jack.

'We don't poach them, sir, we boil them.'

'Not entirely unfunny, Smit.'

'Thank you, sir.'

'Tell Porky not to worry. I won't report him to the coppers.'

Later, the officers sat in the wardroom eating the fish-flavoured eggs accompanied by the cook's freshly baked rolls lathered with butter from Oostewal. 'Food of the gods!' exclaimed Jack.

It was a balmy night and the crew lay on deck taking in the stars. Van Reenen played his harmonica and sailors sang old favourites such as 'Suikerbossie' and 'Sarie Marais'. Jack understood none of the Afrikaans, but the lilting voices that drifted down to his cabin engendered a sense of belonging and a kind of peace he had not known in a very long time. Perhaps he had finally been accepted by his men.

They were singing 'Wish me luck' as they headed for their bunks. Jack looked out of the scuttle. The moon was not yet up and the lagoon was a glistening mirror. Low cloud crept in from the Atlantic. Muffled voices reached him from the mess:

'Wish me luck as you wave me goodbye
Cheerio, here I go, on my way
Wish me luck as you wave me goodbye
Not a tear, but a cheer, make it gay.'

Jack felt a strange yearning, as well as contentment, both somehow interwoven and feeding off each other. There was England and his mother, Dunkirk, the loss of *Havoc*, the fight that had to be won, and this new life. Behind it lay a sense of deep foreboding that the war was about to reach out a hand and touch them all.

CHAPTER 18

It was 22:00 on that calm Sunday evening. Low cloud rendered the night black as coal. *Sturmvogel* approached the South African coast at full speed, her crew at battle stations. On the bridge, Falk watched the steady pulse of Cape Columbine Lighthouse, sweeping its long blades of light across the sea. Although it was ten miles away, he flinched involuntarily as each beam flashed over *Sturmvogel*. All about the ship, pairs of apprehensive eyes scanned the horizon, trying to make out the enemy shore.

Adler stood beside a large open hatchway at the stern, staring at the phosphorescent wake. A row of mines sat on a narrow-gauge railway that led to the opening. Mechanics had spent the day inserting the soluble plugs and screwing on the lead horns. Now they were setting the hydrostats to the predetermined depth. The black seeds were almost ready to be planted in the furrow ploughed by the raider.

Adler looked at the obscenity chalked on the first mine. 'Lingen, you idiot, there is only one *t* in Smuts,' he chided.

Despite the misspelt graffiti, the mine was a thing of beauty. He pictured its contents: desiccator, detonator, primer and 500-pound charge of TNT. The five-inch horns made it look like a lethal sea monster. Inside each horn was a glass tube containing a chemical mixture. If anything bumped the mine, the tube would break, releasing liquid to energise a battery and fire the detonator, igniting the TNT. Adler patted the sphere. Bitter fruit indeed, but oh so ingenious — a marvel of Nazi engineering.

The telephone's loud trilling startled him. It was time. 'We will release the first mine in two minutes,' said Adler. 'At my command.' PO Erasmus and his team took up their positions. Adler held up his arm.

'Let go.' Falk's voice was crisp in his ear.

'Commence laying!' Adler called out, dropping his arm and pressing the knob on his stopwatch. Two mechanics shoved the first mine along the rails; it slid with an iron screech down the chute and tipped off the stern. Adler saw the splash and expanding white rings in *Sturmvogel's* wake before the mine bobbed to the surface. He imagined the sinker's descent to the ocean floor, the mooring wire unreeling as it went. Then a hydrostat gripped the mooring wire and dragged the mine below the surface to a depth that allowed for the rise and fall of the tide. And there it would remain, a lethal dog at the end of a long leash waiting to tear the guts out of a passer-by.

The mechanics rolled another mine into position. Adler tracked the time on his watch, and, at the allotted interval, shouted: 'Release!' Another mine trundled down the chute. PO Erasmus called out the lays: 'Mine three, away … mine four, away … mine five, away!'

Sturmvogel was transforming this patch of ocean into a death trap. Staring aft from the bridge, Falk derived a quiet satisfaction from his work, anticipating the inevitable reports of sinkings. Even if his ship were intercepted by the British, once this minefield was laid at least one vital part of their mission would have been fulfilled.

The raider continued to follow the zigzag course carefully plotted by Bauer. 'Mine twenty-three away … mine twenty-four away … mine twenty-five away…'

Suddenly, a cry of alarm from the crow's nest lookout: 'Fishing boat, port bow, 2,000 yards!'

'Stop laying!' shouted Falk, striding to the bridge wing. The little vessel was almost dead ahead and showing no lights. She looked like a trawler and was fitted with masts and aerials, so she could radio a warning. Her crew might have seen what *Sturmvogel* was up to. Even if they hadn't, Falk could not take a chance. Why had the lookout spotted her so late? Heads would have to roll.

'Starboard forty. Prepare to open fire,' said Falk. 'All guns.' There would be no time to pick up survivors. He gritted his teeth. There must not be any survivors.

Shutters banged open. Blurring hands spun the training wheels as the 5.9s came to bear and settled on the target.

'Open fire!'

The big guns spat gouts of flame in a broadside that lit up the night. Shells streaked low across the water with the sound of tearing cloth. Tracer from twenty mm cannons arced through the air, pouring fire onto the craft. The range was negligible — even rounds from the stuttering machine gun on the bridge wing were reaching the target.

The fishing boat frantically signalled: 'QQQQ. MV *Limpopo* to all ships. Under attack by enemy warship. We are sinking. Position —' Shells ripped into her wooden side, eating the vessel alive. Chunks of her hull flew in every direction.

The breeches of the 5.9s snapped open, more pills were fed into their mouths. The guns coughed again, jerking backwards in violent recoil. The fishing boat disintegrated. Within a minute there was nothing left of *Limpopo*, save for a few brown-skinned bodies, a piece of the wheelhouse and two life rings.

'Course southwest, Cox'n, get us away from here,' said the captain, his face set in a grim frown. Anger and frustration gnawed at him: after all they had endured to get here, they had tripped on the final approach.

Sturmvogel steamed away from the coast, heading southwest. Falk could just make out the flash of Green Point Lighthouse, marking the entrance to Table Bay. Cape Town's lights glowed tantalisingly on the horizon, a city not yet touched by war. He was determined to change that.

Two days later, Falk sat in his chair staring at the Cape rollers that lumbered out of the southwest like footloose mountains. After the sinking, spirits on board were low. He had failed in both his objectives. *Sturmvogel* had managed to lay only half the minefield and they'd been spotted, forcing the unnecessary destruction of a fishing boat close to the enemy shore. The alarm would no doubt have been raised by now and a hunt for the raider initiated. To Falk, it felt as though a mantle of fear, perhaps even guilt, hung over the ship. Maybe he should risk another mine-laying foray to lift the men and complete the task? More daring, closer to Cape Town? Purpose, again, after so much empty ocean.

The three senior officers gathered around the chart table again. 'Let us return, sir,' said Adler. 'Give it a few more days for the fuss to die down. We can lie far off the continent and return at night or under the cover of fog, which is so prevalent at this time of year.'

'I am not sure,' said Falk. 'It is risky. We could round the Cape and try our luck in the Indian Ocean.'

'But, sir, we must focus on the *Schwerpunkt*. The northern approach to Cape Town is where we can do the most damage.'

'Kapitän, if I may,' Bauer interjected. 'I think it's too dangerous. The St Francis Bay area will be almost as profitable, poorly defended, and it's far from a Cape that is on high alert.'

'Ever the circumspect Bauer,' said Falk with a sigh. 'All right, gentlemen, thank you, let me sleep on it.'

Later that night, Falk lay in his sea cabin, weighing the options. Adler was all fire; Bauer all caution. He was inclined to agree with Bauer, but he had as yet made no impact on the Cape, his principal objective. There hadn't been a single report of a sinking and minesweepers were probably already clearing his Columbine field. Falk felt unsettled, demoralised. Perhaps one bold run, close in, then a hasty retreat to the south, far from any sea route or air reconnaissance? Perhaps.

CHAPTER 19

The lighthouse keeper at Cape Columbine had been woken by a rumbling sound to seaward of his station. He got out of bed, put on his boots and stomped down the hallway to the telephone. Contacting Cape Town, seventy miles to the south, he told the Combined Operations Room that there might have been a series of explosions at sea. As he was a known drinker, his story was treated with circumspection. All the same, a mine was suspected.

Given that *Wayfarer* and *Star* were having their boilers cleaned, and *Belle* was helping to sweep the Simon's Town channel, it was decided to dispatch two minesweepers from Cape Town to assist *Gannet* with a provisional search for West Coast mines. In the meantime, seeing that *Gannet* was already in the vicinity, she was sent ahead to scout the waters off Columbine.

Rounding North Head the next morning, Jack set a north-westerly course. There was a light mist and *Gannet* cleaved through a viscous sea. The air was icy and they could hear the faraway moaning of Columbine's foghorn, which sounded like a dying sea creature.

'Wreckage, sir, port bow!' came a lookout's cry.

'Action stations!' Jack barked and the alarm clanged as men ran to their positions. The three officers trained their binoculars on the flotsam. They could see pieces of wood, a spar and half a lifeboat. Jack felt a tightening of his throat: the enemy was surely close.

Gannet slowed then stopped her engine, coasting towards the debris. Jack stared at the ocean's dirty stain. A Carley float packed with *Havoc*'s survivors, the stink of oil, floating bodies. The tidal flow and ebb of unconsciousness.

'Grappling party to pick up flotsam, sir?'

'What's that, Smit?' His voice was a hoarse whisper.

'Grappling party?'

'Yes, Number One, see to it.'

The mist cast an unnerving spell over the scene. The sea was dead calm and the men's voices echoed in the silence of the stopped engine. A life ring was hooked and pulled aboard: 'Limpopo' stencilled in black. A fishing boat, probably out of St Helena Bay. She must have struck a mine. There were obviously no survivors.

Gannet headed south to meet the pair of minesweepers coming up from Cape Town. *Sandvlei* and *Rietvlei* were both trawlers requisitioned from the Kerguelen Sealing and Whaling fleet, a subsidiary of Irvin & Johnson. The two vessels — battleship grey, thin-funnelled and bluff-bowed — appeared over the horizon and joined *Gannet* off Saldanha.

'Comfortable ships compared to ours,' said Smit, looking through his binoculars. 'All fancy mahogany in the wardroom, and headroom for a six-footer like you, sir, unlike *Gannet*. Built by Smith's Dock Company in Yorkshire.'

'Smaller than us, by the look of it,' said Van Zyl.

'Yes,' said Smit. 'Slower too, thirteen knots tops. Quite new and fitted with depth charges. But no asdic yet. Coming soon, they say.'

'You know your stuff, Smit.'

'I know a chap on *Rietvlei*, sir.'

The three ships joined up and began clearing a wide area off the Cape Columbine Peninsula.

Late in the day, *Gannet* put up the first mine on her starboard quarter. Jack called for the flotilla to stop. The mine wallowed in their wake, its demonic horns plain for the sailors on all three ships to see.

'Let the off-watch have a go with rifles,' said Jack.

The small-arms locker was opened and four Lee-Enfields distributed among the hands. The rest of the crew watched keenly from their action stations, despite being ordered to the windward side. Brooke lifted the heavy rifle and tried to aim at the dancing blob, 100 yards to leeward. Both he and the target were moving unevenly. *Crack!* The splash was short. There was a derisive cheer from the boat deck. *Crack, crack, crack*. The sailors fired, and fired again. Failing to take the ship's roll into account, their aim was way off, much to the amusement of the duty sailors.

'Message from *Sandvlei*, sir, "No teddy bear for you at the funfair shooting gallery."'

'All right, enough of this lark,' said Jack. 'Seaman Behardien, your Lewis if you please.'

The machine-gun stuttered into life and water columns sprouted around the mine. After a few seconds, one of the rounds found a horn. There was a thunderous explosion and a tower of water as metal splinters rained down on the sweepers.

Over the next few days, the flotilla swept the Paternoster and Jacobsbaai coast. Although sweeping could be punctuated by moments of terror, it was for the most part monotonous, back-breaking work with little reward. The constant manhandling of serrated wire, the parting and splicing of sweeps, resulted in ripped and torn hands. Endless, accurate station-keeping, dreary food, sunburn — and always the gnawing tension.

A misty afternoon found them working near the end of Saldanha's prospective swept channel. They were completing a northern leg, when the dark shape of a merchant ship loomed out of the murk to the west.

'Flash the interrogative, Bunts.'

The Aldis lamp clattered its question, but there was no answer and the freighter turned away.

'Flash her again: "Make your signal letters, immediate."'

The merchantman slowly hoisted the flags PKQM. Smit looked them up in the register and confirmed her identity as the *Dunedin Queen.*

'I'm not satisfied, Number One,' said Jack. 'There's something odd about her. Bunts, signal the first and second letters of the secret call sign.'

There was no reply. The freighter had turned back to her original course. *How very strange*, Jack thought. Just then, her port side lit up in a series of bright flashes. There was a moment of agonising confusion before Jack realised what he was seeing.

'Good God!' he gasped. 'Sound action stations!' Five columns of water rose like whale spouts ahead of the flotilla.

Alarm bells echoed through the sweepers. Smit dived at the telegraph. Throwing the lever forward, he shouted down the voice pipe: 'Full ahead, Chief!'

Van Zyl grabbed the speaking trumpet and yelled to the afterdeck: 'Cut the sweeps!'

Men scrambled to their stations. Gun crews poured onto the forecastles, pulling on tin hats and anti-flash gear. Jack could taste acid in his throat.

A tower of water grew out of the sea beside *Gannet.*

'Good grief, sir, they've found the range with the second salvo,' said Smit. He looked at his captain and saw the pale face, the horror in his eyes. Jack was frozen. Smit brushed him aside and shouted down the wheelhouse pipe: 'Hard to starboard!'

'Hard astarboard, sir.' February's voice was even and cool, like a steadying hand.

'Midships. No, hard to port!' *Gannet* zigzagged towards the enemy.

Jack closed his eyes and lost his balance as his legs appeared to give way.

'Come on, sir,' Smit said softly, taking him by the arm and pulling him upright. 'Got knocked off your feet there by the sharp turn,' he said loudly for the benefit of the lookouts.

Jack gripped the bridge windbreak with both hands, as though releasing it would scupper him. He stared fixedly ahead, eyes glazed. His face trembled.

'Sir, sir?' said Smit. 'Are you all right?'

'I ... I ... I...'

'Let me help you to your chair.'

Smit prised his captain's fingers from the windbreak and half carried him to the chair. Another salvo tore into the water among the ships.

'Can you... Can you?'

'Captain?'

'If you'd be so good as to... To hoist the battle ensign.'

'Certainly, sir. Hoist battle ensign!' Smit yelled. Bunts was already running aft with the bag.

Brooke turned to see the big white-and-red flag break open and fill at the gaff, snapping in the breeze. 'Blimey, that's the first time I've seen one of those,' he said to Lofty. 'Looks too big for the ship. Sort of gives you a lump in the throat.'

By now, the sweepers had brought their twelve-pounders to bear.

'Range 5,000 yards, open fire.'

Boom! Jack felt the hot flash on his face as *Gannet* shuddered to the recoil. There were two more bangs in quick succession from the other sweepers. Their shells were far wide of the enemy. Jack stood up unsteadily, pressed the engine-room button and put his ear to the voice pipe.

'Sir?' McEwan shouted against the background thunder.

'Everything you've got, Chief. I want all seventeen you promised, and a bit extra.'

'Oi, I promised nothing, Captain. But I'll have a word with ma engine and see what she's willing to give. Short burst, mind!'

Deep in the hull, CPO McEwan watched his dials like a doctor with a feverish patient as steam whooshed into the cylinders. His greasy fingers eased a shining wheel and the revolutions rose. He smiled at his handiwork. 'Like the clappers,' he said to no one in particular.

Gannet's stern sat well down, giving the propeller full purchase. White water peeled from her bows. Her two companions were doing the same over to port, line abreast and slightly ahead of her, but *Gannet* was catching up. They made a proud sight against the powerful foe.

'Sparks!' Jack shouted down the voice pipe, gaining more composure with each minute of the battle. 'Make to Combined Operations Room: "Am engaging enemy raider. Request immediate, repeat, immediate, assistance. Course two-six-oh, speed seventeen." Bunts will bring you our position as soon as the sub has plotted it. Plain language, quick as you like!'

The guns spoke again. In the wireless cabin, Sparks put the mic to his lips: 'Hello Cape Town, hello Cape Town, this is *Gannet* calling Cape Town. Do you read me, over?'

The RT offered only crackle. Sparks repeated the message, his voice strained with urgency.

'Hello *Gannet*, hello *Gannet*, this is Cape Town. I receive you strength three. Over.'

'Hello Cape Town. We are under attack.' Sparks gave their position, course and speed. A shell cleaved overhead like a freight train and exploded in the water alongside. 'We are engaging enemy raider. Over.'

'Thank you, *Gannet*. We will alert Wingfield and Simon's Town. Over.'

Sparks cut the power to the transmitter, opened the voice pipe cover and said: 'Bridge, message to Combined Ops acknowledged.'

'Bunts, please hoist the South African flag on your signal halyard,' said Jack.

'Aye, sir.'

The twelve-pounders were finding their rhythm and range. Splashes straddled the raider. Brass shell cases glinted in the sun as they rolled back and forth across the prancing bandstands. The three sweepers were small, nimble targets, dancing and weaving through the web of enemy fire.

Gannet's twelve-pounder barked again. This time there was a white flash on the enemy ship. 'Yes, we got him!' yelled Jack, banging the rail with his fist. Flames flared, then started to billow smoke. Jack tracked the freighter as it cut across the horizon like a dark island lit every now and then by stabs of orange and gouts of black smoke. His throat was like sandpaper, his head ached. But the rage inside him had found a target at last. And so had the hate.

The raider made a diagonal approach, bringing her full broadside to bear, and was concentrating her fire on *Sandvlei*. Shells fell around the little ship as she ducked and dodged, aiming for the splashes to throw off the German gunners. The 5.9 salvos came at fifteen-second intervals, accurate after so much practice in recent weeks.

The next salvo straddled *Sandvlei*, peppering her with shrapnel. She slowed, falling out of the chase. On her bridge, Captain Morris felt the deck lift and twist beneath him. She'd been hit amidships. A monstrous roaring filled his head. Then silence. He sat up and wiped his face. It was wet with blood. Slowly his hearing returned, the sounds reaching him through a tunnel. The screaming sounded like a wounded pig; the signalman had been ripped open, slashed in half. How could he still be alive? An explosion eliminated the responsibility of writing the dreaded letter.

The next shell struck *Sandvlei* right aft, sending the lookout tumbling through the air. There was a hard thud and he was underwater. Green light and bubbles. His lifebelt brought him to the surface like a cork. But his eyes dimmed as his body bled out through his wounds.

A shell exploded in the bows, killing everyone manning the twelve-pounder. By now, *Sandvlei*'s decks looked like a charnel house. The bosun tended to a wounded sailor on the boat deck whose foot had been severed; the other was hanging on by a few strips of livid flesh. The PO neatly amputated the foot with his seaman's knife and tossed it over the side. Then he applied tourniquets and lifted the lad into a Carley float that was flush with the sinking deck.

Another sailor's stomach had been sliced open. His oppo was crouched over him, trying to hold the intestines in place. With the bosun's help, the mortally wounded lad was also lifted into the Carley. What was left of the crew jumped into the icy water and swam to the half-submerged lifeboat. They clambered in and started bailing with their caps.

The other two minesweepers continued to bear down on the enemy. *Gannet* was straddled; splinters showered her boat deck. Seaman van Reenen slumped in his pom-pom seat.

'Lofty, look, Hans has been hit!' screamed Brooke. The back of the sailor's shirt was peppered with small holes. The gunner was white as a sail and barely conscious. Lofty and Brooke lifted him out of the seat and carried him to the PO's mess. They laid the groaning seaman on a bunk and rolled him onto his stomach. Porky was there in a flash with the first-aid box. Out came the scissors to cut away the shirt.

'All right, lads, back to your station, I'll take it from here,' said Porky.

'Why aren't we hitting the bastard?' Jack's voice was choking. *Gannet*'s twelve-pounder still fired, but more raggedly now. He heard the curses of the loaders, layers and trainers as they toiled at the gun. The clunk of the breechblock.

'Ready!' came a hoarse bark.

'Fire!' The missile streaked across the water.

'Up 100. Shoot!' Again the gun belched and the ship shuddered. Jack had lost all sense of time and place. His whole being was narrowed to a still, angry point on the horizon.

Far below him, the stokers listened to the guns, praying that no shell penetrated their steel box. Brooke and the pom-pom crew had their gun trained as far forward as it would go, but frustratingly couldn't bring it to bear, even if they'd had the range.

Jack looked across at *Rietvlei*. The enemy gunners were concentrating their fire on the Cape Town sweeper, her decks raked with shrapnel from near misses. She was a terrible mess, holes all over and rigging shot away. Her captain raised a weary hand. Jack could make out two bodies on the forecastle, their positions taken by other sailors. Blood leaked from the scuppers.

On *Rietvlei*, Captain Walsh looked down at his fo'c'sle. There was a headless corpse wearing an officer's jacket. A single stripe adorned the sleeve. His trusted number one, his friend.

There was a blinding flash and Walsh crumpled to the deck.

'Direct hit on *Rietvlei*, sir!' cried Potgieter. Jack turned to see the smoking hole behind the bridge. Not a single man was left standing. Her mizzenmast toppled over, bringing with it a tangle of aerial wire. He saw the flash of an axe as a sailor tried to cut it free.

Another salvo streaked in. *Rietvlei*'s bow wave died away and the vessel slewed to a stop. She was settling fast. Still her twelve-pounder coughed from the canting forecastle. Jack saw a figure on the bridge and heard a distant voice shouting through the speaking trumpet. *Abandon*, thought Jack. *They must abandon.*

The raider fired again. Another direct hit. The smoke cleared to reveal men clinging to *Rietvlei*'s tilting deck. The sweeper's depth charges rolled over the side and sank beneath her.

Oh God, please let someone have neutralised them. Jack counted off the terrible seconds in his head.

There was an incandescent yellow flash just below the surface. An eruption of grey water engulfed the stricken ship, rising higher and higher, followed by the blast which reverberated in deafening waves. Then another blast, turning the sea into a feverish storm of atomised water.

When the smoke began to clear, Jack saw that there was nothing left of *Rietvlei*, save for some floating wreckage and a handful of bodies. He shivered as he pictured *Havoc*'s stern pointing at the sky.

Gannet raced on. The raider switched target. One shell passed clean through the sweeper's funnel without exploding. Another struck the water dead ahead. She climbed a welt of white water. Jack was choking with fury; he imagined dark fingers clawing at his throat.

'Sir, we must turn away!' screamed Smit, his eyes wide with panic. 'The raider completely outguns us now! We have no chance!'

'Shut up, Number One, we will fight on!' shouted Jack, wild-eyed. 'Steer straight at her, Cox'n!' he yelled down the voice pipe.

'Straight at her it is, sir,' came the even, disembodied voice.

Shells bracketed *Gannet*, splinters clattering against both her flanks. The next salvo would surely sink them. Jack could taste cordite and bile. He knew he had to turn away.

'Fuck you!' he screamed at the enemy ship. 'Fuck all of you!' Then a look of defeat passed over his face. His shoulders slumped. 'Hard to port, one-eighty degrees. Make smoke.' His voice cracked with emotion. The minesweeper veered away, thick chemical smoke pouring from canisters at her stern, settling on the water and forming a protective blanket.

As *Gannet* retreated behind her acrid screen, the German ship also bore away, sliding back into the mist and laying down a curtain of her own with smoke generators.

With the raider vanished, the minesweeper returned to look for survivors. She was at dead slow, stealing through smoking wreckage. Seagulls and Cape gannets circled the debris, crying plaintively and diving to scavenge on bits of floating meat. The engine stopped and, in the silence, they drifted closer to a group of men. Lines snaked out to drag a raft alongside. Survivors were lifted aboard, the wounded carried to the petty officer's mess. Porky opened his stash of morphia syrettes and worked his way through the badly injured, most of whom were in a state of shock.

At least *Gannet* had scored one or two hits, thought Jack ruefully as he scanned the mist line. The raider would think twice before approaching the South African coast again. He heard the throb of aircraft sent from Wingfield, but in the mist and gathering dusk they'd have a hard time finding her.

'Let's go home, Number One,' said Jack.

CHAPTER 20

HMSAS *Southern Gannet* headed down the coast, nursing her wounds. Jack knew his ship would need time in dry dock for a thorough patch-up. The sweeper was leaking from seals and had nasty shrapnel holes all over her superstructure. A spell in dock would also allow for a much-needed boiler clean.

A crash boat came out from Cape Town to take off the wounded in the dark. *Gannet* pressed on past Sea Point, the dark cliffs of Karbonkelberg and long white sweep of Noordhoek Beach. They rounded Cape Point in the early hours and entered the calm waters of False Bay. Jack looked at the craggy, encircling arms and, just for a moment, had an inkling of what it might be like to belong here. He pictured his father and sister asleep somewhere on the bay's western arm. And a Nazi raider, somewhere to the southwest, bent on taking this away from him. Another image entered his mind: the estate in Hampshire and their old home sitting squarely on the hill, its sandstone façade catching the late afternoon light. The grandfather clock in the entrance hall ticking loudly, portraits of naval Pembrokes lining the walls, the furniture gathering dust. Empty.

'Signal from Simon's Town, sir: "*Gannet* will enter harbour and prepare to blow down for boiler clean. Repair and defect list to be ready for approval by 13:00 today, 4.5.1941. SNO."'

'Number One, take care of the list, will you?'

'Yes, sir.'

The minesweeper drew curious looks as she sailed through the bullnose, peppered as she was with holes and with her plating fire-blackened. She sidled up to the quay where her three sisters were berthed. Mooring-line eyes slid over bollards and fenders brushed the stonework with a wheezing exhalation. *Home.*

Jack immediately reported to the SNO. 'The raider's shooting was accurate throughout,' he said, seated opposite the commodore. 'Her salvoes were fired together and hardly ever out of line. She's obviously fitted with full direction finding.'

'Always damn good gunnery on these commerce raiders,' said O'Reilly, leaning back in his chair. 'It was the same in the last war.'

'She used high-fragmentation shells for the most part: both overs and shorts covered our ships with splinters. They knew exactly what they were about. I reckon she was doing about nineteen knots. An ugly ship, black hull, about 8,000 tons, straight stem, cruiser stern. Two tall masts, one funnel, two shallow well decks.'

'She's probably changed her look completely by now. Did you surprise her?'

'Yes, I think we must have. There was thick fog all morning. I suspect they'd come in to lay mines. Then the fog began to lift.'

'Damned shame about the two lost sweepers, but now we know what we're looking for. I've got ships and aircraft searching in every direction. I'm sure we'll catch her in the next couple of days. You reported that you'd landed one or two punches?'

'Yes, at least one hit aft. She was on fire when we turned away.'

'Good, it'll give our reconnaissance aircraft something to work on.'

Returning to his ship, Jack found dockworkers infesting *Gannet*'s superstructure. Over the next several days, they seemed determined to do more damaging than fixing. Cummins was apoplectic at their dirty boots, the debris left by the welding team and the labourers' casual treatment of his precious equipment. Light fingers were also a problem and, though Jack posted sentries, loose items found their way ashore.

'They're sitting on their arses half the time!' Smit fumed to his captain. 'I even caught one of the rascals fishing over the stern during his "lunch hour".'

'I know, Number One. Carrot and stick, though. We can't be at war with the shop stewards. They'll loosen our seacocks.'

'They have no respect, sir. They're not like us. They're —'

'Listen, bribery and corruption is the way to handle them: a few well-placed cartons of cigarettes, a whisky bottle or two. Let's try to oil the wheels.'

Gannet's crew, on the other hand, appreciated the change of pace, enjoying the normal hours of port routine. Overnight liberty was granted to alternate watches. There was unlimited water from shoreside hydrants, light work during the day and a full night's sleep. It was as good as a holiday.

As the patching up neared completion, Cummins set his hands to making *Gannet* pretty again. The crew spliced wires, scrubbed the decks with sand, wire-brushed all fittings showing rust and touched them up with red lead. The skipper got on with his paperwork and caught up on the latest Admiralty Fleet Orders; Van Zyl went ashore to acquire more charts and a new sextant; Smit saw to stores, and the sparker gave his wet-cell batteries, chargers, transmitters and receivers a thorough service.

Gannet was moved onto the slipway in West Yard for a bottom scrape and the application of anti-fouling to her hull. The men were granted leave while she was on the hard. Some, like the coxswain, went home to their wives. Adam February's leave was entirely devoted to his small family, walking his daughter to and from school and taking the boy fishing on the harbour wall.

Others, among them David Levy, went home to their parents. The Levy villa was a large Edwardian affair in Sea Point. Having phoned ahead to warn them, he took the train to Cape Town station, then a bus to his home. The sailor anticipated a warm welcome and a Shabbat meal with his siblings and cousins. There was so much he wanted to tell them about his scrape with the Nazi ship.

Van Zyl sat in a first-class compartment, hardly noticing the bay as it spooled by. He was returning to a fractured Stellenbosch home, although all he really wanted to do was see Sylvia and walk hand in hand with her through the Gardens again. His eldest brother had fallen in with the Nazi-sympathising Ossewabrandwag, while his middle brother had joined the army to serve up north. His father was a conservative Hertzog man, his mother from a liberal Afrikaner family. Van Zyl dreaded the shouting, the veiled threats and slamming of doors that characterised his visits to the old house on Neethling Street. He secretly hoped his eldest brother was away on one of his torch-bearing Stormjaer 'camps'.

For Cummins, home life had become a trial. His relationship with his wife had deteriorated over the past year. She was a drinker and prone to misplaced generosity where her affections were concerned. Would he confront her this time?

Ellis downed a couple of beers at the Soldiers' and Sailors' Rest Home in Simon's Town, then took a late train to Rondebosch. He dropped his bag at the flat and walked straight to the Pig and Whistle, his local pub. He was well known there, mostly on account of being thrown out for rowdy behaviour. But his presence was tolerated as he was a big spender. On this particular evening, he met a young woman, Belinda, he'd seen around the 'bosch and they got chatting at the bar counter. He separated her from a flotilla of young women and tried to work his limited magic. It turned out she was some sort of secretary, too mousy and thin for Ellis's taste, but he reckoned beggars couldn't be choosers on short leave.

Brooke had waited for most of the men to disembark before heading into town alone. His bell-bottomed trousers flapped wildly as the southeaster propelled him down St Georges Street like a human square-rigger. Just before reaching the station, he turned left up Paradise Road, crossing a hopscotch court chalked on the cobbles.

The house was on the left. White clapboard, green corrugated-iron roof and small sash windows. Brooke stepped onto the veranda, took a deep breath and knocked at the door. A pretty girl opened. She had green eyes, dark-olive skin and wore a see-through white dress. He took off his cap.

'Can I help you, sailor?' she asked with a smile.

'I'd like… I was wondering… Wondering whether —'

'Stop wondering, Dumbo, and step inside.'

She led him down a corridor and into a bedroom. The curtains were drawn, casting a rosy light.

'Business first, please,' she said sweetly.

He fumbled in his pocket for the money.

'You're not going to do an inspection or anything?' he asked.

'An inspection of what?'

'Um… Can we just sit and talk for a bit?'

'Of course, sailor, you're the one paying and we're not busy yet.'

They sat on the edge of the bed and talked like polite strangers. He told her about his home on the East Rand and she talked about her upbringing on a rural mission station before her father died. For a while, they were just two teenagers, the one privileged and white, the other poor and brown.

She took his hand and placed it on her thigh. 'You're running out of time, Paul.'

He reached across and kissed her lightly on the cheek. She turned her head and their lips met. His hand ran slowly up her flank and came to a tentative rest on her breast.

'That's better, sailor boy. Now, let's get you out of that fancy uniform.'

The short period of leave was eventful for many Gannets — but not for her captain. On the first night, Jack had skipped supper with Miss Retief, polished off the better part of a bottle of gin under the fig tree at Belleview and ended up face down on his bed. Trying and failing to get rid of the images of a raider emerging from the mist with him in its sights, the vision of oil-stained men in the water and him sailing on, unable to help. If only he'd realised it was a raider sooner, if only he'd turned away sooner. How many lives might he have saved?

But by Monday morning, he was back on board and at his paperwork, along with supervising the last of the repairs. He could not afford to take any more time off. There was too much to do before putting to sea once more. The raider would lay again, somewhere along the coast, and they needed to be ready.

All the same, Jack desperately wanted to see Clara. He asked to use the telephone at Belleview, Miss Retief eavesdropping from her easel in the next room. Trying to quiet a thumping heart, he called Clara's home in Newlands. Her mother answered and, after a brief but brutal interrogation, put Clara on the line. There were a few clumsy pleasantries, then he blurted: 'Why don't you come down to Simon's Town for a day? I'll organise a temporary permit for you. Take the train. I'll pick you up at the station.'

To his relief, Clara said, 'All right, Jack, I'd like that.'

On Saturday morning, he was on the platform as Clara stepped off the train, wearing a yellow floral dress and white shoes. He kissed her on the cheek and her smile lit up the western shores of False Bay.

'I've organised a picnic,' he said. 'Actually Miss Retief, my landlady, helped me. I thought we might go over to Scarborough. I hear it's a pretty beach.'

'A bit wild and windswept down there. Rather dramatic.'

'But it's such a perfect day, I thought it would be nice to get out into nature.'

Jack had signed out an Austin Ten on the officers' rota system. They drove up Red Hill Road, passed the military boom, and headed over the mountain to Scarborough. The terrain was tufty and barren, reminding him of Scotland, where he'd spent an energetic week with the Oxford University Rambling and Hillwalking Club. The road wound downhill through stone pines and along a valley towards the coast. When they came to a rock in the shape of a camel, they turned onto a gravel track that led to a deserted beach.

Jack parked on a patch of grass and carried the basket and blanket down onto the sand. 'Not a house or a person in sight,' he said.

'It's hard to imagine there's a war going on out there somewhere…' She saw his face cloud over. 'I'm sorry, Jack. Let's forget all that, shall we?'

He opened the basket and took out a tin of cheese and tomato sandwiches, two apples and a bottle of Miss Retief's homemade lemonade. He also brought out his Roberts and binoculars.

'Are you a proper birdwatcher?'

'No, I'm pretty hopeless, but awfully keen. I've always loved animals and nature, especially birds.'

'Not much around here, I would think, other than seagulls.'

'That's where you're wrong. Look over there, in that bush.' He handed her the binoculars and pointed. One hand touched her bare shoulder as he directed her gaze. Clara's skin was satin. 'On the low, left-hand branch.'

'Oh! It's beautiful. What is it?'

'A lesser double-collared sunbird.' He breathed in the scent of her hair.

'All got up in her red and green outfit.' She laid the binoculars on the blanket.

'His. It's a boy.' His fingers brushed the back of her hand.

Clara looked at him and widened her eyes. 'Sandwich?' she said.

He drew his hand away, feeling capsized by her loveliness and confused by her enigmatic expression.

After lunch, they walked barefoot along the beach to the promontory. Emerald waves hollowed and crumpled onto the sand. Jack rolled up his trousers, Clara gathered her skirt, and they splashed through a stream that leaked tea-coloured water into the sea.

'Oh, look at those two birds with the bright pink legs!' she said.

'Black oystercatchers. A mating pair.' He smiled, then, as they walked on, his expression turned serious. His eyes were far away.

'Penny for them?'

'Oh, nothing. The ship, stores, repairs.'

'Jack?'

'What?' he said defensively. They had come to a stop.

'Really. Your thoughts.'

There was a long pause.

'War stuff.'

'Go on.'

'The raider we encountered. I don't think it's gone. Not completely, anyway. I'm sure it will be back to lay more mines, perhaps just ahead of a convoy. Do you have any idea how many Allied ships are rounding the Cape at the moment?'

'Well, yes. My ma works for the SAWAS and keeps trying not to tell me.'

'SAWAS?'

'South African Women's Auxiliary Services.'

'She must be kept busy. Every week more and more ships.'

'So you keep on sweeping.'

'Yes, we sweep and we sweep and we sweep. But I know the Nazi ship is out there, waiting to have another crack. Maybe she's poised to strike at this very moment.' Jack's narrowed eyes scanned the horizon.

They walked in silence to the end of the headland where surf thundered on the rocks and the scent of kelp filled the air. Then Clara turned to Jack and said, 'You're a complicated creature, Lieutenant Pembroke, you know that?'

'No, I'm not.'

'It always looks as though you're carrying too much weight on your shoulders.'

'Last year was hard for me. Bloody awful, actually. Losing my mother…' He bit his lip and looked away. She put a gentle hand on the back of his neck. 'And my ship. I think Dunkirk broke me. The feeling of helplessness. All those men…' In spite of himself, he buried his face in his hands.

'Jack, you're strong, you're brave. Your leg has healed.'

'I'm not brave at all. The leg is better, but the head…'

'Your head looks just fine to me.' She ran her thumb gently along the scar on his temple.

'You don't want to see inside.' His body was shaking. She put her arms around him and held tight, resting her head on his shoulder.

After a long while she glanced up. 'Look, a boat!' She pointed to a grey speck on the horizon.

'A liberty ship, I think.' He wiped his eyes and straightened up. 'Coming in along the southern swept channel.'

'Now, now, Jack, loose lips!' She tried to lighten the mood. 'You know the saying:

'*Girls alluring*

spy for Göring.

Tattle tittlers

help all Hitlers.

Talking loosely

aids the Duce.

You stop talking!

Put a cork in!'

'Good grief, where on earth did you learn that?'

'It's on the wireless all the time. And my ma preaches silence, despite an inability to keep her own mouth shut.'

'Your mother sounds like a force of nature.'

'That she most certainly is. She keeps insisting that I help out with the SAWAS. Do my bit. The fact that I have university work doesn't deter her. I have to wash dishes, make beds at the Soldiers' Club, help take visiting troops sightseeing.'

'I hope they behave.'

'Most of them do. The occasional stray hand. Saturday mornings I assist with street collections: for the Red Cross, for Russia, for "brave little Malta". This morning I got a "special concession" to come and see you. There are no idle hands anywhere within shouting distance of my ma.'

'She sounds like my father.'

'Is he a bit of a martinet?'

'He has very particular ideas about what he wants from his children and how they fit into the great family tradition. I've been a bit of a disappointment to him, unlike my brother.'

'How so?'

'Harry went straight into the navy and has been a brilliant success. I didn't want anything to do with the Andrew. That's why I went up to Oxford, why I tried my hand at journalism.'

'And then the war came to mess everything up.'

'Yes, just about everything.'

Though it wasn't warm enough to swim, they spent the rest of the afternoon on the beach, mostly lying on the blanket enjoying the autumn sun. They were close enough for Jack to touch her, take her in his arms, but something held him back. He'd already let his guard down with her. Perhaps he was afraid of what intimacy might unlock.

They waited for the sun to set before packing up and heading back. The Austin's headlights had narrow blackout slits and emitted a feeble beam. Rounding a bend, they surprised a porcupine, which scuttled from their path. Jack pulled off at the top of Red Hill and they climbed out to look down on False Bay. Searchlights probed the sky above Simon's Town, their eerie fingers stabbing the night.

Suddenly, tracer began to streak into the air from Lower North battery like rows of agitated fireflies. The banging and popping of the guns echoed off the mountain.

'What's going on?' Clara asked, as flak exploded in showers of light above the sea.

'Air-raid drill and live-fire practice.'

'Gosh, it looks like Guy Fawkes.'

'Feels like London.'

She glanced at his face and saw the tautness, the narrowed eyes, the tensing of his shoulders. She laid the back of her hand against his cheek. 'It'll be all right,' she said.

'Will it?' he asked. His expression looked lost. She took both his hands in hers and their fingers entwined. They stared into each other's eyes as the stutter of flak intensified.

'My train,' she said eventually.

Like his captain, Smit had not taken leave and remained on board, not trusting himself ashore and fussing, instead, over the repairs. The shrapnel holes in the hull had been mended with new plates and covered with a fresh lick of paint. Below deck, the overhaul had been more makeshift. Cummins was indignant at the 'slapdash work', but at least they were ready for sea once more.

It was a chill autumn evening and Smit sat in a wardroom armchair beside a stove glowing with orange coals. *Gannet* chafed at the quay as a northwester ruffled the water of the basin, rain pecked at the deck and halyards clinked against masts. He heard the first batch of sailors coming aboard from their leave; the rest would return in the morning. From this vantage, he thought, they didn't seem like such a bad lot after all. Perhaps his captain had been right about easing up on discipline. He looked forward to getting back to sea.

The crew boarded in dribs and drabs and went below. They undressed, taking off their best uniforms and stowing them in lockers or under mattresses. The mess was loud with laughter and chatter — tales of jaunts, conquests, family reunions, pliable women and legendary bouts of drinking.

February appeared in the wardroom doorway wearing a duffel coat. 'Ready for rounds, sir.'

'Aye, Cox'n,' said Smit.

'The duty part of the watch have cleared up the mess decks. Still a bit of a shambles, though.'

'We won't be too hard on them then, will we, Cox'n?' said Smit, putting on his cap.

February raised his eyebrows, not knowing quite what to make of the number one's sudden flirtation with benevolence.

CHAPTER 21

After the fight off Saldanha, *Sturmvogel* had steamed due west into the fog, nursing a flaming boat deck and a destroyed floatplane. Black hoses snaked across the superstructure as the crew fought to douse the fires. The mines were stored in a hold beneath the hangar and if the flames spread, it could prove fatal to the ship. Those firemen who ventured close to the blaze were hosed by the others. Scalded faces and burnt hair were a small price to pay for getting the flames under control.

After three hours, the worst of the fire was out.

The charred bird that had once been their floatplane looked like the remains of a giant's barbecue. Its corpse was tipped over the side. Falk felt the loss keenly. Although the Heinkel had been an unreliable aircraft, it did extend his reach over a vast area. If he were being hunted by enemy ships, eyes in the sky could buy him valuable hours. But there was nothing to be done about it and the damage might have been far worse. At least his ship could fight on. In fact, the blooding had renewed his determination to hit back hard. The enemy captain had been brave, perhaps rashly so, coming straight at him after losing his two companions. Falk had underestimated the South African patrols and sweepers. He would not make the same mistake twice and he wouldn't approach the coast in daylight again, even if the fog was temptingly thick. A reckless part of him wanted to meet that minesweeper again — the *Southern Gannet*, his telegraphist told him — and blow it out of the water.

To avoid naval patrols and air reconnaissance, *Sturmvogel* made a wide detour of the Cape, heading southwest for 500 miles and then turning east. She lay to for a week in those remote southern latitudes, allowing the fuss to die down and taking the opportunity to undergo an overhaul in relatively calm weather. The raider wallowed along in the great watery desert at the end of the world.

All the while, the monotony and uncertainty wore at Sophie Macfarlane's nerves — as did the continuous noise of a warship at sea. Each morning, she was startled awake by martial music and the intercom's infernal blaring: '*Achtung, Achtung, wecken*' for reveille; then came sombre hours of Wagner, '*Backen und Banken*' for meals, news reports from Germany, birthday greetings, jaunty oompah music and, finally, the merciful '*Pfeifen und Lunten aus*'. She passed the time reading in the captain's bunk. Fortunately, the ship's library now stocked a number of English books liberated from *Kimberley Star*. Bauer paid her regular visits, but their short conversations remained awkward and constrained.

Falk himself sat in his sea cabin staring at a bookshelf filled with Schopenhauer, Kant and the unfathomable, damnable Nietzsche. He was struggling with depression and the feeling of isolation, exacerbated by the South Atlantic's bleak wastes. As captain, he stood so far above the men that he was as good as alone on the ship. There was no one he could turn to, no one to confide in — his doubts about the mission, the sea war and about Germany's course that had taken them into the unforgiving shoals of history. Being constantly on the run, always behind enemy lines with no safe harbour for thousands of miles, exerted tremendous psychological strain. He felt it in his bones.

Falk turned on the radio repeater above his desk. The announcer told of more Nazi successes in the Western Desert and a big air raid on Liverpool. The Propaganda Ministry claimed that seven British merchantmen had been lost to mines laid by a German raider off the Cape. Seven! Who said Dr Goebbels lacked journalistic flair? And what about secrecy? Enraged, he switched off the radio. Lies and pyrrhic victories. If the Royal Navy were not destroyed, there would be no 'Thousand-Year Reich'.

He thought about his Number One. Loyal, blind, misguided Adler, a man who'd given himself completely to the cause. He'd fallen for all the pomp and nonsense, the rhetoric and bile. Resentful of the injustices heaped upon Germany, the humiliating reparations and disarmament, the plotting of the filthy Jews. And then there was Bauer: a thinker, a doubter; a more intelligent and refined man, but weak. In a way, his two senior officers perfectly complemented each other. Perhaps they cancelled each other out.

Falk thought, too, about his crew, packed in tiers below him. They trusted entirely in their captain. Why? Because of his track record, his decorations, his Great War glories? Because of the self-same pomp and nonsense? Or did they see something else in him — something even he was blind to? Beneath his feet, in bunks, on mess decks, in hammocks, seated at tables gambling, deep in the thundering engine room … bankers, artists, bricklayers, schoolteachers, chefs, dreamers. Maybe this was indeed a suicide mission. Maybe they were all doomed.

Sometimes the responsibility was simply too heavy.

The raider headed northeast to join the shipping route from Australia, aiming to arrive off Cape Agulhas after dark. In the late afternoon, an Anson flew low over the ship, then circled.

Sailors remained out of sight, apprehensively watching the aircraft from scuttles and hiding places.

With deliberate clumsiness, the signalman flashed: '*Eendracht*, from Perth, bound for Cape Town.' Falk donned an old sailing coat and stepped out onto the bridge wing to wave his cap. Apparently satisfied, the Anson flew off towards the setting sun.

Sturmvogel approached Agulhas from the southeast in windless conditions, shouldering into a muscular swell that was building from the west. Falk timed his run so as to be sixty-five miles from the mine-laying objective at nightfall. The light sea mist and cloud cover suited his purpose as the raider stole towards the Cape, her gun crews closed up. No one spoke in the wheelhouse; there was a forbidding silence below decks. Outside, Agulhas Lighthouse flashed its silver beam, seeming to illuminate the ship with each pass. At 21:30, the first mine was laid twenty miles southeast of the lighthouse in sixty fathoms; *Sturmvogel* continued to drop mines in patterns at six-minute intervals on an irregular, northward course.

At 23:00, when *Sturmvogel* was only five miles from Agulhas, she turned southwest, still laying her eggs as she headed back towards the 100-fathom line. Bauer stepped onto the bridge wing and tossed a couple of lifebuoys, marked *U-68*, over the side. Hopefully they would confuse the enemy, suggesting that a U-boat was in the area. Finally, at 01:20, the raider laid the last of the pattern twenty-five miles southwest of Agulhas, and vanished back into the deep. The deed was done.

CHAPTER 22

The lighthouse keeper at Cape Agulhas was outside taking a leak when he heard a rumbling sound. He reckoned the detonation had occurred about five miles offshore, and immediately contacted Simon's Town. A raider, possibly *the* raider, had laid mines off Africa's southernmost point. Wireless reports warned all shipping in the vicinity to stay outside the 100-fathom line and keep a sharp lookout for drifting mines.

Jack's flotilla was assigned the onerous task of sweeping the Agulhas Bank. Compared to their daily round of False Bay work, this would be a relatively long voyage and they might be gone for some weeks. The ships were carefully prepared, taking on as much fuel, water and ammunition as they could carry. Everything from tinned vegetables to rifle clips had to find a home. Hundreds of twelve-pounder shells were swung aboard and lowered to the ammunition stores where they were grouped according to the different colour rings on each projectile. Sides of beef and sheep carcasses, frozen solid and covered in butter muslin, were delivered to the cooks.

Where the flotilla was headed, the autumn seas took no prisoners. The men's worn-out watch coats had to be replaced with new oilskins and sea-boots, as well as sheepskin coats, balaclavas and gloves donated by the ladies of the SAWAS, who had adopted the minesweeping service. Jack wondered if Clara's mother had been the instigator.

They set sail in the late afternoon. Leaving the bullnose, *Belle* took up her position a cable's length astern of *Gannet.* Behind her, a few minutes later, came *Star* and *Wayfarer*, nosing into the swell and taking up station. They made a handsome sight, heading southeast, line astern, bathed in orange light.

Rounding Cape Hangklip, they were into the notorious Cape rollers. The South Atlantic stretched out like an endless blue desert, reaching all the way to Antarctica. Long, ranging swells picked them up on their stern quarters and lobbed them forward. After a few moments of surfing along with a creamy bow wave, the ships slid off the back of the swell and almost disappeared into the trailing trough, feathery spray breasting the low-cut gunnels. Quartermasters struggled in vain to hold a straight course.

The western sky threw up splashes of colour, like a child let loose with paint. Crews on all four ships stared astern at the fiery display. Standing on the bridge beside his captain, Van Zyl wondered how Sylvia, the art student who'd hardly left his mind for a moment, would render such beauty. Perhaps only in brooding black-and-white like Dürer.

The flotilla drove on to the southeast in the dark. Jack left the bridge and went forward, climbing the ladder to the forecastle, using the barrel of the gun to steady himself as he passed to the prow of the ship. Leaning over the rail, he stared down at the gnashing bow wave, then out at the expanse of sea ahead. *This feels right*, he thought. *This is where I belong.*

He turned around and looked back at his ship. It was as though he'd become its figurehead. The hull appeared to project backwards from his body, an extension of himself. Seesawing back and forth, it knifed through the swell, the mast swinging like a metronome. There was a heady feeling of weightlessness on the crest of each wave. And, maybe, joy. Or a kind of contentment, at least. Up on the bridge, he could see the heads of Van Zyl and two lookouts; below them, the coxswain would be watching his captain from the wheelhouse. February, dependable February, the still centre of the ship.

Perhaps it had been the scrap with the raider, perhaps the hiatus of shore leave and repairs: for the first time, he felt he was truly in charge of *Gannet.*

The white beams of Danger Point and Cape Agulhas lighthouses scythed through the darkness to port. Van Zyl went to the chart table, elbowed his way inside its canvas hood and switched on the lamp. He plotted their position and calculated the time of arrival off the cape.

The flotilla reached Agulhas Bank in the early morning and prepared to sweep a large area fifty miles wide, starting with the inshore shipping route, about five miles offshore. They rigged Oropesa sweeps, with *Wayfarer* ordered to play tail-end Charlie and lay dan buoys with orange flags to mark the cleared area.

'Let go dans,' shouted Captain Wilson into his speaking trumpet. The first buoy dropped from its slip and splashed into dark water, bouncing wildly until the steadying pull of its weight settled the dan. The bosun immediately prepared the next one. After a clumsy start, *Wayfarer* found her rhythm and laid a straight, evenly-spaced row.

Jack surveyed his little fleet, sailing in echelon formation, their Oropesas out on both quarters. Employing this configuration, with each ship tucked inside the line of the float ahead, they could cover a much greater area. The day was blue and temperate, the sea mercifully placid, and the float flags fluttered jauntily in his wake. It reminded him of a regatta.

The ships came to the end of the first sweep, hauled their wires to the short-stay position to avoid fouling the others, and went through the complicated business of turning 180 degrees in echelon formation. Jack watched closely as each vessel wheeled round and got back on station. The manoeuvre was neatly executed. They weren't necessarily ready to take on the *Bismarck*, but they were certainly holding up their end properly.

At noon, *Star* got her sweep tangled on a wreck. For half an hour she wallowed, painstakingly extricating herself, while the other three ships completed a lap. Soon after, *Belle* put up the first mine, which was punctured and sunk by rifle fire.

With subsequent mines, Jack first allowed each ship to have a go with rifles. Striking a mine with a Lee-Enfield from a moving platform was difficult, even on calm days, but it served as a diversion for the crew. If they were unsuccessful he resorted to the Lewis guns. These usually exploded the mine, whether a detonator horn was hit or not. Each sailor had his own special place to take cover when a mine blew up, usually on the opposite side of the vessel. But such protection wasn't available to everyone, least of all the shooter, who had to rely on his tin hat and good luck.

Off-duty men were reluctant to go below while sweeping in a known minefield. It was often cold topside, with a piercing wind from the west. Sailors gathered on the boat deck, on top of the boiler-room casing or around the funnel, for warmth. They smoked, snoozed, chatted about home or played mindless games of 'I spy' and 'Animal, Mineral, Vegetable'. Jack noted with satisfaction how the camaraderie on each ship had grown in recent weeks; the witty banter spoke of generally happy crews.

Each evening, the sweepers found shelter under the lee of a headland, usually in Struis Bay. The next morning, they would up anchor before dawn and head back to pick up where they'd left off the day before.

On the fifth day, *Star*'s sweep wire sliced through a mine's mooring line. The deadly black sphere bobbed to the surface directly ahead of *Wayfarer*, where, due to a heavy swell, it wasn't spotted until the last moment.

'Floating mine, dead ahead!' came the high-pitched scream from a lookout on *Wayfarer*.

'Jaysus, *Star*'s put one up!' cried Seaman Fitzpatrick from *Gannet*'s stern lookout. 'It's gonna be close.'

On *Wayfarer*'s bridge, Captain Wilson watched in horror. 'Starboard twenty, then straighten her!' he shouted into the copper voice pipe. His coxswain responded instantly. 'Can you see it, Cox'n?'

'No, sir,' came the reply up the tube.

The mine appeared briefly on a wave top forty yards ahead of *Wayfarer*, then disappeared again. Wilson thought for a moment of ringing the telegraph for slow ahead, or even full astern, but realised the loss of way would reduce steerage. The mine bobbed on the crest of a swell once again: twenty yards.

'Okay, I see it now, sir,' came a firm voice from below.

Wilson's coxswain knew the ship's niceties better than he did, so he issued no more commands.

'Your judgement then, Cox'n. As you see fit.'

'Aye, Captain.'

Wilson held his breath. The coxswain eased the wheel over and straightened. The mine edged away to port, then sloshed back on a counter swell, seemingly sucked towards *Wayfarer*'s flank. From his position in the wheelhouse, the coxswain could no longer see the mine. He simply had to hold the ship dead on course and pray.

The mine passed within two yards of their port side. Wilson looked down at its Satanic horns: one brush and he'd know nothing more about it.

The coxswain edged her away slightly. The mine wallowed into their wake, missing the quarter by a couple of feet. Wilson knew that if his coxswain had made a more exaggerated turn, the stern would have clipped the mine. He pulled off his cap and ran the back of his hand across a sweating brow.

'Stop engine, let's destroy that revolting thing.' Wilson tried to keep his voice even, despite his rioting heartbeat. 'Number One, please have the telegraphist radio *Gannet* and tell them it's a brand new mine. No sign of rust or weed. Must have been laid very recently.'

'Aye, sir. And a message from Captain Pembroke, sir: "New underpants to be issued to all *Wayfarer*'s crew."'

The next afternoon, they were busy completing the last lap of the day when there was an immense explosion just ahead of *Southern Star*. It appeared to lift the sweeper bodily from the ocean. The ship vanished behind a wall of water darkened by debris. As *Wayfarer* swung away to avoid the scene of destruction, the cascade enveloped her too.

Jack looked on in horror. But, to his great surprise, *Star* emerged from the falling water. She seemed remarkably unscathed, although he knew her men must have been terribly shaken up, especially in the engine room.

'Sparky, please radio *Southern Star*: "Any damage?"'

It took some time before a crackly reply was forthcoming: 'Minor injuries, minor leaks, major miracle. A few stokers who don't know which week of the day it is.'

'Please reply: "Back in Simon's Town we'll put you on the slip in West Yard and have a look at your petticoat. Regrets, you may no longer be a virgin."'

As long days dragged by, Jack began to notice how the constant sweeping was wearing down his men. The frequent manhandling of serrated wires took its toll; one sailor on *Star* had lost two fingers when a cable snapped in heavy swell. The mine pickings grew thinner, the men's nerves more brittle. Back and forth, forth and back, never reaching a destination, never *getting anywhere*. Bobbies on an endless beat with no crooks to apprehend.

'What a way to fight a war, sir,' said Smit.

'It's not exactly glamorous,' said Jack. 'But it's jolly well essential, Number One.'

Jack knew that his men would soon need a break. Up before dawn to weigh anchor and out on the sweep all day, often back only after dark. Watches had to be kept through the night and equipment repaired. When they were too far from an anchorage, they'd steam slowly up and down all night in a recently swept area, hoping no one would bump into a floater.

Each day, a patrolling Maryland or Anson rumbled overhead and the minesweepers would display their identification pennants, more out of formality than any chance of being mistaken for the enemy. The pilot usually came in low and waved. Jack wondered if one of them might be Clara's brother. She occupied most of his non-sweeping thoughts and he ached to see her again.

Sometimes the flotilla encountered fishing boats out of Arniston, working the same patch of ocean but for a different sort of catch. The fishermen would hold up galjoen or yellowtail and the sweepers would sidle over and stop engines.

There'd be a few minutes of rowdy bargaining; cash or barter items such as canned food would pass between the vessels, and half a dozen silver ingots would disappear into the galley. Fresh provisions were running low. There were no refrigerators on the ships so perishables were on their last legs. The cooks seldom managed to get ashore to stock up on large enough quantities of fruit, vegetables and meat, which were hard to come by in the village of Struisbaai. Crews began to show signs of weight loss and fatigue.

And, with the approach of winter, the weather had begun to grow foul. On days when conditions were marginal, they'd set out for a few hours of torrid sweeping, more often than not being forced back to the shelter of Struis Bay. Angry seas often meant that dan buoys dragged or broke adrift, forcing them to repeat part of a sweep. But each day progress was made and the bank was slowly swept clean.

Though the crews were exhausted, morale remained high and Jack saw little sign of shirking or grumbling. Every man in the flotilla knew just how vital it was to make sure that Agulhas, the fulcrum of the continent, was properly cleared. To Jack it seemed as though the men felt the Seaward Defence Force was finally proving its worth.

A bank of charcoal cloud, split by lightning flashes, spanned the western horizon. Jack gave the order, 'In sweeps. We'd better find shelter from that lot.' Bunts responded and the flag hoist was repeated down the line. The winch on *Gannet*'s stern coughed into life and dragged the dripping wire around its drum. Slowly, the Oropesa wallowed closer and was hoisted inboard.

That evening, the flotilla lay at anchor in the lee of Northumberland Point, pinned down by a cold front that tore at the Cape. A strong westerly whipped up an angry chop in the anchorage. The ships creaked and rolled as gusts whistled through their rigging.

Jack stood beside Van Zyl in the chartroom, going over the laps marked in pencil and assessing how much still needed to be done. The sub wasn't always the most reliable officer, but his navigation was excellent. Jack noted with satisfaction how each lap was marked with neat letters, the ships' names on each one. The fifty-yard overlaps as well as the time of the start and end of each pass were all accurately recorded.

Later, the other captains were rowed over to *Gannet* for a chinwag. They sat in the wardroom, heated by the glowing coal stove. A chart was rolled out on the table, the corners held down by a gin bottle, ashtrays and Van Zyl's volume of Rupert Brooke poetry.

'Liberal lashings of gin all round, please, Hendricks,' said Jack to the steward. 'Tomorrow, I want us to start here, at the forty-two-fathom mark, and work east, into the current.' He ran two fingers across the chart. 'If you look closely, you'll see where Van Zyl has marked the mines we've swept so far. From the pattern, I think we can work out the raider's route. She must've followed a zigzag course, starting in the southeast, sailing up to Cape Agulhas and then swinging away to the southwest. Or vice versa.'

The captains talked late into the night. A second bottle of gin made its appearance. Cigarette butts accumulated in the ashtrays and the room grew thick with smoke. It was a chance for Jack to get to know his skippers better, far from the madding brass and formality of Simon's Town. Sven Alstad was a wild and gregarious Viking lookalike with a quick temper and a sailor's superstition. His belly laugh filled the wardroom with contagious good humour. Andrew Wilson was urbane and erudite, forever fiddling with his pipe and always ready with a nugget of schoolboy wit. Louis du Toit was quiet, steadfast and practical, just the kind of chap you wanted on a bridge when trouble was brewing. Yes, Jack thought, he was lucky with his three captains.

The Norwegian tanker rescue and *Gannet*'s brush with the raider also meant that his men took their battle readiness seriously. The Cape's phoney war had come to an end, albeit a lot later than Britain's.

'Next time we see that *ekkel* raider, we'll ram her, *ja*?' said Alstad, nudging Du Toit in the ribs. 'Fix bayonets on our twelve-pounders and we charge!' The Norwegian guffawed and Du Toit turned brick red.

'*Ag* sir, it's not fair.' The young lieutenant appealed to his CO. 'Any skipper could have made the same mistake. It looked *just* like a bow wave.'

Jack smiled and winked at the others.

The incident had occurred on their voyage to Agulhas. Due to engine trouble, *Star* had taken up station at the stern of the flotilla. They were sailing through a patch of mist when *Star* abruptly peeled away at full speed, intent on challenging a suspicious vessel on their port beam. It turned out to be a rock, which *Star* had seemed intent on ramming. Although Du Toit denied this in the strongest terms, he was mercilessly ragged by the other officers and had acquired a host of nicknames, including 'Rammer Louis' and 'Cutlass-and-Pike du Toit'.

Eventually the three captains, none too steady on their pins, were rowed back to their ships. Jack lay on his bunk with the scuttle open, listening to the tinkle of halyards, the brushing of his canvas blackout curtain and sloshing of water down the ship's side. Fido jumped onto the bunk and curled up at his feet, purring loudly. *Gannet*'s two captains, both human and feline, were comfortably content. It was time to get some sleep.

Suddenly, Jack wrenched himself upright with a shout. The sheets were wrapped tightly around him like rope and he pulled them loose. Gasping, he got up and stuck his head out of the scuttle. Bracing air. Moonlight. Stars. He was still afloat. His leg ached and his body was soaked in sweat, as were the sheets.

Hendricks had heard him cry out but did not enter, knowing it was another of his captain's 'mares'. But this one seemed worse. He tapped on the door and opened it a few inches. 'Sorry to disturb, sir. Would you like a nice cup of Milo? I was just making.'

'What? Yes, yes, sorry, thank you, Hendricks.'

'Are you all right, sir?'

'Yes, I'm fine.'

'If you need me, ever, sir. Anytime. You just shout.'

'Thank you, Basil, very kind. Very kind indeed. I'm quite all right.'

CHAPTER 23

Late on Monday night, an urgent message crackled through on the radio from SNO Simon's Town. Brooke and some of his mates gathered in the doorway of the wireless cabin, trying to catch a glimpse of the signal before Sparks dashed to the bridge. Had the balloon gone up, they wondered?

A conference of the captains was hastily called. The cook prepared a pot of coffee and a plate of corned beef sandwiches as the men were rowed across. He took it to the wardroom where the four skippers, as well as Smit, were poring over charts and discussing the operation ahead.

'We've received intelligence that a Vichy French convoy has set sail from Fort Dauphin in Madagascar and is trying to make a dash for Europe around the Cape,' said Jack. 'Looks like four merchant ships escorted by a sloop. As you know, French colonies such as Madagascar are caught between supporting the spineless puppet regime back home and the Free French. They've got Marshal Pétain pulling in one direction and General de Gaulle in the other.'

'So is this convoy an ally, neutral or the enemy?' asked Alstad.

'We treat it as hostile. If the cargo gets through to Occupied France, it will aid the Nazi war machine. Our job is to apprehend them and escort the merchant ships to South African ports where they'll be requisitioned.'

'What about the sloop, sir?' asked Smit.

'I don't exactly know. If she fires on us, we fire back.'

'But those French sloops are well armed. Five-inch guns —'

'I'm well aware, thank you, Smit.'

'Sorry, sir.'

'And the raider?' asked Du Toit.

'It could be in touch with the French. Possibly taking on supplies from them. They might even be sailing together.' Jack noticed his officers exchanging glances. 'The operation is codenamed Bullwhip and will be run by the Royal Navy, not the SDF. Simon's Town wants us to patrol this area.' He placed a hand on the chart. 'From 300 to 500 miles south of us.'

'That's an enormous patch of ocean,' said Wilson.

'It is. But the flotilla will spread out, creating an extended patrol line sixty miles wide, and sail west to east. We'll get help from the South African Air Force, who'll send out long-range patrols. Two cruisers, HMAS *Fremantle* and HMS *Hawksbill*, as well as the AMC HMS *Carnarvon Castle*, are to join us in due course.'

'Some very foul weather coming our way,' said Alstad. 'I don't think I've ever seen the glass fall so fast. We'll be off the end of the Agulhas Bank, right in the teeth of it.'

'Yes, it's going to be a rough ride,' said Jack.

'We might have trouble staying in touch if we spread out too wide,' said Alstad.

'Quite right. I want round-the-clock radio watch and double the lookouts if necessary.'

The steward had found a number of pressing things to do near the open scuttle and soon the mess-deck-gossip telegraph was buzzing. Within minutes, everyone on board knew the nature of their mission. The captains returned to their ships and stokers hurriedly raised steam.

'Weigh anchor, Number One,' said Jack and rang the engine-room telegraph to 'standby'.

PO Cummins was on the forecastle with his anchor party. He engaged the winch and the dripping, weed-covered cable clanked into the anchor-chain locker.

'Up and down!' came the cry from Cummins. Then, 'Anchors aweigh!'

'All right, slow ahead.'

The last of the chain links clinked home and the hook banged snugly into place as *Gannet* began to crease a path across the bay, followed by her sisters. The four dark shapes headed due south. As they cleared the headland, Jack ordered, 'Full ahead.'

Stokers worked their vessels up to maximum speed, pressing every extra revolution from the engines. Propellers increased their beat; quarterdecks sat deeper in the water. The flotilla ploughed into the black vacuum of the night. On each sweeper's bridge, lookouts clad in heavy duffel coats scanned the dark undulations.

'Van Zyl, take a turn around the ship and make sure we're fully darkened,' said Jack. 'And check that everything is securely lashed down that might have an inclination to move about.'

'We're in for a proper blow, then, sir?'

'Aye, Sub, that we are.'

Van Zyl started in the bows and worked his way aft, ensuring that all external lights were extinguished, that deadlights covered the scuttles and that only a small, shaded stern light showed for station keeping. He poked his head into the wireless cabin where Sparks was listening to a lengthy all-ships weather forecast. The sub was alarmed at the severity of the storm warning issued for the Cape coast. He reported the news to the bridge and it appeared to give his captain's already worried expression an even grimmer set.

The swell had begun to build from the west. The sweepers staggered under each watery blow, rolling now through thirty degrees. In the chartroom, Van Zyl wrote in the logbook: *Swell increasing.* Gannet *labouring and taking water over her decks. Barometer continues to fall.*

The ships had the swell on their beams. Sheets of spray wreathed their superstructures, flying across the open bridges and drenching those on watch. Tons of water thundered over the prows, but the shape of the enclosed forecastles and large scuppers allowed it to be shaken off easily. Not for the first time, Jack blessed the Norwegians who'd designed such seaworthy, if wet, craft. With its narrow waist, a whale catcher was more porpoise than ship, often ploughing through the swells rather than over them. At times, he feared they were too submarine-like and might never resurface.

Dawn broke on a tormented ocean lashed by rain squalls. The men on watch squinted at the shortened horizon, their eyes stinging from salty tears. Jack realised that the flotilla was taking too much of a battering from the beam sea, so he made a signal to reduce speed and turn to face the alpine swells.

A three-knot current from the east took up arms against the storm from the west, churning the ocean into a scene from some watery apocalypse. Through the course of the day, wind and sea continued to build. Gusts reached seventy knots, creating a wall of spray. *Visibility reduced to nil at times*, wrote Van Zyl in the log. The other three ships often disappeared from sight. Then a distant mast would be spotted in the murk, or a ghostly shape would punch through a hill of water, before vanishing into a dark valley.

Conditions in the mess decks deteriorated as the sea state worsened. Mealtimes became intricate dances. Brooke made his way up the ladder with his tin plate, hesitating when he saw how water crashed inboard amidships with each roll. He whispered the old sailors' maxim, 'One hand for yourself and one hand for the ship.' In these conditions, he needed three hands. Waiting to time the ship's roll on the up, he sprinted along the waist, but a wave caught him before he reached the galley. His drenched sheepskin jacket now weighed a ton.

The cook worked wonders, managing, against all odds, to produce fairly tasty, reasonably hot meals. Porky spent all day shut away in his coffin-like galley. Every few hours, the steel door banged open releasing a gout of steam and meals for twenty-four men. No one knew quite how he did it.

Brooke propped himself against the half-open barn door while Cookie ladled skilly onto his plate and sloshed tea into his mug. Then the teenager tried to make his way back along the pitching deck, through the hatch and down the ladder to the seaman's mess. Halfway, a wave robbed him of his dinner and he was forced to return to the galley and endure Porky's torrent of abuse before a second helping splattered onto his plate. This time, he made it to the mess. But even eating had become difficult. Each mouthful was taken at the weightless moment on the crest of a swell, then swallowed when the G-forces exerted themselves as the ship dived into a trough.

While on watch, the men wore a strange assortment of garments, from oilskins, windcheaters and duffel coats to balaclavas and tea-cosy caps. Any exposed skin was lashed with icy spray; hands froze and feet skidded on the slippery deck. Injuries started being reported to the bridge: concussion, a sprained ankle and plenty of bruises.

Despite the crew's exhaustion, sleep proved elusive. Lower bunks were soaked, while ratings in the upper bunks feared being ejected and injuring themselves. Stoker Hughes had been seasick from the moment they left Struis Bay. Pale and dehydrated, he held on grimly to the side of his bunk, unable to keep food down. At first, he'd tried to haul himself up the ladder to vomit over the side, but when he grew weaker a bucket was placed beside him. The stoker's aim was not accurate and soon the mess deck reeked. Porky mixed water and glucose powder from the first-aid box, but the patient vomited it straight back up. Cummins ordered that the mess deck be swabbed with paraffin to kill the smell.

The forecastle heads was a no-go zone, with toilet contents sloshing freely about the deck. No one dared go in there, not for anything.

That evening, Van Zyl laboured over his charts: plotting courses and currents, speed and distance made good. Without accurate sightings, it was more guesswork than science. In the wireless cabin, Sparks was catching forty winks. A round-the-clock radio watch was essential but, as the ship had only one telegraphist, Bunts stepped in to let Sparky get some sleep.

Jack had not left the open bridge since Struis Bay and was battling to stay awake. How many cigarettes had he smoked, how many cups of kye had he drunk on this never-ending watch? What if they met the raider in these conditions? The enemy ship must be out here somewhere. They would stand no chance. And what would he do if they met the Vichy convoy? Could he really give the order to open fire on a French ship? And if he didn't find the convoy, what would O'Reilly say? What would his father think?

His eyelids drooped; his mind grew ponderous and his nerves friable. Jack had entered a territory beyond fatigue. Welded to the deck by sodden sea-boots, he clamped his frozen hands to the bridge rail. The storm had transformed him into an effigy. Facing the storm, he registered each wave as a blow to his own body. Jack had become *Gannet*'s brain, her heart too.

That night, the storm intensified. Coming off the middle watch at 04:00, Brooke ran across the main deck to the mess hatch between waves. He wrenched open the weather doors, allowing a cascade of water to accompany him down the ladder. Curses greeted him as he made for his bunk. The storm had transformed the mess deck into a dark, stinking chamber that echoed with the ocean's blows. Nothing was dry anymore, not even his top bunk. Loose items sloshed about in the freezing water, mixed with Hughes' vomit. Under his damp blanket, Brooke braced his knees against the bulkhead to counter the roll and, in a matter of seconds, slipped into a drugged, fathomless sleep.

Starboard watch was shaken at 07:45. Brooke opened his eyes in dread. How could it possibly be time to go back up top? He was famished and knew he needed to get some breakfast down before his watch. Tucking his plate and mug inside his overalls, he made a dash for the galley. But when he got there, he saw that Porky was ladling tinned herring in tomato sauce onto the plates.

'No porridge today, Cookie?' he asked pleadingly.

'Sorry, Pickles, we've run out of oatmeal.'

His stomach revolted at the idea of herring. There was no way he'd keep it down. He retreated to the mess with a mug of cold tea and a slice of stale bread.

On the bridge, Jack was still wedged in his chair. 'Go below and get some shut-eye, sir,' said Smit. 'You'll need to be fresh as a daisy if we make contact with the French.'

'A daisy. What a lovely thought. A yellow one. Pretty petals. She loves me, she loves me not. Oh all right, Number One, if you insist. But call me for *anything*.'

'Aye, sir, that I will.'

Jack looked at Smit, who was staring ahead at the oncoming swell. Perhaps he'd been too hasty in judging his first officer. He did not like the man, but you could hardly fault him on his commitment to *Gannet*. Perhaps likeability didn't come into it.

Jack made his way clumsily down the ladder and collapsed on his bunk. Hendricks opened the door quietly and looked at the figure sprawled on the mattress. The captain had removed neither his duffel coat nor his sea-boots; his face was pale and drawn. There were black half-moons under his eyes, the vein on his temple looked like a throbbing fuel line. Hendricks put two glasses between the fiddles on the gimballed table — one with water, one with raw gin. Gently, he removed the boots and pulled a blanket over his skipper. He switched off the light and closed the door.

The weather worsened. Weary lookouts could hardly keep their salt-encrusted eyes open. Porky gave up on hot food, lest he scald himself while handling the pots. With the galley fire doused, it was bully-beef sandwiches, biscuits and Oros for the crew, or any eats they'd secreted in their lockers.

Conditions seemed to grow colder and fiercer with each hour of southing. The wind howled, moaned, screamed. The swells were taller than even Alstad and McEwan had ever seen. Then, mid-afternoon, a rogue wave caught them on their starboard bow. *Gannet* reared up and pitched, rolling through seventy-five degrees; knocked over to almost her beam ends, she was seemingly on the brink of capsizing. Everyone held on for life that was dear, until the sweeper slowly righted herself.

'We can't take much more of this,' said Jack, back in his chair after a few hours' kip. He bent over the voice pipe and shouted: 'Radio flotilla: "Heave to and ride out the storm. Every ship for herself."'

Out of the corner of his eye, he noticed a monstrous wave. Swollen, grotesque. The crest exploded, forming a great fist of white water. It reminded Jack of Table Mountain, complete with fleecy tablecloth. For a moment, *Gannet*'s captain was transfixed. Then he yelled: 'Hard astarboard, quick as you like, Cox'n!' He grabbed the telegraph handle and rang down for full ahead.

February spun the wheel and watched the bows swing slowly to meet the giant. The wall of black water towered over them, looming ever larger. Its foaming crest appeared somehow suspended in the sky above them. Out of all proportion. Impossible.

They could never survive it.

CHAPTER 24

The wave struck *Gannet* and enveloped the forecastle. To Jack, it appeared as though a dam wall had burst. The Atlantic had boarded his ship. If anyone had been on the main deck, they'd have stood no chance. Jack clung to the rail, bracing himself as the wave detonated on the bridge. He was knocked over and sent sprawling across the deck, his arms finding the telegraph as the bridge was inundated. Jack, Smit and the two lookouts clung on with all their strength, immersed in freezing water, the air wrenched from their lungs.

Jack's grip began to loosen. The weight. The terrible weight of water. He floated free. There was nothing to hold onto, no ship, no help, no harbour. He lashed out in terror, his hands seeking a hold. Nothing. Weightlessness. Was he overboard?

The wave travelled the length of the sweeper, filling the waist and swamping the stern. With tons of water pressing down on her, it seemed *Gannet* would never rise again. Down and down she went, buried under a liquid mountain.

February stood steadfastly at the con, like a statue, one window smashed and water gushing in. He willed the ship to lift. Pulling at the wheel as though it were a joystick, he held the nose true and waited for *Gannet* to come to her senses.

Eventually, as if in slow motion, the sweeper began to rise. Water poured off her like a duck, or perhaps a gannet, as she shook herself free. The scuppers wept torrents as she shuddered to the surface. Her inherent buoyancy and, seemingly, her will, reasserted itself. Water drained down the bridge companionway and four drenched men looked around them, stunned to be alive and still aboard their ship.

Jack stood up gingerly, sensing that he had, somehow, been 'returned'. His teeth chattered and his breath came in short gasps. Horizontal rain stung his face; his eyes leaked. He had survived. His ship had survived. They would fight another day, and another, and he would not give in. Not ever. He smiled at the two lookouts, who also wore strange, disoriented grins.

'Wet up here, isn't it, Number One?' he said. 'Number One?'

'Aye, sir, just a bit,' said Smit hoarsely. He was wide-eyed and shaking uncontrollably.

'The old girl can take a pasting, can't she?'

Smit tried to reply but words would not come.

Jack could not worry about him: *Gannet* was climbing another giant swell. February aimed at the crest and burst through the white water. For a moment, half the ship was airborne, before dropping into the ensuing trough with a bone-splitting crunch that shook her from keelson to truck. Slowed by the body blow, she was caught by an almighty gust that forced her head off the wind.

'She's falling off, Cox'n!' shouted Jack, hanging onto the binnacle, his clothes heavy as armour. February gritted his teeth. The wheel was hard over, but the ship would not respond.

'We haven't got enough steerage way, Captain,' gasped Smit. 'The wind is driving us backwards.'

Unable to straighten, *Gannet* took the next, mercifully smaller, wave on the starboard bow. On the crest, the wind caught her under the bows and forced her over on her beam ends once again. A collective groan and shouting came from the mess decks.

Jack lifted the cover on the voice pipe. 'Chief, can you find a few extra revs in that puffer of yours? We're in a spot of bother.'

'I'll see what I can do,' came the curt reply.

Feeling an increase in the propeller's beat, February spun the wheel in the pit of the trough where there was some shelter from the wind. The prow slowly responded and *Gannet* climbed the slope to face the next curling lip. *Come up, old girl,* Jack importuned the ship.

'Well done, PO!' came a faint cry down the pipe as the sweeper punched through the crest. *Gannet* belly-flopped onto the reverse slope and careened into the trough. Down, down, down she went again, sliding off the back of the wave, sliding off the end of the world.

Jack scanned the horizon. A succession of mountain ranges marched towards them, snow-capped, spine-chilling. The clouds were black. The rain turned to hail, drilling the superstructure with its machine-gun fire. In the wheelhouse just below him, February stood with his legs wide apart, eyes red-rimmed from the strain, holding his course.

Between gusts, February allowed the head to come off slightly on the wave crests. This broke the fall on the reverse slope. Sailing into the trough, he'd straighten up for the next ascent. Captain and coxswain were learning what was needed in order to survive: a little more helm here, more or less power there, how to absorb a breaking swell, how to hit back.

Gannet was hardly making headway, but at least she had steerage way. By now, February was utterly spent, but he remained at his post. Jack did not dare relieve him — this man to whom he entrusted the life of the ship. February stood firm with the gaping mouths of two voice pipes before him, a smashed window to his left and the great dial of the telegraph to his right.

A low sun briefly lit the scene. It looked as though the west had sustained a mortal wound and was bleeding out. Jack knew it was going to be a long, perhaps never-ending, night.

If anything, the weather deteriorated during the night. Ghostly crests glowed in the dark in shades of ivory. Lightning flashes illuminated a maddened sea that boiled and rose and fell and was resurrected again. The sweeper was submerged for interminable seconds; then she'd tear herself free and shake herself off like a dog as water poured from the scuppers. Jack suffered with his ship. He knew the stories of whale catchers that did not come back from such onslaughts, of succeeding waves that refused to let them rise, until they succumbed, foundered, sank. But each time she rose again; each time he felt his agonising doubt ease as her prow lifted.

Somewhere in the middle watch, and far over to port, *Southern Star* collided with an object. A tremendous thud echoed through the hull, which had men leaping to their action stations even before the alarm was sounded.

'What on earth?' cried Du Toit, rushing to the bridge wing and peering into the black cauldron of the night. There was a second blow near the stern, as though the ship had been sideswiped. Du Toit leaned over the side and looked aft. '*Goeie genugtig*, we've hit a whale! Damage report, Number One.'

A young lookout on the quarterdeck saw the leviathan swirling away in the darkness, its carcass lacerated by the propeller, livid chunks of meat peeling from it. It was the most monstrous thing the lad had ever seen. He stuck his head over the stern and threw up his supper.

Meanwhile, on *Gannet*, Jack sensed that the ship was labouring, her prow struggling to lift. He suspected they were taking on water. 'Van Zyl, go below and see if we've sprung a leak for'ard. We seem to be down by the bows.'

'Aye, sir.'

'And take a torch.'

Van Zyl dreaded an odyssey into the ship's nethers. He descended to the chaotic seamen's mess through the hatch in their deck, then down into the black tomb of the magazine. He heard water rushing back and forth and paused on the ladder. Leaning down, he tried the light switch. It didn't work. Flicking on the torch, he pointed the beam into the cavern. The ammunition store was three feet underwater.

With a seaman standing on the ladder shining a light, Van Zyl plunged head first into the water, feeling for the outlets. Groping in the filthy water, his fingers found the problem: rust, loosened paint flakes and assorted gunk had clogged the drains. He dug at them, tearing his fingernails until they bled. Eventually, there was a sucking outrush as water poured down into the bilges.

Drenched and shivering, he scrambled out of the magazine and made his way forward to repeat the process in the cable locker, which had suffered a similar blockage. By the time he returned to the bridge — his body quivering and fingers bleeding — he was done in.

'Blockages cleared, sir,' he said weakly.

'Well done, Sub. Now go below, get out of those wet clothes and have a rest on your bunk. You deserve it.'

'Thank you, Captain. I'll get cleaned up, but it's not yet time for a rest.'

Another dawn, another watch. The weather had eased considerably, and Porky had managed to relight the galley fires. *Gannet* and her three sisters were raggedly line abreast, sailing towards a salmon sky. They had reached their patrol area and were heading due east at seven knots. Large seas from astern made steering difficult, each swell trying to elbow the ships off their course.

Weary lookouts scanned the horizon, sweeping their binoculars through sea and sky. A large bird, planing along the lip of a swell, pricked a moment of interest. 'Wandering albatross, dark upper wings and body, must be immature,' said Jack. Then it was back to innumerable shades of grey.

'Ten minutes to go!' came the call from the duty watchman down the hatch.

Brooke opened his stinging eyes. Not again! It seemed impossible. He had just closed them. How had four hours passed so quickly? He clung to his pillow for a few more moments, then swung his aching body down, making sure he didn't tread on Van Reenen, inert in the bunk below. The body of his oppo emitted a whining sound, like that of a neglected puppy.

'Come on, Hans, let's grab a quick cuppa,' Brooke said.

'*Nooit,* just shoot me rather,' came the mumbled reply. 'I can't do this anymore.'

Sailors were trying to pull on boots with one hand while sipping their coffee. Brooke filled his mug from the pot and added three heaped spoons of sugar and a dash of condensed milk from the tin. A dazed Van Reenen sat upright on his bunk, his hair pointing in every direction. 'Come, Hans, you're gonna be late,' said Brooke. 'The Jimmy will have your guts.'

'Fuck the Jimmy,' mumbled Hans.

Brooke dragged on his oilskins, then followed the rest of the watch up the ladder. Thank goodness, the new day seemed brighter. His duty lookout position was the quarterdeck. Once again, he mistimed his run along the ship's waist and reached the stern sopping wet.

'You look like a drowned mongoose, Pickles!' said the lookout he was replacing.

'It's my luck and my lot.'

'Enjoy! I'm off to a soggy bunk.'

Brooke called into the voice pipe: 'Bridge, aft lookout relieved.' Difficult hours lay ahead. Viewed from the quarterdeck of a small whaling ship, the deep South Atlantic was a terrifying place. Brooke watched, mesmerised, as teetering waves approached *Gannet*, lifting her up and sweeping beneath her counter at the last moment. He felt utterly alone on his platform, a few feet above the raging sea. He thought of the Bible classes he'd abandoned in his early teens. Perhaps this voyage was a good time to take up praying again. 'For those in peril on the bloody sea,' he said aloud.

At last, apart from the occasional rogue wave, the weather began to improve. With an easing of the sea state, Cummins took stock of damage. *Gannet* was as much of a shambles above deck as below. The Carley float frame had buckled, the log line had been ripped away and a ready-use ammunition locker had gone over the side.

The other three ships had also sustained damage and injuries to crew. Rolling to forty degrees, *Wayfarer* had lost most of her dan buoys and sinkers. One sailor had been thrown against a ladder and fractured his leg. *Wayfarer*'s binnacle had come adrift, snapped from its mountings when a wave broke over the bridge. *Star* was suffering engine trouble, but was still able to hold station. Her funnel sat askew, like a jauntily cocked hat.

Belle's lifeboat had been torn from its davits and gone by the board. Most of her wheelhouse windows were shattered. All the sweepers had lost stanchions, awnings and rigging; rails had twisted, screens were smashed.

Gannet's crew was in a trancelike state of exhaustion. Jack fought to stay awake. He sat slumped in his chair and kept nodding off, only to be roused by a dose of spray. He must keep alert, focused. The raider. The French. He might have only seconds to make a decision.

'Seaman Hughes would like to put in for a transfer to the army, sir,' said Cummins, appearing on the bridge.

'Seriously, PO, how is the lad doing?'

'He's turned from green to white, which is always a good sign. And he kept his breakfast down.'

'That is good news.'

'Why don't you go and get some shut-eye, sir?' said Smit.

'Aye, Number One, perhaps a catnap.'

'With Fido, sir?'

'If she'll have me. Get Seaman Brooke up here, he's got bloody keen eyes.'

A few moments later, the sailor clattered up to the bridge.

'Brooke, by my calculation, we could be pretty close to the Frog convoy and the visibility is much improved,' said Jack. 'You've got the best eyes. Put them to work.'

'Carrots, sir.'

'What's that, Brooke?'

'My mum fed me lots of carrots. Good for the eyesight.'

'Ah, good for your mum,' Jack said, smiling and shaking his head. One minute later, he was fast asleep in his bunk with Fido purring beside him.

Smit sent the young lookout up the foremast for a wider view. Given the ship's exaggerated rolling, Brooke had a terrible time of it. Often he'd find himself dangling over wild ocean with the *Gannet* a small, vague afterthought at the periphery of his vision. Eventually, he had to be brought down. Grey-faced and shaken, he was sent below to recover.

At midday, February tapped on Jack's door.

'Yes, what is it now?' came a befuddled response.

'Smoke to the southeast, sir.'

CHAPTER 25

Jack hauled himself from the depths of sleep, slowly climbing the Jacob's ladder towards consciousness. Smoke? Hand over hand, out of the Carley float and up, up to that other world. To the southeast? Smoke! He wrenched himself upright in the bunk, feeling his bones creak, his leg pulsing like a lighthouse.

'What?' he exclaimed.

'Lieutenant Smit's compliments, Captain,' said February, his ear against the door. 'He said to call you. Smoke, sir, far off yet.' His tone was warm, almost maternal. 'Sorry to disturb.'

'That's quite all right, Adam. Step inside. How many ships?'

'Probably five, sir, still hard to tell,' said February, opening the door.

'Have I slept long?'

'A few hours. We didn't want to bother you.'

'I'll be right up. Carry on.'

On the bridge, Jack trained his binoculars on the smoke.

'I think there was possibly a sixth ship, sir,' said Smit.

'Sixth?'

'Yes, far to the south of the convoy. A lookout thought he might have seen something. Gone now.'

'Why didn't you tell me immediately?' Jack snapped.

'You've just got here, sir.'

'Damn it all, Smit! That's the first thing you should have told me.' Jack swept the southern horizon.

'Could it be the raider, sir?'

'Anything's possible. But now we've got our hands full with these Frogs. Can't go chasing ghosts. Sparks, make to SNO Simon's Town: "Sighted Vichy convoy. Four merchant ships escorted by one French sloop in position 40° 15' South 23° 47' East. Course west, speed eight knots. Minesweepers to shadow them."'

The rest of his scattered flotilla closed with *Gannet*. As they drew nearer the convoy, action stations was sounded. Excitement coursed through tired crews like an injection of gasoline. The off watch dragged overalls and oilskins over their undergarments, grabbed tin hats and scrambled to their positions. In a handful of minutes, all four ships were closed up.

The weather was turning foul once again. By late afternoon, visibility had dropped to one mile. The French ships increased speed and turned south.

Darkness fell and rain began to pour. Jack's task was to track the convoy through the night and wait for heavier units to join them the next day. He ordered that two sweepers take up station astern of the Frenchmen and one on each quarter. He must not lose them in the dark.

The convoy doused its lights and made course and speed changes during the rain squalls, trying to throw off its pursuers. But the flotilla closed to within a few hundred yards, and each sweeper chose a ship to tail. *Gannet* and *Belle* clung on like limpets, while *Star* and *Wayfarer* occasionally lost their quarries and had to regroup using RT.

At sunrise, Jack signalled the French sloop: 'Heave to and allow boarding parties onto your merchantmen.'

There was no reply. What to do? He wanted to call up Simon's Town but thought better of it.

'Repeat the signal, please, Bunts.'

After a few minutes, the sloop responded by radio: 'This is the captain of *Loire*, escorting a sovereign French convoy. We carry no contraband, only foodstuff for the French people.

This is my word of honour. In consequence, I cannot accept any diversion.'

'Fucking French honour: what the hell is that?' Jack banged the rail with his fist. 'Bunts, make to *Loire*: "You will heave to and allow boarding parties immediately."'

There was another long pause. All gun crews were closed up and tension mounted as the stand-off continued. *Gannet*'s boat was prepared for lowering. Finally, a signal flashed from *Loire*'s bridge. 'We are returning to Madagascar. Do not attempt to hinder our progress.'

The convoy began a ponderous 180-degree turn. Jack fought to control his rage. After all the BEF had done in France. After Dunkirk. Now these Vichy turncoats…

'One round across the bows of the leading ship, please, Gunner,' Jack yelled into his speaking trumpet. 'As close as you like!'

The twelve-pounder coughed and moments later a pillar of water rose ahead of *Cap Ferrat*. The French convoy slowed to a halt. *Loire* stood off to one side. Jack was well aware that the sloop outgunned the South African whalers. An uneasy quiet descended on the scene. He must keep a clear head; react decisively to each twist in this confrontation.

'I intend to board your ships with armed guards and send them to Cape Town for examination,' came the signal from *Gannet*. 'You must not interfere with this operation. Lower ladders immediately.'

Strange signal flags were hoisted on *Loire*. 'TZ, sir,' said Bunts. 'Very odd. It means, "My radio is not working."'

'But we know jolly well their radio is working,' said Jack. 'Must be a private, coded signal. I wonder what it means.'

As *Gannet* came abreast of *Cap Ferrat*, there was a flash, followed by a loud explosion and billowing smoke. So that was the coded signal.

'Sabotage!' said Jack. 'Bastards. Van Zyl, we'll get you aboard her as soon as we can. Looks like the Frogs are trying to scuttle.'

'Sir, the French are abandoning ship on the opposite side!' cried Smit.

'Let's drive them back on board. They won't want to be stuck on a burning ship. Take us around to her starboard side, Cox'n,' Jack said into the voice pipe. 'Bring her in nice and close. PO Joubert, stand by with .303s and Lewis guns.'

'But sir, we can't fire on the French,' said Smit. 'They're our allies!'

'Allies, my arse, Number One. Seaman Potgieter, a single round in the water ahead of the lifeboats.'

The .303 cracked and there was a splash in front of one of the escaping craft. The oars flailed, hesitated.

'Closer, please, Potgieter.' Jack's anger had brought a cold decisiveness.

Another splash clipped the water near the leading boat. It was enough. The Frenchmen turned about and hastened back to their ship. Scrambling up the side, they were forced to fight the fires they'd started.

'Number One, make a general signal to all the French ships that if anyone tries the same trick they'll get the same response.'

Gannet's boat swung out on the davits and an armed party climbed aboard as soon as it touched the water. *Wayfarer* and *Star* trained their guns on *Loire*, lest she try to interfere. The sloop moved behind one of the freighters, making a clear shot impossible.

Van Zyl checked his Webley revolver, then jumped into the boat and took the tiller. He sat with his shoulder pressed against Cummins, who had a rifle propped between his knees. His heart pounding, Van Zyl gave the command: 'Give way together.' Four oars found their purchase and, after a few ragged strokes, their rhythm. The little boat pulled away from *Gannet*, rising and falling on the swell like a scrap of flotsam dwarfed by the vastness of the ocean. Van Zyl pictured the chart: they were in a rowing boat 500 miles from home. If anything went wrong… He tightened his grip on the thwart.

The white blades dipped and heaved, dipped and heaved. Van Zyl felt lightheaded — the exaggerated motion of the boat was nauseating. The rowers were eyeing him as they heaved on their long oars. Could they see his fear? As *Gannet* shrank, the French ship grew, smoke pouring from her stern. Soon, the merchantman towered overhead, blotting out half the sky. Van Zyl's mouth was dry. He pulled his revolver out of its holster. Would they dare to open fire on the South Africans?

'It'll be all right, sir,' whispered Cummins. 'We'll have you covered. So will the *Gannet*.'

Van Zyl nodded, not trusting his voice. The boat drew alongside the steel skyscraper. He mustn't misjudge the timing. Pushing the tiller over, he called out: 'Easy, boat your oars!'

The seamen heaved their blades inboard and the bowman grabbed the Jacob's ladder just as the rowing boat connected the merchantman with a thump of wood on metal.

'Right, men, follow me!' Van Zyl clutched the swaying ladder and began to climb, just as debris rained down on them. Cabbages, rotten tomatoes, eggs, even a spanner. A lobbed potato looked just like a hand grenade. Then a pail of garbage was tipped over the side, landing in the boat. The crew let go and hastily pushed off. Van Zyl was left alone on the swaying ladder. He felt a wave of terror. Should he keep climbing or jump and swim for the boat? He heard rifle cracks from below and bullets ricocheted off the hull above his head. Resistance from the ship abruptly ceased.

The panting sub reached the gunwale, pulling himself over and dropping onto a deserted deck. Heart hammering in his ears, Van Zyl remained at a crouch, revolver aimed at a nearby hatchway. A few moments later, his men began thudding to the deck beside him, rifles unslung and at the ready. There was no Pembroke or Smit to give instructions. His mind was racing. What should he do?

'PO, take three men aft. Get that fire doused. Use Frogs at gunpoint if you need to.'

'Aye, sir!'

'The rest of you, come with me. We must make sure they don't try to sink her. Let's check below first.'

They clattered down a steel ladder into the deserted engine room and spread out, searching for scuttling charges. Turning a corner, Van Zyl stopped dead. On the next deck down, he spotted what looked like a long thin snake. Glancing to the left, he saw it was a fuse, hissing as it burned towards an explosive charge lying beside the boiler.

Panic clawed at his throat as he sprinted along a gangway and down a ladder, his footsteps echoing in the metal chamber. Any moment now, the engine room could blow. Leaping to the deck, he dived for the charge, almost landing on top of it. What now? How did one extinguish the fuse? There was no time to think. He took a chance, ripped the fuse from the device and threw the coil to one side, where it continued to spit and spark. He looked up to see Behardien and Van Reenen staring wide-eyed down at him from the gangway.

'All right, you two, I think we're done here,' Van Zyl said with a trembling voice. 'Come with me to the bridge.'

Van Zyl's shaky legs led them up a ladder to the wheelhouse, only to find the door jammed. He could see figures inside.

'Bloody hell, I've had enough of these Frogs!' Van Zyl cocked his revolver and butted the door with his shoulder. It gave a little. Then he launched himself at the door with all his might and it gave way, to the sound of splitting wood. He tumbled into the wheelhouse, falling at the feet of the Vichy skipper. Behardien and Van Reenen followed him in, aiming their rifles at the Frenchman's chest.

Van Zyl stood up with as much dignity as he could muster. The French captain towered over him, a thin fellow with a handlebar moustache and close-cropped grey hair. He wore a food-stained reefer jacket and white flannels.

'*Capitaine, je voudrais* ... um...' Van Zyl had done a year of French at Stellenbosch before joining up. But his course had failed to prepare him for ship requisitioning.

'Don't bozzer, Lieutenant, I can speak English.'

'I am placing your ship under arrest, Captain.' Van Zyl's voice was high-pitched and angry. His eyes darted around the wheelhouse, looking for potential danger. 'Your crew will be confined to their quarters for the present and placed under guard. Your signalman will notify my ship that *Cap Ferrat* is secured.'

'I must protest —'

'Don't, Capitaine. You and your chief engineer will accompany me to my ship. You are both under arrest.'

'But you cannot —'

'A small word of advice, sir. Do not antagonise my captain. He lost his last ship at Dunkirk, *comprenez*?'

The Frenchman did not answer.

Loire circled the convoy and approached *Gannet* with all her guns trained on the sweeper. Jack watched her anxiously while trying to keep an eye on the other seven ships of his moving chessboard. The situation seemed poised to slip out of his control at any moment. What if the other merchantmen tried to scuttle? All the sweepers would have to send boarding parties and *Loire* would have the advantage.

Jack's shirt was soaked with sweat. He put the speaking trumpet to his lips: 'PO Joubert, prepare to fire on the French sloop! Load high-fragmentation shells and aim at the bridge.'

'Captain! Aft lookout here,' came a shrill cry from the voice pipe. 'Large vessel approaching, green one-seven-oh.'

The raider. They were done for.

Jack dashed to the bridge wing and saw a dark shape to the north. The enemy ship was close. At any moment, she would open fire. Focusing his binoculars on the speck, he felt a surge of relief that left him momentarily lightheaded. It was the eight-inch cruiser HMAS *Fremantle*. The cavalry had arrived, and not a moment too soon. Within a few minutes, he could make her out clearly, lit by the low sun. She presented a handsome sight, her peeling bow wave spread like the wings of a white dove.

At 09:10, HMAS *Fremantle* joined the flotilla, followed shortly thereafter by the cruiser HMS *Hawksbill*.

'Message from *Fremantle*, sir: "Well done, *Southern Gannet* and minesweeping flotilla. Needle in a haystack. I am taking over command. One sweeper to shadow each ship if they attempt to scatter. *Hawksbill* to dispatch boarding parties to all four ships and relieve *Gannet*'s men on *Cap Ferrat*."' The cruiser captain then addressed the *Loire*. 'Please confirm that you will order the convoy to Cape Town.'

The Frenchman replied: 'I confirm that I am absolutely unable to do so. My convoy will return to Madagascar.'

Both the cruisers' guns were now trained on *Loire*. 'If you refuse, I shall be compelled to sink you. I am giving you five minutes.'

After four and a half minutes, *Loire* signalled the French ships to accept boarding parties and stood off to the south. But her captain must again have conveyed some private signal. There was an explosion on *Champagne*.

'Quick as you can, let's help get those sailors from *Hawksbill* on board,' said Jack.

Gannet raced to the three boats, tossed them lines and towed them hastily to the French ship. Just before the minesweeper struck the merchantman, Jack ordered a sharp turn and let go the boats, which glided up to *Champagne*. Armed sailors soon swarmed over the side and shots rang out. There was another detonation and smoke billowed from *Antoinette*. Boats from *Fremantle* rushed to board her too.

Within minutes, resistance had ceased and damage-control parties were being ferried across from the warships to prevent any more destruction. Status reports flashed across to the cruisers: the Vichy-sympathising chief engineer on *Champagne* had detonated charges in her engine room and tried to destroy the steering gear. *Basque* had been in the process of setting scuttling charges, but a revolt by her stokers had prevented serious harm. *Antoinette*'s sailors had set fire to her cargo. The French crews — some willing, some at gunpoint — were enlisted to help put out fires.

By mid-afternoon, all four freighters had been saved, although there was considerable damage. *Champagne* was the worst off, with her engines out of action and the steam steering gear badly mauled. She would have to be taken in tow by *Hawksbill.* All merchant captains and chief engineers were placed under arrest.

Loire stood further off and, once the situation was beyond saving, turned about and headed back to Madagascar. Jack watched the Frenchman disappearing over the horizon: what a strange, hamstrung, conflicted war those Vichy sailors must be having. He didn't envy them the complexity of their fight. Jack thought of Dunkirk and his last glimpse of the French coastline. Nothing but sadness and loss there.

His flotilla and his men had done well, though, and Van Zyl had not let him down. The storm and this engagement had welded them together. Was the ache in his chest perhaps the beginning of pride? But exhaustion was the overriding feeling, like a sea anchor dragging him down. Maybe some rest, soon, but not quite yet.

Their return to the Cape was a slow procession. The minesweepers were joined by the armed merchant cruiser HMS *Carnarvon Castle* and escorted the merchantmen back to Table Bay. HMAS *Fremantle* returned to her patrol in the southern Indian Ocean and HMS *Hawksbill* took up the rear, towing *Champagne* at snail's pace. All four Vichy ships were claimed by the Royal Navy as prizes on account of their resistance and attempted sabotage. The crews were to be either interned or deported.

On board the sweepers, the encounter with the convoy had exhausted any reserves the crew might have had left after battling the storm. Two slow days of northing passed in a haze of four-hour watches and drugged sleep. The airless mess decks had turned rancid; no one had had a chance to wash himself or his clothes properly since leaving Struis Bay. Given the fairer weather, some attempt was made to clean up, wet clothes and equipment laid out on the decks to dry.

Everywhere on *Gannet*, men slept. Even McEwan was slumped against a bulkhead beside his engine, dead to the world. Stoker Jantjies took the opportunity to draw a penis and two hairy testicles on the Scotsman's dome with an indelible pen. Despite all the sniggering, McEwan didn't become aware of the artwork until they reached port.

One benefit of the cold weather had been the preservation of the ice block in the box on the boat deck. Porky was now able to produce a hearty stew from the lamb he'd been saving. For pudding, he treated the men to canned fruit smothered with Nestlé cream from a tin. It was the only culinary highlight. The rest of their meals mostly comprised corned dog and 'hard-tack' ship's biscuit. The ever-creative cook repurposed the bully beef into curries, rissoles and even a passable cottage pie.

On their last night at sea, Brooke was on the starboard bridge lookout when he noticed light on the water.

'Fire, sir, green one-one-oh!'

Van Zyl was officer of the watch and spun around, ready to sound action stations. Then he exhaled. 'It's the moon, Seaman Brooke.'

'Oh, yes, sir. So it is. Sorry about that.'

'Easy mistake to make, Pickles.'

Brooke turned in astonishment. The officer had used his nickname. Van Zyl winked at him, then returned to the binnacle.

As they neared the peninsula, three patrol vessels came out from Cape Town to take over escort duty. The flotilla peeled away and entered False Bay's swept channel. The crews felt like battle-hardened navy men returning from a long fight in —

and with — the South Atlantic. Could it only be a fortnight since they'd left Simon's Town?

Fido emerged to sun herself, and McEwan appeared on deck looking grimy and pale — like a subterranean Morlock from the science-fiction novel he'd been reading. He ambled over to where a group of sailors sat watching the western flank of False Bay coast by.

'Well, lads, I'd be happy to stand you lot to a round of drinks when we get in. I think we all deserve it.' A cheer erupted from the scruffy crop of sailors, along with some banter about 'dickheads' and 'knob-domes'. McEwan didn't notice.

'Aye, Chief, and maybe we'd all better get ourselves cleaned up or they won't let us ashore, let alone into the NAAFI canteen,' said Cummins, grinning. 'A good old scrub all the way from the tips of our toes to the tops of our noggins!'

Sub-Lieutenant Van Zyl and four seamen stood beside the twelve-pounder at their harbour stations. The sweeper took a wide turn, passed the boom and chugged through the bullnose. Fore and aft parties readied themselves with the mooring lines. In a few minutes and with minimal fuss, *Gannet* was alongside, followed in short order by her three sisters.

CHAPTER 26

Four days after laying the mines, *Sturmvogel* was cruising far to the south of the continent when Telegraphist Becker intercepted a British message. It warned all vessels to keep clear of the Agulhas Bank: a mine had detonated itself in shallow water and ships were instructed to remain outside the 100-fathom line until further notice. *SKL* confirmed the report over the radio, stating that a mine had broken free and self-detonated.

'*Gottverdammt*, these shitty mines!' said Falk, leaning over the chart, his face scarlet with anger. 'What species of invertebrate supplies us with mines that are this sensitive? I *knew* they were a mistake.'

Adler tried to mollify his captain: 'Sir, we were assured that these are the very best and the very latest the Reich —'

'Then why on earth are they primed to detonate when they break free? That might be appropriate in the North Sea, where opposing sides use the same patch of water. But down here, every bloody ship is an enemy!'

'Should we try again, sir?' asked Bauer.

Falk looked surprised. 'Yes, Oberleutnant, that is exactly what we are going to do. Let's give the South Africans a couple of weeks to sweep Agulhas, then we shall return and lay again. In the meantime, we will keep to the far south.'

Falk had originally hoped to catch the Norwegian whaling fleet returning from the Antarctic, but he'd arrived in the South Atlantic too late in the season. However, Becker picked up a promising radio transmission from one of the Norwegian factory ships, the *Pingvin*. Due to engine trouble, she had been forced to take shelter among the Prince Edward Islands and was undergoing lengthy repairs. Falk set a south-easterly course, hoping to catch her still there.

For days, the raider made heavy weather, corkscrewing her way through a gale of Wagnerian proportions. Shambling up and down interminable swells, her stern would hang in mid-air for agonising moments, the screw thrashing free of the water, before crashing down in an explosion of spray. The storm increased in ferocity, the waves grew taller, and the ship took a terrible beating. During a lull, they met a Vichy French convoy and exchanged information with the sloop *Loire*, its escort. Then *Sturmvogel* pressed on, deeper into the southern wilderness.

For Sophie, the storm's ferocity was barely credible. She had to grip the sides of her bunk to stop being hurled to the deck. Books took flight from the shelves, bottles and glasses shattered. Heavy coats streamed at right angles from their hooks. Drawers shot out from the chest and the wardrobe banged open, spilling its contents until the captain's quarters resembled the aftermath of a blitz. Yet for the Allied prisoners in the hold, it was far worse. They had little to hold onto and were thrown mercilessly about the deck.

Finally, the storm began to ease, then died away quite suddenly. The sun sank into the clouds behind them as the raider approached Prince Edward Island — the most likely refuge for a stricken ship. The serrated peaks of Marion Island lay to the southeast. Night fell swiftly. *Sturmvogel*'s upright prow sliced through dark water, shaving the island's north shore. The crew had not been this close to land since leaving the Kattegat. They could smell the ammonic stink of guano and the island's earthy, vegetable musk — perfume to nostrils that had forgotten the scent of land. Waves detonated on a black coastline, snow-capped peaks were dimly visible in the night sky. The cry of seabirds filled the air.

'All guns load, load, load! Semi-armour-piercing shells.'

The raider eased closer to the shore, low cliffs looming on the starboard beam.

'Headland coming up, sir,' said Bauer. 'The bay beyond it is the best anchorage.'

In the captain's cabin, Sophie clumsily donned a lifejacket and sat in an armchair listening apprehensively as the raider made ready for battle. The soles of her feet registered the deck's increased vibration as *Sturmvogel's* engine worked up to full revolutions. Nervous energy seemed to be pulsing through the ship. Then the armament shutters banged open giving her a start, the sound echoing off the shore.

Standing behind his captain on the bridge, Bauer thought of the young woman below. Why had he convinced the captain to keep her on board? If only he could protect her.

The raider cleaved round the headland, her guns searching for a target. And there she lay: the *Pingvin*, at anchor, brightly lit and at their mercy. She was modern — tall-flanked with two funnels side by side, a forest of short derricks and a wide slipway at her stern.

'Got him!' cried Falk, clapping Adler on the shoulder. 'A valuable prize and a sitting albatross, eh?'

'Do not use your wireless!' flashed the raider's warning, repeated over the radio. 'This is a German cruiser. Prepare to accept a boarding party. If you resist, I will open fire.'

The Norwegian captain was roused from his bunk by a terrified signalman and appeared on the bridge in pyjamas and dressing gown. 'Do as they say,' said the bearded giant, his voice hoarse with emotion. 'There is no way to stop them.'

Sturmvogel's anchor chain rattled out in a cloud of rusty red dust as her hook plunged to the sandy bottom. The grating sound was music to the crew's ears; they had not heard their anchor since the Baltic, months before. Many had thought they would never hear it again. And here was land. Land once more, so close you could almost lean out and touch it.

Bauer led the boarding operation, which deployed both launches. *Pingvin*'s gangway had been left down with a boat tied on — the Norwegians had obviously been sending parties ashore. It made Bauer's life much easier. But his palms were sweating as he fidgeted with his Luger. Was Sophie watching the scene from her scuttle? And what, exactly, did she feel for him?

Bauer timed his jump as the first launch bumped against the gangway. He scrambled up the ladder, followed in quick order by a line of armed sailors. Reaching the deck, he gave the blubber boiling plant and open cookers a quick glance, then found a companionway to the bridge and raced up a series of ladders, his heart pounding in his ears.

Moments later, Bauer burst into the wheelhouse, flanked by four boarders armed with Schmeissers. Standing before him was a big Norwegian, shoulders back and defiant, despite his pyjamas and bare feet. 'You will be treated well, Captain. No one will be hurt as long as you obey orders.'

'You are Nazi savages,' the Norwegian said in broken German, his lip quivering with rage.

'No, Captain. We are conducting ourselves according to the rules of war. Your ship is a legitimate prize.'

The aging skipper had been too shocked to take the customary precautions. Bauer's search party retrieved the captain's papers, decoding books and a transposition table of the Merchant Navy Code. Once the ship was secured and the prisoners confined to a hold, a prize crew was transferred to *Pingvin*. Bauer returned to *Sturmvogel* with the intelligence booty, including a set of charts, some with Cape Town's swept channels still marked in pencil. He reported to Falk on the bridge.

'Sir, she is carrying nearly 11,000 tons of whale oil, over 5,000 tons of fuel and a crew of 140 with provisions for three months.'

'Very well done, Bauer. She is a rich prize indeed. And the intelligence material is invaluable. This is fine work.' For once, Falk was smiling.

'Thank you, Kapitän.'

'We will transfer what we need and send her to Bordeaux with Oberleutnant Lange and the prize crew. And, Bauer, I want the girl to go with them. The doctor says she has recovered enough.'

'Sir —'

'Bauer, you will not say another word. The girl must go.'

The two vessels lay at anchor beside one another for a few days while *Pingvin*'s repairs were completed. *Sturmvogel* took on fuel, leaving the factory ship with only enough in her tanks to reach France. A gunnery fire-control position was set up on a volcanic mount, so that the 5.9s could fire over the hills at a ship approaching from the west while the raider herself remained unseen. The men were allowed ashore to stretch their legs. They enjoyed a picnic on a pebbled beach, using stores plundered from *Pingvin*, and organised a game of football on an uneven patch of marshy ground. One party visited a bay where they photographed each other with king penguins. Seaman Detmers tried to ride an elephant seal, but it did not end well.

Bauer walked through a mire, the mud sucking at his boots, and climbed a hill to take in the view. From up there, his crew were no bigger than ants. Shouts from the football reached him faintly on the breeze. The two vessels looked like toy ships pinned to a sheet of blue that stretched into the distance, into forever. Insignificant, those two floating hives were no more important than the soaring albatrosses above, or the fur seals on the beach below. No greater, no higher up life's mysterious ladder, than the swaying kelp that stroked the shallows or the lichen encrusting the boulder on which he sat.

Once all the sailors had returned on board, it was time to weigh anchor. And Sophie needed to be transferred to *Pingvin*. Bauer knocked on the door. There was no answer. He turned the handle and opened it a crack.

'May I come in, Fräulein?'

'Yes, Friedrich, you may.'

She was sitting in the captain's armchair, her cheeks showing something of their old rosiness.

'We have prepared a bag with some food and clothes. I hope they fit.'

'It doesn't matter if they don't. I won't be stepping out much.'

'You must take good care of yourself. It is a long voyage to France through enemy waters, but Lange is a fine captain.'

'Enemy waters for you, not for me.'

'You are right, unfortunately.'

'Perhaps we shall meet again, Friedrich. You never know.'

'I do not think so.' He looked disconsolate — and very young.

The ship's horn sounded, its baritone voice echoing off the cliffs. *Pingvin* responded with her own sonorous booming.

'Let me help you.' He took her arm and led her out of the cabin to the gangway. She was dressed in the same clothes — now washed and ironed — that she'd come on board in. Only the shirt was ill-fitting. It was one of Bauer's.

At the brow, she turned to face him. A line of sailors at the rail watched them curiously. 'So long, Lieutenant Bauer,' she said, shaking his hand. They looked into each other's eyes for a few seconds.

'*Auf Wiedersehen*, Sophie. One day. Maybe.'

CHAPTER 27

As the flotilla would be in port for a few days before returning to Agulhas, Jack was desperately keen to see Clara again. Lieutenant Wilson had told him about a dance for officers of the armed forces at Kelvin Grove Club, so, at the first opportunity, he phoned the house in Newlands. Mrs Marais answered.

'Oh hello, Jack. Clara was just talking about you.'

'Your daughter has told me lots about you too, Mrs Marais. Especially your SAWAS work.'

'Just doing our bit, dear. We've got another big convoy in town.'

'The logistics must be a nightmare. May I speak to —'

'You have no idea. When a convoy leaves, it's as though a locust swarm has passed through Cape Town.'

'Mrs Marais, I —'

'There isn't a tomato or a lettuce leaf to be found. Think about it, Jack, a ship like the *Queen Mary* wants 144,000 eggs.'

'May I please —'

'Oh, yes, of course, dear, here's me rattling on. I'll call her.'

Clara finally came on the line.

'I missed you,' he said.

'Missed you too.'

'I was wondering… There's a dance at Kelvin this weekend.'

'I know, my ma is helping to organise it.'

'So, would you —'

'Like to risk dancing in the vicinity of your feet again?'

'Yes, I know, um —'

'Of course I would, silly!'

It was agreed that he would pick her up on Saturday at eight.

Dressed in his best uniform, Jack took the train to Newlands. The Marais home was close to the station: a rambling house in a garden that backed onto the Liesbeek River. Opening the gate, he walked up a winding path through beds of tall hydrangeas. On the veranda, he straightened his tie, then tapped the doorknocker. A statuesque woman with grey curls opened.

'Jack, good to meet you in the flesh.'

'Good evening, Mrs Marais.'

'Clara isn't ready yet, I'm afraid. Come through to the lounge.'

The room had dark stinkwood furniture, Persian rugs, a piano and a grandfather clock. A large Pye wireless sat on the mantelpiece blaring the SABC's 'Snoektown Calling'. Mrs Marais switched it off and took a seat in the armchair. Jack perched on the leather sofa.

'A little sherry, perhaps?'

'I don't —'

'I'm having.' She proffered a winning smile.

'Oh, all right, that would be lovely, thank you.'

She rang a bell and the maid arrived with a decanter and two glasses.

'How are you enjoying South Africa, Jack?'

'Very much indeed. It was good to get out from under the Blitz. I think I can do my bit just as well at the Cape. As you are doing so admirably with the SAWAS.'

'Yes, well, it keeps me on my toes. In fact, SAWAS has enlisted 100 girls for tonight's dance at Kelvin and I've organised an excellent band, Raye Levine and her dance orchestra. I do hope you enjoy yourself. Kelvin has a beautifully sprung ballroom floor. Clara tells me you're an enthusiastic dancer.' Mrs Marais had a wickedly innocent smile.

'You mentioned there was a convoy in town?' he said, hastily changing the subject.

'Yes, a big one. They've dumped 30,000 troops on me who all want pampering, girls, films, food. We're laying on additional trains, buses and tickets purchased in bulk. We've arranged for farmers to bring in extra produce. Bakeries are working through the night. Eggs and bacon are a favourite — our hens also have to work overtime. I've seen soldiers devouring half a dozen eggs in one go.'

'There's a terrible shortage back in Blighty.'

'You'll be pleased to know that SAWAS has adopted the South African minesweeping service.'

'Yes, I heard, thank you.'

'We'll be sending you lots of woollen goods, and our girls will write letters to your sailors.'

'I know my men really appreciate it.'

Clara entered the room wearing a glamorous full-length pink satin dress. For a moment, Jack could not find any words.

'You can take the car, Clara.' Mrs Marais filled in for the tongue-tied lieutenant. 'Back by midnight, *skapie*.'

'*Ja*, Ma, just like Cinderella,' Clara said, pecking her mother on both cheeks.

It was a short drive to Kelvin Grove.

'Did you see the cartoon in the *Cape Times* on Wednesday?' Clara asked as they turned into Campground Road.

'No, I seldom get the chance to read newspapers.'

'It showed a strapping Royal Navy sailor in bellbottoms walking hand in hand with a tiny chap in tropical rig, representing the South Africans. Over his shoulder he had a rod with four toy ships in the shape of fish. The caption read: "Catch of the day: something Vichy!"'

'Very clever.'

'The little officer in the tropical rig looked just like you. Well, to my eyes anyway.'

Clara parked the Plymouth under a palm tree and the pair joined a queue beside the gabled portico. They were handed glasses of punch at the door and found a table beside the dancefloor. The ballroom was already nearly full: officers in dress uniform and young women in long dresses.

'Tonight, we *are* going to dance,' said Clara. 'A lot.'

'Oh dear, I'd like to blame my last performance on the dicky leg, but the fact is I'm just not very good.'

'Practice, Jack, practice. Come on, let's give it a go.'

The band was playing a series of Paul Jones round dances which gave everyone the opportunity to change partners and helped break the ice. As things became increasingly rowdy, Jack found that he was rather enjoying himself.

After a while, the couple paused for another glass of punch, but were interrupted by a waltz.

'This one, I know how to do: one-two-three and a one-two-three,' said Jack. 'Put your drink down. Let's grab it while we can.'

He took her in his arms. She was light as air, her movements fluid as they glided across the floor. Having set his mind to it, he was doing all right.

'Not bad, Jack, have you been practising on the deck of your boat?'

Jack just grinned. He felt emboldened to ask a question that had long been on his mind. 'By the way, who was that chap you were with at Admiralty House?'

'That was Henry, one of my brother's flying pals. I've known him for years.'

'Just a friend?'

'Ye-es, a close friend. You're rather nosy, Jack. We hardly know each other.'

'I intend to jolly well change that, Miss Marais.'

Clara smiled her charming, inscrutable smile and his head spun with the waltz, the flickering candlelight and the dreamy unreality of it all.

It was suddenly, incomprehensibly, 11:30. By then, Jack had struggled manfully through the rumba and the foxtrot, but best of all, he'd been with Clara, without interruption, for three blissful hours.

She drove them home, where they stood on the garden path for a long time talking.

He took her hand. 'I know I made a hash of things the first time we met. And the second. And probably even the third. But I so enjoyed this evening. I hope we can do this again sometime.'

'Yes, Jack, that would be nice.'

'Clara, I know you think I'm a bit stuck-up and a bit serious.'

'A bit?'

'All right, quite a lot. But I had rather a rough time before I came out to the Cape. And having a first command has not been easy.'

'Are those violins I hear?' She smiled up at him. 'What were you just saying about being a bit serious?'

'It's just that … I really do like you. Very much.'

He looked down at his shoes to hide the emotion in his eyes. She reached out and touched his cheek.

'Clara, is that you?' It was her mother calling from the darkened stoep.

'*Ja*, Ma, I'm coming. Just saying goodnight to Jack.'

'Don't go,' he whispered.

'I have to go.'

'We're going back to sea for a long —'

She was in his arms, her lips against his, soft and searching. He pressed her body to his. They kissed ravenously, achingly.

She pulled away. 'Jack, I do have to go.'

'I know.' He held both her hands, their fingers entwined.

'Phone me when you have liberty again.' With that, she let go and disappeared up the garden path, seemingly swallowed by the hydrangeas.

CHAPTER 28

'Stop engine!'

The flotilla was off Cape Agulhas once again, midway through a long sweep. *Gannet*'s trembling died away and she idled to a halt in a glassy sea. The otter had fouled something. Since they were in a suspected minefield, chances were the fouler was deadly.

The Indian Ocean was like velvet — an unruffled navy blue. Only the low pulse of the other ships disturbed the morning's stillness. A hoist of signal flags announced that *Gannet*'s sweep was out of action. The other three ships flew answering pennants and hove to, wisps of steam leaking from their exhausts as they wallowed in the gentle swell.

'Don't ask her to dance, she might be prickly,' came the flashed signal from *Wayfarer*.

'No chance,' answered *Gannet*. 'I like them thinner and not wearing widow's weeds.'

Jack lit a Cavalla and ran a finger along the scar on his temple. What should he do?

'I'll go, sir,' said Van Zyl.

'What did you say, Sub?'

'I'll go and have a look. Might be snagged on a wreck or fouled by fishing nets.'

'Are you sure? We could just sever the line.'

'No, sir, we've lost too much gear already.'

Jack weighed up the offer. Van Zyl was probably right: so much damage had been caused by fouled sweeps, and mines destroying floats and kites, that they were in danger of having to return to Simon's Town before completing the job again.

'Very well, let's give it a go. But we need you in one piece at the end of this. Don't do anything silly.'

'No, sir, not on your life.'

A few minutes later, *Gannet*'s davits swung outboard and her boat was lowered. PO Cummins and Seaman Ellis rowed Van Zyl over to the bobbing Oropesa. The crew had gathered on the main deck or taken cover behind gear as far away from the potential detonation as possible. Jack watched through his binoculars, feeling a sense of foreboding. Why had he given in and allowed his second officer to go? It wasn't worth the risk.

Jack clenched his teeth as the boat drew level with the Oropesa.

Van Zyl had also begun to regret his rash suggestion. What on earth had he been thinking? In the bottom of the boat lay a marlinspike and various tools, including a butcher's cleaver provided by Porky, in case the obstacle needed to be cut free. They looked like the implements of murder. Van Zyl peered into the inky water, numb with apprehension. It was too murky to make out the problem. He pulled off his clothes and laid them on the sternsheets. He was already shivering and not only from the cold. Glancing back at *Gannet*, he saw his captain watching. Van Zyl felt the sharp sting of misgiving.

'Good luck, sir,' said Cummins.

Giving a thumbs-up, Van Zyl lowered himself gingerly over the side. The water was freezing. Every instinct told him to climb back in the boat. Tipping forward, he dived down the wire, swimming breaststroke, kicking hard and going deep until his lungs were bursting. Nothing. He rose to the surface.

'Can't see a ruddy thing down there, PO,' he gasped.

'Temperature, sir?'

'Arctic.' His teeth chattered. He'd begun to hyperventilate.

'Give it up, sir. Just now you blow us all to high heaven. Let's cut our losses and cut the sweep.'

'I'll have another go.' Van Zyl took a gulp of air and dived. This time he went deeper and spotted the dark orb snagged beside the otter. For some reason it hadn't exploded. He kicked back to the surface.

'It's a mine all right, PO,' he blurted. 'Give me that cleaver and let's see if I can't dislodge it from below. The thing's hanging on by a thread.'

'Be careful, for heaven's sake, sir.'

'I'll try to cut it free. Row a little way off, PO. You don't want the thing surfacing underneath you.'

Van Zyl took a deep breath and dived again, swimming down the wire towards the dark sphere. All of a sudden, the mine broke free and shot towards him like a big rubber ball. He gave a few panicked kicks as the spiky rocket hurtled past him and burst to the surface, fifteen yards from the boat. Van Zyl swam to the surface to find Cummins and Ellis in a state of mild shock.

'Bloody hell, sir! Bloody, bloody hell,' said Cummins as his unsteady hands helped Van Zyl aboard. They rowed back to the ship in stunned silence.

The trembling sub was helped aboard, wrapped in a blanket and given a few slaps on the back. Cummins ushered him below to the engine room and through to the stokehold where he was left to thaw out in front of the furnaces. Van Zyl could never have imagined himself enjoying the engine room so much. A pleasantly painful tingling announced the return of blood to parts of his body that had resigned themselves to wartime austerity.

Soon, Van Zyl heard the stutter of machine-gun fire, followed by the mine's detonation. It was as though *Gannet* had been struck by a giant sledgehammer. For a few moments, he was quite deaf and the stokehold appeared to be vibrating. It took a while to realise that the end of the world had not, in fact, arrived. At least he now knew what it would be like to stick one's head inside Big Ben when it tolled.

The flotilla completed a long sweep that brought them far to the east of Struis Bay. As it was a Sunday, Jack decided to stop work at lunchtime and anchor for the night in Marcus Bay. There was a fishing village on the headland at Arniston and a pleasant beach, or so Van Zyl assured him.

'I have an uncle in Bredasdorp. We used to go swimming at Waenhuiskrans in the summer holidays.'

'Where's Waenhuiskrans? I didn't see it on the chart.'

'It's another name for Arniston. It literally means "Wagon House Cliff". There's a big cave near the anchorage.'

The flotilla steered towards a cluster of thatched, whitewashed cottages on a bluff above a bay of emerald water. Through his binoculars, Jack scanned the low, limestone cliffs and row of brightly coloured fishing boats drawn up on a slip.

Anchor chains clattered through the hawse pipes and the sweepers came to rest in the lee of a rocky headland. Skippers granted their crews a few hours of make and mend, and Jack's old bathing costume fluttered from the gaff to indicate that swimming was permitted. Soon men were diving into the luminous water — even Smit pulled on his maroon trunks and jumped in. A makeshift water-polo game was arranged with the crew of *Belle*. As the water was cold, the game was short, with the Belles emerging victorious. A jovial bunch of swimmers climbed back on board and sponged themselves down with fresh water in the forecastle's washroom.

The cook had asked Sparks to radio ahead and arrange for fresh provisions from a farmer friend of Van Zyl. Porky and Van Zyl rowed ashore under cloak-and-dagger secrecy and returned from Kassiesbaai beach with a mound of food hidden under a tarpaulin. That night's dinner was going to be a surprise.

Jack, too, took the opportunity to have a swim. He changed into bathing trunks, climbed onto the rail and executed a graceless swallow dive. He swam towards the descending sun and the rocky ledges that lined the cliff. The exercise felt good for his leg. Treading water, he admired the scene before him. Tendrils of smoke drifted from the thatched cottages, a dog barked, someone in the village was playing an accordion.

Jack turned to look at *Gannet*. How could he ever have found her unattractive? Now he wouldn't swap her for HMS *Hood* (may the good ship's soul rest in peace). With her high whale-catcher bow, low-slung midriff and cruiser stern, *Gannet* was a handsome vessel in her own modest way.

More even than the ship, it was her hodgepodge South African crew that he'd grown attached to. In a matter of only a few months, the odd assortment of men had been moulded into an effective sailing unit. Schoolboys, a lawyer-to-be, a motor mechanic, shop assistant, train driver — no doubt the odd petty thief. But good men. The grind of daily sweeping and the moments of terror had done their work.

The sun dipped behind the headland and Jack swam slowly back to his ship.

Porky had managed to procure a whole sheep from the farmer. Supper that night was roast lamb with Yorkshire pudding and flavoursome gravy. There was a loud 'Three cheers for the cook' as the men ate their meal topside, not wanting to miss the pyrotechnic sky. Van Zyl brought his gramophone up to the boat deck and Cummins did the cranking. Tommy Dorsey's band had the whole crew singing along to 'Blue Moon' as the lights of Arniston waltzed in the shallows and the smell of grilling fish wafted across the bay to the sweepers.

Before turning in, the men asked Stoker Hughes to recite one of the bawdy poems he'd memorised for just such occasions. 'Give us the one about Eskimo Nell!' cried Lofty.

'Aw, not that one again!' Hughes groaned.

'Come on, Spikey, we love you, honest,' said Lofty.

'Spikey, Spikey, Spikey!' came the chant from the others.

'Oh, all right then, listen up:

'*Gather 'round, all ye whorey!*
Gather 'round and hear my story!
When a man grows old, and his balls grow cold,
And the tip of his prick turns blue,
Far from a life of Yukon strife,
He can tell you a tale or two.
So pull up a seat, and buy me one neat
And a tale to you I will tell,
About Dead-Eye Dick and Mexican Pete,
And a harlot named Eskimo Nell...'

CHAPTER 29

Sturmvogel was back in South African waters. Approaching from the southeast, she simulated a freighter inbound from Australia. The raider was disguised as a Panamanian ship and had acquired a coat of brown paint, green-and-white funnel bands, an extra mast and sham patches of rust appropriate to a tramp steamer plying South Atlantic routes. Her deck armament was concealed behind screens now emblazoned with the words 'General Motors New York'. Nearing the continent, a lookout sighted the mast of another ship, which he reported as a merchantman. Falk was committed to a quick Agulhas run and decided not to turn away, relying on their disguise. Too late, the lookout's mistake become apparent.

'Kapitän, it's an enemy cruiser!' came the cry.

'*Verdammt*!' Falk banged the bulkhead with his fist. 'Battle stations! Bauer, put the codebooks in a weighted bag. Wireless Officer Zimmermann must have his most powerful transmitter tuned to the Berlin wavelength and be ready to give *SKL* our details. Prepare to scuttle. Adler, tell the crew to be ready to abandon ship.'

'But, sir —'

'Do not worry, Korvettenkapitän, we will fight first. But she is a cruiser and *Sturmvogel* must not be taken.'

'I think she's HMS *Durban*, Danae-class, light cruiser,' said Bauer, looking through his binoculars and consulting the recognition charts pinned to the bulkhead. 'About thirty knots, six-inch guns.'

'Thank you, Oberleutnant, we might just have a chance against one of the Danaes if she comes too close. They're old ships — Great War vintage.'

When the cruiser was five miles away, she flashed the signal 'NNJ'.

'What does it mean, sir?' asked Bauer.

'He's requesting our recognition signal,' said Falk. 'Many merchant ships are clueless, so let's try to bluff it. Give our ship's name and see how she responds.'

The signalman flashed, '*Bahia*, Panama,' with slow, deliberate clicking of the shutters. There was a long pause. Below decks, the tension was thick as fog. Gun crews crouched at their weapons, praying they would not be called upon to use them.

'He's thinking,' said Falk. Every eye on the bridge was locked onto the grey mote on the western horizon. *Sturmvogel* ran up the Panamanian flag to the gaff and Bahia's recognition signals amidships — 'PKQY', just as they were listed in Lloyd's.

'Where from?' came the cruiser's flashes.

'Melbourne,' said Falk.

'Where bound?' Signalman Weber replied.

'Montevideo.'

There was another interminable pause. Falk watched the cruiser's six-inch guns tracking *Sturmvogel.*

Below, the crew peered nervously through portholes where they could, or relied on messages from the bridge. Each man had his survival kit, a lifejacket and a few personal belongings tucked into pockets: a photograph, letters, chocolate. Many turned to prayer, or to the rosary, making any number of unrealistic promises to their deity.

'I wish you a happy voyage,' came the eventual response.

'Thank you. Same to you.' The enemy cruiser changed course and sped off to the northeast, disappearing into the dusk. Falk looked around at the men in the wheelhouse. Their faces betrayed the draining away of pent-up strain. It had been too close for comfort. He would lay one more minefield, he decided, then shift his area of operation to the central Indian Ocean.

The sea was calm and phosphorescence lit their wake; Cape Agulhas Lighthouse could be seen from fifty miles out. The evening was luminous, too clear for Falk's liking. Fortunately, there was a cold front on the western horizon, which would mask his withdrawal.

'Release!' Sailors at the stern heaved on their jacks as the first mine squealed down the tracks and tipped over the side. A moment later there was a splash in their creamy wake. The box-shaped sinker and mine disappeared in a shower of water stars.

Falk stood looking aft, his hands behind his back. He pictured the mine sliding into the inky depths, parting from its sinker and rising towards the surface. A deadly hat trick. Now you see me, now you don't, now you're dead. The first mine was ready, primed, lying in wait for an enemy ship. Just then, he had a clear picture of his three daughters in their Lübeck beds. The grandfather clock ticking in the hall. A scene of eternal, loving peace. The image sent a chill of terror through him.

Jack's flotilla had spent the day sweeping to the south of Cape Infanta. An icy breeze blew from the west, precursor to an approaching cold front. They were heading for the shelter of St Sebastian Bay in the late afternoon when a coded message with a priority rating beeped in the wireless cabin. Sparks grabbed his pencil and wrote down the ciphers. Sensing the urgency, he quickly thumbed through the codebook.

'Enemy ship suspected in area...' The captain of HMS *Durban* had had second thoughts about the Panamanian freighter he'd spoken earlier, and had radioed headquarters to check on her legitimacy. Simon's Town had in turn called up C-in-C South Atlantic. *Bahia* was meant to be in the Caribbean.

Sparks scribbled the co-ordinates and sprinted to the bridge. 'Urgent message to *Gannet*, sir.' He handed the flimsy to his skipper.

Jack took one glance and said, under his breath, 'The raider, it's got to be.' His mind was racing. The chance to hit back. This was it. 'Van Zyl!' he bellowed.

The sub-lieutenant scrambled to the bridge, received instructions and dashed to the chartroom, where he hastily plotted the co-ordinates, then reappeared on the bridge. 'Yes, sir, our sector.'

'All right, then. Make to flotilla: "Line abreast, patrol due southwest, suspected raider in vicinity."'

The Aldis lamp clacked out Jack's signal and he watched the acknowledging dah-dit-dahs from the other ships. Southwest they sailed, into the gathering darkness. The men stayed at action stations longer than normal, on edge in the dusk, then stood down for supper. Jack doubled the lookouts after dark and continued to scan the horizon with his binoculars, unwilling to leave the bridge even for a moment.

It was after midnight and Falk stared at the black outline of the enemy coast. Low cloud, a few scudding stars. Another set of mines was ready to be laid. Then came the cry from his lookouts — vessels to seaward.

Falk knew he was trapped: four sweepers silhouetted against a rising moon. Obscured by the headland, the raider had not been spotted. But not for long. Falk knew he had to strike first. The night of his dread had arrived.

'Full speed ahead, hard aport,' he ordered.

The telegraph in the engine room jangled and the brass pointer jerked to 'full ahead'. Chief Engineer Fuchs leapt from his stool and bellowed at his men. The ship worked herself up to full revolutions, the screw's hammering vibration transmitting itself through the hull. Even up on the bridge it felt as though *Sturmvogel* were tearing herself apart. Rivets protested, wood creaked and the deck shook as the raider's prow split the ocean into peeling white sheets. Gun shields clattered open, exposing her fangs.

A star shell fired from the raider whined overhead and burst its magnesium radiance above the minesweepers. Silver light inundated sky and sea. To Jack, caught in a moment of terrifying confusion, it appeared surreal — the glare too bright, the shadows too black. His flotilla was perfectly illuminated for the German gunners. The rippling flashes of a full broadside lit up both the distant raider and the underbelly of the clouds.

Sitting ducks. Action stations sounded through the sweepers as the first rounds streaked in. There was a mad clattering of feet as sailors grabbed Mae Wests and tin hats and sprinted to their stations.

'Emergency full ahead!' Jack shouted down the voice pipe. 'Hard astarboard.' *Gannet* slewed round in a tight arc. 'Bunts, make to flotilla: "Attack line abreast."' Where *Gannet* had been the lead ship, she was now at the tail of the group.

Jack heard Smit speaking into the voice pipe. 'Make to Combined Operations Room: "Enemy raider in sight. Minesweeping flotilla engaging." Give our speed, course and position.'

'Bosun, run up the battle ensign, if you please,' said Jack.

A few moments later, the big flag bobbed up the mast, a white smudge in the darkness. Water plumes rose between *Wayfarer* and *Star*; men on both vessels fell to the deck as shock waves punched their ships. *Wayfarer* was lifted out of the water. Jack watched anxiously as her prow emerged from the collapsing spray.

'Open fire when you're ready, Guns!' he called through the speaking trumpet. There was a flash of orange as the twelve-pounder banged, sending a waft of nostril-stinging cordite across the bridge. Jack's throat constricted, a feeling of being strangled.

The pom-poms could not be brought to bear and were still out of range. *Crash!* The twelve-pounder spoke again. 'Guns, put one star shell in the spout, 6,000 yards, green ten!' he shouted.

Seconds later, the horizon lit up. Jack could see the enemy clearly, a distant black shape spitting fire. Five white columns stood up like evil water sprites, bracketing *Wayfarer*.

'Cox'n, steer towards the explosions!' shouted Captain Wilson as his ship weaved this way and that, trying to loosen the German gunners' grip.

Jack knew he had to close the range, or they'd be picked off. He called down to the engine room for the kitchen sink. McEwan responded immediately, driving his engine to its limit, beyond its limit, risking disaster for a few extra revolutions.

Jack's mind was clear. This time, he would not turn away. He tried not to think of the raider's superior armament and speed. His legs shook, but he clamped his jaw shut, grinding his teeth. He focused his whole being on the enemy.

Below him, PO Joubert stood on the forecastle yelling fire orders in a high-pitched voice: 'Load, load, load!'

Cloete crouched over the traverse handles, his eyes glued to the sighting telescope. 'On, on, on!' he cried.

'Fire!' screamed Joubert. A tongue of flame and whiplash slam as the twelve-pounder recoiled on its springs. The empty brass case, like a spent husk, slid out of the breech and clanked to the deck in a cloud of fumes.

'Load, load, load!' A sailor grabbed another shell from the ready-use locker to feed into the breech.

Jack peered anxiously through his binoculars, watching for the fall of shot. A small feather rose well short of the target.

'Up 400!' came the cry.

Shells rained down around *Wayfarer* like hornets. Her hull clanged as holes were punched through the plating. Captain Wilson kept weaving erratically, but it was only a matter of time.

An ear-splitting *crack!* Jack watched in horror as *Wayfarer*'s prow erupted in flame. Deadly fragments flew in every direction. The gunnery officer was swept from the bandstand in a broken, cartwheeling mess. *Wayfarer*'s forecastle had been transformed into an obscenity of blood, severed limbs ... pieces of flesh that had, moments before, been men.

Another shell found its target. The coxswain died instantly as a splinter pierced his heart. *Wayfarer* carved an arc to port and came to a stop. Captain Wilson dragged himself towards the binnacle, an unlit pipe still clamped between his teeth. The lookout sat in a pool of blood staring at the place where his legs used to be.

The next shell penetrated deep inside the hull. The effect was catastrophic — a flash of light at the core of the explosion, and then the ship reared up, breaking its back. Funnel, masts and deck plating were hurled like chaff into the sky. When the hateful squall subsided, there was no ship to be seen, just a chunk of her stern, barely afloat. Debris and body pieces splashed into the sea like the Devil's manna.

Watching in horror, Jack beat the rail with his fist.

Glancing to starboard, he saw that *Star* had been straddled, disappearing behind two columns of water. He held his breath. The pugnacious prow burst out of the maelstrom and her gun spat fire. His heart lifted. *Good for you, Du Toit!*

Van Zyl appeared on the bridge. 'No damage, sir, other than a few holes. No leaks either.'

Another bang.

'*Star*'s been hit, Captain!' cried Smit. 'She's on fire.'

Jack turned to see ugly fingers of flame around *Star*'s wheelhouse. But her twelve-pounder fired again and the thunder rolled over them. The gun crew were still at it. There was a glint on the enemy superstructure, then smoke. They were hitting back. But the raider had found the range on *Star* and fired once more. The sweeper was hit amidships, below the waterline. She slowed, listing heavily to starboard, until she came to a halt and began sinking. Jack watched as codebooks were dumped over the side in a weighted bag.

Star's deck was littered with dead and wounded. Sailors lowered the boat, others manhandled a Carley to the rail. The engine room was a disaster — steam pipes had burst, ejecting scalding air. Water gushed in from a large hole. The ladder had been blown free of its fastenings. The only surviving stoker was trapped. Sobbing, he knew he was doomed. *Star*'s bosun was about to abandon ship when he heard a keening sound from below. He called a sailor to help him wrench open a grating and grabbed the badly scalded stoker, borne aloft by the rising water. As they pulled him up on deck, the skin of his forearms came off as easily as silk gloves.

The next shell hit the wheelhouse. Du Toit was thrown twenty feet into the air and landed on the listing main deck. He watched the perpendicular chaos with a misty detachment. A figure crawled past him. It was his second in command, Forsythe, his right-hand man. Forsythe turned to him, but he was without a face. The skin had been burnt clean away, leaving only loosely spaced holes.

Then slowly everything righted itself. Either that, or the ship had heeled over. This impression was reinforced by the objects sliding past him. A block, a shell casing, a hand. Now he was sliding too, into the scuppers where an assortment of goods covered him. Water lapped at his body. A fog descended and he blacked out, unconscious when the foremast fell on him, crushing his ribcage.

Southern Star rolled over, briefly exposing her keel before sliding into a vortex of smoke and debris. Survivors in the water cheered *Gannet* as she swept past, still bowling at the enemy, her singed battle ensign standing out stiffly.

Shells from the raider continued to arrive with a wheezing rush. One of them exploded alongside *Gannet*, transmitting an almighty shudder that reached from her keel to the inside of Jack's skull. An avalanche of water cascaded down on *Gannet*'s forecastle, knocking some of the gunners off their feet. The sweeper bounced across angry water as though driving over rocky ground.

Jack heard a heavy thud to starboard and the high-pitched whistle of escaping steam. *Belle* had been hit behind her funnel and was visibly slowing. Her mizzenmast toppled over, draping the rigging across her boat deck in a mess of halyards and aerial cables.

'Bunts, make to *Belle*: "Can you keep up?"'

Alstad flashed an immediate reply: 'Sorry, main steam pipe hit. Taking water. Over to you, Jack. England expects...'

Bang! Gannet's bridge lit up as though a flashbulb had gone off. Jack was thrown to the deck. Smoke curled around him; there was a ringing sound and a terrible shaking that seemed to come from inside him. He crawled to the voice pipe and used it to pull himself half upright. He was disoriented, lightheaded. 'Damage report, engine room.' His voice was hoarse, choking on the smoke.

'All right doon here, I s'pose,' came a wobbly voice.

Jack realised their gun had stopped shooting. 'Number One, why aren't we firing, for fuck's sake? Number One!'

He raised himself to look over the windbreak. The forecastle had taken a direct hit and was now an abattoir. Four men lay around the twelve-pounder, their bodies cut to ribbons. Only PO Joubert stood in their midst, stunned but unscathed. Shells and brass casings rolled from side to side around him as the minesweeper pressed on, toothlessly, towards the raider. One figure got up and staggered towards the open breech, mortally wounded and half blinded. He clutched a shell in his sound arm; the other was severed at the elbow and dangled at his side in strips of flesh.

'Number One!' yelled Jack.

'Smit has been hit, sir,' said Van Zyl, coming up the ladder.

Jack looked around the bridge as if seeing it for the first time. He stared at his two officers as if through gauze, not immediately comprehending. Van Zyl was kneeling over Smit, who appeared to have a hole in his stomach. The starboard lookout was slumped in the corner. Half his head was missing, pieces of his brain spread across the deck boards.

Jack reached for the speaking trumpet: 'Cookie, get up here with your first-aid kit, now!' The portly AB came clattering up the ladder. 'Look after Number One!'

Jack's mind had begun to clear. With nerves screaming like an air-raid siren, legs trembling and fists gripping the windbreak, he stared in hatred at the approaching raider as *Gannet* continued her erratic zigzagging. *Belle* had fallen far astern and was largely out of the fight. *Sturmvogel*'s broadsides crept closer, her gunners now free to focus on a single target. The sweeper's twelve-pounder was quickly manned by a scratch crew. This motley bunch of non-gunners was the last sting in the flotilla's tail.

Another salvo rumbled over them like a freight train and exploded in the sea just astern of *Gannet*. White-hot splinters sprayed the deck. A shower deluged the poop deck, tasting more of cordite than seawater.

'Hard aport!' shouted Jack.

Anticipating the order, February had already begun the turn. As the sweeper heeled over, describing a sickening curve, a pair of shells exploded in her wake. Jack had judged the turn to precision. Now they were close enough for the lighter guns of both ships to join the fight.

'Secondary armament, fire at will,' ordered Jack. He'd committed everything. There was no turning back. He sensed a great howling within, like the sound of a Stuka wedded to his own rage, his burning will.

Gannet's pom-pom opened up, followed by *Sturmvogel*'s twin thirty-seven mm and then her twenty mm cannons. Tracer shells arced lazily skyward, then rushed down, tormenting the sea around the sweeper. At first, Lofty and Brooke's fire was more accurate than the German's. The pom-pom immediately found the raider, spitting a stream of shells across the enemy's superstructure. The German's secondary gunners struggled to lock onto the tiny, weaving target. Tracer hosed the water around *Gannet*. Then they found her. The sweeper clanged and thudded under a stream of lead that turned metal to sieve.

On the forecastle, Potgieter was killed instantly by a twenty mm round through the groin. A wounded PO Joubert wrenched the smoking body from the twelve-pounder and took his place at the gunsight. Behardien left his Lewis gun and, despite a shoulder wound, ran to the forecastle to assist; Hughes emerged from below to help load. Joubert had the raider's bridge in his sights. He reached for the firing lever and pressed. The shell spiralled in a great parabola towards the enemy and found a fortunate home, exploding just forward of *Sturmvogel*'s funnel.

'A hit!' Van Zyl yelled maniacally. Jack's expression was set in a savage grimace.

Shrapnel tore through the raider's wheelhouse. Falk dropped to one knee and doubled up. A sailor was screaming that he'd been blinded.

'Kapitän!' cried Bauer. 'Are you all right?'

A stain spread across Falk's shoulder and chest. Agony was etched on his face. 'Hard aport,' said Adler. 'Keep her zigzagging.'

'Lift me up, Bauer,' said the captain, his face white.

'Sir, you are badly injured.'

'Maybe. But that doesn't matter. Must save the ship. Make smoke. Get away to the south.'

'No, we will destroy them first,' said Adler coldly. 'This one and the damaged one. You are not in a fit condition, Kapitän. I am taking command.'

'Turn away, damn it!' hissed Falk. 'Make smoke. A single sweeper will not follow us.' His voice came in painful gasps. 'Don't risk a crippling hit. Our only hope is … is to get … to get far south … by dawn.' Falk slumped in Bauer's arms, his gaze fixed on his second officer.

'Sir, sir —'

Falk's eyes registered nothing.

'Damn it, Adler, you heard him.' Bauer's voice was quaking.

'The Kapitän is dead. I am in command.'

'You bloody fool.'

'If you say another word, I will have you court-martialled when we return to Kiel.'

'Return?' spat Bauer, an incredulous expression on his face.

Although two German guns were out of action, the rest still fired. Blue-white tracer lines streaked in flat trajectories across the wave tops. Their splashes crept across the water to pluck Joubert from his position. 'Get to the fo'c'sle, Sub,' said Jack. 'See what you can do.'

Van Zyl scrambled down the ladder and across the deck. Hughes rammed a shell into the breech. Van Zyl slipped into Joubert's position and peered through the sights. It took a moment for his vision to adjust to the misty glass. Then he saw it. A gash in the enemy's side, just aft of the main superstructure, revealed a row of black pods illuminated by lights within the hull. A last roll of the dice. He spun the wheel and trained the crosshairs on the hole. Van Zyl wiped the sweat from his eye and took careful aim. Left a little. Left a little more. Now!

He pressed the firing lever. A dazzling muzzle flash. The sight pad smashed his eye socket as the gun recoiled on its springs. Van Zyl reeled backwards and fell to the deck as though he'd been punched. Cordite seared his nostrils. Without earplugs, he was momentarily deafened. Rubbing his black eye, he sat up and looked at the raider. There was no sign of a hit. His shot must have gone high.

Despair engulfed him.

Then he saw a sparkle, followed by a blinding flash and a roar. A hit! He'd hit the raider! Fire spat from the hole in the enemy's side, followed by the rumble of persistent thunder, rising to a crescendo. The mines detonated in a chain reaction, followed by the boilers. *Sturmvogel* atomised in a terrific eruption. Van Zyl stared in bewilderment: his act had reaped catastrophe. A ball of orange flame climbed into the sky, swirling and seething in its own mushroom cloud.

Shock waves swept over *Gannet*, hurling men to the deck. The air filled with raining metal that splashed into the sea around them, hissing like meteorites. When the iron hail subsided, Jack's shaky voice called down to the engine room: 'All right, Chief, you can take the kettle off the gas.'

'Hell's bells, thank bloody Christ,' McEwan replied, 'we were havin' ta hold the engine together with our bare hands.'

Silence enveloped the ship. What was left of the gun crew stared at each other, aghast. Around them were piles of spent shell cases, wounded sailors quietly moaning, and the dead. Porky and Brooke moved among them with a first-aid box. Some of the men were crying. Porky shook Van Zyl's hand: '*Wel gedaan*, sir. Very well done.'

'Thank you, Porky,' Van Zyl said hoarsely, his ears still ringing. 'It was just a lucky shot.'

CHAPTER 30

From a corner of the darkened bridge came the gentle murmur of Porky's voice, bent over Smit and pressing a bandage to his stomach. A partly inflated lifebelt served as a pillow. Jack noticed the cook slipping a morphine tablet under Smit's tongue. It looked like an act of intimacy, almost religious.

'How are you feeling, Robert?' Jack knelt beside his first officer.

'Stomach, sir, the leg too … so cold, my hands are numb.'

Jack took Smit's hand and squeezed it. Feeling for the leg wound, his fingers probed the darkness and Smit gave a terrible moan. There was no leg there. Jack found a torch and switched it on.

'Porky, a tourniquet and all the bandages you can get!'

The cook disappeared down the ladder and was back in a trice. He cut away Smit's trouser leg. The thigh was a mess of livid meat. Shrapnel splinters had entered the bone. The strips of hanging flesh made Jack want to retch as he and Porky tied a tourniquet above the wound. Then they bandaged the stump as best they could. Brooke held a torch over the gruesome scene.

'Hang on, Robert,' whispered Jack. 'We'll soon be heading home. No more mucking about with sweeping. Let's get you below to your bunk.'

'No,' Smit moaned. 'Must stay.' He was ashen-faced.

Jack placed a hand on Smit's forehead and left a smear of blood: Smit was ice cold, his skin like putty. Porky returned with two blankets. Jack held a mug of rum to Smit's lips and he took a small sip, then coughed it up.

'Sir, I know I'm not … I'm not…'

'Don't talk, Robert, rest now. We got the raider.'

'I've always tried to do my duty … for the *Gannet*.'

'I know, I couldn't have done it without you. You've been the rock.'

'Sir? I thought —'

'Don't think, get some rest. We'll be alongside in no time and get you patched up.'

Smit tried to smile. 'So bloody … cold.'

'Porky will get more blankets. We'll put you to bed. You did very well, Number One.'

'Did I … really?'

'Yes, really.'

'How's he doing, sir?' Van Zyl bent down and switched on his torch. Shocked, he quickly turned it off again.

'Porky, organise a stretcher and some men,' said Jack. 'Let's get Lieutenant Smit to his bunk. Look lively.'

Gannet sailed towards the scene of destruction as hoses sprayed down her own steaming scars. Their searchlight played across the water, illuminating a shattered life raft, debris and black-humped bodies floating face down. A few survivors splashed about in a skin of viscous oil. The enemy. To Jack, they looked more like dying fish than humans. Some of them clung to wreckage, others bobbed in their Mae Wests. Red life-lights shone like fireflies on the water, most of them belonging to corpses.

'Prepare to pick up survivors, Sub.' Jack's voice was devoid of emotion.

'Aye, Captain.'

'What are our casualties?'

'Seven killed, five badly wounded, a few bumps and bruises, sir.'

'Names of the dead?'

'PO Joubert, Ellis, Cloete, Hofmeyr, Potgieter, Plato and Fitzpatrick.'

'Lofty?'

'Aye, a good man, sir.'

'That he was. The others too. Thank you.' Jack turned away. There was a long silence. 'Once we've picked up survivors, we'll go back and help *Belle*. Try to have the blood on the bridge mopped up. Oh, and get Sparks to whistle up Simon's Town and send someone out to take off our wounded.'

They had no trouble from the dozen prisoners who were dragged aboard, most of them black with oil and unable to lift themselves. The Gannets showed no animosity towards the defeated. Wounded Germans were given first aid, the rest herded to the quarterdeck where they were put under armed guard. The only officer among them was escorted to the bridge.

'Your name?' asked Jack coldly as he stared at the tall, blond, but very bedraggled, representative of the Aryan race.

'Oberleutnant Friedrich Bauer.' His voice was barely audible.

'You will make a list of the survivors: name, rank and serial number. Any resistance from your men and they will be shot. Understood?'

'Yes, Kapitän, there will be no trouble.'

'Trouble. That's rich: trouble!'

'I do not understand. We are an auxiliary cruiser of the Kriegsmarine.'

'No, Sub-Lieutenant Bauer, you are Nazi lowlife conducting a deceitful war.'

'Kapitän, sir, this is not true. We are navy men. Men of honour.' His eyes were pleading.

'*Dismissed*.'

Bauer stared at the deck, his shoulders bowed. He turned slowly and was escorted down the ladder.

Cummins appeared on the bridge with a damage report: 'The galley is wrecked, the lifeboat and one of the Carleys are riddled with splinters. Unusable. We're taking water from two holes below the waterline, but the pumps are holding. Just. Jantjies has managed to plug one of the holes. The other's a bit hard to get to. Splinter scars everywhere, but none mortal.'

'Thank you, PO.'

Gannet had turned about and was heading for *Belle*, which had made engine repairs and was able to achieve quarter steam. Alstad had limped over to pick up the survivors of *Star* and a lone survivor from *Wayfarer*, Seaman Bairstow. A bobbing hat, pieces of driftwood, a rugby ball, two Oropesas, a pod of dan buoys — all that remained of half the flotilla. As *Gannet* drew alongside, *Belle* slowed to a stop.

'What's wrong now?' shouted Jack through the speaking trumpet.

'Propeller shaft seized,' called out Alstad. 'We might need a piggyback. She's taking water, but the pumps are holding. Oh, and thanks for swatting that Nazi fly. It was starting to irritate us.'

'Don't mention it. All in a night's work.'

Cummins supervised the party on the quarterdeck preparing a towline. *Gannet* wallowed beside *Belle*, now sporting a fifteen-degree list, and instructions were shouted between the ships. With both vessels rolling heavily, it was a thorny business made more difficult by the darkness. A weighted heaving line arced through the air and struck the head of an unsuspecting sailor on *Belle*. The grass-line was attached to a coir rope that floated, which was in turn attached to a three-inch steel-wire hawser.

'Heave away!' called Cummins. The towing hawser was dragged across by a row of men in a slipping, cursing tug of war. Finally it was fed through the fairleads and secured.

'All fast!' came Cummins's cry from *Gannet*'s quarterdeck and Jack ordered dead-slow ahead. The tow rope rose dripping from the sea and stiffened. *Belle* began to inch forward as *Gannet* raised her revolutions.

'Keep an eye on the tow and let me know if it gets bar taut,' Jack called aft through the speaking trumpet. 'Where are we, Sub?' he added.

'Off the southern tip of Africa, sir,' said Van Zyl.

'Thank you, Smart Aleck, a tad more specific would be helpful. Get on with it.'

'Aye, Captain.' Van Zyl scurried down the ladder to the chartroom. After fiddling with dividers and a stubby pencil, trying to gauge the effect of the current and their erratic course during the fight, he came up with a position twelve miles SSW of Cape Agulhas, which he reported to his captain. They motored steadily into a long swell, making for False Bay at a genteel four knots. Two seamen did their best to clean the bridge of blood, flesh and the spilt brains of the lookout. Seven bodies were laid out in a row on the main deck, covered with blankets.

'I don't think it would go amiss to splice the main brace,' said Jack to no one in particular. 'Porky!'

Minutes later, the cook walked through the ship pouring liberal tots of rum from a copper jug. 'Up spirits, lads,' he said. 'Warms the cockles of your heart, or thereabouts for those that don't have one.' He looked kindly at Brooke, whose head was wrapped in a blood-soaked bandage. 'Here you go, Pickles. You bloody well deserve a nip.' The teenager offered a crooked grin, his lips still trembling.

The middle watch found the sweepers south of Danger Point. Jack stood on the bridge gazing at the swells raking in from the west and thinking of the men he had lost. Two ships, two trusted captains and so many crew. His throat was tight, his eyes glistened.

Eventually, the black of the night gave way to dark grey, then he began to make out the horizon. The east wore a pale opalescence, followed by the first shades of pink as dawn broke astern of them.

By now, men were dozing everywhere. Jack was slumped in his upright chair, barely conscious. Signalman Gilbert lay curled up in the corner of the bridge, sound asleep. Van Zyl sat with his head resting on the chart, snoring loudly.

Jack roused himself and scanned the north, noting the pale crags of Maanschynkop on their starboard quarter, his mind slowly making its calculations. He nodded off again.

There was a tap on his shoulder and he jumped. 'Mug of kye, sir.'

'Oh, thank you, Porky.'

The sweet, sticky chocolate warmed his throat. It tasted alcoholic. The cook winked. 'I added a bit of sauce, sir.'

'Good man, just the ticket.'

The sky brightened and a tangerine sun lifted above the village of Hermanus, a white crusting on the shoreline. *Belle* was dipping and rising in their wake. Jack thought of Clara, still asleep in her downy bed in Newlands — her blonde hair draped across a pillow, her gentle breathing, the impossible smoothness of her skin. The gulf between that apparition and the savagery of all he'd witnessed seemed as wide as the universe itself. He ached for her.

Jack became aware of the large bulk of February standing behind him at the back of the bridge, like a guardian angel. He felt more reassured by the man's presence than he would care to admit.

'Vessel fine on the starboard bow, sir,' said the coxswain.

Jack roused himself to proper wakefulness. 'How long have you been standing there, Adam?' he asked without turning around.

'Most of the night, sir.'

'You think I can't command my own ship without your bloody help?' he said irritably.

'Yes, sir.'

Jack turned to look at his coxswain. February didn't take his eyes off the horizon. What was the old trawlerman thinking? His craggy face gave nothing away.

'You're damn right, Cox'n.' He felt a wave of exhaustion pass through him. 'I can't.'

At that moment, Jack felt the absence of Smit keenly. Even if they didn't get along, Smit knew what was what. Their differences now seemed trifling.

'Simon's Town calling us on the RT, sir,' said Sparks up the voice pipe. 'Do you want me to switch it over?'

'Aye, do that please, Thomas.' Jack took the hand microphone from its box and a metallic voice crackled in his ear.

'Pembroke, it's Commodore O'Reilly here. I've received the situation report. Are you all right, over?'

Jack slid the switch to answer: 'Yes, sir, we got knocked about a bit, *Wayfarer* and *Star* are lost. *Belle* in tow. The raider is sunk. Over.'

'Good man, very well done.' O'Reilly's voice was full of feeling. 'Godspeed and a safe return. I'm certain there'll be a gong in this for you. Over.'

'For the crew, sir, not for me. I couldn't have done it without them. Over.'

'Of course. But you too, Lieutenant, you too. Over and out.'

Gannet and *Belle* continued their slow plod towards Cape Hangklip. The headland that marked the eastern portal of False Bay stood up from the Atlantic like a shark's fin, reminding Jack of Gibraltar and the Pillars of Hercules. What was it Van Zyl had said about Greek mythology? Something about the Cape being known as Adamastor, a cantankerous god guarding the tip of Africa.

'Sub, I'm going to check on Robert again,' said Jack into the voice pipe. 'Come up and keep an eye on *Belle*. We don't want that tow parting.'

'Aye, Captain,' said Van Zyl.

Smit lay in his bunk, the stump of his severed leg swathed in a wad of red bandages. Porky sat beside him. Smit was taking short, shallow breaths.

'How's he doing, AB?' asked Jack.

'Not good, sir,' whispered Porky. 'Not long now, I think.'

Jack pulled a chair closer and took Smit's hand. 'Can you hear me, Robert?'

'Yes,' came a faint rasp.

'We're nearly home. There's a rescue boat coming out from Gordon's Bay.'

'Cold. Cold.'

'Another blanket, Porky.'

'Sir … sir…' Smit opened his eyes wide.

'Yes, Robert?'

'I…'

Porky leant in close and took Smit's wrist, then placed a hand on his neck. He straightened up and shook his head. 'He's gone, Captain.'

Jack bent forward and laid his forehead on his first officer's shoulder, the palm of his hand on Smit's chest.

On deck, the air was warmer and the winter sun cast a bright, clear light. Jack pushed back the hood of his duffel coat and reached for his cap. It was battered and oil-stained. He held it in his hand for a moment, running his thumb over the tarnished badge, feeling the ragged ends of the gold wire. A tired, careworn, seagoing cap.

After *Gannet*'s crew had a makeshift breakfast, a crash boat arrived to take off the wounded and the prisoners. The dead remained on the main deck under tarpaulins. An hour later, *St Dogmael* came fussing down the bay, pushing a portly bow wave ahead of her like a maritime bulldozer.

'I see you have a cripple; may we assist?' flashed the rescue tug.

'No, thank you,' replied *Gannet*. 'We can manage.'

'As you wish. But we'll hang around, just in case.'

Ahead of them, Roman Rock Lighthouse rose like a white obelisk. Simon's Town took shape, looking like icing at the base of a chocolate mountain. Over to port lay Milkwood House, a white speck above its crescent beach. He pictured his sister on the veranda with a book, Rachel in the kitchen, his father in the study.

Seaman Brooke was at the helm, bandaged head and all. A reliable lad. One of his dependables.

The steward appeared on the bridge with a tray of steaming mugs.

'Thank you, Hendricks, just what the doctor ordered,' said Jack. 'Tell me, is Fido doing all right after last night?'

'She's on your bunk, sir, snoring loudly. I think she slept through the whole thing.'

'Good for Fido, she's a trooper.'

'Aye, she is, sir. Do you think we can get her signed up?'

'What do you mean?'

'Like Just Nuisance.'

'I don't think there's ever been a Wren cat before.'

'Maybe your dad could put in a word, sir. The Admiralty might look favourably on a battle-hardened cat. You know, one with combat experience, rather than an overfed, lazy, shore-based dog.'

'You might have a point there, Hendricks. I'll look into it.'

The pair of sweepers, with *St Dogmael* taking up the rear, approached the harbour entrance. 'Stop engine.' The hawser was released and dragged aboard. As the tug drew alongside, Jack called through the speaking trumpet. 'All right, *St Dogmael*, you can take over babysitting.'

'We'll see *Southern Belle* bathed, powdered and put to bed on the slipway in West Yard,' came the shout from a bearded sea dog on the tug's bridge. 'Enough excitement for one war.'

Gannet turned towards the harbour entrance at dead slow.

'Sure you don't need some help, Captain?' came a shout from the tug's skipper. 'I hear you do harbour stations at full ahead!'

'Cheeky bugger, isn't he, sir?' said Van Zyl.

'Takes one to know one.'

'Not true, sir.'

'It is true, Number One.'

Van Zyl looked to his captain, a shocked expression on his face. Jack nodded. Smit was dead. *Gannet* had a new first officer. Van Zyl turned to stare at the town, his eyes brimming with tears he would not allow. Not here, not now.

Jack saw that a convoy was in and the harbour was crammed with warships. There would have to be much saluting as the sweeper crossed the basin to her berth in the far corner. The crew would need to be on their toes. He glanced down at the harbour-stations party mustered on *Gannet*'s forecastle beside the seven corpses under tarpaulin. They were perhaps the scruffiest, dirtiest, worst-turned-out sailors he'd ever seen, but he could hardly have felt prouder.

He walked to the bridge wing and gazed back at his ship. She was a mess. Gaping shell wounds, burnt plating, a smashed lifeboat, holes peppered in her funnel and across the entire superstructure. She looked as though she had no right to be afloat. He felt tremendous sadness, and relief.

The destroyer HMS *Hadrian* and cruiser HMS *Yorkshire* were tied up on East Wall. HMS *Carnarvon Castle* was berthed to starboard. Jack noticed that sailors had lined the guardrails of all the warships. He heard a few cheers from a group of dockworkers at the bullnose. The cheering was taken up by each ship in succession. Hats were raised as the sound grew. The basin echoed with voices. Ship's hooters and horns took up the cry, the baritone booming of *Carnarvon Castle* drowning out the others. A colosseum indeed.

'Sir, the flags are dipped!' cried Bunts. 'They're saluting *us*! What must I do?'

'Acknowledge them, Gilbert.'

'Aye, Captain!' A smiling Bunts lowered the ensign in recognition.

Beside the four empty sweeper berths, Jack spotted a staff car. He could just make out the four figures standing on the wharf. His father and the commodore were side by side, for all the world like old friends. Next to them were two women, their dresses bright against the drab naval buildings. Both were waving. One looked like his sister. He picked up binoculars to identify the second and focused the lenses. Clara. He ran his finger gently across the scar on his temple.

'Would you take a look at that,' he said under his breath. Then he turned to Van Zyl. 'So, Number One, not such a bad showing for a boring old sweep.'

'No, sir. As a matter of fact, not boring at all.'

Bunts was eavesdropping as he folded away his signal flags.

'We've lost two brave ships, but our work has only begun,' said Jack. '*Wayfarer* and *Star* will be replaced, and we'll be sweeping again as soon as the old girl is patched up. So will *Belle*.'

'Aye, sir, sweep, sweep, sweep,' said Van Zyl. 'The housemaids of the Atlantic.'

'And none can do without us,' whispered Bunts.

GLOSSARY

AB — Able Seaman

AMC — Armed Merchant Cruiser

ack-ack — anti-aircraft (guns)

the Andrew — nickname for the Royal Navy

Asdic — an early form of sonar used to detect submarines by the reflection of sound waves

A-sweep — a sweep wire strung between two minesweepers sailing line abreast

BEF — British Expeditionary Force

Bosun (or Boatswain) — usually a petty officer, responsible for the efficient seamanship functions of the ship

Bunts — signalman specialising in visual signals such as flags, lights and semaphore (literally 'bunting tosser')

corned dog — tinned bully beef

CPO — Chief Petty Officer

Davy Jones's locker — the bottom of the ocean; the grave of those drowned at sea

dhobi — washing, from the Hindi word for laundry

ERA — engine room artificer

Hilfskreuzer — German auxiliary cruisers disguised as merchant ships and used for commerce raiding

HMAS — His Majesty's Australian Ship

HMSAS — His Majesty's South African Ship

HMS *King Alfred* — training depot in Hove, Sussex, for officers of the Royal Navy Volunteer Reserve

housey-housey — bingo

Jack Tar — seaman of the Royal Navy or merchant marine

the Jimmy — also known as the First Lieutenant, Number One or Jimmy-the-One; the second-in-command of a warship
Killick — Leading Seaman; the name refers to a small anchor and is the symbol on the badge of a leading seaman
kye — sweet hot chocolate, often served on board at night
Mae West — nickname for an inflatable life jacket
NAAFI — Navy, Army, Air Force Institutes (military shop/recreational establishment)
OKM — *Oberkommando der Marine* (Nazi Germany's Naval High Command)
oppo — chum, special friend, buddy (literally your 'opposite number', the person on watch when you are off)
PO — Petty Officer
pongo — soldier; slang for any member of the British Army (troops rarely washed in the field, hence 'where the wind blows, the pong goes')
pusser — Naval slang for anything that is military-like or service issue
RN — Royal Navy
RNVR — Royal Navy Volunteer Reserve
RNVR SA — South African Royal Navy Volunteer Reserve
RT — Radio-telephony
Schwerpunkt — 'centre of gravity'; a popular term used by German strategists denoting concentration on and maintenance of the objective
SDF — Seaward Defence Force; forerunner of the South African Navy
skilly — a broth, typically made from oatmeal and water, flavoured with meat
SKL — *Seekriegsleitung* (operational staff of *OKM*)
SNO — Senior Naval Officer

Snoektown (or Snoekie) — sailors' nickname for Simon's Town

Sparks — radio operator; telegraphist specialising in wireless communication

splice the main brace — the order given to issue a ship's crew with alcohol

tiddly sailor — neat and tidy; in his best uniform

HISTORICAL NOTES

The Jack Pembroke series follows the young lieutenant's naval career through World War II, beginning in South Africa. During the war, enemy submarines, raiders and mines sank more than 150 ships in local waters. It's an episode in the country's history that went largely undocumented and today very few people are aware of the deadly battles that took place within sight of the South African coast. I wanted to dramatize this episode in our naval history.

South African ships operated alongside Allied vessels in many theatres, not only in coastal waters. They fought in the Mediterranean, off Madagascar and in Burma, and Jack Pembroke will find himself in the thick of it in future novels. World War II was a fascinating period in South African history, when the country was still umbilically linked to Britain, but with the rising tide of Afrikaner nationalism threatening radical change. It was a time of rapid growth and optimism, despite the war. The country's trajectory would be irrevocably altered in 1948 with the coming to power of the National Party and the institution of apartheid. Far from the mass destruction of Europe, the South African war years, then, offer a moment of nostalgia and, ironically, hope.

My family has a 200-year-old holiday home in Simon's Town, so I've watched the comings and goings of warships all my life, and spent much time bobbing about the waters of False Bay on anything that floats. Something of the Royal Navy atmosphere persists in this delightful town and its museums and archives are a treasure trove for amateur historians like myself. Even a walk down the high street transports you back to a time when Jack Tars thronged this southern port … and it's a simple trick of the imagination to find yourself following in Jack Pembroke's footsteps, on his way to board the *Gannet*.

A NOTE TO THE READER

Dear Reader,

Thank you for taking the time to read the first Jack Pembroke naval adventure. I do hope you enjoyed it. I will be tracking Jack's story through World War II and although each novel in the series may be read as a stand-alone, the next one will follow on directly in time from *The Cape Raider*. It will tell the story of U-boats operating off the South African coast during the winter and spring of 1941, attempting to disrupt Allied convoys bound for North Africa. Jack and the good ship *Gannet* will head to sea once more to try to stop this mortal threat.

In this series, I have chosen a British hero and placed him on a South African ship in a Royal Navy base at the southern tip of the continent. It has provided me with the opportunity to marry parts of my own background: my time in the South African Navy as a citizen-force officer, my university education in England and my love of the Cape and its stormy ocean.

Since I was a boy, I've adored nautical yarns and grew up reading the likes of Alexander Fullerton, Nicholas Monsarrat, Patrick O'Brian and Douglas Reeman. But I always lamented the fact that none of these naval adventures were set in my home, the Cape, despite the presence of an important Royal Navy base in Simon's Town. The Jack Pembroke series is an attempt to bring the South African maritime story of World War II to life. Future books could see Jack serving in the Mediterranean at Tobruk, Malta, Sicily and Greece, and even in the oft-forgotten Madagascar campaign.

Nowadays, reviews by knowledgeable readers are essential to an author's success, so if you enjoyed the novel I shall be in your debt if you would spare a moment to post a short review on **Amazon** or **Goodreads**. I love hearing from readers, and you can connect with me through my **Facebook page**, **Instagram**, **Twitter** or my **website**.

I hope we'll meet again in the pages of the next Jack Pembroke adventure on the high seas.

Justin Fox

SAPERE
BOOKS

Printed in Great Britain
by Amazon